For Watson, who was my companion on our many walks, and who listened patiently to my ramblings about Geordie.

The PEREGRINATIONS of GEORDIE STUBBS, ROGUE

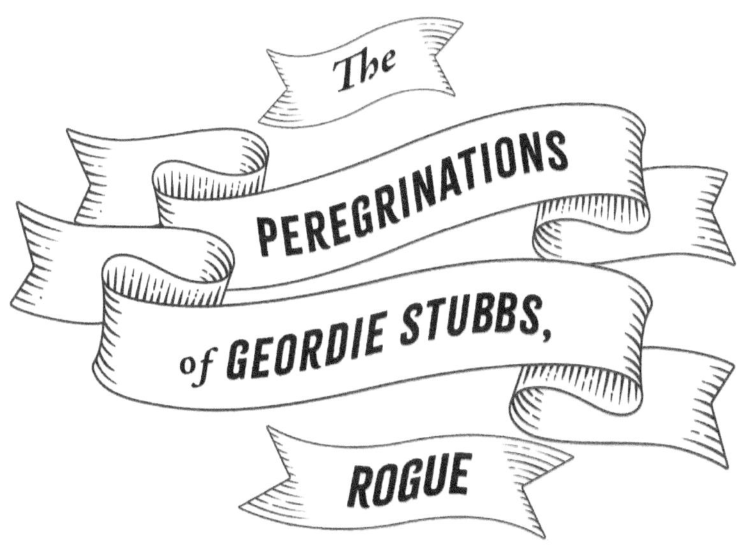

John Tully

ASHWOOD
PUBLISHING

ISBN (print): 9780645913729
ISBN (ePub): 9780645913736

Published by Ashwood Publishing
Cradoc, Tasmania

www.ashwoodpublishing.com.au
info@ashwoodpublishing.com.au

Set in 11.5/16 Minion Pro
Cover by Susan Young

This is a work of fiction, and the scenes described are entirely the fruit of the author's imagination. While it includes scenes involving real historical figures, the actions and words depicted are entirely imaginary and are not in any way intended to represent the real actions, speech or opinions of these persons.

The quotations on Munich beer in chapter 33 are from H.L. Mencken, 'The Beeriad', *The Smart Set: A Magazine of Cleverness*, John Adams Thayer, New York, April 1913. Available at The Modernist Journals Project (searchable database), Brown and Tulsa Universities, ongoing. www.modjourn.org. The quote on the American public in chapter 37 is also widely attributed to Mencken although the exact wording seems to have evolved.

The Frank G. Bruner quotation in chapter 56 is from 'The Primitive Races in America', *Psychological Bulletin*, 1 October 1912. American Psychological Association.

 A catalogue record for this work is available from the National Library of Australia

I told the Secretary he could not pardon him without a
favourable report from the judge; besides, he was a fiddler, and
consequently a rogue, and deserved hanging for something else;
and so he shall swing.

– Jonathan Swift, *Journal to Stella*

Geordie: 1. A native of the Tyneside conurbation and
immediate environs in NE England. 2. The dialect of English
spoken by Geordies. 3. Tyneside and Scottish diminutive of the
given name George.

Peregrination: a long trip in which you travel to various places,
especially on foot.

– Cambridge Dictionary

A Note on the Characters

Peregrinations is a work of fiction. Writers, however, are like magpies, picking up all kinds of trash and treasure, storing it away, and recycling it. This includes people from books or real life who have stuck in the writer's imagination. Although most of the characters in the book are fictitious, some are based on real historical figures. Nancy Wake, for instance, was very much a real person – and an admirable one – and I hope that my portrayal does justice to that thoroughly decent and brave woman. The scenes in which she appears are, however, imaginary. The Feuersteins in Akron, while inspired by the founding families of the Akron tire and rubber industry, are in no way intended to represent any of the real people involved. Other reconstructed figures are less sympathetically portrayed. I make no apologies for treating Nazis, Nazi sympathisers, and Spanish fascists in an unflattering way. Again, however, the scenes in which they appear are imaginary.

Hobart, Tasmania, Winter 1954

Big Tommy Cresswell trudged up draughty Campbell Street as the dawn light smudged the horizon in this wintry little city at the edge of the world. The mercury had fallen to below freezing overnight, so Cresswell was hunkered bearlike inside his thick warder's greatcoat. His destination was the sandstone Georgian pile of Her Majesty's Hobart Gaol; a human warehouse in which six hundred crims were sleeping in their slots. Waking them was a highlight in the dreary sameness of his days. He entered the iron gates, pulled on his peaked warder's cap, and nodded to his colleague Mick Burr, who was bolting a mug of scalding tea.

'Freeze the balls off a brass monkey,' Cresswell said, blowing on his hands.

Burr winked slowly like a bluetongue lizard and croaked: 'Gunna have some fun today, mate.'

The warders' eyes swivelled to the cell block where wee Geordie Stubbs coughed and stirred under his coarse blanket, chasing the elusive remnants of a dream that had featured a bairn, a fiddle, and a Baby Austin two-door sedan. Cresswell looked inside the cell, his dull eyes set so close together that they could peer simultaneously through the spy hole, and bellowed 'Getcha black arse outta bed!'

Geordie obeyed mechanically, pulling on the khaki prison shirt and trousers and grey jumper, nervous of the warder's uncertain temper. Still groggy with sleep, he stumbled along as Cresswell steered him by the elbow down a whitewashed corridor and across an internal courtyard to where Mick Burr was waiting, jangling a bunch of iron keys. Were they moving him, he wondered? Instead, Burr unlocked another door with a theatrical flourish and Creswell shoved Geordie roughly through. One of them flipped a switch, and electric lights flickered into dull yellow life. Geordie espied a flight of steps leading to a dark wooden shed.

'Up you go,' Cresswell ordered, with another shove for encouragement.

An awful realisation hit Geordie – he saw the dangling noose! The lever! The trapdoor! He could almost feel the crunch of his neck breaking and his body rotating at the rope's end. Were these fucking bozos going to hang him here and now? His knees went to water and Cresswell's sneering laugh echoed off the bare walls, his black shadow huge in the dim light of the low wattage bulb. Burr had mounted the scaffold and was beckoning to Geordie to join him.

The ghastly tableau seemed frozen in time, but eventually Burr came down the steps with an evil grin on his reptilian features. 'Carn, darkie,' he sniggered, seizing Geordie by the arm and propelling him back out towards the iron gate. 'Just a little rehearsal, like.'

Geordie's mouth opened and closed, but he was speechless. He did not resist the men's pushing and shoving and scarcely took in his surroundings as they propelled him back to his wing of the prison, which was stirring into life. Big Tommy pulled a newspaper from the back pocket of his blue serge trousers and waved it in Geordie's face.

'*Mercury's* callin' ya the Beast of Bronte.'

'Reckon you'll cry for Mother, ya black bastard?' Burr jeered, miming placing a noose round Geordie's neck, the knot correctly positioned under his left ear.

A sudden punch to the kidneys caught Geordie off guard and left him gasping for breath.

'Ya little black Scotch bastard,' Cresswell hissed. 'You done them sheilas like you done that poofter Giblin up at Bronte! Next time we take you up there it won't be no rehearsal.'

The door thudded shut and Geordie slumped on his three-legged stool. The pain was ebbing, but his heart was still thumping.

Ten minutes later the morning was in full swing. The place was run like the military by numbers and strict routine. Governor Dan Hornblower had been an admiral or something, the crims reckoned, and Geordie wondered if the screws piped him aboard of a morning. Keys rattled and doors were banged open. 'Cocks off, socks on!' Cresswell shouted at the prisoners, as he did every morning and thought it was funny every time. A pair of white-haired trusties wheeled a cart surmounted by a stinking bin and the crims tipped the contents of their slop buckets into it. Geordie joined the line of convicts shuffling down to the muster yard, where they stood at attention while Principal Officer Don Markwick and his underlings did a head count. Satisfied, Markwick ordered the crims to march off for breakfast, but then pulled Geordie aside.

'Important visitor for you today, Stubbs,' said Markwick, chewing on something Geordie thought might be cud. Markwick didn't say who this personage might be, and Geordie knew better than to ask.

Seated at the mess table, Geordie poked at the lumpy porridge. He nibbled a slice of half-burnt toast, smeared it with industrial jam and sipped gingerly at the lukewarm black tea the crims swore was laced with libido suppressant. Geordie sighed: to think that he, George William Marmaduke Stubbs, who had trained under the great chef Auguste Escoffier, was reduced to consuming such awful swill! The ghastly meal over, he returned to his cell and read the Bible, the only book Markwick allowed him until library day. Geordie wasn't religious, but he had found much of the good book to be damned good poetry. A lot about prisoners in it too. He laughed out at loud at Psalm 146's optimistic claim, 'The Lord sets prisoners free.' At that the cover over the spyhole clicked open and Cresswell peered monocularly through. 'What's so funny?' he snapped. Geordie ignored him, then fell into a reverie: Tyneside, wandering, Annie and the bairn, forks in the road. The peace and quiet didn't last long. Keys rattled, and Cresswell's bulk filled the doorway. 'Gerrup!' he shouted and jerked his head for Geordie to follow.

Bronte Park, Tasmanian Central Plateau,
April 1954

One glorious autumn day when the sun shone brightly in an azure sky, time clerk Dessie Delphin was out walking his cocker spaniel Dinah when she suddenly rushed off, barking madly. Normally quietly obedient, she refused to return, and stood near a thicket of gorse, wagging her tail and growling. Dessie saw the Blundstone-booted feet first, and when he grabbed the dog's collar and parted the bushes, he saw the rest – and wished to Christ he hadn't. It was young Giblin, one of the civil engineers. He was lying very still and when Dessie forced himself to look closely, he saw that the back of his head was lying in a pool of blackening blood. Dessie vomited when he saw the flies and maggots. There was a knife embedded to its bakelite hilt in the poor bugger's chest, too. Mumbling half-forgotten prayers, Dessie slipped the lead onto Dinah's collar and scrambled up the hill to the police station, gibbering like a madman. Doc Bryant had to slap his face before the big Sergeant, Stan Alomes, could get a sensible word out of him.

Dessie had known the victim by sight – a quiet bloke who kept his own company, didn't drink in the Hydro's 'wet canteen', didn't go to the two-up or place bets on the horses with the town's SP bookie, and spent his off-duty weekends in Hobart, presumably with his mum and dad. He had been working on the Pine Tier Dam and had been a competent civil engineer and liked well enough by the workers, although there were certain *whispers* about him. He hadn't been to work that day, which was unusual, the ganger on the dam told the gawping drinkers in the bar.

Sergeant Alomes secured the crime scene with a bit of old rope and Doc Bryant certified the death. A rectal thermometer reading allowed an estimate of the time of decease and the body was stretchered up the hill to the medical centre, where it joined the corpse of a poor fellow killed in a tunnel collapse. Four hours later two hard-faced detectives arrived from Hobart and booked accommodation in the staff house, where they were joined by the new government pathologist, Peregrine Rowley-Samuels. Samuels carried out an autopsy the next morning and confirmed the obvious: as Stan Alomes had surmised, the victim had been killed by a massive blow to the back of the head. Rock fragments embedded in the skull indicated that the blow had been inflicted with a lump of the local dolerite rock by someone of considerable strength; which suggested that the murderer was a male. Rowley-Samuels believed that Mr Giblin was already dead when the knife was driven into his heart. 'Bit of overkill,' he remarked with a nervous, snorting laugh that contrasted with the sorrow in his eyes. Disturbingly, though, he added – wiping his spotless glasses and adjusting his bow tie – someone had methodically tortured Mr Giblin before the blow to the head finished him off. Defensive wounds on his hands suggested that he had attempted to ward off his attacker. Sniffing about like bloodhounds, the detectives found a blood trail through bushes, which suggested Lance Giblin had tried desperately to escape his tormentor.

The detectives soon established a firm lead. A kitchenhand called Darryl Hall – nicknamed Elvis because of his winklepicker shoes and Pompadour hairstyle – told them he had seen the chief cook, 'that fuckun darkie Geordie Stubbs', leaving the scene of the crime. Elvis added that he had overheard Geordie arguing with Mr Giblin the previous night and that it had sounded like they had come to blows. He knew it was Stubbs because of what he called his 'Scotch' accent. This was strong proof that Geordie Stubbs was their man, the detectives believed. The cook's knife, too, was potent evidence, and now reposed in an evidence bag awaiting fingerprint analysis. The detective inspector sent his underling over to the Works Industrial Office, where he questioned the boss, 'Grinner' Newcombe. Grinner praised Elvis Hall as an exemplary employee who was overdue for promotion. As for Geordie Stubbs: 'The little bastard's been trouble from the word go,' he snarled. 'Doesn't surprise me what he's done and I hope he swings for it.'

Little Geordie's ears had pricked up when he heard the two detectives talking as they crunched over the gravel towards his 'camp', as the single men called their little cabins. He never forgot a voice and what he heard paled his brown face almost to an allowable shade of White Australia Policy pink. The sight of the beefy, red-haired man standing there filled him with dread. Like most people, he felt a frisson of guilt when he saw policemen, and he had more reason than most for it. But surely, these coppers weren't going to pin the murder on him …?

'I'm Detective Inspector Verte and this is Detective Constable Edensor,' the boss detective growled, his accent English Home Counties. When he had ascertained Geordie's identity, he launched into the time-worn formula: 'George Stubbs, I am arresting you on suspicion of the murder of Lance Allan Giblin. You do not have to say anything, but it may harm your defence if you do not mention when questioned something which you later rely on in court. Anything you say may be given in evidence against you. Do you understand?'

Geordie managed to choke out that yes, he did understand, but surely … No, it couldn't be … but it was the same flaming red hair, bulldog jowls and big shoulders straining the seams of the Harris tweed jacket … But something wasn't quite right. The man's face was pudgier for a start, and he was too young, but the name was the same – *Verte!* – and he was an Inspector with a Pommy accent to boot!

The inspector was regarding Geordie curiously, as if he were wondering where he'd seen him before, and at a nod from his boss, Edensor carried out a rather perfunctory search of the cabin. He sneered at the violin sitting in its case at the back of the table and made miaowing noises.

'Careful with that,' said Geordie as Edensor opened the case and pretended to play the instrument.

'Stradivarius, is it?' Verte jeered.

'No, but it's valuable.'

'Humph,' Verte grunted. 'Best put it down, Roy.' He had turned his attention to the sketches of local characters and landscapes tacked on the walls. 'Artist, are we?'

Geordie shrugged and the detectives lost interest. Edensor handcuffed Geordie and they walked him the two hundred yards to the police station, where big Stan Alomes was waiting with a sceptical smile on his broad face.

'Gotcha man then? He's never given me no trouble, but then youse'd know best.'

'Yeah, the black bugger done it alright,' piped up Edensor – eager to assert his CIB superiority over the country copper. Edensor had a slight English accent, but Midlands, Geordie thought, not Home Counties like Verte. He turned to the inspector: 'Anyway, we'd best get him in the car, sir. Long drive ahead an' the weather's gunna turn bad.'

They bundled Geordie into the back seat of their car – a spanking new pale blue FJ Holden. Fresh off the production line at Fisherman's Bend, the cars were Australia's pride, and Edensor, clipping one of the handcuffs to a ring set next the back door, looked disappointed when Verte jumped into the driver's seat and started the car. The inspector kept peering at Geordie in the rear vision mirror. Geordie was used to this – he was a memorable sight with his dark complexion and thick red hair – and stared right back. Then it came to him – not only was the detective's face fatter, and his age surely wrong, but his eyes were the wrong colour! Those of his long-ago nemesis, the crack thief-taker who had hunted him so relentlessly 'in another life', had been icy blue and besides, the man was dead, and Geordie did not believe in reincarnation.

Almost simultaneously, the inspector's brown orbs widened with the realisation that his prisoner was the same little bastard who had spoiled his father's near-perfect arrest record and driven him to jump into the black Thames. He had sometimes wondered what had happened to the criminal the English papers had called the Human Fly, and now he had him bang to rights!

Hobart, April 1954

The interview room in Hobart's Liverpool Street nick stank of sweaty feet, stale cigarette smoke, and – Geordie was sure – of desperation. DC Edensor sat him down on a hard chair and left him to stew; a common police ploy, Geordie knew. An hour crept by, then another. Night fell and Geordie sat in the dark, craving a cigarette.

Eventually, Inspector Verte stomped into the room on his size thirteen brogues, followed by his grinning offsider, who flicked on the lights with a theatrical flourish. Verte made a great show of flipping through a manila folder and peering at Geordie over the reading glasses he had donned. He angled the desk lamp at Geordie's face, like the Gestapo did in films, and demanded to know why he had done it. Geordie stoutly declared his innocence; he had never spoken to Giblin and knew him only slightly by sight. Verte sneered and pressed him harder to confess.

'How do you explain this?' He slapped the kitchen knife onto the table. 'It was found at the crime scene. It's got your initials burned into the handle and your fingerprints are all over it.'

Geordie rolled his eyes – an arresting sight. 'Howay man, it was taken from my cubby in the kitchen. Anyone could have nicked it.'

Verte snorted contemptuously. 'For God's sake, man, we have a sworn statement that you were seen leaving the scene of the crime. You were also overheard arguing with the deceased the night before the murder. How do you explain that?'

'There was no argument, man, and anybody who says different is a bloody liar!'

'Where were you when Mr Giblin was murdered?'

Geordie was vague about that. Verte noticed him looking shifty and tried a new gambit; a nice confession would wrap it up so he could get to the pub before closing time.

'Word has it that Lance Giblin was a poofter,' he said. 'You're an arse bandit too, aren't you? We think you met him by the creek for sex and things got out of hand.'

'Haddaway. I had no idea that he was camp, and I'm a ladies' man myself.'

'Go on!' joshed Verte. 'A man has needs. There's only married women up there in Bronte. Admit you did it and we'll put in a word for you. Nice cup of tea and the Detective Constable here will prepare the paperwork.'

Edensor nodded vigorously. 'Go on, matey. You can always plead diminished responsibility.'

'Lovers' tiff,' Verte agreed. 'Crime of passion. Jury'd buy it, and you'd maybe go down for manslaughter.'

'I am not responsible for the poor man's death.'

At this rate they'd be here until after the pub closed, so Verte suddenly roared with a ferocity that startled even Edensor: 'You're a lying black bastard!'

Edensor joined in. 'Lemme givvum a smack, Sarge!' he demanded, rolling up his sleeves and baring his crooked teeth. 'Bastard's gaggin' for it!'

Verte shook his head irritably. Much as he wanted to give the little bugger a slap, he was mindful of Superintendent Doughney's recent memo warning about over-use of the third degree. 'It's Inspector now, Constable!' he hissed in an exasperated aside.

After a while, Geordie tired of the game. 'Haddaway and shite,' he declared, folding his arms. Verte had him locked him up for the night and then hurried around to the pub. A couple of quick beers restored his equilibrium, and he went home feeling that he'd earned his money.

The next morning, Superintendent Doughney informed the press that 'a male was helping police with their enquiries', and that a conviction was likely. Magistrate Merv Crisp shook his head sadly when Stubbs appeared before him charged with Lance Giblin's murder. He remembered 'sentencing' him several years ago to twelve months on the Hydro for a drunken hotel brawl and regretted that it had not worked out well. He refused bail and remanded him in custody. Throughout the proceedings Geordie maintained his innocence but did not or could not provide an alibi, much to his solicitor's exasperation.

Hobart, Winter 1954

The case was a sensation across the country. The Hobart *Mercury* headlined it and an angry mob swirled around the Campbell Street entrance to the gaol, demanding that the 'Beast of Bronte' be hung, drawn, and quartered, even if his hapless victim was a homosexual, which they were prepared to overlook in the interests of 'justice'. There had been a spate of murders on the island and in the court of public opinion, Geordie Stubbs had committed the lot. It was obvious, said newly elected Alderman Audrey Amos, the spokeswoman for the hanging party who had got up a petition demanding draconian new laws. The police tended to agree given the similarities between the crimes, but their standards of evidence were a little higher. Inspector Simon Verte chafed. He was determined to pin another four murders on 'that bloody darkie': one at New Norfolk, another at Queenstown, a third at Hobart, and the last – of a beekeeping Welsh hermit – at Mount Arrowsmith. The snag was that although the other victims had been tortured and stabbed to death, the fingerprints found at the scene of those crimes did not match those of Stubbs, nor anyone else who was 'known to the police'. Circumstantial evidence suggested that

Stubbs had been in New Norfolk and Hobart around the time of the murders, but he denied ever having ever set foot in Queenstown and there was no evidence to suggest that he had. Verte toyed with the idea that Stubbs had an accomplice but again he had no proof. A nosey reporter called Karl Wollig overheard DC Edensor expounding this hypothesis in the Royal Exchange Hotel and the article he wrote for *The Mercury* – 'Did the Beast Act Alone?' – uncorked a fresh flood of public hysteria.

Dermot Lindsay, Geordie's defence brief, sighed in exasperation. He had been hired by Geordie's good friend Harry Rolls and was one of Tasmania's best advocates, but he was having a hard time with this client.

'Okay, Geordie, let's start again,' he sighed, stubbing out his umpteenth Senior Service – the supposed 'perfection of cigarette luxury' – and running a hand through his thick black hair. 'I can't help you if you don't tell me everything.'

Geordie shrugged and puffed on his cigarette. He was sitting while the lawyer paced the room, snorting like an angry bull. Dermot tried again. 'Look Geordie, mate, you're just not capable of doing what was done to Lance Giblin. I've spoken with Harry and your other cobbers, and they say you haven't got it in you.'

'"There's no art to find the mind's construction in the face",' said Geordie.

'Chrissake, mate, don't start spouting Shakespeare at me,' grumbled Dermot. 'Much as I love the bard, he's not much use to us now.'

'Well, Mr Lindsay, who knows what any of us are capable of? We think we know a person and then everything we know is thrown into question.'

'Jesus Christ, man, would you listen to yourself. Stop the ragged arse philosophy and this devil's advocate nonsense. Look, unless you have a plausible alibi, before too long they will come one morning and drag you to the hanging shed, drop the noose round your neck, and bang' – he clicked his fingers – 'that will be the fucking end of Geordie Stubbs!'

'Haddaway, Dermot. You think I divvent knaa what's waitin' for me? I think that—' He was suddenly overcome by a coughing fit.

The lawyer looked alarmed. 'Jesus, Geordie,' he said. 'We'll have to get you seen by a doctor.'

'Not much point now, bonnie lad.'

Dermot shook his head and leaned down on the table to collect his papers. 'I have to go now,' he said, 'but if you want to tell me what you're not saying, you can contact me any time.' He consulted his watch. 'Pub time Geordie. I still hope to sink a few beers with you sometime and go out to visit the nags out at Elwick and put on a few bets.' He banged on the doorframe, shook hands with his client, and went out through the door Warder Burr was holding open for him.

The Giblin murder was an open and shut case. The prosecutor didn't have to try very hard to convince the jury of the Beast's guilt, and although Dermot Lindsay strove valiantly to cast doubt on Elvis Hall's testimony, Geordie Stubbs could not or would not say where he was when the murder was committed. Dermot despaired and went on a bender after the jury delivered a unanimous guilty verdict. Over in Melbourne, the public hangman looked forward to collecting his fee and booked his ticket on SS *Taroona*. The little man was going to swing so that law-abiding Tasmanians could sleep peacefully in their beds. Mr Justice Peter Dicer, however, was somewhat of a liberal among his reactionary colleagues, and the whole business had given him migraine. The murder had been so ferally brutal that His Honour wondered about Geordie's sanity. Before donning the black cap, he would commission a full psychiatric report and then decide on the most appropriate course of action, which just might be confinement in the secure ward for the criminally insane at the Lachlan Park Hospital.

Dicer's request landed on the desk of Doctor Stuart Hetherington, a psychiatrist who had rooms at a prestigious address in Macquarie Street. Hetherington was ambitious and, he liked to think, more than competent. He had completed his basic medical training in 1933 at the University of Melbourne and gone on to specialise in psychiatry after a stint in the Royal Australian Army Medical Corps treating patients suffering from shellshock. He was the logical choice, because he was experienced in advising courts whether felons awaiting sentence exhibited any mental or cognitive impairment that should be considered in sentencing. A concatenation of Tasmania's misfits, psychopaths, dipsomaniacs, dullards, and assorted sad cases and 'no hopers' had passed under his forensic gaze, some of them for a second or third time, or from the same family. These outcasts were grist for Hetherington's intellectual mill. He had studied the Miller Report, submitted to the Tasmanian Parliament almost thirty years earlier, which had found significant levels of mental retardation and borderline intelligence in the contemporary prison population, together with smaller than average brains. Hetherington suspected that such traits were widespread in the colonial population, and that differences with the population of the 'old country' would be marked.

He had written a few well-received scholarly papers for medical journals, but his magnum opus was in gestation – a book on the criminal and anti-social traits within the contemporary Tasmanian population inherited from the transported convict gene pool. The study had been suggested by an eminent colleague – the first professor of psychiatry in Spain – who had taken Hetherington under his wing when he was on sabbatical leave in Madrid. Tasmania, Professor Vallejo Nájera enthused, was a marvellous eugenics laboratory.

The book he felt sure Hetherington would write would amplify the celebrated US studies of the degenerate Kallikak, Jukes, and Ishmael families. Once it was published, Hetherington's career would blossom. He coveted the directorship of the Lachlan Park asylum and fretted for the incumbent to retire to his hobby farm at Sandfly. He'd spread rumours about the boozy old bastard – some true – but to no avail. The director stuck to the job like a limpet, but Hetherington hoped his fondness for the bottle would eventually create a vacancy. He was convinced he was entitled to it.

Hetherington was indefatigable. Whenever a convict died behind bars, he would attend the autopsy, anxious to examine the brain for physical evidence of moral degeneracy, and he itched to obtain permission to run a pair of phrenological callipers over the skulls of all living inmates of Her Majesty's Hobart Gaol, if not the entire Tasmanian population. Critics sneered that researchers such as Doctor Hetherington found what they wanted to find, but he was not deterred.

Hobart Gaol, Winter 1954

The city's guardian mountain was carpeted thick with snow and the air smelled of iron. Miss Marjorie Sproule was walking through central Hobart from her boarding house in Battery Point, her sensible shoes click-clacking on the frost-rimed streets. Some loafers wolf whistled as she passed their lodging house, but she ignored them. The walk saved on tram fares and helped pay for the book she had on order from Fuller's, the city's best bookshop. She was dreading another visit to the prison and had earlier contemplated calling in sick to avoid it, and in truth the thought of the sights and smells of the penitentiary did make her feel nauseous.

Alas, there it was: Her Majesty's Hobart Gaol, as solid as the towering mountain from whose flanks its stones had been hewed. Its lines were classical Georgian, but Miss Sproule knew it to be a place of squalor and misery that mocked the idea of rehabilitation. She walked slowly to the main entrance, which was set between two handsome octagonal double-storey colonial gatehouses. Everyone – prisoners and warders, priests, solicitors, doctors, undertakers, and corpses – entered or left through the two sets of iron-barred gates. Her boss, Doctor Stuart

Hetherington, was already waiting, and although she was ten min-utes early, he was peering irritably at his watch. Hetherington was a very fussy man and would often complain to Miss Sproule of some supposed act of negligence by his housekeeper, his marsupial face puckered in a peevish rictus. Now, as he waited at the prison gate, he was picking at a splodge of egg yolk on the blue of his Hutchins Old Boys' tie – Mrs Rattray's fault, no doubt. He rapped on the outer gate and a white-haired screw trotted out of the gatehouse and opened it for them.

'Mornin', Doctor, miss,' he croaked, touching the brim of his cap as if it were a forelock.

The old screw had somehow kept a kindly face, wrinkled like an old apple. Miss Sproule took in the fruit-salad spray of campaign ribbons on the warder's chest – Gallipoli 1915, Dublin Easter 1916, Fromelles, the winter of the same year – and her thoughts turned to her beau, dead these past ten years on the Kokoda Trail.

A younger screw scurried up and took the doctor's Gladstone bag up the spiral staircase to the interview room. Hetherington followed, two steps at a time, preening as he caught sight of his reflection in a window. He was, Miss Sproule knew, a fitness fanatic and had taken his daily plunge in the freezing Derwent as dawn was breaking. She guessed it was a self-imposed penance for the drinking problem he thought she didn't know about. Now, briskly towelled and breakfasted, dapper in his uniform of blue blazer and buff cavalry twill trousers, he was anxious to begin his first interview with the prisoner the press had dubbed 'the Beast of Bronte'. He was proud of the muscular torso he had maintained since his rugger bugger days and had no idea that people called him Kanga after the Winnie the Pooh character. Miss Sproule smiled inwardly: he really did resemble a Bennett's wallaby, *Notamacropus rufogriseus*, but his eyes were gimlet-sharp, his manner brusque, and his tone peremptory. Nevertheless, she detected a faint smell of beer on the old hypocrite's breath. The file on the so-called

Beast was in his briefcase, which the obsequious warder handed him at the door of the interview room before hovering about like a porter waiting for his tip.

The so-called Beast was already seated at the interview table; an arresting presence despite his tiny stature. He would be lucky to be five foot tall, Miss Sproule estimated. His breath was steaming, and he was shivering, for it was as cold inside these stone walls as it was outside. As if on cue, an ancient convict shambled in bearing an armload of kindling and paper. He stooped arthritically but set the fire expertly in the grate, and the warder struck a match to light it.

Miss Sproule had scanned the police report on the Beast's crime before filing it away and knew the gist of it – a particularly vile murder in a hydro-electric construction town on the Central Plateau. She took in Geordie Stubbs's head of thick red hair, greying at the temples, under which one startlingly green eye and one blue eye stared from a face the colour of her polished Tasmanian Oak dresser. Heterochromia, the medical notes had said, with slight exotropic strabismus in the left orb. Two warders – Cresswell and Burr – were lumbering about, fastening chains around the Beast's ankles, their features betraying a common ancestry with some of those they kept under lock and key. The little Beast raised an eyebrow at the sight of them. 'Heads on them like boarding house puddings,' he muttered, fumbling for his sack of tobacco. When Hetherington suggested the shackles were unnecessary, the warders shrugged gracelessly and stomped out through the door leaving a faint trail of sweat and flatulence in their wake. Meanwhile, the fire was crackling in the grate and as it was slightly warmer, Miss Sproule took off her cardigan and draped it over the back of her chair. She was in her late thirties, but had retained her severe, rather good-looking features, short fair hair, and a fine-boned, intelligent face.

Mr Stubbs really was very small, a veritable manikin. There was a wiry strength in his body, but he sat mildly, basking in the heat of the now blazing fire, with a slight moue of amusement playing on his lips as he rolled a thin cigarette from the coarse prison-issue tobacco. Miss Sproule, meanwhile, had taken out her stenographer's notebook and pencil. She knew the horrid details of the murder off by heart.

Hetherington dropped Geordie Stubbs's file on the desk before him with a thud. It comprised half a ream of double-sided foolscap paper: a record of police interviews, witness statements, court proceedings and the verdict, and personal documents seized from the Beast's quarters at Bronte Park. An appendix covered the other murders of which he was prime suspect.

'The Court has appointed me as an expert witness to prepare a mental evaluation as part of your pre-sentence report,' Hetherington began, glancing at the door to make sure the warders weren't eavesdropping. 'My secretary here, Miss Sproule, will be taking shorthand notes.' Miss Sproule sat by the window, the light bringing out the amber tones in her face – not that the doctor had ever looked closely at his employee.

The Beast blew a shrewd plume of blue smoke towards the nicotine-stained ceiling, tapped his temple, and winked with his good eye. 'Why aye man, ye're a "trick cyclist".'

His voice was a low, singing rumble rather than the piping tones you might expect from such a bantam of a man. His singsong accent was Geordie, redolent of the coaly Tyne and the salt wind off the North Sea, not 'Scotch', as the local rag had misinformed its readers. He folded his arms and winked again.

Hetherington gave a strained smile. Prisoners usually greeted him with either sullen taciturnity or obsequiousness, but there was no deference in Geordie's tone.

'That's one way of putting it,' he agreed, adopting a jolly-hockey-sticks tone, and tapping his notes into order. 'Yes, for my sins I'm a psychiatrist.'

The Beast raised an eyebrow and waited while the doctor pretended to initial some passages in the margins of his documents. Silence is a stock-in-trade of the alienist's toolkit, and normally only the most obdurate or stupid people can resist filling it with words, but the Beast puffed calmly on his cigarette, with one ruddy eyebrow interrogatively raised. Irritated, Hetherington scrutinised his features, taking in the high forehead and the wide, sardonic mouth. The broken nose hinted at a history of pugilism – and perhaps other things. The red hair, too – another abnormality, because they weren't many with that colouration. He took up his Parker fountain pen and scribbled a scarcely legible note.

Meanwhile, the silence yawned. Hetherington pointedly cleared his throat. Miss Sproule smiled nervously, eyeing Stubbs as a sparrow watches a hungry alley cat.

'Now, my man,' said the doctor briskly. 'You are George William Marmaduke Stubbs?'

'Aye, that's me,' the Beast agreed. 'Quite a mouthful, eh? I go by Geordie, by the way. Geordie the Geordie, like.'

The doctor's question was rhetorical. There was a copy of the prisoner's birth certificate in the thick folder. George William Marmaduke Stubbs was born on the eighteenth day of January 1894 in the town of Felling in the parish of Jarrow in County Durham, northern England.

'So that makes you sixty years old?'

'Aye, that's wight, Doctor,' the prisoner concurred.

Aha! The doctor's ears pricked up at the speech impediment – rhotacism, or in the vernacular, a lisp, in which a person cannot properly pronounce his r's. He found this in combination with the prisoner's strabismus and other bodily imperfections to be highly significant. He jotted another note and glanced back down at the birth certificate, which named William Hector Stubbs, a 48-year-old coalminer, and Catherine Sarah Stubbs, née Allen, an 18-year-old domestic servant, as the Beast's parents. Geordie agreed they were and volunteered that the family had lived in the pit village of High Fell on the outskirts of Felling.

Geordie ground out his cigarette in the yellow Pimm's No 1 ashtray and watched the doctor keenly, the cast in his eye slightly disconcerting. He looked Hetherington squarely in the face – or at least his 'good' green eye did, while the blue one squinted slightly out through the barred window with its view of a slice of brumous sky above Mount Wellington. Over the next few hours, Hetherington – and Miss Sproule – learned a great deal about Geordie's early years. They had a long lunch break that day as Hetherington had some urgent business to attend to. Miss Sproule took the opportunity to go for a walk on the Queen's Domain, the large area of bushland on the city's edge, and Geordie spent the time reading the Bible in his cell.

'Do you sleep well, Stubbs?' Hetherington enquired when they resumed, not from any concern for Geordie's welfare but to ascertain his mental state and see perhaps if he showed any remorse for his crime.

Geordie raised an ironic eyebrow: 'Well doctor, I divvent sleep so well, what wi' bugs in the cot and what's waiting for me along yon prison yard.'

Hetherington offered to prescribe sleeping pills, but Geordie shook his head and Hetherington invited him to continue, with his fountain pen poised above his notebook. Miss Sproule puzzled over the dialect words but transcribed them phonetically.

'Anything more you would like to tell me about your birth?' asked the doctor.

'Ye want to look back to "the stars that reigned at my nativity", eh?'

Hetherington frowned, not getting the allusion, but forgotten in her corner, Miss Sproule wrote 'Faustus' in the margin of her notebook. At this point Stubbs burst into a fit of coughing and Hetherington asked the turnkeys to bring in some water. Stubbs waved it away. He didn't trust the screws not to spit in it, and as the short winter day was ending, Hetherington shut his notebook and announced that they would conclude the session. For a man convicted of a capital crime, Stubbs was in good spirits. Hetherington wondered if he was in a dissociative state and wrote a last-minute note to investigate this in a future session.

The doctor opened his car door deep in thought, not quite aware of the drenching winter squall buffeting the Hobart streets. The weather had taken a turn for the worse that afternoon, with sudden savage squalls of rain deluging the city. As he went to start the car, he noticed Miss Sproule standing outside the prison gatehouse, attempting to prevent her umbrella from turning inside out in the wind. He wound down his window and offered her a lift, which she accepted gratefully, for she was dripping wet.

'You know,' he said, as if it were a revelation when she slid into the passenger seat. 'You have never said where you live!'

Miss Sproule smiled wryly. In fact, he had never asked, although she had worked for him for many years. Perhaps the man thought she was warehoused somewhere and wheeled out for his convenience! Still, he had noticed she was getting drenched in the filthy weather, and for that she was thankful.

'Oh,' said Hetherington. 'Battery Point. That's on my way!'

The route took them past the Sullivan's Cove wharves, which were crowded with ships. When they stopped at a red light, they saw a seething mob of waterside workers milling about on the wharf. A tall, rangy man was haranguing them through a bullhorn and some of the wharfies were brandishing placards. The rain didn't seem to be deterring them at all.

'Not another strike,' Hetherington muttered. 'The Waterside Workers' Federation at it again. It's a Communist front and it leads these wharfies by the nose. If I had my way, they would get a taste of the baton and I'd bring in men who want to work.'

Hetherington was shocked when Miss Sproule, sitting straight-backed in the passenger seat, dared to disagree. 'My dad's a wharfie up in Launceston. He's a good man. Wharfies work hard but they're treated so badly that it's no wonder they go on strike.' Hetherington drove on in silence after that and grunted a goodbye when he let her out at the corner of Hampden Road. He wondered if the woman was a Communist herself, for as Prime Minister Menzies said, the Reds wormed their way into responsible positions to rot the state from within. Straight out of Lenin's revolutionary textbook. Hetherington had a motion on the threat of communism up at the annual general meeting of his club that very evening, and he was looking forward to speaking to it. The sight of those wharfies had quite got his dander up.

After he had dropped her off, Miss Sproule sat in her first-floor room in Mrs Mahoney's 'Superior Boarding House for Respectable Ladies' in Hampden Road. Night was drawing a veil over Battery Point's roof-tops and chimney pots, but she was thinking of Geordie Stubbs and didn't take in the view. He didn't seem like a murderer, but perhaps things would become clearer as he related his story. Meanwhile, it promised to be another dreary evening, punctuated only by dinner, served promptly at 6:00 p.m. in winter and 6:30 p.m. in summer. It was Friday, and as Mrs Mahoney was an observant Catholic it would be vegetable soup and a main course of poached fish in white sauce, with chocolate pudding and custard to follow. A brass clock ticked on her mantelpiece; the fireplace long since replaced with a single bar electric heater, which struggled against the chill. Pulling on a woolly jumper, she sat at her escritoire, and surveyed the photographs lined up neatly, each one sitting on an embroidered doily next to stacks of books and writing paper. A sepia-toned photograph of The Cor-ner on Cape Barren Island hung on one wall – a family heirloom inherited from Nanna Everett – but pride of place was given to the framed portrait of a serious young man in army uniform and slouch hat. Lieutenant David McDougall was twenty-four years old when he was killed in action in 1942, at Oivi-Gorari on the Kokoda Trail. Next to it was a snap of the lieutenant arm-in-arm with a younger Miss Sproule taken when he was on leave from Puckapunyal. The couple were smiling happily. He had proposed and she had accepted.

The dinner gong interrupted her reverie.

~ 5 ~

Hobart Gaol, Winter 1954

Hetherington was in good humour the following Monday morning, after a weekend's fishing down at Eaglehawk Neck. He felt he had spoken eloquently at Friday night's club meeting, which had voted unanimously to send a strong statement to the local newspaper condemning the waterfront strike and linking it with the communist threat in French Indochina. The motion also lamented the failure of the 1951 referendum to ban the Communist Party and called for a second vote. He didn't feel the need to mention this to Miss Sproule, who had been very frosty since their recent disagreement. She needed to be put in her place, he thought, and he wondered about what subversive political opinions she might harbour behind those guileless blue eyes.

Miss Sproule was angry, but not with him – she knew he was incorrigible – and was glaring at the two screws Burr and Cresswell, whom she thought of as the Lizard and the Monocle. Geordie was already in the interview room. The fire was unlit, and the room was dank and cheerless. The doctor insisted that the fire be lit before he would begin the session. He frowned at the livid bruise on Geordie's cheekbone and scowled at the smirking warders.

'I've been in solitary confinement,' said Geordie, fingering the bruise gingerly. 'I refused to go to the Sunday service, so they gave me a little encouragement, like.'

'But attendance is compulsory,' Hetherington observed, lips pursed. 'I'm afraid that the prison has strict rules about this. May I ask why you are creating such a fuss about it?'

Geordie managed a wry smile. 'The head yard screw Markwick let me borrow some books from the library. I found some Charles Dickens and Walter Scott. Anyway, I was just looking forward to a quiet read when them bozos come round and said it was time for chapel.' He jerked his thumb to the door to indicate who he meant. 'Bastards frogmarched me there.'

'Are you religious?' Hetherington demanded.

'Well,' Geordie replied, stroking his chin. 'To me, religion is a childish toy and there is no sin but ignorance.'

The psychiatrist scrawled something so savagely in his notebook that the nib went through the paper. A smile flickered briefly on Miss Sproule's lips. *Doctor Faustus* again. Stubbs rolled one of his prison issue cigarettes and leaned away from the fire, which was crackling merrily. Either the Lizard or the Monocle audibly farted outside the door. Miss Sproule hoped it was cold out there. Hetherington harrumphed a bit before asking Geordie to tell him something about his early childhood. None of what the little man said seemed to make the doctor happy. He seemed amazed that Geordie's father, Billy, had never physically chastised his putative son; his own father lived by the rule that to spare the rod was to spoil the child and Hetherington believed it had been character-building. Perhaps if Billy Stubbs had been more responsible, he mused, his son might not have turned out the way he did. Hetherington's questions were probing, and Geordie volunteered information even when the doctor hadn't asked.

The Lizard and the Monocle were smirking when they next delivered Geordie to the interview room. They plonked him down on his chair and winked at Miss Sproule as they left the room. Hetherington scanned Geordie's face for signs of assault, but apart from the earlier bruise, which was fading, his brown features were unmarked. Geordie muttered that he had spent the night in the punishment cells on bread and water because he had again refused to attend religious services.

'But why do you do it?' Hetherington was genuinely puzzled. 'Surely, it's not worth all the bother?'

Geordie sucked on the Craven A the doctor had given him and blew out a cloud of smoke before replying. 'Because it's mumbo-jumbo.' He chuckled. 'We are supposed to have separation of religion and state, don't we?'

'You went up before Governor Hornblower about this?'

'Aye, but he refuses to listen. I said that as they are going to hang me, they should leave my soul in peace, but he's a stickler for the rules. I've demanded to see my lawyer about it. Anyway, it's not your concern, Doctor.'

Hetherington believed that Geordie Stubbs's atheism was his concern, but he refrained from further comment.

Geordie had a broad smile on his face when the screws brought him in the next morning. 'My lawyer, Dermot Lindsay, gave that Governor a right bollocking. Hornblower didn't take kindly to it, but Mr Lindsay threatened to take it to the High Court. The Constitution prevents the authorities from imposing any religious observance – even on us crims. Hornblower backed off and now they allow me to stay in my cell while the others go off and bother God.'

Hetherington said nothing, but he was not happy with this radical ratbaggery. He would most certainly mention it in his report to the judge. When they broke for lunch, he nibbled on the egg and lettuce sandwich Mrs Rattray had prepared to spare him the unpalatable prison fare. Miss Sproule ate her sandwiches in the University Garden and read a chapter of Camus's *The Plague*. Back in the prisoners' mess, Geordie pushed his plate aside, squinting at the grey thing that wobbled obscenely on his plate. His neighbour grabbed the saveloy, devoured it in three bites, and mopped Geordie's plate with a slice of bread.

After lunch, Geordie continued his account of his childhood. Hetherington listened carefully and despite his determination to remain objective, he found himself warming to the little man's tale. Geordie boasted that he had been a pretty baby, but there was a self-deprecatory edge to his storytelling.

High Fell, County Durham, 1892–93

By his own account, Geordie was an inquisitive child. He had been in a hurry to leave his mother's womb and had taken a keen interest in his new surroundings. Old Fanny Urwin, the midwife, reckoned he had winked at her when she was cutting the umbilical cord, but his young mammy, proud though she was of the bairn, believed the wink was due to wind, or that Fanny's prodigious intake of gin had affected her eyesight. Catherine had given birth at home in Calcutta Row, a terrace of miners' cottages abutting the High Fell colliery railway line on the outskirts of Felling, an industrial town on Tyneside. She was pleased to have avoided the infirmary, not least because the Russian influenza pandemic was turning hospitals into charnel houses. She must have wondered what life had in store for the infant, for even today Tyneside is an anthracite-hard place, far from the picture-book England of gardens and soft green lawns.

Catherine had come to Tyneside with her family from Derry in Ireland in the spring of 1892, when she was sixteen years old. Her mother had died some years earlier during a cholera outbreak and her father, Timothy Allen, had been blacklisted back home because of his outspoken socialist politics and activism in the Associated Society of Blacksmiths. He found work at the High Fell colliery and the family moved into a company house in the nearby village. Catherine secured a live-in position as a skivvy at Lambton Hall, the ancestral seat of the Cholmondley-Devereaux family, which sat atop a hill at some remove from the sights and smells of the River Tyne. She had unusual features for those dour northern parts, with jet-black hair, bright green eyes, and a dark complexion such as is often found in Sicilians and Maltese. Her employers, the judge Sir Cuthbert, and his good wife Lady Agatha, were oblivious to such pulchritude, but their strapping red-haired son Jeremiah had noted her charms. The boy was supposed to be reading Greats at Oxford, but horses, the hunt, tennis, beer, and girls took precedence over study. Indeed, he had been rusticated from Balliol the previous year for drunkenly abusing the Master and sneaking common tarts into the Junior Common Room and hanging their knickers on the clock tower. The judge had to call in many favours to persuade the Master not to send him down for good.

Jeremiah had slouched into the Hall one afternoon and tossed his tennis pullover in Catherine's direction, with the drawled order to 'get it washed'. After a few steps he had turned and ogled her shamelessly. When she next saw him, he was dressed up in a foxhunting turnout of scarlet jacket and he turned a leg clad in canary-yellow breeches to impress her. After that he contrived to bump into her whenever she was alone, and she heard him drawling away about her with his friend Horatio Bowes-Lyon, a scion of the coal-owning family with blood ties to Buckingham Palace. Catherine was flattered by Jeremiah's attentions, but she knew he was playing with her. Her mammy had warned her about the men from the Big Houses back in Ireland who had deflowered maidens on their wedding eves not so many years past.

She tried to avoid Jeremiah until he went back down to Oxford, but she could not always hide behind the French cook's hefty posterior. One sultry May evening, when she was serving dinner, she was uncomfortably aware of the hot glances he was casting in her direction. She thought she heard one of the Bowes-Lyons boys whisper that it was time for Jeremiah 'to bed the darkie' but couldn't be sure. She tumbled into her bed that evening and watched the thunderstorm that was raging outside her attic window. She snuffed out her candle. Rain began to fall, and when she drifted off into a fitful sleep Jeremiah's voice woke her. She had no idea of the time and wondered where she was. This was her room, she realised, fully awake … The Young Master … It was dark … What was he doing here? She wasn't a complete eejit … She knew … The springs creaked under his weight as he sat heavily on the end of the bed.

Afterwards, she lay silent with her face to the wall. Jeremiah fumbled in his riding breeches, and she heard coins clinking as he dropped them on her bedside table. She did not sleep again that long night, but lay listening to the rain, sobbing and praying to the Virgin Mary. She was soiled. Unclean. How could she find a husband? With the watery dawn came resolution. She should not beg God's forgiveness, for Jeremiah had forced himself on her. There was a word for what he had done, though it had never crossed her lips. She hurled his filthy coins out the window into the rain, dressed quickly, and lit her candle to find the way down the back stairs. Soon she stood trembling at Mrs Campbell, the Scottish housekeeper's, door and gave it a tentative knock.

'Ach, whatever do you want, child?' demanded Mrs Campbell, her voice thick with sleep. 'What un-Christian time is this to come knocking on doors?'

She invited Catherine in and busied herself making a pot of tea.

'Now, lassie,' she said, wide-awake now and encouraging, proffering cup and saucer. 'I'll sit here quietly, and you can tell me why you have dragged me from my bed at this heathen hour.' When Catherine had finished, Mrs Campbell's face was set. 'Leave it wi' me hen,' she said. 'I'll make things right for you.'

Lady Agatha denied her son would do such a thing, but Mrs Campbell was quietly persistent. Her employer sat at her desk with her face in her hands, her red tresses awry. It all fitted: the serving girls who had left in a hurry without collecting their money, always when Jeremiah was home; the dark mutterings she had half-heard on the stairs; the whispering voices stilled as she came past; her own dark thoughts buried for too long. She would warn Jeremiah against any further scandal and would keep her eye on him whenever he was in the house. She summoned the miscreant to her sitting room and gave him a tongue-lashing that echoed inside his empty head all the way back down to Oxford.

The damage, however, was done. Catherine missed her period and three weeks later, she awoke feeling nauseous.

Mrs Campbell had another urgent conference with Lady Agatha, who insisted that marriage was out of the question. A youthful lapse must not destroy a life. Surely a marriage might be arranged to someone of a suitable station? Mrs Campbell knew there was no arguing with her employer. Sir Cuthbert conferred in his club with Mr Rupert Bell, a coal owner and ironmaster in whose business he had invested a goodly sum, and who could be relied upon for discretion. The judge would provide a lump sum to a suitable suitor and subsidise the child's care until it came of age, whereupon he would arrange a final payment and send it out into the world, duty done. Bell knew just the chap, a thrifty middle-aged bachelor who worked as a corporal, or under-deputy, in the High Fell pit, and who owed him a big favour. So it came to pass that one autumn day, Catherine Allen and Billy Stubbs exchanged vows in St Crispin's Anglican Church. Catherine's father did not approve of the match but there was little he could do about it. Billy took two days' leave from the pit – his lost wages provided for – and the couple honeymooned in a guesthouse at Whitley Bay. It was debatable which was more afraid of the other.

~7~

High Fell, County Durham, 1894–1907

Born hairless as an Xoloitczuintli pup, baby Geordie soon sprouted a thatch of luxuriant red curls and developed his mam's bright green eyes; or one of them at least, for the other was blue. His skin was dark, a throwback to his African ancestors. Catherine doted on him despite the manner of his conception, and Billy Stubbs, his putative father, always treated him with gruff affection. Catherine had managed to conceal the facts of her son's conception from her family and didn't feel any guilt about doing so. Being wed in a Protestant church, though, made Catherine imagine the black pit of Hell so vividly that she smelled the smoke and cinders. In fact, the smell came from locomotives hauling coal wagons past the house, but visions of eternal fire and brimstone tormented her.

Severe though the faith of her fathers could be, Catherine was a good Irish Catholic girl. Billy had taken it for granted that the baby would be baptised by the Anglican vicar. She agreed, but one winter's day, she wrapped wee Geordie in a thick shawl and trudged a mile or more through the snow to have Father Flynn baptise the bairn into the One Holy Catholic and Apostolic Church of Rome. Thus, when she stood before St Peter, she could argue that she had done her solemn religious duty. Her agnostic father, Tim, joked that it meant Geordie had a bob each way in the spiritual stakes.

The child was an early walker, and this caused his mother constant worry. Other small boys wanted to be omnibus drivers or sea captains, but he wanted to be a mountain climber. There are no mountains on Tyneside, but he clambered to the top of the pit heap and had to be rescued by a pit deputy. Catherine was angry. 'Just you wait until your da gets home,' she said, but Billy just laughed. He never hit the child, though he was a tough old pitman and there were many around who held that to spare the rod was to spoil the child. Another time, Catherine's neighbour, Elsie Ross, came thumping on the door to complain about what Geordie and her daughter were doing. 'Missus Stubbs!' she shrieked. 'Them un-Christian bairns is doon the lonnin showin' each other their private parts!' Annie, the Rosses' girl, became Geordie's closest pal when they started school. With her apple cheeks and thick black hair, she looked like an angel, but the appearance was deceptive, for she and Geordie were always up to some devilment or other.

When he turned five, Catherine took Geordie to the National School on the Felling main road. After bribing him with his favourite sherbet lemons, she entrusted him to the care of the infant mistress, Miss Beryl Preedy, a refined spinster who looked down her long nose on the Geordies. After an hour of fidgeting through lessons Geordie decided he had had enough and went home, declaring that as he had been to school and did not like it, he would stay at home. Catherine had to drag him back kicking and squealing to Miss Preedy's dubious care. The teacher laboured hard to wean the pupils off 'slang', as she called the local dialect, but she did not try to spark any love of learning in her charges. Despite this, having an autodidact for a grandfather gave Geordie a head start. Tim Allen had an impressive library and was always holding forth about education for the working class.

Usually, the children did their sums and writing with chalk on slates, but on those occasions when Miss Preedy doled out paper, pens, and ink for the inkwells, she was impressed despite herself with Geordie's calligraphic ability. Geordie also found it very easy to copy her beautiful flowing script. He was fascinated by atlases and would pore over maps highlighting in pink the Empire on which the sun never set. He hoped one day to visit those places. He also excelled at drawing and had the uncanny ability to capture the look of a person or an object in a few quickly sketched lines. He could calculate sums in his head long before Miss Preedy worked them out with pen and paper. He was a very bright child, but she never liked him. He was, however, very popular with the other children, both for his natural friendliness and for the madcap antics that kept them amused.

Geordie's parents did not know what to make of his report cards. Miss Preedy noted that 'whenever there is some mischief afoot, Master Stubbs is always to be found.' Nevertheless, she admitted that if he behaved himself, she could see him becoming a pupil-teacher. Geordie also discovered that he had considerable musical talent. His granda had been a fiddler of some renown back in Ireland and he was delighted by the interest Geordie took in the instrument. Under Tim's patient eye, Geordie learned some reels, jigs, and slow Irish airs. When he turned ten, Tim presented him with one of his own fiddles and it was afterwards the boy's most treasured possession.

Geordie's best friend after Annie Ross was the family's fox terrier, Barney, who had been Billy's dog before he and Catherine were wed. The time came, of course, when the dog died, and Geordie was inconsolable. It happened not long after his twelfth birthday. He came home from school and Barney didn't run out to meet him like he always did. It was the cancer, Billy reckoned. Billy cared for the boy as if he were his own child. He loved walking and most Sundays, when Geordie was big enough, they'd go for long rambles in the fells, often taking Annie with them. Windy Nook was a favourite in all weathers. In summer, they would leave early and walk as far as Waldridge Fell, which was above the valley at Chester-le-Street. Catherine would cut them some sandwiches and they'd have a flask of cold tea like Billy took down the mine. Billy loved nature and was a good teacher. He knew the names of all the plants – bracken of course, but also hairgrass, heather, bilberry, the various types of ferns, the sphagnum moss round Wanister Pond. They would sit quietly in the oak or alder trees, and he would point out the names of the birds like the Green Hairstreak and the Stonechat. He even knew the names of the insects because when he was a boy, he'd known an old schoolteacher who was an expert. Another place was Beacon Lough, though the lough was long gone. Hazlett's Pond, they'd called it, after a highwayman they'd hung there years before. When it was clear, which wasn't very often, you could see as far as the Cheviots up on the Scottish border.

Billy could never abide cruelty. One day, Geordie and some other children were tormenting a mad old woman. Kids would throw stones at her door and shout things at her. They thought she was a witch. Billy caught them at it, and he took Geordie straight home and gave him a real talking to. The poor old creature had never been the same after her husband had died down the pit. The strong had to protect the weak, Billy said. Geordie left her alone after that and would intercede when the other children harassed her.

Geordie was a good scholar, and in a more equal world he could have mastered any profession. Alas, working-class kids seldom stayed on at school. Their parents couldn't afford it. Socialists like Geordie's grandfather argued for longer schooling for all, but the High Fell people knew that it wasn't something that was going to happen anytime soon. That was the general situation, but in Geordie's case particular circumstances hurried things up. Towards the end of 1907, the days were shortening and there were thick frosts on the fields. Guy Fawkes Night was coming, and the miners had gathered fallen branches, broken furniture, and whatnot for the huge bonfire they would light to burn the effigy of poor old Guy; barring the Labour members like Will

Thorne and Keir Hardie, the only man ever to enter Parliament with honest intentions, Tim reckoned. It was a fine time for all, especially for the children, who eagerly looked forward to the fireworks. Billy had purchased a stack of rockets, Catherine wheels, roman candles, jumping jacks, bangers and the like and stashed them in the coalhouse. The devil got into Geordie. Early one morning, he sneaked out with a load of gunpowder from the fireworks, which he'd poured into a cardboard box. He put this in the staff lavatory at the school and laid a fuse he'd made by soaking paper with wet gunpowder and letting it dry. Then he sneaked back home for breakfast.

He left as usual for school after submitting to a kiss from his mother, cut across some waste ground and hid behind a hedge. He knew that his old nemesis, Miss Preedy, was in the habit of visiting the lavatory before classes began. Everything went according to plan, at least at first. Miss Preedy was just stretching out her hand to the door when the gunpowder exploded. She screamed and ran back to the schoolhouse just as the other teachers came running out to investigate. The poor woman had wet herself with fright. Geordie was delighted, but an old man had seen him setting the charge and he informed the headmaster. Mr O'Neill expelled Geordie on the spot and the local constable warned that any future misbehaviour would result in charges laid.

Billy was furious and swore that the boy would 'gan doon the pit'. For once, he refused to listen to Tim Allen. Catherine begged him to give Geordie another chance. He could enrol as a pupil-teacher in the next village, she said, but Billy would have none of it. 'Stubbses has elwis bin mining folk!' he shouted and went out to the pub, taking it for granted that his wishes would prevail.

Hobart, Winter 1954

Geordie had been surprisingly willing to talk, but he had been strangely reluctant to discuss the actual murder.

'You've been fairly honest and open with me,' Hetherington said. 'So, I must ask: is there something you're not telling me?'

'Howay man, I must have killed him, mustn't I?' Geordie retorted. 'The court found me guilty. Why don't we just leave it there? When you make your report, the judge will pass sentence. I'm guilty of so much anyway and when I go, my death will not amount to much. 'The stars will move still, time will still run, the clock will strike.' *Doctor Faustus* again, noted Miss Sproule and Hetherington shrugged.

Hetherington whistled as he headed for his club. The case was providing some very interesting material. The session had revealed a marked dislike of authority and the social system on Stubbs's part. The fireworks incident showed an audacious flair for crime from an early age. He was also struck by the fact that Stubbs was a born actor. He had put on an array of voices and accents—English upper class, Irish, and Scots, besides his native Geordie. Hetherington would have to be on guard against the little man's wiles. The manner of Stubbs's conception also appeared to have weighed heavily on him. Hetherington wondered about the transmission of Jeremiah Cholmondley-Devereaux's character to his biological son – if Mr Stubbs's account was accurate, that was, and his mother had not been a tart out to snare a man of higher social standing. That persistent cough though – it was most likely caused by smoking, but perhaps there was some underlying cause?

Hobart Gaol, Winter 1954

The prison ablutions block was known as 'Ringworm Alley' by both crims and screws, and it was to this dismal shanty that Geordie Stubbs and the other inmates in his wing went for their weekly baths. The plumbing had possibly been state-of-the-art back in Queen Victoria's day, but it taxed the ingenuity of the prison maintenance man to keep it in operation on bath nights. An ancient hot water cylinder coughed and gurgled, and sometimes actually did work but often it either scalded or froze its victims. Occasionally, the drains would block up and dirty water would run out into the exercise yard. The insalubrity of the place was sometimes raised in the State Parliament, but as the public didn't much care what happened to the criminals after they were banged up, nothing was ever done.

The ablutions block was also dark, which made it difficult for the warders to see what their charges were up to.

Geordie placed his scrap of towel on the rickety bench and walked naked into the crowded shower bay. His sensitive antennae detected an indefinable menace in the air, but he was anxious to sluice off the week's grime.

At first, he thought someone had punched him in the back. Then there was a sharp, unbearable pain, followed by a flurry of blows. He tried to turn but his attacker had seized him by the neck and again and again drove something sharp into his torso. Geordie screamed and had collapsed in a bloody heap when the old warder supposedly standing guard noticed what had happened, by which time the knifeman had vanished into the steam. The screw frantically blew his whistle, and a phalanx of baton-wielding colleagues came rushing in expecting to find a riot in progress. Geordie was seriously injured and was fast losing consciousness, so they stretchered him out of the annex and into an ambulance, which screeched off to the Royal Hobart Hospital with its siren wailing.

Geordie, by now semi-comatose from massive blood loss, was taken directly into Casualty, where the young doctor on duty did his best to stem the bleeding, gave him injections to quell the pain and counter tetanus, and whisked him off for an x-ray. 'You're a very lucky man,' said the doctor. 'If the knife had gone in just a fraction to the side, it would have severed your spine. Had that happened you would never have walked again. There is some bad news, though. Some of your internal organs are badly damaged.' Geordie nodded his thanks and slipped into oblivion as the morphine took hold. The surgeons were worried that his wounds would become infected and although they strove mightily to repair the damage it was touch and go whether he would survive the frenzied attack. He was wheeled into a ward with tubes protruding from various parts of his body while nurses fussed, and an armed warder stood guard in case by some miracle he ran off.

When Inspector Simon Verte arrived, hoping to question Geordie about the attack, he was seen off by the formidable Sister, and beat a tactical retreat to the prison. Governor Hornblower was pessimistic that any of the prisoners would talk, but the inspector was relentless. The lights of the prison interview room burned late into the night. The screws dragged sleepy crims from their slots and paraded them before the inspector, who questioned them at length about what they had seen. The air was blue with cigarette smoke and Verte's temper was only just held in check as prisoner after prisoner denied seeing or knowing anything about the attack. Finally, disregarding Superintendent Doughney's instructions not to lay hands on suspects, Verte got Roy Edensor to rough up a couple of the weaker looking crims, using the old coppers' trick of placing a telephone directory on their abdomens and giving them a good belting with a truncheon. It hurt but left no marks. The trouble was that most crims lived by a strict code of omertà. Others either feared the retribution of their peers more than they feared the screws and police, or genuinely knew nothing. It was close to midnight when the screws ushered in a weedy little fellow for the penultimate interrogation of the long night. Verte and Edensor took one look at the mouth breather and exchanged knowing glances.

Wayne Standage was shit scared because his cellmate had told him about the phone book and baton treatment. To his surprise, the red-haired inspector smiled and offered him a cigarette.

'Go on, Wayne,' Verte prompted. 'It's tailor-made, not like the rubbish you get in here.'

Standage reached out a trembling hand and took the smoke, worried that it was a trick, but the little copper stepped up and lit it with a silver lighter. The big copper was looking at something in his notebook. It didn't look like they were going to give him a good hiding.

'Now, Mister Standage, you've been a naughty boy,' said Edensor, wagging a finger. 'Hitting your girlfriend! Nicking things from the swimming pool lockers, too. Help us and we'll get you transferred up the prison farm at Hayes. It's a cushy number and you're due for release soon, so how about it?'

'Wayne, Wayne! We know you know who stabbed the darkie,' put in Verte. 'Look, it's just a matter of what we call corroboration. You know what that is?'

Standage sucked on his cigarette and shook his head.

'What it means, son, is that your cobbers have already told us who stabbed the fellow. We just need to hear it from you as' – he made air quotes – 'corroborating evidence.'

Standage started to blab, and the detectives arrested Danny Belbin, aka 'Piano Teeth', a 26-year-old Moonah boy who was doing a long stretch for aggravated burglary. Danny's peculiar dentition explained his nickname – black teeth alternating with yellowish-white ones like an old piano keyboard. This, together with a pair of enormous bat-like ears and a snub nose, made a disturbing impression. When Danny realised there was no point in denying he'd done it, he sucked on his ciggy and declared that 'the cunt got what was comin' to 'im.' Verte pretty much agreed. Piano Teeth's big sister, Shirley, had been raped and stabbed to death on her way home from Cadbury's chocolate factory. She had led a blameless life. She had sung in the Presbyterian Ladies' Choir and baked lamingtons and scones for the Country Women's Association. She had prayed for her brother to go straight and visited him every week in prison. The public was outraged, assured by the young alderman Audrey Amos that Geordie Stubbs was the killer.

'I didn't have no choice, did I?' Danny insisted, baring his teeth as if inviting them to play 'Chopsticks' on them. 'I'd be a dog if I didn't stiff the darkie, wouldn't I?'

The shiv – the crude but effective homemade weapon used in the attack – sat bagged and tagged on the interview room table. Principal Officer Ron Markwick had found it in a drain. Piano Teeth described how he had stolen a piece of wrought iron from the prison workshop and sharpened it on the sandstone wall of his slot. He'd carried it to the showers in his rolled-up towel and sneaked up behind Geordie and stabbed him over and over. He regretted that his victim was still alive. The detectives charged him with attempted murder and Governor Hornblower put him in solitary confinement on bread and water for a month. His enhanced status as Shirley Belbin's righteous brother who had 'given the darkie what he deserved' was almost worth the long stretch he knew would be added to his existing sentence. But if Geordie died, Piano Teeth could expect the gallows. Nothing was worth that! To the inspector's credit, he did ask the governor to transfer Wayne Standage to the prison farm. Snitches got short shrift in Campbell Street.

Royal Hobart Hospital, Winter 1954

Geordie lay perilously close to death in his iron hospital bed. He was drowsy from the morphine and spent much of the time in a reverie about his past – some of which he had revealed to the psychiatrist during their sessions in the prison. Outside the art deco hospital building, life went on. Men and women hurried to or from work and the days gradually lengthened. With the Beast out of circulation, the fear that had gripped the city ebbed away. Karl Wollig interviewed some of the medical staff and the article he wrote for the local rag predicted that Geordie would cheat the hangman by dying first. Stuart Hetherington was surprised to feel more than mild regret at what had happened to the little brown man, but he pushed the feeling aside. He was a man of science, after all, and had to maintain a professional distance. Then again, Stubbs might recover, and the interviews could resume.

After the attacks, it appeared that the clock had struck Stubbs's final hour. There was little point, therefore, in writing the report for Justice Dicer, but Hetherington's observations would still, he felt, form the basis for an article in *The Lancet* or the *American Journal of Psychiatry*. The man had displayed deviant behaviour from an early age.

Geordie, however, was a tough old bird and he confounded the hospital doctors' gloomy prognoses. One morning he sat up and announced that, as with Mark Twain, reports of his death had been exaggerated. The doctors stood round his bed, prodding and poking, and hemming and hawing among themselves. He was still in pain, but they took him off the critical list, and removed some of the tubes that festooned his body.

A few days later the hospital rang to inform Doctor Hetherington that Mr Stubbs was fit enough to be interviewed for short periods. Worried by the dangerous prisoner's recovery, the authorities redoubled security. When Hetherington and Miss Sproule arrived, the Monocle was sitting just outside the ward nursing a Webley pistol in his large hands, and the Lizard was patrolling the balcony with a rifle. Geordie was propped up in bed reading an old copy of the *Australasian Post*, which he tossed aside dismissively. He looked almost pleased to see his visitors.

'Why aye, it's like the Ritz here,' he joked. 'I have the whole ward to meself, and the nurses are nicer company than that lot over in Campbell Street. Pity about this, though,' he said, raising his left arm, which was shackled to the iron bedframe. 'Did ye bring grapes by any chance?'

Hetherington smiled and busied himself with his folders. Geordie winked at Miss Sproule. She blushed and sat with sharp pencil poised to record the proceedings. Over the next week, Geordie was in full flow, for he was a born raconteur who obviously loved an audience and was not too choosy about who was in it.

High Fell, 1907–08

Geordie's mother was a quietly stubborn woman and fiercely protective of her errant son. Whatever her husband said, Geordie would not go down the pit, and his granda, Tim Allen, agreed. Catherine walked the three miles to Lambton Hall in the rain and asked Mrs Campbell the housekeeper if she could see Lady Agatha. It was quite irregular, Lady Agatha sighed, but she received Catherine in her private sitting room. Rooks cawed in the fine old trees surrounding the hall. Rain dripped from the eaves and splashed onto the broad walk alongside the house. Catherine stood tongue-tied before her former mistress, dripping rainwater onto the fine Persian carpet.

'Well, Catherine,' Lady Agatha said. 'Do tell me what it is you want and be quick about it!'

'L … Lady Agatha,' Catherine began, her Irish accent strong. 'I'm after walkin' three miles to see you … I'm very grateful for what ye've done for us since … since …'

'Yes, I'm sure,' Lady Agatha cut in. 'Just tell me what it's about.'

Catherine begged her former employer to help Geordie find a position more attuned to his abilities. He was, she said as she proffered his school reports, a clever lad. Especially good at the mathematics and all. Sure, he'd made a mistake, but he deserved a second chance. And he was—

Lady Agatha held up a hand. She was shocked to learn what had caused her secret grandson's expulsion. She didn't promise anything, but she listened and made some starchily sympathetic noises, concerned, despite the class and race prejudices drilled into her, about a lad who was after all her own flesh and blood. Catherine went away feeling better than when she had arrived.

Lady Agatha broached the subject with her husband that evening. Whatever his faults, Sir Cuthbert had never forgotten his familial responsibilities, and was troubled to think of his grandson working as a trapper boy down the High Fell colliery. He had heard that almost one quarter of the Tyneside miners did not live past their thirty-fourth birthdays and shuddered to think of his own flesh and blood buried under a mile of earth, blown to smithereens in a firedamp explosion, or dying of black lung. The next evening, the judge spoke with his pal Rupert Bell over port and cigars at their club. Bell, a tweedy wee man with a pipe always stuck in his mouth, was not without a sense of humour and he guffawed when Sir Cuthbert related the incident which had caused Geordie's expulsion from school.

'Hmm … the darkie's good at mathematics you say?' he ruminated, sipping his whisky. 'Well, I might have just the thing for him. We have a vacancy coming up for an apprentice colliery mechanic at the High Fell pit. If he keeps his nose clean, perhaps we'll make an engineer of him.'

The two men clinked glasses and Geordie's fate was sealed. In the interim between his expulsion from school and starting at the pit, he earned his keep at a variety of odd jobs around the village: running errands, bringing coal in for old biddies, sweeping the saw-dusted floors of the 'Seven Seas', and suchlike. He also made money busking with his fiddle in the Gateshead High Street, playing such tunes as 'The Nine Points of Roguery' and 'The Donegal Reel' with rather more passion than skill, but still entrancing the crowds of shoppers and belying his tender years.

Geordie's first day of work – Saturday 18 January 1908 – had dawned cold and dark, with a freezing wind blustering off the moor. Billy Stubbs fell in with his workmates as they trudged through the village. He was now over sixty. His hair was white, he complained of aches and pains in his back and limbs, his fingernails were rough and misshapen as horn, and his hands were twisted with Dupuytrens's contracture. Coal dust was embedded in the skin of his face, and he had a persistent, hacking cough. He was tough, but he was only made of flesh and blood.

'Eeeh, Billy,' said another old collier, noticing the small figure hanging back in the gloom. 'Ye've got the boy along now.'

'Aye. His first day and not before time.'

The day before, Billy had accompanied Geordie to the colliery offices to witness the boy sign his apprentice's indentures. To Billy's surprise and embarrassment, Rupert Bell, the coal owner, was there to sign on the company's behalf. Bell gave no indication that he remembered Billy's spot of bother fifteen years before, which had involved lowered trousers and an undercover policeman in a Newcastle public lavatory.

The High Fell offices stood on a slight rise behind the pit headstock and the engineers' workshops. Under hissing gas lamps, clerks pushed tall piles of paperwork around on slanting desks. It was all aromatic, polished wood and gleaming glass, kept spick and span by the charlady. Mr Bell's office, which contained a handsome American roll-top desk and swivel chair, was the inner sanctum of the mine, seldom entered even by pit deputies or overmen such as Billy Stubbs. Billy and his son had entered the room tentatively, Billy self-conscious about the pit grime ingrained on his hands, and Geordie subdued perhaps for the first time in his short life. Bell scrutinised the boy's features: he had the same blazing red hair as Sir Cuthbert's wife and son, but he was short and slight, and lacked Jeremiah's mad blue eyes. Or rather he did have one of them. Although he was not a coal-black African, it was plain to see that negro blood ran in his veins. The clerk, a pimply young swell with pomaded brown hair and pince-nez glasses, pushed the indenture papers across the desk with a supercilious smirk, and Bell solemnly addressed the nervous pair on their responsibilities to the firm and vice versa.

'This document,' Bell said, 'legally binds you, young Stubbs, to faithfully serve your time for seven years, and reciprocally, it binds the firm to train you to be a first-class mechanic by the end of it.'

The speech over, Bell stood back and warmed his backside at the fire, all the while sending out villainous smoke clouds from his pipe. The document was written in the pompous legalese of the era and by signing it Stubbs agreed to live a wholesome life, with 'no fornication, gambling, or taverns.' He signed in his beautiful copperplate, and Billy scrawled his name and splashed a couple of inkblots across the paper, and Rupert Bell added his own signature with a flourish. Business concluded, the head clerk ushered the proletarians from the office much as one might shoo away a pair of stray cats. The next seven years of Geordie Stubbs's life were settled, or so it seemed.

The workshop to which he reported the next day was a long, red brick structure, blackened by rain and soot, standing adjacent to the boiler house, which smoked and throbbed twenty-four hours a day, providing steam for the winding engine and the workshops. Inside, he glimpsed a row of large lathes, driven by endless leather belts from a drive shaft that ran the length of the building. Strange machines gnawed on iron and steel, spewing out swarf, and down the far end was the blacksmith's shop where his grandfather Timothy Allen hammered billets of white-hot steel to make horseshoes, tools, machine parts and the like. There were large double gates on one side of the workshop, with railway lines leading to where a locomotive's innards were scattered, with some fitters standing by, ready to begin work.

An old labourer pointed Geordie in the direction of a wooden stairway that led up to some glass-fronted offices. The largest office bore a varnished wooden nameplate, embossed with MR CYRIL TOWARD, ESQ., CHIEF MECHANIC in gilt lettering. A reedy voice bade him enter. Toward was mid-fiftyish and rotund, with a puce complexion, a shock of white hair, and a silver moustache. He was wearing a collar and tie and a waistcoat with fob watch, and his bowler hat and overcoat hung on a peg in the back of the door.

'Harrumph,' Toward grunted. 'Ye'll be Billy Stubbs's boy, Tim Allen's grandson.'

He said nothing more, but rocked from foot to foot, looking Geordie up and down, sucking from time to time on a cigarette and tut-tutting as he did so. Because of this strange vocal mannerism, the workers called him 'Tut', but only behind his back. After some more tutting and harrumphing, he cleared his throat.

'Haddaway back doonstairs.' He pointed with the glowing end of his cigarette. 'Report to yon Yorkshire tyke warmin' his arse at the brazier. That's him. Mister Armstrong, the charge hand.' With that, Tut jerked his head towards the door to indicate that the audience was over.

The Yorkie Tyke, Mick Armstrong, was indeed warming his skinny backside while studying an engineering blueprint. He did not look pleased to see Geordie. He was aged beyond his years, with a yellowish complexion that hinted at chronic digestive problems and a fondness for the bottle. Some people have lived-in faces; Armstrong's badtempered mug looked almost died-in, and Geordie thought a smile might well have cracked it to reveal the bones beneath.

'Who t' fuck are thee, then, boy?' Armstrong muttered in his Yorkshire accent. 'You look like summat t' cat dragged in and there's summat wrong wi' your eyes.'

Geordie informed the chargehand that he was the new apprentice, reporting for duty as Mr Toward had ordered. He had hoped to be set to work with the fitters repairing the railway engine, but Armstrong took him over to a young man who was collecting his tools from a locker.

'This,' said Armstrong, 'is Frankie Cunningham. Now keep thy nose clean and do what Mr Cunningham tells ye. Tha'll be goin' down the pit to help 'im repair a pump.' He paused and essayed a joke: 'Now, Frankie, mind ye don't lose him in the dark, what wi' his colour!'

It had begun to rain, which made Geordie keen to get to the shaft, although he was full of apprehension about descending into the mine. Some boys he knew from school were picking out slate and pyrites from tubs of coal on a raised length of rail track. They were called 'wailers' for some reason and they looked cold and mournful. Dressed in filthy shirts and torn breeks, they stared with blackened faces and shivered in the wind and rain. Save for the intervention of what must have been Geordie's guardian angel–or his mam – that would have been his own fate. He felt guilty that he'd avoided that, but there was no way he'd have swapped their situations.

There was a slight rumble as the cage came to bank below the mine's headstock. The banksman seized the heavy concertina-wire doors and heaved them open, nodding to indicate that they should enter. The mechanic and apprentice were the only passengers in the cage, which sat trembling beneath their feet. Next, it plummeted into the hole that bored three thousand feet down into the earth's crust, leaving Geordie's stomach up at the headframe and causing his ears to pop. Eventually the headlong descent slowed, and the cage bounced on the wire ropes suspending it from the winding engine far above. Frankie bade Geordie take the toolbox and follow him into the gloom. There was a strange smell and young Geordie was surprised to find it very warm after the freezing temperature on the surface. They had to walk for what seemed like miles, the last part of the journey in a stooped position to avoid bashing their heads on the roof of the tunnel. In the distance, they could hear picks striking rock, the ringing of shovels

on piles of coal, the echo of voices and the occasional whinny of pit
ponies. Geordie frowned: poor beasts, condemned to spend their
days underground. It was cruel.

After fixing the pump, they sat down on some pit props to eat their
'bait' and sup their bottles of cold tea. Frankie explained that he was
the shop steward for the Colliery Mechanics' Union and that Geordie
should not hesitate to seek him out for advice. Geordie was distracted.
Could he ever succeed as a colliery mechanic? The place terrified him,
and if Satan himself had come walking down the tunnels from the
mine workings, breathing soot and sulphur, he would not have been
at all surprised. It was growing dark when they handed their discs to
the lamp man back at the surface, and thus ended Geordie Stubbs's
first day at the colliery.

High Fell, 1908–11

Miserable Mick Armstrong soon singled out Geordie for sadistic attention. He was a lay preacher for some gloomy sect and could be heard of an evening ranting in the Felling High Street and believed 'darkies' were fit only to be the hewers of wood and drawers of water described in the Bible. The mechanics advised Geordie to ignore the 'foreign' chargehand: 'Aye, he's a reet micey old bastard, the wazzock's always gannin radgie. He'll find a new victim soon enough.' But he did not. He had two cronies, Adam Tudge and Scott Joyce, and they too joined in the sick fun. One day, they grabbed Geordie and dragged him behind the lavatories. He bit, screamed, and struggled to get free but they debagged him and smeared his private parts with engine grease. 'Blackie's cock and balls the size they say?' Armstrong chortled. Geordie got his own back, though. He riveted Tudge's tool-box shut one evening and smeared old sump oil in Joyce's sandwiches. Miserable Mick had instigated the greasing, but Geordie knew that revenge is a dish best taken cold.

Around this time, early in 1911, Geordie's uncle Anthony grew tired of the sea and found employment as a ropeman in the local collieries.

As strong as his father, Tim, but half his age, he too still spoke with a thick Irish brogue. Geordie's granda was a fierce socialist and a dedicated fiddler, but Anthony didn't take anything too seriously, except the horses. Early in life, he had caught the gambling bug. He borrowed money from his mother's purse to put on a horse that was a sure thing. Alas, the horse had stumbled in the final straight, and Anthony had run away to sea to avoid her wrath. He was happy to introduce Geordie to the pleasures of the racetrack.

One spring day, Geordie took what the colliers called a 'St Monday holiday' and accompanied the reprobate to the racecourse in High Gosforth Park: a breach of the strict rules of his indentures. The racecourse entranced him – the bookies shouting the odds, the thunder of the horses' hooves on the turf, the punters cheering or hissing, the smell of beer, horse sweat, strong tobacco, fish 'n' chips doused in salt and vinegar. It rained heavily, but Geordie didn't notice. He put a sizeable wager on Prince Wilhelm, a horse so-called because of its alleged noble German ancestry. The horse was an outsider, but Anthony had studied its form and reckoned it would beat the odds. The horses galloped round the muddy track, their jockeys not sparing the whip. The favourite, Bold Schemer, was leading but as they came into the straight Prince Wilhelm passed him to win by a good length! After that, Geordie haunted the racecourse but after Tut Toward gave him a 'hurry up notice' to improve his attendance he had to place bets with the local bookie. He would bet on anything and there were any number of takers in the mechanics' shop to put money on whatever daft thing he had dreamed up. He didn't always win, and this was to have unpleasant consequences.

Meanwhile, he got even with Miserable Mick. The whole pit was looking forward to the ninth of June, when foot runners would race a 5.9-mile course from Newcastle to Blaydon. It was a big day in the Geordie calendar, with thousands of men, women, and children 'gannin alang the Scotswood Road, to see the Blaydon Races'. Geordie went with Billy and his mam and was enthralled by the acrobats, illegal card games, Gypsy fortune tellers, fiddlers and Northumbrian pipers, strolling players, and the stalls selling Geordie 'scran' like parkin cakes, claggum, singinghinnies, pan haggerty, pease pudding and stotty cakes, together with fish 'n' chips, beer, stout, Vimto and lemonade. There was a boxing tent where local lads could try to best the proprietor's professional bruisers: big, sad men with cauliflower ears, broken noses, and masses of scar tissue on their beetling brows. Geordie considered running a book on the outcomes of the matches but the regularity with which the challengers were knocked onto the canvas convinced him it wasn't a good idea. The crowd was getting bored with these one-sided contests so the proprietor, an Irishman who called himself Doctor Jarlath Ronayne, invited all comers to come to the ring and there to challenge anyone in the tent to a few rounds. The ensuing bouts were lacklustre affairs characterised by a lack of skill that diluted the venom with which the contestants attacked each other.

To Geordie's surprise, Miserable Mick Armstrong climbed through the ropes and donned a pair of gloves. 'Little darkie over there with the red hair!' shouted Ronayne. Armstrong, who was hopping round the ring in some kind of mad war dance, was twice Geordie's age and much taller and heavier, but memory of the greasing incident dragged Geordie from his reverie, and he skipped into the ring. When the bell clanged, Armstrong rushed straight away at Geordie, his arms windmilling, but the boy was twice as fast and agile. The first round ended inconclusively. Armstrong had landed a blow on Geordie's shoulder, but otherwise both were unscathed. Geordie calculated that if he could keep out of reach, his opponent's strength would begin to ebb. Mick charged out again with bloodlust in his eyes when the bell went for the next round.

'Come on,' he snarled. 'Box proper!'

Geordie concentrated on conserving his energy and dodging

Armstrong's wild punches. By the middle of the next round, the chargehand was breathing heavily, and spraying snot and saliva over the ring. Geordie jabbed him hard in the belly, danced backwards, ducked in under his flailing arms, and hit him hard on the chin. Mick collapsed and lay unmoving on the canvas. Doctor Ronayne counted him out and raised Geordie's arm above his head. 'It was David and Goliath!' he shouted to the cheering crowd. 'The little darkie gets the £5 prize for his courage and skill!'

The match was the talk of the village. Armstrong gave notice at the mine and moved back down to Yorkshire. With their patron gone, Tudge and Joyce kept a very low profile, but Geordie neither forgot nor forgave them for what they'd done. One day, they arrived at work to find official embossed High Fell Colliery Co. Ltd. envelopes in their lockers. Inside were letters purporting to be from Cyril Toward. These informed them that because of their poor workmanship their services were no longer required. The signatures appeared to be authentic. Mr Bell himself interrogated the clerks one by one but concluded that although they all had the means and opportunity, they lacked the motive, not to mention the imagination. Geordie had discovered a new talent for forgery but was careful to keep it secret.

Catherine hadn't dared watch the boxing match, but she was proud of her son – he was just a little chap, but he was brave, and he'd given that bully what for. Despite this, she didn't want her son to go in for the boxing, because it was so violent. Billy had other ideas. 'Now Geordie,' he said. 'First thing Sunday, we'll gan doon to the boxing gym in Gateshead. You're a reet natural, but you still need lessons.'

Alas, the family's jubilation did not last long. One morning when Catherine was getting the breakfast, she dropped a plate of porridge and slumped heavily into her chair by the fire. 'My insides feel all wrong,' she moaned. 'I'm so sorry.' Her face was bathed in sweat and she doubled up from the pain.

Billy was used to giving orders down the pit, so he took charge.

'Divvent worry aboot us being late,' he said. She'd always made light of illness, but this was serious. He picked her up and carried her up to bed, shushing her feeble protests, and bade Geordie run the three miles to the doctor's surgery in Felling.

Doctor Belasis arrived shortly afterwards in his pony trap and tramped heavily upstairs. All too many of his profession looked down on the poor, but he was a conscientious and humane man. 'Now, deep breath in and hold it,' he said, listening carefully through his stethoscope, and making a thorough external examination. He came back downstairs looking pensive.

'I'll not deceive you,' he told Billy, sipping the tea Geordie had provided. 'Your wife is seriously ill. It appears to be some kind of blockage of the intestines. There is a great deal of swelling and the discomfort and pain will be intense. She must rest and refrain from all domestic duties.'

'Aye, Doctor,' Billy agreed. 'We'll have to get Mrs Ross in to help … but will she get better?'

'I was coming to that. The only way we can diagnose the problem with any certainty is to take her to the Royal Victoria in Newcastle. She'll have to go under the knife, I'm afraid.'

Catherine would not hear of it. Two of her aunts had died on the operating table, and she was terrified that the same thing would happen to her. Billy thought he could talk her round, but she was a stubborn woman. The doctor left after writing a script for laudanum and promising to return in a day or so.

Billy worried himself sick and Geordie fell into dark depression. The poor woman bore her illness stoically. She insisted getting up and doing her household chores as usual, but the day came when she could no longer rise from her bed. One day, she bade her son come close so that she could whisper in his ear. 'I want you to have this, *acushla*,' she murmured, proffering a faded photograph. An insolent young swell stared back from the curling paper. He was carrying a tennis racquet and had a towel draped over his shoulders. His eyes, hooded and watchful, were not smiling.

'Who is it, Mam?' Geordie inquired, making to pass the photograph back to her.

'Nay, son,' she countered, placing it on his palm and closing her hand over his. 'It's your *real* father. Billy's a good man, so he is. He's looked after us all these years, but *this* man, Jeremiah Cholmondley-Devereaux' – she said the name with an uncharacteristic sneer – 'is your …' She burst into a fit of coughing, but after she had sipped some water, she continued. 'Jeremiah's father, Sir Cuthbert, paid us an allowance for your keep, but they got off lightly. Lightly, d'ye hear?' She appeared to be drifting off into sleep, but before Geordie could go, she seized his hand, her eyes dark moons in the fitful light. 'By rights, son, ye're Jeremiah's heir,' she whispered. 'Don't ever forget it. They owe you, son, the Lambton *bosthoons* owe you. Now, play me something nice on your fiddle.' He played one of her favourites: Carolan's 'Eleanor Plunkett', a beautiful slow air, full of yearning Celtic melancholy.

'That's grand,' she said, settling back on her pillow. The next morning, she died; a young woman of little more than thirty-five years.

Billy planned to bury her according to the Anglican rites, but Father Aloysius Flynn was a force of nature and would have none of it. Even the most rabid Presbyterians turned out for the funeral at St Oswald's Catholic Church in Wrekenton, and then crowded into the Stubbs house for tea, cakes, and sandwiches. Geordie didn't feel much like socialising. He slipped out the back door and went for a walk as night was falling. He had no conscious destination, but his feet carried him to a small hill where he had often played as a child. He trudged along, lost in gloomy thought, but stopped at the sound of light footfalls coming up the path behind him. Like most miners, he was superstitious and in the gathering dark, he recalled the stories of ghosts that haunted the lonely fells. He called out again and this time a familiar voice answered. It was Annie Ross, his childhood pal.

'What are you doing here?' he demanded. 'I mean, lassie, it's no place for you to be walking about at this hour.'

'Divvent be sae daft, man!' she remonstrated. 'I know this place like the back of me hand – as ye well know, Geordie Stubbs.'

And so she did; she had been a real tomboy and his best friend. Together, they had climbed every tree for miles around, scrambled up the sheer walls of the abandoned quarry, fished for tiddlers in the burn behind the village, scrumped apples from nearby farms, roasted stolen tatties over fires in a ruined byre, and scared the living daylights out of old wifies by leaping out of bushes at them in the gloaming. Whatever devilment Geordie had been up to, she'd been in it and had initiated enough of it herself. She had been a skinny wisp of a thing, her black hair cut short, her knees covered in cuts and bruises, running barefoot in all weathers, shouting like a banshee. Now, despite the fading light, he saw that she was a beautiful young woman.

'I'm sorry about your mam, Geordie,' she said, her big blue eyes shining. He wanted to cry, then, and she enfolded him in her arms, stroking his hair and whispering softly.

Everyone said they made a handsome pair: her lustrous black hair contrasting with his flaming ginger mop and exotic complexion. They went dancing and for long walks around the village, arm in arm. They took the tramcar to Gateshead High Street and over the river to the horses, though she couldn't see what he saw in the so-called sport of kings. One day, when they were lying in each other's arms, she hinted at marriage. He said nothing, but something froze inside him. He had never planned to stay at High Fell. His mind went back to the school atlases with the splashes of pink around the globe – places that he longed to see, their exotic names calling – Zanzibar, Cayenne, Durban, Hong Kong, Hawaii, Van Diemen's Land, Bombay and many more! Marriage would mean staying in Calcutta Row forever, working in the mine and fathering a brood of village urchins who in time would themselves work for Rupert Bell or the Bowes-Lyons family in the mines.

Geordie had always assumed that once he had served his time, he would leave Calcutta Row and see the world. There would always be work for mining mechanics in distant lands – the Rand, perhaps, Broken Hill, Potosi, Butte Montana – and his skills would be transferable to ships' engine rooms and any number and type of manufactory: sugar mills in India, rubber mills in Malaya, shipyards in Baltimore, San Francisco or riverboats churning the wide Yangtze. Maybe driving a locomotive over the prairies or driving cattle across the red plains of Australia. The voices of distant lands were calling. He wondered if he loved her. She was as the Geordies say, a reet bra lass! He was fond of her and the mere thought of her shapely legs and pert breasts filled him with lust and he wondered if that had anything to do with love. Even if it did, was it enough to make the thought of staying in High Fell palatable? He pondered these questions interminably.

One day when they were sharing a bottle of stout on the old settee, Annie announced, 'I've fallen wrang, Geordie. I've missed me monthlies twice.' Geordie was stunned. There could be no doubt about it. She was pregnant. She never told lies. Now she was looking at him as if to say, what next, Geordie? His mind raced. There was a doctor in Newcastle they said terminated pregnancies. But no, he wasn't sure about that and besides, Annie was a Catholic and she would never consent to it. So then what? The bairn was his. She'd never even look at the other young men of the village. He would have to do the right thing and marry her. He kissed the top of her head and hugged her protectively, but he felt the wide world slipping away from him – all his plans to travel coming to naught – he'd have to stay in High Fell for the rest of his life.

High Fell, 1911

Annie was not Geordie's only problem. A few weeks earlier, the Gorringe twins had accosted him outside the Miners' Welfare one evening. Donny stood by, cracking his knuckles while Lonny shirtfronted Geordie. They were a hulking pair of Cockney thugs, horrible types, both with mouthfuls of misshapen teeth stuck higgledy-piggledy in their gums like the tombstones in a photo Geordie had seen of the Jewish cemetery in Prague. They wanted the money he owed their boss. He'd known it was a risk borrowing from a gangster like Ebenezer Richardson, but he needed the money to pay off his gambling debts. He promised to pay half the next pay Saturday. Lonnie leered and shook his loaf-shaped head.

'I don't fink so, mate,' he snarled. 'Mr Richardson says time's up. You'll pay us the full instalment, like, or you'll wish to Christ you had!' With that, he punched Geordie in the gut and his brother kicked him in the face for good measure. They left him gasping like a fish for air on the pavement, dripping blood from his nose, which seemed broken.

Ebenezer Richardson ran a stable of bookmakers at the Newcastle racecourse. He also raced greyhounds and fed their carcasses to the pigs on a farm near Chollerford when they failed to perform. Rumour had it that several of his human victims had also met this fate. He owned a string of pubs, brothels, and a loan-sharking business, and fenced stolen goods via a pawnbroker's shop in Gateshead High Street. The exorbitant interest he charged had dwarfed Geordie's original debt. His enforcers carried sets of brass knuckles and knives, wore steel-capped boots, and didn't hesitate to use them on defaulters. Rumour had it that the Gorringes sometimes dispatched recalcitrant debtors with a captive bolt pistol. Geordie was in for it unless he could raise enough money to repay Richardson by the end of that week. He had never again managed a big win like the one at his first race meeting, and there was no way he could meet the next instalment. It all swirled round in his brain that night. He would nod off and wake up, sweating, seeing Lonnie's or Donny's grinning face. Towards dawn, he had an idea.

The next night, when Billy had retired to bed, Geordie crept out and sidled along the lanes in the dark. He had a duffel bag over his shoulder and had improvised some burglar's tools. Catherine and Billy had always been honest people and they had drummed it into him that theft was wrong, but he would have to steal to pay off his debts. The neighbours wouldn't have anything worth stealing so when the moon rose, it found him lurking out the back of a mansion in Saltwell Park, a leafy suburb of Gateshead. His knees were knocking together, but he vaulted over the wall and into the dense shrubbery. After scanning the windows for any sign of light or movement, he emerged onto a wide lawn, all senses tingling. He tried the first window. It was locked, but the second one he tried slid open and he climbed into the scullery. Encouraged by the silence, he removed his pit boots so that he could creep soundlessly around the house. In the moonlight through the windows, he saw a tall kitchen dresser full of silverware. Alas, he failed to see some large cooking pots sitting on a low table. The resulting crash froze his blood! He tried to grab the runaway pots rolling across the floor but in his haste, he dislodged a cast-iron frying pan and it landed on the flagstones with an enormous clang. He listened. There were muffled footsteps: someone was coming downstairs, so he fled out the scullery window, quite forgetting his boots. Gas lamps flared, and a posh Dunelmian voice roared, 'Who's there?' The back door creaked open and Geordie half-turned to see a large form clad in a nightshirt. 'Stop or I'll shoot!' roared the figure as Geordie scooted across the lawn, which glistened in the moonlight. There was a loud bang and shotgun pellets tore through the bushes, but he was over the wall and pelting away down the lane. He got back to Calcutta Row as dawn was breaking, bootless, his feet cut, swollen and aching. His attempt at burglary had been a farce.

Geordie dreaded the thought of another attempt, but the image of Richardson's goons concentrated his mind. Late the next night he slipped on his spare boots and crept out again, thankful that the heavy fog that had rolled off the river was muffling his footsteps. He calculated that his intended victims of the previous night would not dream he would dare return. Before long, he was back skulking in the thick shrubbery of the victims' garden. The light burning in one of the top floor windows went out soon enough. He waited half an hour, his mouth too dry to chew the crust of bread he had brought to keep up his strength. The fog thickened, dampening any noise as he crept over the lawn and muffling the creak as he jemmied open the window. This time, he was careful to avoid obstacles. He opened the kitchen dresser and lifted out the cutlery. He left the house as silently as he had entered it and was soon on his way back home through the fog.

He took the stolen silverware to the pawnbroker's shop in Gateshead High Street. The shop was seedy, with a line of people queueing out the door and into the street, all with a hungry look about them. There were wives with their husbands' best suits – pawned for a few bob until they could redeem them next payday – and old men with bits of junk that the pawnbroker's men sneered at. Boys with bits of tat that they'd probably stolen. The suits were draped on wooden hangers and hoisted up towards the ceilings before the women shuffled off, counting a few coppers in their hands. When it was Geordie's turn at the counter, the assistant took one look at the silverware and jerked his head to the side. 'Gan o'er there, man,' he hissed, indicating a door set into the side of the vestibule.

The man who received him in the office was Ebenezer Richardson's brother, Mattie, a nasty little stinker who wore a suit in a vain attempt to look respectable. Mattie took one of the spoons and bit the handle with pointed teeth. Satisfied, he bade Geordie unload the lot onto the desk and separated it into piles, all the time nodding his head and licking his thin lips. He named a price. Geordie gasped, but the pawnbroker shrugged. 'Take it or leave it, man,' he said. 'Ye're in nee position to bargain.' It was daylight robbery, but Geordie agreed to the price. There was enough to cover two instalments on the racing debt, which would give Geordie time to figure out some way of paying back the lot.

'Wait,' Mattie ordered as Geordie went to leave. 'I'll take whatever you can get off your hands. Good stuff only, mind ye.'

Geordie became an expert burglar. He was nimble, skilful with his hands, and small enough to squeeze through narrow openings. He could cross creaky floorboards without making a sound. Locks sprang open with the picks the Richardsons supplied. His most extraordinary ability, however, was the skill with which he could scale sheer walls to giddy heights to access high windows. The Richardsons fenced everything they could get and even though they took a hefty commission, Geordie was able to clear his racing debts and start a nest egg. Soon, the *Evening Chronicle* was warning its readers to be vigilant against the master criminal they were calling the Human Fly.

The *Chronicle* was not the only institution taking a keen interest in the crime wave. Stung by the newspaper's dismissive accounts of their detective skills, the Gateshead police had doubled patrols and carried out dawn raids on likely culprits. They felt the collars of quite a few local criminals, but the burglaries continued. Exasperated, Chief Constable Rutherford brought in a crack London investigator, Detective Chief Inspector James Arthur Verte, and installed him with great fanfare at the Swinburne Street police station. Verte stormed through Swinburne Street like a human whirlwind, leaving distressed constables mentally shattered in his wake. He bawled out the detective squad and threatened to put them back on the beat and bring in men from London unless they lifted their game. The duty sergeants learned to fear his wrath and to try to gauge his mercurial moods and anticipate his demands. He reduced one old boy to tears for using pins instead of paper clips and blasted another for speaking 'incomprehensible Geordie gibberish'. Constables dozing off in previously safe locations were hauled to their feet and reprimanded. At least one peeler retired early. 'Howay, man,' said another constable, summing up subaltern opinion in the station, 'It's gettin' worse than Turkey.' Even the chief constable thought it was all a bit much, but he let Verte get on with it, being – not that he would admit it – afraid of the man.

The *Chronicle* ran a long interview with the inspector, replete with a grainy photograph that showed a beefy thirtyish man with ferocious bulldog jowls, a beetling brow, and ice-cold eyes. There was a suggestion, too, of a misshapen nose feathered with fine veins. The photo didn't do justice to his hulking presence, but it was intimidating enough. Yet even those who had suffered his wrath admitted that he was a brilliant detective. Verte adhered to the principles of scientific detection, but like most good thief-takers, he possessed sound gut instinct. If the crime wave continued, it was only a matter of time before he got his man, the *Chronicle* reckoned. His arrival, however, coincided with a winning streak for Geordie at the horses. The burglaries stopped abruptly and left the Chief Inspector spinning his wheels. Nevertheless, he did not sit idly in his office twiddling his enormous thumbs but ordered the Swinburne Street detective staff to bring in their snouts for questioning. None of them knew much, but he gleaned enough to suspect that the Human Fly had links to the gangster Ebenezer Richardson and that he lived somewhere in the Felling district. He had also deduced that given his mark's climbing skills he was a young man and – from the dirty pit boots he had left at the scene of his first burglary – a miner. It was also rumoured around the quays and riverside lanes that the cat burglar was a coloured man. They were not so unusual on the Tyne, for ships came there from across the wide world, and the descendants of lascars and others were to be found close to the docks. Coloured colliers, though, were rarer than virgins in Ebenezer Richardson's knocking shops. Verte mounted a big map of the district on his office wall and stuck pins in it to mark the Human Fly's burglaries. Bulldog-like, once he had sunk his teeth into a case, he would never let go.

One day, the *Chronicle* published a cheeky letter that had been postmarked at Newcastle and written in beautiful copperplate script. 'Chief Inspector Verte's abilities are overrated,' it taunted. 'The Great London Detective is no match for me, the mighty Human Fly. Chief Constable Rutherford is advised to send him home and hire a competent thief-taker.' Geordie couldn't help it. The old devilment had got into him, even though – or perhaps because – subjecting the inspector to public ridicule would only intensify his obsessive quest. There was a great deal of sniggering at Swinburne Street too.

Verte was so enraged that Rutherford feared he might succumb to apoplexy and insisted that he take some leave. Home down in London for a few days leave, Verte made his wife's life a misery, finding fault with everything she did. The food was too salty. It was not salty enough. This stuff was not mulligatawny! He disliked haddock. Why the hell didn't she serve Eton Mess the way he liked it? He didn't care for the sponge cake. He wanted a piece of fruit cake. She would have to slip out and buy some because she hadn't baked. Why wasn't the fire set in the grate? What kind of wife was she? He spent his days in the pub, returning only for meals and to sleep, and she breathed an enormous sigh of relief when he took the Flying Scotsman up to Tyneside to resume his investigation into the crimes of the Human Fly. His twin boys, Simon and Claude, shed tears, though, for they idolised their father and dreamed of following him into the thief-taking profession.

Verte went straight to his lodgings from the train station, humming tunelessly to himself and looking forward to kicking arse at Swinburne Street the following day. He'd teach them to laugh at him behind his back, the insolent Geordie bastards! His flat was cold and cheerless, but the charlady had set the fire and he lit it hurriedly, cursing the provincial weather and the Geordies. He had called in at the local chipper and after wolfing down his cod and chips he downed several pints of the strong local ale. This lifted his mood. He would catch the Human Fly, he felt sure, and make him pay for his insolence. He drank several more pints and when the ornamental Town Hall clock struck midnight, he crawled into bed feeling fuzzily contented and was soon sound asleep.

Geordie Stubbs was lurking in the shrubbery outside Verte's bedroom window. He'd been watching the flat on and off for some time and had hatched an audacious plot to needle the detective. Verte had left a couple of gaslights burning, so Geordie could see inside. Howay, man, he marvelled; from the empty bottles on the table, it seemed that the old boozer had drunk at least ten pints of ale and from the tremendous racket of his beer-fuelled snores he was unlikely to wake. Geordie tiptoed to the door and picked the lock. He sniffed the air: something was burning. The sot had neglected to put the fireguard back in place and some red-hot embers were smouldering on the carpet. Geordie scooped them into the coal scuttle and replaced the guard. He stood stock still, his hearing preternaturally acute. Verte snored on so Geordie crept over to where the policeman had left his tweed coat and trousers on the back of a chair. His fingers deftly located what he was looking for and seconds later he had closed the door behind him and was on his way home. Most insolent of all was the caricature he had left on the table, of James Verte snoring abed with his mouth gaping open under his bulbous nose.

Verte's face went puce with rage and embarrassment when the chief constable handed him a copy of the *Chronicle* a day or so later. He'd kept quiet about the cartoon. There, on the front page, was a photograph of his bloody warrant card! The accompanying article informed readers that the Human Fly had lifted it from Verte's coat while its owner was in a drunken stupor. There was also a sketch of the inspector comatose with drink, similar to the one Geordie had left in Verte's flat. Verte wanted to arrest the editor, but Rutherford sensibly vetoed the idea. Verte would just have to swallow his pride and get on with the job of tracking down the brazen thief. He would give Verte a month and if the Fly was still at large after that, he would send him back down to Scotland Yard and bring someone else in. There was some snickering as Verte trudged back down to his office, but the ferocious look on his face quelled any thoughts of insubordination among the lesser ranks.

High Fell, early 1912

Geordie was dreaming that his grandfather was hammering a billet of white-hot iron on an anvil. The banging became insistent. What? No ... Not the blacksmith ... He awoke with a start. Someone was thumping on the front door! Cursing, he made his way downstairs in the freezing dark and flung open the front door, and there was Annie, about to drop the knocker again. She had wrapped herself in a shawl and her face was drawn and pale in the flickering light of the lantern she held aloft in her left hand.

'What brings you here, hinney?' he gasped. 'Is it the bairn already?'

'No, ye daft bugger! We'd best gan doon to the mine,' she said. 'There's been an explosion!'

Explosion? Billy! His Da! He was on the nightshift! Geordie threw on his clothes and ran with Annie down the dark street towards the pithead. Other families were converging on the mine gates too. You could smell the smoke before you saw it billowing up the pit shaft and swirling round the headstock into the black sky.

'I divvent sleep well,' a woman was telling anyone who might listen. 'I went doonstairs to make a cup of tea and heard this sort of muffled bang and then a terrific roar. I just knew it were the mine! Ma man's in there!' She dropped to her knees, whimpering. Strong arms lifted her up and led her gently away.

High Fell was what the colliers called a 'fiery mine'. Rupert Bell had pooh-poohed the miners' fears, but just days before, when Geordie was carrying out minor repairs on an underground electric pump a mile underground, he had heard hissing and bubbling noises behind the rock walls. The tunnel floor had been heaved up a good two feet by what the colliers call a 'bag o' foulness' – a build-up of firedamp. Davy safety lamps had been mandatory since a disaster in a Felling mine a century earlier, but the introduction of electric pumps had brought the possibility of sparks igniting the gas.

A group of miners were already under the headstock when Geordie and Annie arrived. They were demanding to descend into the mine to help, but the banksman, Moses Parker, held them back. 'It's nee good,' he insisted; the cage was stuck in the shaft. They would have to enter the mine via the downcast shaft. Over forty years earlier, a heavy steam engine had fallen into the Hartley mine's shaft and trapped over 200 miners down below. After that, Parliament required mines to have at least two shafts so that miners could be rescued in the event of accidents. Now, there were almost fifty men and boys down the pit, including Billy.

The downcast shaft was situated beyond the colliery offices and workshops, in the lee of the dim bulk of the pit heap. The odd wisp of smoke escaped from the shaft, but it was nothing compared with what was belching up the main shaft. There was no shortage of volunteers to descend into the pit: the imperative to help your workmates was drilled into these men almost from birth. They knew that those trapped below would do the same for them were their roles reversed. Geordie never forgot that black day. There was no afterdamp, but one hundred feet along the inbye leading from the bottom of the shaft to the mine workings, the roof had partly collapsed from the huge force of the explosion. Geordie and his mates had to remove the mass of debris blocking the tunnel with their bare hands, as a spark from a shovel striking rock could trigger another explosion. More men arrived and they made rapid progress, all the while aware that the roof could come down again. Nevertheless, they broke through to the other side and crept along the tunnel. There were no signs that the fireball had come this far, probably because there was a very wet section of tunnel up ahead and it had extinguished the flames. They began to call out, hoping to hear answering voices, but the mine was silent, save for the drip of water from the tunnel's roof and the occasional creak of a pit prop settling. Fifty yards further along, their headlamps picked out the first bodies of men and pit ponies burnt or suffocated to death. There were no survivors. The rescue party took fifty bodies or and parts of bodies to the surface and laid them in a makeshift mortuary under flapping canvas. Women keened and big tough colliers cried. Geordie Stubbs was able to identify Billy by the twisted frames of the reading spectacles he had carried in his breast pocket.

Night had fallen by the time Geordie got home to Calcutta Row. He had just enough energy to wash off the worst of the pit grime before falling into bed. That night he had vivid nightmares. He was in the pit, about to be engulfed by a fireball generated by a spark from the pump he had been working on. The Devil was laughing over his shoulder. He tried to scream but could not make a sound and awoke sweating despite the chill bedroom air. He had not hesitated to descend into the mine to assist with the rescue, but he could not shake off the premonition of doom.

After the inquest, which concluded that all fifty deaths were the result of an explosion of gas caused perhaps by an electrical fault or a malfunctioning Davy lamp, there were fifty funerals, and fifty cruelly battered bodies were lowered into a line of new graves in the Heworth cemetery. Geordie carried on as usual, saying nothing, but thinking more and more of leaving. Annie, too, was becoming increasingly insistent about marriage. The pregnancy was now very visible, and her mam was threatening to pay Geordie a visit to make him face up to his responsibilities. He had reluctantly carried out a few more nocturnal burglaries at Richardson's insistence, but he knew he had gone too far in taunting that London detective, James Verte. One Saturday afternoon, a little man even smaller than himself sidled up in a pub on the Gateshead High Street.

'If ye know what's good for ye, ye'd best lie low,' the fellow advised. 'Inspector Verte knows that the Human Fly lives near Felling and he has all the footpaths watched. Now, if ye happen to know who the Fly is, ye'd perhaps be tellin' him this.' He paused and rubbed his thumb and forefinger together, so Geordie gave him a coin and he continued. 'Ye'll knaa aboot yon Jennings gadgie in America?'

Geordie had heard. A jury had found Thomas Jennings guilty of murder based on newfangled fingerprint evidence, and he was hanged. Scotland Yard had trained three of the four expert fingerprint witnesses at his trial.

'Why aye, man,' the man whispered. 'They say Inspector Verte has brought up fingerprint experts from the Met.' With that, he vanished like an evil spirit on the moors, leaving Geordie playing with his beer glass, lost in thought.

Shortly afterwards, he was out walking with Annie on the fells. She poked him in the ribs. 'Howay man,' she prompted, 'ye're in a broon study, Geordie Stubbs.' They were at their favourite place, with a view over the fields beyond the pit towards Lambton Hall and across to Beacon Lough. A gentle breeze was blowing away the last of winter and in a sheltered place a clump of daffodils was flowering yellow against a grey stone wall.

'I'm sorry, hinney,' he replied. 'I just canna get what happened at the pit out of my mind.'

A bird was singing its little heart out in a ragged tree on the hillside, but Geordie could see little reason for such joy. The pit crouched always, a dark succubus, eating at his soul. The miners were a superstitious lot. After the explosion, the mine lurked in his mind like the Portobello Braag, a shapeshifting goblin that haunted the fells and lured men to their doom. It was almost as if it possessed a malign personality. More prosaically, he was afraid of another visit from the Gorringe twins. He had sworn to stop the burglaries, but his debts to Richardson were piling up again following a run of bad luck at the horses. He also had the bloodhound Inspector Verte on his trail, and Annie had point blank demanded that he marry her. It was in this state of mind that he recalled his mother's dying words about the young master of Lambton Hall and resolved to pay him a visit.

The next Sunday morning, he walked from High Fell to the Hall, rehearsing what he would say to the Cholmondley-Devereaux bastards. By the time he walked up the long gravel drive he had worked up a fine head of resentment. Lambton Hall was an imposing structure built from hard Northumberland sandstone and capped with dark Welsh slate. It stood four storeys high with corner towers, a crenellated façade, and tall windows reflecting the sunlight like mirrors. Geordie hesitated when it came into view through the spring foliage of the grounds, but when he thought of his many problems, he pushed on, determined to interview Sir Cuthbert. He was overtaken by a procession of pony traps and other carriages, whose occupants gazed at him curiously: a coloured man in the Durham countryside was as rare as an Eskimo in Northumberland Street. The so-called great and good of Northumberland and Durham were arriving, and the turning circle in front of the main doors was clogged with their vehicles, around which liveried footmen and stable boys were fussing, watering horses, and parking their traps.

One of the servants – a snooty fellow dressed in butler's waistcoat and tails – minced up on polished black pumps as Geordie entered the circle. 'Your business, fellow?' he demanded, raising one eyebrow.

Geordie cleared his throat, drew himself up to his full height, which was considerably less than that of his interlocutor, and declared that he wished to speak with Sir Cuthbert about a private matter. The butler waved a dismissive hand and laughed in his face. 'Pooh! Sir Cuthbert is indisposed,' he snapped. His extended arm invited Geordie to leave.

'In that case,' Geordie said, 'I'll see his son instead. I've come quite a distance and my business won't detain him long.'

'And what, pray, is your business?'

'Tell him,' said Geordie, 'that a close relative wishes to speak to him on an urgent matter.'

The butler took a sudden double take before backing off and trotting up the wide stone steps into the hall. Some minutes passed. The sun crept high into the sky. The warm weather had returned early as it sometimes did. Bees buzzed in the flowerbeds lining the drive, and more gentry arrived and alighted from their carriages. Instead of entering the hall, they made their way around the side of the house, drawling away to themselves, leaving their conveyances to the servants to deal with. They ignored Geordie, a truculent black plebeian bantam standing with folded arms at the foot of the steps. The butler emerged from the front door and jogged in the direction in which the guests had disappeared. He crooked a finger in Geordie's direction and jerked his head in the universal 'follow me' gesture.

A large red and white candy-striped marquee had been erected on the lawns behind the hall, overlooking an ornamental lake on which some waterfowl were swimming. Guests stood in groups, drinking from champagne flutes and nibbling canapés offered on silver trays by maids in black-and-white uniforms. Gales of laughter wafted across the lawns and a Hooray Henry type was holding forth to a circle of admiring young women about how the Huns had best not push their luck with John Bull. Geordie might have stopped to listen – it was a recently elected Tory MP declaiming about the Kaiser – but the butler bade him follow round the back of the hall.

'The Young Master will see you in the conservatory,' he said, raising a quizzical eyebrow and indicating a large iron and glass structure – a smaller cousin of the Palm House in London's Kew Gardens, but imposing enough to Geordie, who had never been to Kew. The white-painted iron door swung open on well-oiled hinges, and Geordie passed into a sudden dense humid heat and the smell of rampant vegetation and humus. Jets of fine mist sprayed down from pipes crisscrossing the high glass ceiling and fronds of ferns and other plants pressed down as he made his way along a pathway into the interior of the structure. The heat was stifling, and just as he was considering a quick retreat a fruity upper-class voice bade him venture further into the interior.

'I always knew you'd turn up one day.' Jeremiah Cholmondley-Devereaux sat astride a heavy iron chair at a matching table. He was a portly, middle-aged fellow with flaming red hair streaked with grey, above a florid face running to fat. Despite the humid heat, he was nattily dressed in a three-piece tweed suit and did not appear to have broken a sweat. Two mad blue eyes stared at Geordie as he took a seat. The fellow took a sip from a glass of something at his elbow.

'Oh, I say,' he drawled. 'You're Catherine's brat and no mistake about it. I don't mind saying, you've caused me a great deal of grief over the years, especially with Mater.'

Geordie said nothing, and his silence seemed to unnerve the man.

'Yes, yes,' Jeremiah blustered. 'I must say, it's strange to see you at last. But here, you'll have a glass of this punch, will you not?' He poured Geordie a liberal measure from a cut glass jug and pushed it over the table. 'I always wondered about you, but I've been abroad, you know. Malaya mostly, which is why I prefer to sit here in the warm and to hell with my sisters' silly friends.'

Geordie drank thirstily and jiggled his glass to indicate he wanted a refill. 'Yes, I'm Catherine's son,' he said, 'and you are my natural father, which is what I wished to discuss with you.'

Devereaux nodded. 'By Jove! Your voice is an echo of my own, save that it's Geordie!'

Geordie looked him in the eye. 'I'll not beat about the bush. Your Da – my Granda that is – provided us with a stipend, but he got off lightly. I have no wish to remain long in your company. I know the way I was conceived, but for all that, I am your son and I want more adequate remuneration than what Sir Cuthbert arranged.'

'By Jove!' Devereaux snorted, his mad blue eyes flashing. 'You come in here and start demanding—'

'Just a portion of what I am owed,' Geordie cut in. 'I'll speak plainly. History has a way of repeating itself and I have got a girl pregnant. I'm not concerned with myself, but I want to make sure that she is provided for – she and your grandchild, for that's what the bairn will be. I cannot remain in these parts. Once I have your word, like, I'll leave and never trouble ye again.'

'But this is preposterous!' shouted Devereaux. 'Why, you're nothing but an upstart, the son of a mere serving wench who, who—'

'Then a fine story it will make in the papers,' Geordie retorted. 'Son of a baronet works doon the pit while his father lives in luxury! And a bairn gans wi'oot! The choice is yours … Father.' He spat out the word.

Devereaux slumped in his seat and all the heat drained from his voice.

'Very well,' he muttered. 'If you put it that way, we can reach a … err … an arrangement. I'll have my solicitor draw up a contract. The mother and child will be provided for, and you will undertake never to set foot in this house, nor to make any further claim upon me or my family.'

He turned back to his drink – one of many, no doubt, that he would have that day – and indicated with a sidelong nod towards the door that Geordie was dismissed.

'The butler will see you out,' he muttered, for he had to have the last word.

Geordie felt nothing for Devereaux, but he was worried that he might have inherited some of his weaknesses. These matters preoccupied him as he walked back to High Fell, ruminating on the nature of the British class system, and whether he could judge the man.

A week later, just as the sun was rising over the eastern fells, Geordie slipped out of the house in Calcutta Row and crept off down the lane between the house backs. He carried his mother's small cardboard suitcase and had a navy duffel bag slung over his shoulder. It contained some clothes and his fiddle. He left in the nick of time just as the Gorringe twins arrived down the end of the street. The money he owed their employer was safely stowed in a cotton money belt around his waist and he was determined they would not have it. The twins hammered on the back door, shouting threats and waking the neighbours. Geordie paused on the hillside amid the gorse and looked back at the village. The Gorringes were kicking in the back door of his house, and as he could also see something they couldn't, he sat down behind a tree to watch the fun. Inspector Verte and a posse of uniformed police officers had drawn up in pony traps at the front door and were peering through the letterbox, no doubt calling his name.

Curtains were twitching all up and down the street and one or two old biddies had come out of their doors to gawp, and their hope of a delicious scene was soon rewarded. Verte ordered one of his strapping constables to put his boot to the door and it splintered open. They stormed inside just as the Gorringes came in through the back door. Geordie could hear yelling and the sound of crockery breaking and then one of the twins came out of the back door with two constables at his heels. They rugby-tackled Gorringe and gave him a good hiding and afterwards carted him and his brother off in handcuffs. The altercation perhaps compensated to some degree for Verte's failure to arrest the Human Fly. Geordie crouched down for a while longer in the gorse, but the fun was over. The twins were trussed up like chickens in the back of one of the traps while Verte rampaged through the house. The inspector came out waving his arms about and ranting about the Fly, but after a while he calmed down and the police drove off towards Gateshead with their captives.

Geordie's destination was south. Anywhere south. Once out of County Durham, he would travel on foot and by whatever lifts he could beg to save his precious funds. A knot of regret gnawed at his chest. He was leaving Annie and the unborn bairn, but then they would be provided for until the child was of age, for the Cholmondley-Devereaux family solicitor had drawn up the contract as Jeremiah promised and an addendum negotiated with the ageing Rupert Bell allowed them to live rent free in the Stubbs house in Calcutta Row. Geordie had raised the idea in a roundabout way of them both leaving, but Annie would have none of it. Her mam was poorly, and her da had black lung – a lingering death sentence. His conscience was almost salved by the knowledge that Annie and the bairn would receive an income, but he knew that he was deserting them.

York, 1912

Geordie had no clear idea of his destination when he arrived at the Chester-le-Street main line railway station. He had never travelled much farther than Newcastle or Sunderland. He stood dithering near the ticket office, unable to make up his mind before shuffling up to the counter, and he only half-noticed a shifty little ferret of a man standing there watching. After tossing a coin, Geordie bought a second-class single ticket to York, while the shifty man strained to overhear the brief conversation with the ticket clerk. The ferret slipped off with a sly leer as Geordie sat in the draughty waiting room considering the enormity of what he had done. Normally, he was an alert young man and would have recalled the same ferret lurking around the Gateshead lanes and running errands out at the racecourse. Now, however, he had too much on his mind. He remembered Billy and Catherine's insistence that he had to live honestly and to do the best for other people. And yet he had sneaked out on Annie and left her to face the consequences. He was a cad. A coward. A disgrace to his sainted mother's memory. And what of the wailers shivering at the pit head: they'd have given anything for the chance to learn a trade, but he'd thrown his apprenticeship away and it served him right that he too could only expect to work as a labourer. He realised he was muttering to himself, so he looked around to make sure he'd not been overheard. The sun was shining through the windows of the waiting room and it hit him that he would never have to go back down that awful black sunless pit again. It had devoured Billy and left Annie's da gasping for air; but he was free! And why should he worry about Annie? The Lambton Hall people would provide for her and the bairn. He lit a cigarette on the strength of that and was feeling a bit better about his betrayal when the train puffed up to the platform.

The slow train dawdled along, stopping at even the smallest stations, so it was late afternoon when it pulled into York. He saw a tangle of medieval streets in the shadow of an enormous cathedral. A heavy, sweetish smell hung in the air, competing with the stench of smoke, steam, and cinders from the railway. Outside, electric tramcars rattled past, clanging their bells, and a lamplighter was on his rounds, lighting the gas lamps on cast iron stanchions along the street. A thin, greasy rain had begun to fall as he shouldered his duffel and picked his way through knots of pedestrians towards the centre of the town. He crossed an iron bridge that spanned the slow-moving River Ouse, and was soon lost in the lanes, over which ancient houses cantilevered crazily above the dirty cobbles.

It seemed like a fine town. He was in search of lodgings and after rejecting a few dirty dens, he found a suitable room near the Shambles in a tall house run by a no-nonsense woman of what the French call 'a certain age'. It was small, but clean, with a neatly made-up bed, a table and chair, and mullioned windows reaching out almost as far as those of the house opposite. For a reasonable sum, the woman – a widow whose name was Mrs Mosby – undertook to provide Geordie with half board and to clean the room. He paid in advance and retired to bed and slept until daybreak. When Mrs Mosby brought breakfast, he inquired whether she knew of any work available in the town.

'Eeeh, lad,' she replied, her voice broad Yorkshire. 'I cannot say for sure, but Rowntree's is allus seeking hands. They're out a bit on the Haxby Road. Tha might find summat there. Then there's Terry's, t'other chocolate manufacturers down at t'other end of town. It all depends, I suppose, if tha hast a trade or not.'

He did have a trade, of course, or near enough, but there was little chance of finding work as a fitter given that he had walked away without completing his apprenticeship. The Amalgamated Society of Engineers jealously guarded its time-served members' interests and if he did manage to find an engineering job it would be in a small, non-union workshop. The product of a tight-knit community for whom the union was almost sacred, Geordie wasn't yet ready to violate its laws. There was no work on offer at Rowntree's and none at Terry's either. Nor was there anything going in the big sugar refineries and flourmills. A villainous-looking fellow standing outside a small engineering shop heard Geordie's Geordie accent and told him to 'piss off, yer black bugger, there's nowt 'ere for foreigners,' after which he returned to his lodgings feeling a trifle depressed.

'Tha might try the railway carriage works,' Mrs Mosby advised. 'One o' my neighbours' husbands says that they're taking on new hands. Tha'd best look smart though, as there's many in the town in search of work.'

The next morning, Geordie set off for the workshops, a sprawling complex of red brick buildings on the Holgate Road. A clerk in the office directed him to the electric car shop and he presented himself to the foreman and inquired if they had work. The foreman was a bald little fellow, clad in a grey dustcoat, who stood at one end of the long building where they manufactured electric passenger trains for the Tyne railways. Geordie had difficulty understanding the man – Sammy Sutcliffe by name – both because of his thick Yorkshire accent and because of the pipe that appeared to be permanently wedged between his teeth. No, Geordie said, he had never worked in a carriage shop before, but had been a fitter's helper in Clarke Chapman's engineering works in Gateshead and had come down to York to be near his widowed sister, who had taken ill with rheumatic fever. Making up stories came naturally to him.

'Tha'll do, lad,' mumbled Sutcliffe, chewing on his pipe. 'Tha can start on the morrow as I have a vacancy for a sweeper.'

A sweeper! It was a big comedown for a tradesman, but it was paid work. Geordie figured he could save his pennies for a decent nest egg and then move on down to London to take his chances there. He had never taken much notice of the situation of the helpers in the High Fell workshops, even though he knew that the older ones knew more than he did about engineering. Now he was a labourer himself – and the very lowliest of the men in the Holgate Works. His tools of trade comprised a broom, a shovel, and some cleaning rags. Sometimes, Sutcliffe would direct him to clean the row of privies stinking out the back of the workshop. The clock had never ticked round as slowly as it did in that place, although the only clock in the workshop was in Sutcliffe's office, an elevated hutch overlooking the shop floor. Sutcliffe seemed pleased with his work, however, and when the old fellow who looked after the tearooms retired, he put Geordie in his place and directed another labourer to the sweeping and bogs.

The days piled up into weeks, then months, and soon the rainy Yorkshire winter had set in. The days shortened, and in the evenings, Geordie was happy to retreat to his room at Mrs Mosby's, eat the tasty meals she prepared, and read by gaslight as the rain pattered on the mullioned windows. One morning, snowflakes fluttered down in the cones of light spread by the gaslights. Spending little on amusements, he had saved an appreciable sum of money. Soon he would be on his way south. Another day, when the men were eating their lunches,

Geordie overheard them discussing a problem with the gears of the car they were working on. As he'd worked on repairs to the High Fell locomotives, the answer to the problem was easy for him.

'How dost tha know that sonny?' asked one of the fitters.

Geordie thought quickly. 'I worked as a fitter's mate up on Tyneside.'

'Nay, tha art not just a labourer, lad. I'd wager tha were an engineer back up where tha comes from.' Geordie denied it, but the man touched the side of his nose and went back to work. After that, Sammy Sutcliffe also looked at him thoughtfully, and Geordie knew he would have to leave – he'd left his work at High Fell and broken the conditions of his indentures. It was only a matter of time before he would be unmasked. He'd have to leave York sooner than planned, and travel far away where there was no chance of being recognised.

He'd left it too late. One dreary grey afternoon, two bulky figures loomed out of the fog as he was crossing the bridge to the old town. He thought of running, but they were upon him in a flash. It was the bloody Gorringe twins, Lonnie and Donny, the Cockney thugs with their grinning gobs and cold eyes! They pinioned his arms and shoved him into a narrow alleyway. A fist knocked the wind from his lungs, and a boot connected with his chin as he doubled up wheezing and sputtering. The ferret, he thought – it must have been the little weasel he had half-noticed at the Chester-le-Street station who had informed on him.

'Fought you could 'ide, didya?' snarled Donny or Lonnie. 'Mr Richardson ain't too 'appy wiv ya welchin' on 'im!' Another fist crashed into Geordie's jaw, sending him spinning into the wall.

'Nah, young Stubbs. You can take us wiv ya and give us what you owe. That or we'll kill ya.' They dragged Geordie upright, pretended to dust him off and handed back his cap. 'Don't even try to muck us abaht, neither.'

'How … how did ye find me?' Geordie wheezed when they rounded the corner into the street.

'Nevva you mind,' one of the goons replied. 'Let's just say we 'ave our means.'

Mrs Mosby was not at home when they reached the Shambles. Not wishing to risk another beating, Geordie took the money from where it was hidden under the mattress and handed it to Donny or Lonnie, who hovered at his elbow with sharp eyes.

'You'd better not be 'oldin' aht on us, nah,' said the thug, peeling through the banknotes and counting out the silver on the table. They promised they would be back to get the rest he owed and left with a parting punch to the gut. 'Next time we won't go so easy on ya.'

Mrs Mosby pursed her lips when she saw the state of him, and his workmates were curious about his bruised face. He was feeling very sorry for himself but if he thought things couldn't get worse, he was dead wrong.

A few days later, a familiar figure strutted past the workshop door. Geordie did a double take, then sidled out of sight. His eyes hadn't deceived him – it was his old tormentor, Miserable Mick Armstrong, the former mechanics' chargehand at High Fell! By dint of oblique questioning of his workmates, Geordie ascertained that Mick was foreman over the maintenance engineers, whose workshop stood some two hundred yards away. It was only a matter of time before Mick saw him. The Gorringes had taken his savings and would be back for more. His wages were meagre. He was trapped.

~14~

York, December 1912

The Lord Mayor's Mansion House was a gorgeous Georgian con-fection. Sitting on St Helen's Square where Coney and Lendal Streets meet, it had been the home of York's lord mayors since the mid-eighteenth century. Mrs Mosby had said the house held a trove of priceless jewels and silverware; much of it displayed in glass cases to those privileged to gain entry to the house, and some of it used at official banquets reserved for the town's Quality. The current lord mayor, an overweight, bald, white-bearded old Freemason, had made a fortune as a coal, sand and lime merchant at Monk Bridge and had used it to lever his way into political power and to buy a knighthood along the way. A renowned trencherman, he ate his way through enormous meals in the company of his rich and powerful friends. On hallowed occasions, an enormous silver tea urn would take pride of place on the blinding white tablecloth. It was worth a fortune, both for the precious metal it contained and for its exquisite design and execution by a master silversmith. Normally, it sat locked away on satin drapes behind glass. Geordie had salted all this information away, with vaguely felonious intent. He could not know at the time that it would be easier to burgle than he'd thought.

There was a clerk in the offices of the carriage workshops who went by the name of Norman Barnes. Barnes was a long, gloomy, cadaverous middle-aged cove, who always wore a threadbare grey suit which was baggy about the knees and shiny in the arse, and smelled of tobacco, sweat and mothballs. This Barnes had lodgings close to Geordie's and they often found themselves walking back and forth to work together. Looking back, Geordie realised that the man contrived to walk with him. One pay Saturday, Barnes invited Geordie for a drink in the Red Lion, an ancient half-timbered pub on the banks of the River Foss. Having nothing better to do, Geordie accepted, and they found a quiet table in the snug. Barnes had unwinking blue eyes and a shrewd way of looking at people, almost as if he were contemplating eating them. He took a long pull at his ale, smacked his lips, and opined that he didn't think Geordie was a mere labourer. Geordie shrugged and applied himself to his drink, wincing from a cut lip that the Gorringes had inflicted.

'Word has it,' said Barnes, looking round to make sure that no one was listening. 'Word has it that you took a beating because you couldn't pay t' bookies what tha owes.'

How the devil does he know that? Geordie wondered, studying Barnes's sly face.

'Eeeh, well lad,' said Barnes with a wink and a smile that revealed long yellow teeth. 'A pair of Cockney hard men was sat right where tha art now. Right nasty pair of thugs too. After a few drinks they wasn't too partickler about who heard what they was sayin'. They buggered off back north, but they reckoned they'd be back to finish what they come for.'

Barnes finished his drink and wiggled his glass, signalling for a refill. After the barmaid dumped two fresh glasses on the table, he whispered, 'They said summat about the Human Fly and you being a fiddler too.'

Geordie felt sick with dread, but Barnes gave him a reassuring pat on the shoulder. 'Nay, lad. Don't worry,' he said. 'I'll not shop thee. I was thinkin' we could do business together, like.'

Geordie inwardly sighed with relief, took a sip of ale, and asked Barnes to continue.

'Well lad, as the saying goes, I hide in plain sight. Ask anyone and they'll tell thee "Norman Barnes is a respectable, God-fearing man." I don't flash me money about, and I live modestly.' He winked. 'Thing is, I have me own firm if tha gets my meaning. I'm the brains of the outfit. I plan the jobs and t'others carry 'em out. We stash the proceeds in a hall out Holgate way and when the heat dies down, I know where to place it. I've never been caught and have no intention of that ever changin'. Now, young lad, I'm impressed with what we might call your curriculum vitae. So, I've been thinkin' that mebbe we could be partners?'

'Right, Mr Barnes,' said Geordie. 'So, if I agree, what's the plan?'

'Call me Norman, please. Now, chances are ye've heard of the Mansion House treasure?' Here his eyes glittered. 'Well, I have a man on the inside. Everythin's planned, but what's missin' is somebody wi' the Human Fly's skills. I tek it tha'rt interested?'

Geordie was. He was flat broke, was paid a pittance, and feared that he might soon end up dead on the riverbank if he couldn't find the money to pay off the Gorringe gorillas. Barnes extended a bony hand over the table and Geordie shook it solemnly. They arranged to meet a day or so later. Barnes intimated that he had an inside source and promised to provide Geordie with plans of the building and other vital information.

Geordie took advantage of the moonless night to creep past the line of carriages unseen by the coachmen huddled in their capes, awaiting their masters carousing inside the building. He sidled round to the back of the house. As Barnes had promised, someone had left a window ajar high up on the top floor. Just to the left, an iron drainpipe plunged four storeys to the yard at the back. If the pipe was sturdy, Geordie would have no difficulty in swarming up and swinging over onto the window ledge to let himself into the building. He vaulted the brick wall enclosing the backyard and was soon scaling the wall, climbing by holding onto the pipe and pushing the narrow toes of his plimsolls into the crevices in the brickwork. The pipe held – the solid work of Sheffield ironmasters – and he scrambled across the windowsill to find himself on a dark landing between floors. Here and there, a board creaked under his weight but the racket from the banquet hall muffled any noise he made as he tiptoed down the staircase. The room next to the banqueting hall contained the treasure he was seeking. The revellers came and went via the front stairs so there was little chance that he would be surprised about his nefarious business.

Geordie had brought a stub of candle and when he lit the wick with a Lucifer, he was astounded to see mounds of treasure glistening in the light. There were some richly decorated ceremonial swords – one said to have been owned by the Holy Roman Emperor Sigismund – a set of shining golden goblets, piles of jewels laid out on dark satin, and a large silver basin of fine workmanship. Most of it was locked in glass cases, but his set of picks made short work of that. Soon he was stuffing handfuls of jewellery into his bag. The gold objects were heavy, but he selected some goblets and added them to the haul. On a whim, he seized hold of the silver basin and shoved it into the duffel. It was bulky, but too good to leave behind. The silver tea urn must have been in use next door and would have been too big and heavy anyway. He closed the door and began to mount the stairs. The revelry continued. Someone dropped some plates and there was a gale of laughter, so loud that he didn't hear the man descending the stairs until he was abreast of him.

Geordie's heart stopped. His mouth went dry and he stood stock-still like a frightened rabbit. Flight was impossible with the stout figure blocking the way up the stairs. He saw Chief Inspector Verte in his mind's eye. So much for Norman Barnes' planning. But to his great surprise and relief, the man held up a friendly hand, and waved him past with a wink. Barnes had been as good as his word! Geordie breathed a half-forgotten prayer and soon was sliding down the drainpipe with the duffel heavy on his shoulders. He vaulted the rear wall, crept catlike in the shadows past the waiting coachmen, and slunk across the iron bridge, but not before stopping to wait for the knocking of his knees to abate.

Out in the rundown premises in Holgate, Norman Barnes feasted his eyes upon the haul. 'O yes! O yes!' he muttered as he fingered the loot. 'Beautiful work. Most beautiful work!' His eyes opened wide with alarm, however, when he pulled out the silver basin. 'O dearie me,' he squawked. 'I'd never be able to place this!' He fixed Geordie with a frightened blue eye, and whispered, though none could hear. 'This, my friend is the fookin' King James II chamber pot! Tha must tek it back!'

'Haddaway man,' Geordie retorted. 'I canna take it back. The place will be crawlin' wi' peelers!'

'Well, just dump it anywhere, like,' ordered Barnes. 'Mebbe down by the river. Just dump it man, quick smart!'

Geordie agreed, but not before Barnes promised to pay him a tidy sum for the other merchandise. He told him to return the following evening for his money. 'Just … just tek that bloody thing away!' He prodded the silver basin with a bony forefinger.

Geordie chucked the offending object off the bridge, where it rolled down the bank and came to rest in some cow parsley. The next morning some urchins found it and sold it to an old man, who planned to use it as a drinking vessel, not knowing that the Merry Monarch had once voided his royal excrements into it. When news spread of the daring burglary of the Lord Mayor's Mansion House, the old man's wife seized the pot and dumped it in a nearby street, from whence it was retrieved by the peelers and restored to its rightful place, albeit a trifle battered and smelling of Yorkshire ale.

After that, events had spiralled out of control. Late in the day after the burglary, Miserable Mick Armstrong came into the electric car workshops to arrange for some repair work on an overhead gantry. He saw Geordie pretending to sweep the floor, and it did not take long before recognition dawned. Geordie saw Mick and the workshop foreman, Sutcliffe, talking and nodding their heads, and giving him sidelong glances. At knock off time, Sutcliffe and Miserable Mick were waiting by the time clocks. 'Eeeh, Cyril, or whatever tha name is,' said Sutcliffe, looking grave. 'I'll see thee first thing in the morning in my office.' Armstrong said nothing, but he was staring hard with a carnivorous look about him.

The game was up. Geordie returned to his lodgings, packed up his gear and paid Mrs Mosby what he owed. He told her he'd found more congenial work in Liverpool. He intended to collect his money from Norman Barnes and get as far away from York as possible, but not in the direction of Liverpool. Barnes's yard was dark and silent when Geordie arrived. A fine rain was falling, and the smell of the sweet factories hung heavy in the night air as he knocked and waited on the doorstep. There was no answer and no light in the windows. He waited a good hour after the appointed time before it dawned on him: Norman Barnes had no intention of paying him! Geordie had only a few shillings to his name. He couldn't return to work at the carriage works now that Armstrong had fingered him, so he shouldered his duffel, picked up the suitcase, and walked back along the Holgate Road to the station, where he bought a ticket for Peterborough, as far as he could go on what little money he had. He spent a cold and anxious hour in the waiting room, but the London train pulled in on time and he clambered gratefully into a third-class carriage.

Stevenage and St Albans, early 1913

The Scottish railway conductor was incensed. 'Ye canna travel past Peterborough wi'oot payin' the proper fare!' he ranted, his face as red as Geordie's hair. 'I've a mind to hand ye over to the reelway polis!'

'Eeh, I'm sorry.' Geordie looked contrite. 'I must have dozed off, and now I don't know what to do. I'm supposed to start work in the morning at Peterborough and bring the missus and bairns doon when I get settled in. I've been without work and this job were a godsend.'

Hearing this, the conductor softened, picturing his own tribe of weans in the wynds of Auld Reekie. Class solidarity trumped his obligations to the North Eastern Railway Company. 'Och, laddie,' he sighed. 'Ye're living proof that Geordies are nothing but renegade Scotsmen wi' their brains bashed oot! I'll let ye oot at Stevenage. Ye'll have to get the 10:23 back up the line to Peterborough.'

The Stevenage station was windswept, cold, and deserted when Geordie alighted, with no intention of catching the 10:23 back up the line despite the ticket the conductor had slipped to him. The sole porter on duty ignored Geordie, and the man in the ticket office was fast asleep, snoring with his mouth open. Stevenage seemed little more than a large village, with a few gas lamps hardly lighting up the broad High Street that led past a row of shops and brick houses. Geordie had never heard of the place, and it seemed devoid of life. Even the pubs were shut, their signs creaking in the wind. He wandered around the empty streets, wondering where to spend the night. An owl hooted. The wind blustered. The moon rode out from behind the clouds and revealed the façade and sharp steeple of an ancient church set atop a massive square tower. A faint light glowed inside the stained-glass windows. On impulse, Geordie pushed on the massive oaken church door, which swung open on well-oiled hinges. The inside smelled of cold stone, beeswax, and incense: High Church, he reckoned, but perhaps the vicar would have sympathy for a man down on his luck.

'Who's there?' demanded a peevish upper-class voice. Its owner came out of the shadows behind a massive pillar: the vicar or a curate with his dog collar shining in the light cast by a candle he held in one hand. He had a supercilious horse face under a bald cranium that glowed pumpkin yellow when the light caught it.

Geordie had some vague notion of churches as sanctuaries, so he asked if there was a place he could sleep for the night. He would be gone in the morning, he added.

'Well, you'll not find one here,' harrumphed the priest. 'Cut orf.'

'A corner out of the wind would suffice.'

'Look, my man,' brayed the vicar. 'Be orf with you now before I call the police!'

Geordie turned on his heel and hefted his luggage, but he knew his scripture. 'Whoever is kind to the poor lends to the Lord,' he quoted, 'and he will reward them for what they have done.'

The vicar reacted like an old crone imagining someone was interfering with her knickers drawer. Geordie had bested him verbally but any joy he gained from the altercation soon evaporated. He went outside to find a thin rain was leaking from the sky; the kind the Geordies call a mizzle. It would soon soak him to the bone. He sought what shelter he could under the spreading limbs of a lime tree on the village common and sat on his bag to work out what to do next, careful to remove his fiddle first. The church clock struck twelve. He was dog-tired after a long day. It seemed an age since he had fled the carriage workshops and the scrutiny of Miserable Mick and Sutcliffe. He dozed off with his collar turned up against the wind, dreaming that his mother was admonishing him for abandoning Annie and the bairn.

A beam of bright light shone into his face. 'You! That's right, you! Wake up!' roared an angry voice. Geordie woke up dribbling and someone seized him by the arm and dragged him to his feet.

'Is this the one, vicar?' asked the voice – a foreign sort of a voice, like they spoke in London but more countrified.

'Yes.' It sounded like 'Ears.' 'That's the darkie who came sneaking into my church.'

The torch was lowered, and Geordie saw a massive form clad in a shiny blue cape covered in droplets of rain: a peeler, wearing a blue helmet with the silver insignia of the Hertfordshire constabulary. Next to him stood the vicar with the sanctimonious horse face, a long finger pointing at Geordie. At least he had a bed for the night, although it was only in a dirty cell in the local police station. The charge, a fat old sergeant told Geordie, was vagrancy – wandering abroad without visible means of support. He was a rogue and a vagabond. He booked Geordie as Cyril Toward, bade him goodnight, and took his bags 'for safekeeping'. Geordie slept the sleep of exhaustion and at dawn a surly turnkey brought a mug of sweet tea and a bowl of congealed porridge.

'Ye'll be up before the beak first thing, so make lively,' ordered the turnkey. 'Mister Small don't like no cheek. His gout plays merry 'ell, an' 'e don't like Scotchmen.'

'But I'm a Geordie.'

'Same fing. Makes no diff'rence.' The gaoler turned on his heel.

Later that morning, Geordie appeared before Magistrate Jerome Small, a long, thin, dyspeptic beanpole of a man with lynx-like tufts of white hair sprouting from his ears and a humourless smile fixed on his face like a baby suffering from wind. His gout had indeed been playing 'merry 'ell' if the stricken look on the face of the prisoner who was being led from the dock was anything to go by.

'Who's this?' snapped the beak, fixing Geordie with a malignant eye.

Upon learning Geordie's putative name and offence, Small's face contorted as if he had smelled something bad. British justice was done within five minutes. He sentenced Geordie under the Vagrancy Act to one month with hard labour in the St Albans County Gaol. The Act existed to punish 'any person wandering abroad and lodging in any barn or outhouse, or in any deserted or unoccupied building, or in the open air, or under a tent, or in any cart or wagon, not having any visible means of subsistence and not giving a good account of himself or herself.' Naturally, any Tory vicar, capitalist, politician, or member of the gentry would suffer the same penalty should they commit the same crime.

A heavy depression descended over Geordie as he entered the studded oaken gates of the St Albans gaol, to which they had conveyed him in a closed police cart. He signed for his possessions, stripped, and dressed in coarse prison garb. He was now, the reception screw informed him, Prisoner 8881, and he'd best not forget it.

The days were all the same. Screws rapped with heavy keys on the doors of the slots – their version of reveille – at 5:00 a.m. They roared like maniacs if beds were not made up in apple pie order. The prisoners ate awful food in silence under their vigilant gaze. Worst of all was the task of picking oakum. Seated on hard wooden benches, they worked in silence unpicking old rope, first into strands, then into individual fibres, with the eagle-eyed screws on the lookout for slackers. Fingers bled. Tendons ached. Arms screamed with pain. A young boy cried but there was no pity.

Geordie's ordeal ended suddenly. On his third morning at the oakum picking, a screw led him off to the prison kitchens. 'Noo cook fer ye, Mr Throgmorton!' bellowed the screw. Cook! Geordie gasped. He could scarcely boil an egg. A huge man he took to be Mr Throgmorton bade him don an apron and look lively. This Throgmorton was at least six and a half feet tall and broad in the beam, with an ample belly that protruded from his unbuttoned uniform jacket like a bullfrog's pouch. He wore a permanent scowl on his fleshy face, and Geordie was afraid of his massive hands, which hung like legs of lamb from his ape-like arms. He sat Geordie on a stool next to two large buckets and a pile of potatoes.

'Git peelin', gingernut,' Throgmorton ordered. 'If I sees ye slackin' orf, I'll kick yer black arse inter the middle o' next week!'

Geordie sat obediently and contemplated the task before him. To his surprise, he could wield the peeling knife dextrously and he had finished the task before the ogre returned.

The kitchen was a smelly basement, full of steam and heat. Prisoners scurried around in the semi dark, occasionally bumping into each other, and bawling out oaths that even Geordie as a former colliery man found foul. There seemed to be no rhyme or reason to the layout of the place. One man boiled up what smelled like meat and offal in a huge pot. Another chopped up mounds of vegetables and yet another stirred up something muddy in a tureen, pausing now and again to pick his nose and examine the findings. Right in the middle, a prisoner had his arms immersed to the elbows in a huge sink. The water, Geordie noticed, was full of bobbing bits of food. Cobwebs hung from the low ceiling and greasy water slopped about the floors. There were things in corners that he didn't want to think about. He wondered what was worse – picking oakum or slaving in Throgmorton's filthy domain. For the rest of the day, Throgmorton assigned him to chop turnips on a greasy board and drop the pieces into reeking buckets. It was a wonder that the whole prison didn't succumb to food poisoning.

Early the next morning, Throgmorton tripped on a bucket and fell headfirst into the side of one of the gas stoves. He didn't get up, but as none of the other prisoners attempted to help him, Geordie went over and gently shook the man.

'Leave 'im be!' grunted a coarse voice. 'It's no concern of yours.'

'Man's an arsehole,' added another prisoner to general muttered agreement.

'I divvent doubt it,' said Geordie, 'but if we don't help, they'll say someone hit him on purpose.'

There was muttered agreement and having ascertained that Throgmorton was alive, albeit unconscious, Geordie went to the door and banged on it with a dirty saucepan until a screw came to see what the commotion was. Two screws carried Throgmorton away on a stretcher and after a while, Deputy Warden Oakeshott entered the kitchen, accompanied by a trio of underlings. A rat scurried across the floor. After venturing into the middle of the room, and gazing round with a look of horror on his face, he approached Geordie.

'You seem like an intelligent man,' he observed. 'Maybe you can make some sense of this place because I can't.' Geordie was noncommittal, aware of the eyes of the prisoners judging him, but Oakeshott persisted after conferring with his escorts. 'Tell me, Number 8881, what do you need to run this place properly?'

'Well, sir,' Geordie replied, 'if I'm not mistaken, we'll need disinfectant, buckets, carbolic, and scrubbing brushes. I can't see how we can easily re-organise the cooking, but we should make sure that all the pots and pans are washed properly.'

The kitchen hands threatened mutiny to begin with, but when they had cleaned up the filth, they agreed that it was a more pleasant place to work, and they began to treat Geordie with grudging respect. The rates of illness among the prisoners soon declined and the quality of the food improved. The day of Prisoner 8881's release came. He was marched from his cell to the gaol's reception room. 'Sign 'ere for yer fings,' mumbled a screw, shoving a heavy ledger towards him. Geordie signed and pocketed the few farthings that constituted his earnings. The screw jerked a thumb towards the exit, which was guarded by a massive colleague who smelled of pomade. Before Geordie reached the exit, however, Deputy Warden Oakeshott entered the room in a rush.

'I say, Toward,' said he. 'I would like to thank you for turning things around in the kitchen. Mr Throgmorton was a, err, law unto himself, but things are now on an, err, even keel. If you like, there is a job for you here in charge of the kitchens.'

Geordie did not like, although he thanked the Deputy Warden courteously, touched his finger to his cap and left the premises. He emerged into a fine spring morning. Birds sang their hearts out in a chestnut tree. The sun shone brightly. People went about their business unhindered, passing through doors without waiting for screws to open them, joshing each other good-naturedly without fear of being told to shut it or they would be in solitary on bread and water.

Geordie spent his prison earnings on a pot of tea and a fresh baked currant bun, served by a smiling woman who chattered about the weather. Best of all, he was closer to London, which a milestone informed him lay twenty-five miles away in a southerly direction. He set off at a brisk pace, anxious to leave the County Gaol far behind. Soon, he was out in open countryside, whistling as he walked, and was halfway to Watford. He felt he could have walked all the way to London, but when an open-topped Austin lorry drew up, he leapt aboard. The driver, who introduced himself as Bert Dawkins, was hauling a load of coal to Ealing.

Dawkins was an affable chap. He told Geordie he 'talked funny' and asked about his colour but meant no offence by it and questioned him with interest about what it was like 'Up North in Scotland.' When the lorry spluttered into Ealing along the Great West Road, he offered to drop Geordie off at a hostelry where they served a good pint.

'Here we are, mate,' said Dawkins, coasting the lorry to a halt. 'Dracula's Castle, we calls it!'

Four storeys high and bristling with pointed towers and elaborate pediments, the neo-Gothic confection could well have housed Bram Stoker's famous vampire. Polished windows reflected the western sun, giving it a slightly sinister air. Under the colonnaded entrance, a top-hatted commissionaire awaited well-heeled guests. Geordie gave Dawkins a quizzical look, but the driver laughed at his confusion.

'Nah, mate. Doncha worry. The hotel's posh alright, but your money's good in the public bar!'

With that, he gave Geordie a thrip'ny bit to spend on whatever took his fancy, tipped his finger to his cap, slid the lorry into gear and took off to make his deliveries.

Geordie was humbled by the man's generosity. He had seen men at their worst in the gaol; now he had encountered a man so open and honest that he viewed himself critically – and did not much like what he saw. Pushing the thought aside, he opened the frosted glass doors of the pub, looking forward to a pint of Mr Fuller's best ale.

Ealing, near London, 1913

The Dracula's Castle bar was all dark wood, polished glass and gleaming brass. It smelled of beeswax and fresh beer, and warm sun was streaming in through the tall windows. Geordie ordered a pint of Fuller's Chiswick Best from the pretty barmaid, took an appreciative sip, and walked over to sit on a leather banquette. The bar was otherwise empty save for a young man reading at a corner table. Geordie took a long pull of beer, wiped his mouth, and looked around. The reader did not appear to have noticed Geordie, so engrossed was he in his book, but when he took a sip of his red wine, he looked over and nodded affably. He looked like one of the 'Chinamen' Geordie's uncle Anthony had encountered on his voyages around the world. Small and slim, with thick, jet-black hair parted on the left-hand side, he had piercing dark eyes and a full mouth. He was clad in kitchen whites with a dusting of flour down the front, a little like a German Christmas cake, a *Weihnachtsstollen*.

'Good afternoon,' he said, closing his book with a piece of paper at the right page. 'Have you come about the job?'

'Job? What job?' Geordie asked, his ears pricking up.

'Well, there's a vacancy in the kitchen if you're interested.' The man spoke good English with what seemed a French accent.

Geordie was interested, and he could now say that he had worked in a kitchen – albeit not precisely where. He had only a few coppers to his name and no job or lodging. Even with summer not far away, the thought of cold nights in 'Hotel Stars' or another sojourn in gaol did not appeal. Without a union card, his chances of employment as a fitter were slim. The young man invited him over to his table. His book was in French, something to do with '*La Question Coloniale*,' whatever that was.

'The head chef will be here soon,' said Geordie's new friend, extending a slim hand over the table. 'I am Nguyễn Tất Thành.' This didn't mean much to Geordie, who must have looked puzzled, for he slowly repeated it.

'Oh,' Geordie replied. 'Very pleased to meet you. My name is Toward. Cyril Toward.' He almost added 'Tut', the nickname of the mechanics' supervisor back at High Fell.

'Well, Cyril' – the man smiled – 'your glass is empty.' With that, he collected the glasses and went to the bar, just as a remarkably fat man burst through the pub doors, huffing and puffing like a steam locomotive and seeming to want to be in five different places at the same time. The two men spoke together, and the fat one looked appraisingly over his shoulder at Geordie.

Nguyễn, it transpired, was the pastry cook and the fat man was Mr Percy Gastrell, the head chef. He agreed to hire Geordie on a month's trial. According to popular wisdom, fat men are jolly fellows, but this Gastrell blew hot and cold. Some days he raced around the kitchens in a mad lather of sweat, cursing the sous-chefs, laughing, peering into tureens, and bringing himself to the brink of a seizure. At other times, he was morose and uncommunicative, indicating tasks by pointing his finger and by other gestures, sometimes obscene. He made sure, however, that the kitchen was spotless and under his tutelage Geordie progressed from peeling vegetables and other menial tasks to preparing rich sauces for the fish and meats served up to the well-off guests in the hotel's ornate dining room – or *salle à manger* as Percy Gastrell called it. In one of his expansive moods, Gastrell praised Geordie as a 'natural' and promised him a permanent job when his month's trial was up. Nevertheless, the work was relentless, and each evening Geordie welcomed his bed, which was upstairs in the servants' quarters in the attics. Often, he was too tired to play his fiddle. Sometimes he dreamed of Annie and the bairn and woke bathed in sweat. Most afternoons, he would join Nguyễn in the bar for a quiet drink before the evening rush.

Nguyễn also taught him to play chess and told him something of his life. He came, he said, from near a city called Hanoi in a faraway country called Tonkin. He had worked his passage around the world on ships, sometimes as a stoker, sometimes in the galley. He had been to Paris and even worked for a while in New York. Geordie had always been interested in geography, so he looked up the whereabouts of Tonkin in an atlas in the guests' lounge.

'Tonkin belongs to France,' he told Nguyễn, anxious to show off his new knowledge.

Nguyễn's eyes narrowed. 'No, it does not! The French invaded my country, and they steal our wealth. We were long an independent state …'

'Well, then, if you're not French, you must be Chinese.'

'We drove out the Chinese and we will defeat the French too!'

A quiet and reserved young man, he seemed to glow with an inner fire when he started on about his country. On Sundays, they would sometimes take long walks on Ealing Common, and he would explain mysterious words such as colonialism, imperialism, and socialism.

Some of the High Fell miners were socialists, although Geordie had never bothered to find out exactly what it meant. His granda was one. The secretary of the Durham Mining Mechanics' Association, Mr John Wilkinson Taylor, was a socialist too, and sat in the parliament in London. It seemed that Nguyễn wanted to make a socialist of him, but Geordie was merely expressing polite interest.

Summer ended, and autumn came and went. The year drew to a murky close. Thick fogs descended over West Ealing and rain fell relentlessly, soaking the tennis courts and ornamental gardens out the back of the hotel. Percy Gastrell fell into a state of unrelenting gloom that increased with the shortening days and long nights. He became increasingly snappish with the kitchen staff, finding fault when none was warranted. He drove serving maids to tears and kitchen hands to quit. When a Cockney sous-chef spoke back, he sacked him and declared he would do the same to anyone daring to emulate such insolence. Nguyễn quietly remonstrated, but Gastrell turned on him in a rage, declaring him a Chinese heathen who would best mind his manners when addressing a white man. He would have sacked Nguyễn too but desisted when he realised that he would be without a pastry cook in the busy Christmas season. Nguyễn seethed with quiet rage. He was the equal of any white man, he declared, and he would not tolerate racial prejudice from anyone. Besides, Gastrell was quite mad and was getting worse. Nguyễn believed he suffered from what the French called '*la folie circulaire*' and needed urgent treatment by an alienist. Nguyễn begged him to seek help, but the man was beyond reason.

The following Sunday, Nguyễn did not take his customary walk with Geordie on the common but took the train into the city, and Geordie stayed in his garret room, played his fiddle, and read the volume of Shakespeare's plays that his friend had loaned him. Nguyễn came back late that afternoon and handed in his notice. He had found employment in a grand city establishment and there was a berth for Geordie too if he wanted it. Geordie had also wearied of Gastrell's intemperate moods and foul abuse, so he too gave notice. The fat man pleaded for them to stay but they refused. On a bright winter's day, with frost sparkling on the roads under a hard-blue sky, the two friends bade farewell to Dracula's Castle and took the train to central London.

The Carlton Hotel, London, 1913–14

Geordie had looked forward to the journey into London. Ealing was a bustling town, but it was dwarfed by the city a radical writer had dubbed 'the Great Wen'. Some six and a half million souls called London home and it grew relentlessly, sprawling out like some enormous, hungry amoeba, engulfing villages, fields, woods, and smaller towns. Geordie's train trundled through many stations along the nine miles to the centre, passing open fields, lines of tenements and smoking factories, crossing over canals and other railway lines, the density of settlement increasing all the while. Visibility was poor because of the smog – a choking, yellowish fog consisting of water vapour and the noxious exhalations of millions of coal-burning domestic and industrial fires – and other things Geordie didn't want to think about.

Alighting from the train at Charing Cross Station, Geordie and Nguyễn threaded their way to Haymarket through the crowds thronging the Strand and Trafalgar Square. The smog muffled the sounds of traffic and was so thick they did not see the colossal stone building that was to be their home and place of work until they were almost upon it. Some eight storeys high, the Carlton Hotel stood at the corner of Pall Mall and Haymarket and made Dracula's Castle seem puny in comparison. Later, when strong winds blew away the smog, the upper reaches of the huge building came into view – lines of dormer windows set in mansard roofs, elaborate pediments, bell roofs, and two towering domes topped with pointed cupolas. Well-dressed people were entering the Theatre Royal, which shared an arcade with the hotel, to attend a matinee performance of Shaw's *Pygmalion*. The presence of a bedraggled flower girl in the street outside was, as Nguyễn observed, a real irony.

The pair were received individually by the maître d' in a small office off the Palm Court. Elegantly got up in a tuxedo, this person gave the young man he believed to be Cyril Toward a searching once-over before bidding him take a seat and solemnly shaking his hand. 'Mr Nguyễn comes highly recommended,' he said, 'so we are very happy to take you on probation. We are very cosmopolitan here, so your colour is not a problem.'

He gave Geordie a run-down of his duties as a commis chef in the hotel kitchens and proposed a modest, but acceptable remuneration. Geordie was familiar with the job title, although Dracula's Castle had not employed anyone in that role. Should Geordie prove his worth, he could expect increments as he worked his way up the kitchen hierarchy. A small room and meals were available at a nominal cost. If he agreed, he could sign the requisite paperwork and commence duty at six o'clock sharp the following morning.

'I should warn you,' the maître d' confided, 'that Monsieur Escoffier is an extremely exacting employer who will not accept sloppiness either in work or appearance. That said, you should consider it a privilege to work under him, and if you apply yourself, you will find the work congenial and will learn a great deal.'

Geordie signed as Cyril Toward – the signature indistinguishable from that of his former boss – and was handed over to an underling to be kitted out with kitchen whites and sheets, blankets and whatnot for his room. His garret was reached by interminable staircases, each progressively narrower. It was equipped with an iron-framed bedstead, a small but serviceable wardrobe, a tiny writing table, and an ancient washstand (but not running water). The little window was slightly ajar and through it, muffled by the fog, came the noises from the street far below, with pigeons cooing on the sill. He had finally made it to London, and he looked forward to his new job and to exploring the city in his off-duty hours. Calcutta Row and the High Fell Colliery seemed impossibly distant, both spatially and temporally. He spent the evening reading a translation of Victor Hugo's *Les Misérables*, which Nguyễn had recommended, pondering its message of sin and redemption. The guilt and pain he felt at abandoning Annie and the bairn was never far below the surface.

When he reported for his first day's work, the sheer size and complexity of the kitchen left him stunned. Every surface was spotlessly clean, with gleaming rows of copper-bottomed pans and other utensils reflecting the pale winter light shining through the large windows. Dracula's Castle was nothing like the foetid den that served as the kitchen in the St Albans County Gaol, but it had still been a chaotic place, with cooks shouting and swearing and cutting sanitary corners when there was a rush on. Here, in contrast, everything ran like clockwork and the staff were working methodically to prepare the breakfasts for the hotel's numerous guests. Geordie was standing there feeling like a yokel, wondering what was required of him, when an important personage glided up beside him. Geordie had to tilt his head back to look up into the person's face.

'Good morning,' boomed the personage in slightly Cockney tones. 'I'm Mr Lorimer, the sous-chef and you, I take it, are Cyril Toward.'

Geordie agreed that he was and shook the man's hand. Lorimer bade him sit on a kitchen chair and towered above him like a white painted pillar-box. 'Now, young Toward,' Lorimer intoned, looking down his long and rather pointed nose. 'I want you to forget ever-fing you've learned in other establishments, or virtually ever-fing, and to familiarise yourself with the way we work.' He gestured expansively round the kitchen. 'You'll note that there is no unnecessary movement, and everyone is at their allotted station. There is none of the pointless rushing 'ere that you find in other establishments, and none of the foul language and dirt. Here, we hate dirt like sin. Like sin, I say! We work here strictly according to M'sieur Escoffier's brigade system. M'sieur Escoffier is the chef de cuisine, but 'e leaves the day-to-day running to me, and it is to me that you will report. Nevertheless, there are others above you in the 'ierarchy.'

Here he paused and pointed upwards. Geordie nodded and then cast his eyes around the kitchen. A figure was hard at work, stooped over a stove preparing eggs.

'That man there is Mr Morris. He is one of several demi chefs in the kitchen and he will be your immediate supervisor. Morris 'imself reports to Mr Dudgeon, who is one of three chefs de partie who report to me as the sous-chef.'

If Geordie had imagined he would perform similar tasks to those he had carried out at Dracula's Castle, he was mistaken. Although as a commis chef he was not a lowly scullery hand, he was Ron Morris's labourer, sent this way and that to bring ingredients, ordered to wash down oven tops, chop onions and whatnot; in short, a dogsbody. However, this Morris intimated to Geordie that he would soon be leaving to take over a pie and mash shop in Stepney. Mr Lorimer kept a sharp eye on the staff. He was so impressed with Geordie's work that when Morris left, he promoted him to the vacant position as demi chef. This caused considerable resentment among other lowly staff members, who muttered that Toward was a Johnny-come-lately who had sailed in and taken what was rightfully theirs, and a fiddle-playing darkie to boot.

Worse, however, was the attitude of Barry Dudgeon, who clearly feared that Geordie coveted his job as chef de partie. He was, in the Cockney argot, 'all marf and no trahsers' – a man as small as Geordie, but with a big complex. He contrived to find fault with Geordie's work whenever he could. He was too slow, or too fast, or too slapdash, or too finicky. Dudgeon's aim, it was clear, was to force Geordie to leave. Geordie discussed the matter with Nguyễn, who worked as a patissier elsewhere in the kitchens, and his friend's advice was forthright. He didn't like sneaks, so complaining to Lorimer was not an option, and there was no union. Cyril could either find employment elsewhere or confront Dudgeon outside of working hours and prevail on him to back off.

Geordie did not have to pursue any of these courses of action. One day, he noticed a man watching him from behind a bench near the main doorway. Although the man was so short that he could barely see over the bench – and indeed was no taller than Geordie himself – he had the air of authority about him. The little fellow was wearing a flat cap over a full head of grey hair, and he sprouted a thick, neatly trimmed moustache. His dark suit was immaculate, bespoke from Savile Row.

A colleague nudged Geordie and whispered, 'Mind now. It's Monsieur Escoffier himself, back from New York!'

Aged in his late sixties, Auguste Escoffier was legendary among chefs, hoteliers, and their well-off customers. The French press praised him as '*le roi des cuisiniers et cuisinier des rois*.' Aboard SS *Imperator*, Kaiser Wilhelm told him, 'I am the Emperor of Germany, but you are the Emperor of Chefs.' Escoffier had devised the brigade system following a stint cooking for the French army brass in the Franco-Prussian War. Nineteenth-century kitchens were filthy and chaotic places, but under Escoffier, the father of haute cuisine, order and cleanliness prevailed.

Lorimer, Geordie noticed one day, was conversing deferentially with the Great Man, and they were both casting glances in his direction. After several minutes of this, Lorimer beckoned Geordie over, and stood ready to translate, for Monsieur Escoffier spoke no English, or pretended not to.

The little man spoke rapidly, and Lorimer translated. 'Monsieur Escoffier bids you welcome to the Carlton and has heard many good things about you.' Geordie was surprised that he, a lowly demi chef, had come to the Frenchman's attention. 'You have a natural talent, he says. He tasted one of your sauces and found it to be very agreeable …' Escoffier spoke again in rapid French, this time with a frown. 'However,' Lorimer continued, 'you must never forget to keep things simple. We use only the finest ingredients – meat, fish, fowl and so forth – and we must be careful not to smother 'em in over-elaborate sauces and flavours. He stresses that sauces should be smooth, light – but not liquid – glossy to the eye and decided in taste.' Lorimer paused, and the Great Man continued, this time with a slight smile. 'He says that if our young friend bears this advice in mind, he will go far.'

With that, Escoffier nodded and turned on his heel, and Geordie went back to his station. As he mulled this over, he noticed Barry Dudgeon glaring at him with hatred. Some weeks later, Geordie was promoted to chef de partie and Dudgeon resigned. It seemed that young Geordie Stubbs was destined for great things, and at night in his attic, he dreamed of becoming a chef de cuisine like Auguste Escoffier. Burglary was a thing of the past; of that he was sure. He could never forget Annie and the baby for long. He wondered what she had called him or her. In the dark hours, his unquiet conscience would tear the crusted cicatrice which expediency had plastered over their memory. In his wilder moments, he dreamed of writing to Annie and asking her to come to London. Cold reality, however, told him that she would never forgive him and that even if she did, she'd insist that he return to Tyneside. She had a strong sense of duty, and she would not compromise on her responsibility to her parents. Besides, he was a wanted man up there and the taste of prison at St Albans had convinced him that a stretch was to be avoided at all costs.

He threw himself into his work. While cooking was for most people a job or even a chore, for Geordie it was a vocation, a calling, and a passion. The job had unleashed a creative potential that surprised him. His old life seemed far behind him, and he marvelled that the hands he now kept fastidiously clean were once soiled with grease and coal dust, and that he could hardly boil water without burning the pan. Had he really been the Human Fly, who had once scaled sheer walls to relieve householders of their valuables? Had he been the man diddled by Norman Barnes? Was he the burglar who stole the King James II chamber pot from the Lord Mayor's Mansion House in York? He shuddered with revulsion at the thought of the St Albans prison, with its noisome kitchens and the horror of picking oakum. He had toyed with the idea of a flutter at one of the London racecourses but managed to suppress the urge when he recalled the earlier consequences of his addiction.

He found London fascinating, delightful in all its moods and seasons – save for the slum rookeries into which he had strayed on occasion. He spent much of his free time exploring, often in the company of his pastry cook friend Nguyễn, walking the Embankment, strolling on Hampstead Heath, or disappearing into the labyrinthine lanes of the City. Nguyễn was intrigued by his fiddling and became so fond of Celtic airs that he made a study of O'Carolan and his music.

Nguyễn took him to cosmopolitan meetings with socialists, radical trade unionists, Irish republicans, suffragettes and anti-colonial agitators from India and Africa, but although he found such gatherings interesting, he had no desire to become an activist for any cause. He had also started walking out with a young woman who worked in a milliner's shop near Trafalgar Square. Nineteen years old and comely, Violet Devenish-Meares came from a minor aristocratic family fallen on hard times. For Geordie, Violet was an impossibly exotic creature. A flighty spitfire, haughty and fiercely independent, she led him a merry dance, which he tolerated because he found her so fascinating. She laughed at his Geordie accent, and he suspected he was for her an adventure with a bit of rough, a darkie too, before she found someone closer in station to herself. In truth, too, he never planned anything too serious with her.

The London Reception Centre, August 1914

The idyll ended abruptly. Buildings, as Miss Preedy had maintained in her Bible classes at the High Fell National School, had to sit on solid foundations. The fine building that Geordie was making of his life was built on sand. In August 1914, his past caught up with him again. Nguyễn and his friends had been warning for some time about the danger of a major war, but Geordie, like many others, did not pay much heed to their dire forecasts. When war broke out between the Allies and the Central Powers in late July 1914, he shrugged and continued working. Everyone was saying that the war would be over by Christmas and there seemed to be plenty of recruits, many of whom marched off through cheering throngs in nearby streets.

It was yet again a case of 'See the Conquering Heroes Come!' Posters of Field Marshal Lord Kitchener demanded that young men do their duty by King and Country, and newspaper headlines condemned the invasion of Belgium by 'Kaiser Bill's Huns.' None of this impressed Nguyễn, who scoffed that the same 'poor little Belgium' was guilty of mass murder and forced labour in its African colony. Geordie did not know what to think. He could not fault his friend's arguments, but he was not immune to the call of patriotism.

The war was good for the Carlton's business as many officers called to the colours came there to dine before their postings across the Channel. One afternoon, Geordie left the kitchens, intending to make his way to his garret room to change before meeting Violet at a Lyons teashop near her work. The hotel was packed with guests and diners, many of them in uniform. He turned a corner and saw, to his horror, a man he recognised as Detective Chief Inspector James Verte! Verte was entering the Palm Court tearooms, conversing with an army officer. Geordie slackened his pace and tried to melt into the throng of people, but Verte suddenly turned his head and caught sight of him. Geordie could almost see the cogs and levers working inside the detective's head and he knew with dreadful certainty that it would not be long before Verte placed him. Geordie thought quickly. He had to get out fast, so he sprinted up to his room, changed into street clothes, and packed his duffel bag with spare clothing, a few books, personal documents, and money. He leapt down the servants' staircase three steps at a time and exited into an alley behind the hotel, in his haste knocking over a tramp rummaging through dustbins. Too late, he realised he had left his fiddle behind.

Meanwhile, Verte was quizzing the maître d' about the star employee known at the Carlton as Cyril Toward. Verte had already telephoned the local police station to send round some constables to search the premises. They turned Geordie's room upside down and worked methodically through the staff quarters, rousting startled off-shift waiters and cooks from their beds, demanding if they had seen the criminal. They looked in water closets, invaded the staff dining rooms and even ventured perilously onto the rain-slicked rooftops. A sergeant grilled the old tramp whose dustbin investigations Geordie had rudely interrupted. Still indignant, the vagabond pointed the way 'the darkie' had fled. James Verte seethed with cold anger, furious that his quarry had once again eluded him. For his part, Nguyễn Tất Thành smiled to himself at his friend's escape.

When he left the alley, leaving the tramp cursing volubly behind him, Geordie had no clear idea of where he should go. It was a drizzly, muggy day, with the river shrouded in dense fog. He trotted along the Embankment towards Big Ben, drawn to some noisy commotion ahead, anxious to hide in crowds. To his consternation, he realised that the crowds were milling around a building that he recognised as New Scotland Yard, the central police station! A lengthy crocodile of young men snaked along the pavement and spilled out onto the cobbles, undeterred by the drizzle, which had turned to greasy rain. A sign hung over the main doorway proclaiming the place was now the LONDON RECEPTION OFFICES FOR ALL BRANCHES OF THE ARMY & SPECIAL RESERVE, with an invitation to ENQUIRE WITHIN. Geordie's brain worked with lightning speed. He needed to get off the streets and Verte surely would not expect him to turn up at Scotland Yard. He fell into line with the recruits shuffling towards the doorway. There were howls of outrage and fisticuffs when two men tried to jump the queue, so Geordie decided not to try the same trick.

Half an hour passed. The rain fell steadily but failed to dampen the enthusiasm of the men in the queue. Another half-hour later, Geordie stood before a harassed old army sergeant sitting at a table. He gave his real name in response to the soldier's demand – a double bluff, he reckoned – and produced his birth certificate. The old man laboriously wrote down his details, gave him a slip of paper with his name written on it and ordered him to wait his turn outside a large, curtained-off cubicle. Once inside, a doctor's assistant put him on a set of scales and measured his height. At 5'2", he just met the minimum requirements for new recruits and even then, had to stand on tippy toes. Next, an army doctor tested his eyesight, after which Geordie stripped and coughed on command as another khaki clad quack lifted his testicles. The cast in his eye didn't faze them. Apparently judging him healthy cannon fodder, the doctor scribbled something on a pad and ordered him to dress, after which he walked to yet another table, where he stood before a bored officer. A little corporal ordered him to salute and stand at attention, after which the officer asked his civilian occupation.

'I'm a chef,' Geordie replied, adding 'sir' at the corporal's barked command.

'Chef?' The officer raised a superior eyebrow, looking at him with the kind of smile that gentlemen reserved for amusing specimens of the hoi polloi. 'Heated up some beans, did we? We'll put you down as cook. Dismissed.'

The corporal pointed him towards a small room, where a few recruits were standing around looking lost. Another officer ordered them to each take a Bible and repeat an oath of allegiance, in which they collectively swore to 'faithfully defend His Majesty, His Heirs and successors … against all enemies' and promised to obey the authority of all set over them and to serve for the duration of the war.

Five minutes later, Geordie found himself standing in an internal courtyard along with fifty or sixty other new recruits, being harangued by a sergeant major who was puce-faced with anger at the sight of them. They were disgusting bastards fit only to clean shithouses and were a disgrace that their fuckin' mothers 'ad ever give birth to 'em, he ranted in a curiously high-pitched voice. Next, he screamed at them to get up quick smart into the back of some lorries covered in khaki tarpaulin, which were then quickly driven off through an archway into the cobbled street. Geordie's companions lit up Woodbines and observed each other warily, the sergeant major's insults still ringing in their ears. An hour earlier, they had reckoned themselves heroes, but he had other ideas of their worth. It had all seemed a bit of a lark, but now the full import of what they had done began to sink in. They had left homes, tearful wives, children, sweethearts, and parents and were now in a strange organisation that was nothing as they had imagined it to be. Private Geordie Stubbs, however, was glad to be lost in this anonymous mass of bewildered humanity, and he had suffered worse abuse in the St Albans Gaol.

Where the trucks were headed, none of them had any idea, but as they passed well-known landmarks, the bolder ones opined about possible destinations and the men began to chatter together. They had already accepted that it was not their place to ask questions. All were working-class Londoners and they swapped chitchat about people and locations in the city. Several men had agreed to join up together. It seemed most had had something to do with food in civilian life. A couple were butchers. Another a fruiterer. Two were bakers. There were a couple of Billingsgate fish porters and some others had worked in alehouses. Several were waiters, and most had been cooks of one type or another. The dark-skinned Tynesider Geordie Stubbs was a curiosity among these denizens of the Great Wen, and he kept silent as the lorry trundled along through the endless suburbs. The rain pattered on the canvas roof, and houses and factories flashed by. They left the city behind, and the lorries bumped and rattled along narrow country roads. Groups of women stood in villages waving Union Jacks and knots of small boys cheered and hurrahed the heroes as they passed by. They were heading west under a darkening sky and Geordie fell asleep clutching his duffel bag. Night fell. The rain stopped. He awoke then lapsed back into sleep and woke again when the rain returned with increased vigour. Many of his companions were snoring, although a few held whispered conversations, their cigarettes glowing in the dark. Geordie had quite lost track of time when the lorry slowed at a checkpoint. Dimly, through the rainy darkness, Geordie could make out lines of tents flapping in the wind. The lorry stopped abruptly, and a stentorian voice roared at the men to get out of the fucking truck and fall into fucking line quick smart!

~ 19 ~

77th Regiment Barracks, Wiltshire, 1914

What a shower of shit!' the voice roared as the recruits jumped from the truck and formed a ragged line. The voice was Cockney, and it was anything but friendly. 'What the fuckin' hell am I supposed to do with you lot?' it demanded. The NCO bent down from his considerable height to peer into the face of a small man trembling at the end of the line. 'What's your name, Sonny Jim?' he demanded.

'Err, I'm Billy 'Opkins.'

The NCO went almost apoplectic with rage. 'Billy 'Opkins, SIR!' he roared, pausing so that his victim could correct his error.

He repeated this performance up and down the line, becoming progressively angrier at each encounter. He towered over Geordie, who gave his name and remembered to call his tormentor 'sir'.

'Well fuck me!' the NCO exploded. 'Wot's that language you're speakin'?'

'Err, Geordie, sir,' Stubbs replied, trying to avoid the spittle flying from the man's mouth.

'Fuckin' Geordie, 'e sez. Sounds more like fuckin' Nor-Fuckin'-Wegian to me. Fall out Stubbs, yer red-haired blackie twat until I decides wot to do wiv ya.'

The lunatic, they learned, was Regimental Sergeant Major Clark; 'no fuckin' e!' He had what he considered the distasteful job of turning this 'pitiful crowd of fuckin' waiters and kitchen wallahs into soldiers'. He marched the new recruits over to a wooden barracks hut, seeming to forget Geordie standing at attention in the rain. Inside the hut, Clark roared at the men to strip off their civvies and don temporary 'Kitchener Blue' uniforms. As many as three-quarters of a million men had volunteered in the first month of the Great War and the army struggled to cope with the demand for uniforms.

'Makes youse look like fuckin' postmen,' Clark jeered. He broke off when he pretended to remember Stubbs standing in the rain. 'Getcha black arse over 'ere,' he roared. Geordie sidled over, and Clark looked him up and down and sighed, jerking his thumb at the pile of uniforms. 'You annoy me, Stubbs,' he said. 'You really do.'

When the recruits were dressed and had shouldered blankets and other kit, Clark marched them across to a large, three-sided shelter and lined them up, all the while strutting up and down with his swagger stick tucked under his arm, roaring obscenities. Geordie wondered if he were enjoying himself.

'Now, you useless arseholes is mostly gunna be regimental cooks,' Clark said, 'but before youse lift a fryin' pan or boil an egg it's my job to train youse to be proper soldiers just in case Jerry interrupts while youse are makin' the fuckin' dinners. Over there,' he added, pointing with his stick at a line of tents, 'is yer quarters. Now it's gettin' late so when I gives the horder, you'll get your horrible arses over there and grab some sleep. Reveille's at five a.m. sharp and God help any of youse who sleep in.'

With that last threat, he dismissed the dazed recruits and they scurried off gratefully. It had been a shocking introduction to the training camp, which sat on a miserable plain somewhere in Wiltshire.

Things did not improve the next day. After reveille, the new recruits lined up for a quick catwash in cold water in a jerry-rigged ablutions tent. Rain had seeped in under the canvas and after the men had finished splashing themselves at the sinks, the ground was unpleasantly muddy underfoot. Geordie was the butt of a great deal of mirth, most of it good-natured, and he took it in good spirit. His outlandish accent was noteworthy, his colour also, but his most bizarre attribute – in his companions' eyes – was that he had changed into pyjamas before retiring to bed.

'We knew you Scotchmen wore kilts,' one joshed, 'but not that you wore clothes to bed.' They refused to listen to his protestation that he was a Geordie, not a Scot. 'Same diff'rence,' they joked, and from then on it was a 'fact' that he was a Scotchman.

This interlude was short-lived, for RSM Clark burst into the tent roaring and screaming for them to get their sorry arses over to the mess tent even though they weren't worth feeding. Geordie had dined on worse, but his time at the Carlton had spoiled him. The army breakfast consisted of a dollop of lumpy porridge and a slice of cold toast and slimy jam washed down with a grey liquid that might have been tea or coffee or something else. Afterwards, Clark marched them at the double to the latrine tent and ordered them to shit. There was no privacy. The bogs, as the men called them, consisted of a long plank on which they perched above a ditch sprinkled with lime. Everything had been thrown together in great haste to accommodate the recruits flooding into the army's centres.

After this disconcerting experience, Clark lined them up on the parade ground, screaming at them to stand up straight and form straight lines. They had been issued with wooden dummy rifles, and now learned how to slope arms, ground arms, and present arms, to march in step, and obey all other commands. Clark's flood of scatological invective never stopped, and again he singled out Geordie for special attention. He was a gormless twat. A useless little Geordie prat. A stupid wog. A disgrace to King and Country, and a skiving, conniving little halfwit who would never make a soldier. It was bad enough that he spoke Geordie, but worse, he had a bloody lisp. Clark hated Geordie with a passion, so much so that he thumped him round the back of the head and made him quite literally see stars.

The sight was salutary for the others. They lined up straighter and responded immediately to Clark's bellowed orders. When he called them a shower of shit and asked what they were, they responded dutifully that they were a shower of shit – Sir! – and Clark was almost mollified. This parade ground drill went on for days on end, for the RSM was attempting to instil into each one of them what the enemy called *Kadaverdiszipline* – to obey orders instantly and without question.

Occasionally, a gawky young officer would watch proceedings, and they learned that he was Second Lieutenant Gilbert Coker-Williams, himself a new recruit but the old soldier Clark's nominal superior. They dubbed him Jumbo, because of his sticking out ears and long nose, and they made elephant noises when he was in the vicinity. To say that Jumbo was an idiot is a gross understatement. He owed his rank to the British army's rigid caste system, which recruited ex-public school-boys for officer grades and relegated the others without exception to the other ranks. The recruiters even had a list of 'acceptable' schools.

After several weeks of this marching and drilling, Clark (now known as Nobby behind his back) took his recruits to the firing range and issued them with the army's standard Lee Enfield bolt-action rifles. These they fired at cardboard silhouettes of German soldiers in Pickelhaube helmets. Nobby threw up his arms in horror at his men's appalling marksmanship. He whacked hopeless cases over the buttocks with his swagger stick and flew into such rages that they suspected – and rather hoped – that he would have a seizure. During such rages, he was likely to punch the nearest recruit in the face. Geordie, however, was a natural sharpshooter, despite the cast in his eye. After a couple of practice shots, he never failed to shoot his 'Germans' straight through the heart – or the head if Clark demanded it. Geordie's sharpshooting abilities should have endeared him to the sergeant major, but it was not so. Nobby, if anything, hated him even more.

Next, Clark showed the men how to fix their wicked 17-inch Pattern 1907 bayonets and they practised eviscerating straw men, egged on by the sergeant major to scream demonically as they did so. Geordie hoped that he would never have to inflict such hideous wounds on a living person – and that he would never be on the receiving end of a Hun's bayonet – but he thrust and bawled as ordered.

'Harder!' screamed Clark. 'Louder! You're nothin' but a pack of o' girls and poofs! You've got to stick it hard into their guts and twist to pull it out!' 'You hafta hate the bloody Huns!' 'Loathe the whole filthy lot of them! KILL! KILL! KILL!'

This bloodthirsty malarkey alternated with crawling over improvised assault courses – scrambling over nets with fixed bayonets wearing full combat kit, fording streams, and crawling along with bellies pressed to the ground while some regulars sprayed real machine gun bullets over their cringing heads. Then there were the route marches of varying lengths with full packs and tin helmets in the rain or under the hot sun, during which several men fainted and were revived with streams of water and curses by Clark and the grinning regular corporals who assisted him. Each night, after a gobbled meal, the recruits collapsed onto their cots and fell fast asleep, too tired to worry that the rainy days had generated thick mud that coated their tents and blankets, and that this would enrage Clark.

Clark was indefatigable, shouting orders, prodding the recalcitrant or incompetent with his swagger stick or voiding torrents of foul oaths into their exhausted faces. He would irrupt without warning into their tents, screaming and pulling blankets off improperly made beds and hurling them into the dirt. These scrawny little denizens of the London lanes, however, were becoming fighting fit – prime meat for what Geordie called the army's greet hungry gob.

Geordie was the best soldier of the lot, but Clark still hated the sight of him. On the slightest pretext, he would make him shoulder a pack filled with bricks and run round the perimeter of the camp until he collapsed from exhaustion. 'I don't like you, gingernut,' Clark said with a wince. 'I don't like you at all.'

Geordie reciprocated the sentiment. In fact, he detested the bastard, and each night before he dropped off to exhausted sleep, he dreamed up exquisite torments to avenge himself for the outrages the man visited upon him and his mates. He contented himself by drawing a savage caricature of Clark and pinning it at the entrance to the mess tent. Clark ranted about it and although he gave Geordie searching looks, he had no proof that he was the culprit.

Geordie had become friendly with two of the men; a mournful Mile End baker called Grossman, whom Clark picked on because he was Jewish, and a happy-go-lucky youth called Roger Allsopp, who had worked in the family greengrocer's shop in Notting Hill, and who Nobby loathed apparently because he was always happy. Albert Grossman was an old man by the detachment's standards – not far from his thirtieth birthday – and he confessed to Geordie that as a socialist, he was in two minds about the war, but as his brothers had joined, he too had lined up outside the London Reception Centre.

One day some weeks after arriving in the camp, Clark informed the men that they had a day's leave – and should think themselves lucky that the colonel was so good-natured because if it was up to 'im such a shower of shit would have no leave for the fuckin' duration. He meant it, too.

Geordie and his two mates trekked three miles to the local village pub, claimed a table in the snug, and proceeded to down several heavenly pints of the local ale. The barmaid was a bonus, for she was a handsome young woman and fond of a laugh and she appeared to view them as heroes. The trio quite forgot about the training camp for some time, but eventually Albert Grossman posed the question that had been on their minds: what were they going to do about that bastard Nobby Clark? Their period of training was almost over, for it was past St Crispin's Day and there was an autumn chill in the air. Soon, no doubt, the army would ship them off to Belgium or France.

'Fuck 'im,' opined Roger Allsopp with a grin, finishing his pint. 'The fucker's just not worth it, and we'll be gorn soon.'

Grossman disagreed. Clark was a sadist who took delight in humiliating the men and his victimisation of young Geordie was a disgrace. He conceded that it was the man's job to turn raw recruits into soldiers, but he went over the top.

'Well, it's true too that he don't like you 'cos you're a Jew, and he don't like Geordie 'cos he's a Scotch darkie,' Allsopp admitted. 'He don't like me neither although I never done nothing wrong.'

'He's evil,' said Grossman. 'You're the opposite of what he is, so he hates you for it. He can't stand it that you're good-natured and he wants to make you as bad as he is.'

The three friends supped their pints in silence for a while after that, alternating between gazing out over the village green and ogling the barmaid. Geordie set down his glass and announced that he had an idea for revenge on their tormentor. They tossed the idea around for a while and shook hands on it before making the long trek back to camp, each of them imagining themselves back in civvies.

The Clark Bastard – as the trio often referred to him – was a human metronome who never did anything spontaneously. He was anally retentive to an abnormal degree, noted the well-read Grossman. Clark had forgotten there ever was a time when he was not a soldier, and Geordie joked that the man had been born wearing khaki and sporting a rifle. He did everything by numbers, in army argot, at the same time and in the same way. Thus, every Saturday evening, he walked to the village pub and drank a skinful of ale before staggering back to his bunk in the camp. The barmaid disliked him because of his off-colour remarks and dirty eyes. The old misanthrope went alone, drank alone, and came home alone, sozzled.

The following Saturday evening was dark but dry, with a fitful wind thrumming the tents' guy ropes. Clark dismissed the men after an epic rant and set off on the double soon afterwards, after ordering some corporals to pester the men. As usual, Clark had not returned at lights out and the three friends knew that it would be another hour before he re-appeared.

Silence fell over the tent city, punctuated only by snores and men talking in their sleep.

'It's time,' whispered Grossman, shaking Allsopp and Geordie awake.

They dressed quietly, furtively left the tent, and stationed themselves in the shadows close by to where they knew the Regimental Sergeant Major would pass. Five minutes later, right on time, Clark's tall form hove into view, staggering from side to side. The man was drunk, mortaliously so, as Geordie called it in his dialect. He was singing 'Mademoiselle from Armentières', quite out of tune, and accompanying the filthy song with hiccups and stupid giggles. Drunk as he was, he didn't see his three sworn enemies come up behind him. They pulled an empty flour bag down over his head, gagged him and tied his hands behind his back. Next, they pulled and shoved him over to the stinking jakes and with a whispered one-two-three! dumped him in the cesspit, where he landed with a disgustingly satisfying squelch.

There was hell to pay the next day. The entire squad was hauled up one by one before Jumbo and the Lieutenant Colonel, but no one knew anything. The colonel, a relatively harmless old bird called Tambling-Goggins who had served with no great distinction in India, was inclined to view the whole business as a bit of a joke, and Coker-Williams was a blithering idiot who could only open and close his mouth. It was left to a crusty old major named Daniel Andrews to ask cogent questions, but even he could get nothing out of the men, most of whom really knew nothing. Geordie, Allsopp, and Grossman lied with straight faces and expressed their horror at the incident. The recruits never saw Nobby Clark again. His replacement, a knee-creaking Glaswegian recalled from retirement called Anderson, was old school but fair by army standards. He roared a bit but lacked his predecessor's viciousness and he did not pick on individuals. Maybe he was wary, too. He grinned lopsidedly when the men called Geordie a Scotchman and gave him a wink. He drilled the men daily and by this stage, they obeyed automatically as good soldiers of His Majesty. A fortnight or so later, after the arrival of cold rains portending winter, the squad was packed into lorries and driven away, probably for one of the Channel Ports, Anderson confided.

The following day, a touring car pulled up and discharged Detective Chief Inspector James Verte at the administration building. He was too late to apprehend Geordie, and Colonel Tambling-Goggins refused to tell him anything, citing operational reasons for his secrecy, and ordered Verte off the premises, tut-tutting about civvies' insolence.

The Western Front, 1914

The Channel port was clogged with lorries and humble wagons. His Majesty's Troopship *Tuscania* lay at the dock with steam up, absorbing a steady stream of men and equipment. Dockers swung heavy crates into her waiting holds, followed by the guns, which they stowed safely for the short voyage ahead. Geordie and his companions jumped from their lorry, ready to wield ladle and spoon, fork, and pan – and perchance bayonet – for the glory of His Majesty King George V. They were members of the 77th London Light Infantry – dubbed 'Old Muvver Goggins' Fusiliers' by the recruits. The sea frothed grey and sullen, and many of Geordie's companions would be sick from the ship's incessant rocking before it berthed at Calais.

The voyage itself was short, but so great was the crush of ships on the French shore that they had to ride at anchor overnight, and the Tommies dozed on their kitbags, grumbling about the delay. Had they known what lay ahead they might not have been so keen to get ashore. Late next morning, the ship inched into the harbour, where the process that had taken place on the English shore was reversed and the assorted paraphernalia of war were disgorged onto the French dockside. The men marched through the town, their rifles slung over their shoulders. The townspeople lined the streets, clapping and cheering, some of them throwing flowers at the troops, and the soldiers' hearts swelled with pride. They cheered old Colonel Tambling-Goggins as he rode past on a grey horse, and he acknowledged them with a snappy salute. When he was out of earshot, someone began to sing their unofficial regimental song: 'We're dirty old Bamboozliers/ We're Muvver Goggins' Fusiliers/ Yer dear old muvver's worstest fears!' The townsfolk applauded, thinking it was a patriotic song.

A troop train was waiting at the station and the Fusiliers climbed aboard and filled it to overflowing. It rolled out into the countryside, which was dead flat, like Essex. The chimneys of destroyed houses pointed skyward, the walls blasted open to reveal furniture and wallpaper fluttering in the wind – disturbingly like their kids' dolls' houses. The tang of smoke and cordite still lingered. Night was falling when they reached their destination: a nondescript Belgian town somewhere inland from Dunkirk. A chill wind was blowing, a distant rumble came from the east, and they could see flashes of light on the far horizon. Some dirty British and French soldiers were sitting around on the platform smoking cigarettes. Some had bandages covering their heads or arms or legs. They were dog-tired and did not have the energy to answer tomfool questions. 'You'll find out soon enough,' was the refrain. After some minutes, a grizzled old NCO strode up and marched them along a sunken lane, past darkened farmhouses to the ruined shell of an old building beside a stand of trees. The rumble of artillery was closer now and they could sometimes make out individual explosions from falling shells.

'Latrines are behind the building,' the sergeant said gruffly. 'Youse'll sleep inside wiv them wot's already there. Mind youse don't tread on anyone. They don't like it.'

He turned on his heel and was soon out of sight in the darkness. Geordie and his companions found a place, spread out their capes and wolfed down their Maconochie beef and vegetable stew, eaten cold with Huntley & Palmer's rock-hard biscuits.

'Could be worse,' sighed Roger Allsopp, tilting back his canteen for a last mouthful of water. 'I'm just off to the karsey and then it's goodnight from me.'

The shattered building soon resonated with snores, the guns' rumble tapered off, and Geordie fell into a dreamless sleep. It was still dark when he awoke to hear a rough voice shouting to get up. Ablutions were a bit of a splash from a standpipe. The dawn light revealed they were in what had been a farmyard and grain mill. The rough voice belonged to Sergeant Wilson, a stocky middle-aged man who oversaw the field kitchens.

'I'm no fuckin' Escoffier,' he said, 'but I'm the boss round here. What we do first is to prepare the breakfasts for the blokes up front in the trenches. When we've done that, we can think about ourselves.'

There were two field kitchens, each mounted on iron wheels and equipped with cylindrical metal chimneys. Both were already smoking. The food was cooked with whatever fuel was at hand, in this case bits of old timber cannibalised from the derelict farmhouse. The cooks ladled the porridge into canisters and runners took it to the men at the front. In a corner of the farmhouse, there were stocks of tinned food, biscuits, and stone jars marked with the mysterious letters SRD.

The German offensive had petered out and the conflict had settled down into a war of attrition, with each side digging itself into a deeper and more elaborate system of trenches. The men had little idea of where they were, but they were in fact in a small slice of Belgian territory close to the Pas de Calais. The field kitchen – and the trenches before it – lay in a salient that bulged deep into the German lines. From time to time, the generals sent men 'over the top' into the barbed wire and mud of no-man's-land, where thousands of them were cut down by machine gun fire.

Sergeant Wilson selected Geordie and Allsopp – both small

targets! – to drag the heavy canisters of food on little carts to the trenches, which lay half a mile or so from the field kitchens. When they set off, the German artillery opened up as if on cue, sending shells whistling overhead or exploding with a deafening roar and throwing up great clouds of dirt and dust. Geordie had never been so terrified in his life, not even when he was a mile underground at High Fell with the threat of a firedamp explosion. The soldiers grabbed the unappetising food hungrily. Bone-weary from lack of sleep and living on their nerves, they gave the briefest nods of thanks as Geordie and Allsopp divided the gruel up into their mess tins. They had been up most of the night repelling an attack.

Sergeant Wilson was unimpressed by their account of the artillery barrage. 'That's nothin',' he shrugged. 'Just wait until Jerry lets fly with his heavy artillery – howitzers like Big Bertha … Now, when you're ready we've to scrub out the canisters, then youse can grab a bite to eat.'

This was the pattern of their days. Sometimes, a howitzer shell passed overhead sounding like a locomotive. The explosions left men with ears ringing and bleeding. Or a 'Jack Johnson' shell would explode nearby, releasing huge amounts of black smoke. It got colder too, with constant rain turning the ground into a quagmire and flooding their dank quarters. Geordie knew, however, that they had it easy compared with the poor devils in the trenches. Wilson rotated his men between different jobs, so after delivering food for a week, Geordie was set to work preparing the dinners. He chopped up vast amounts of meat and vegetables on an old farmhouse table, wondering how they would cope with flies in the summer months, and dumped the bits into a black pot that bubbled like the witches' cauldron in *Macbeth*. It was basic food, utterly without flair and apart from salt and pepper it was devoid of condiments. Most days, loaves of bread would arrive from a central field bakery and these, along with stew and potatoes, were the staples of the soldiers' diets. Tea, rum, and cigarettes served to make the conditions at the front slightly more bearable when they could be delivered.

Geordie had landed in the middle of a giant human slaughterhouse, for not a day went by without the bodies of the dead, the dying, and the wounded – some horribly maimed – brought by stretcher-bearers from the front. There was nothing romantic about it and the cheering crowds who had welcomed the war and sent the soldiers off with flowers and kisses seemed impossibly distant. Albert Grossman said it was barbaric insanity and should have been banned. As in other armies sent across the Channel in times gone past, 'Arms were from shoulders sent/ and Scalps to the teeth were rent,' but at least there was morphine for the 'basket cases' smashed up by the death machine. You did not need to die to get to hell. The memory of field surgeons wearing bloodstained aprons, wielding saws and knives like butchers, gave Geordie nightmares for a long time afterwards.

Late one autumn afternoon, a column of walking wounded hobbled into the farmyard.

'Look lively!' shouted Sergeant Wilson. 'Give these men some food and water.'

Geordie and his mates rushed to comply, ladling soup into bowls or holding pannikins of water to the men's mouths. The soldiers were silent when Allsopp joked that they had free tickets back home to Blighty. Geordie attended to a big man who had a bloodstained bandage covering his left eye and NCO's stripes on his arm.

'He don't speak,' said a man on crutches. 'Shellshock.'

Geordie managed to spoon some soup into him.

He whispered: 'I know you, darkie.'

It dawned on Geordie this shambling hulk had been the dreaded RSM Clark at the training camp in Wiltshire. Clark's hands had begun to shake, and he sat down heavily, with thick tears trickling down his cheeks. Geordie grabbed a clean rag and washed away the grime from his face. When the wretched column shambled off, Geordie stood for a long time watching them, not trusting himself to speak.

The 'other ranks' knew nothing of where they were or how the war was going – and soon learned not to ask. Consequently, idiotic rumours circulated: a seaborne attack was planned somewhere up the Belgian coast; America would soon enter the war; the Russians had invaded Germany; the brass had a secret weapon that would enable the Allies to breach the enemy lines and march on Berlin. Silliest of all was the rumour that some spies – two cats and a dog! – were crossing between the lines during the night and feeding vital information back to the Huns' High Command. The brass issued orders to trap the animals about their nefarious business.

Despite the mud and horror, Christmas was coming and there was a palpable sense of excitement in the air. And then a miracle happened: on Christmas Eve the guns fell silent and the staff returning from the front reported that the soldiers on both sides had emerged from their trenches and had shaken hands. They exchanged plum puddings for Stollen, the German Christmas cake. There was talk of a football match, won by the Germans by two goals. It had started when the Tommies had heard their enemies singing 'Stille Nacht':

> *Stille Nacht, heilige Nacht,*
> *Alles schläft; einsam wacht*
> *Nur das traute hochheilige Paar.*
> *Holder Knabe im lockigen Haar,*
> *Schlaf in himmlischer Ruh!*
> *Schlaf in himmlischer Ruh!*

The British soldiers had sung 'Silent Night' in English. Albert Grossman was a Jew, but the tears poured down his cheeks, and he wondered why both sides should not lay down their weapons and refuse to fight anymore. The generals were furious, and governments outraged. On Boxing Day, the guns roared again. Albert Grossman was stirring a kettle of meat and vegetable stew and looking forward to a transfer to the field bakery when a shell blew him into a thousand fragments. Geordie was lucky to have gone to the latrines.

Albert's death plunged Geordie into deep gloom – and cold rage. Fuck Goggins and his stupid Fusiliers, he raged. He heaped insults on the governments that had started the insanity and scoffed at the crowned idiot to whom he had sworn fealty. With dyspepsia of the soul, he recalled the words that had swirled from the London churches when the young men marched off to war:

> *See, the conqu'ring hero comes!*
> *Sound the trumpets! Beat the drums!*
> *Sports prepare! The laurel bring!*
> *Songs of triumph to him sing!*

He wondered why he had not kept walking past the London Reception Centre. He hated the army and thought of deserting, but the penalty was the firing squad. Perhaps there would be a chance of reassignment to a safer job. Was he a coward? He thought not. He had many times taken rations to the front under fire and had never baulked from his duty. He just could not see the point of this madness – and he had no intention of shooting any Germans. He worked like an automaton, slicing meat, dragging canisters of food, numbed to the stink of shit and the sight of maggots feasting on blood, intent on somehow surviving the manmade hell. One day, he vowed, he would go back home to High Fell. See Annie and the bairn. Perhaps she would have him back.

Cardonald, Scotland, 1915

'Eeh, ye've torned yeller, pet!' Annie Ross's mam observed as she pushed tea and toast across the table to her daughter. 'Anyway, eat up, lass, or ye'll be late.' Adjusting her hair in the mirror after the meal, Annie saw what her mother had meant. Her face was bright yellow, and her hair was starting to go the same way. She gently loosened the bairn's grip on her leg, kissed her and told her to be good for her gran, and was half-running down the lane to her work at the National Filling Factory in Cardonald just outside Glasgow. She clocked in and was soon hard at work, pouring the liquid TNT into the brass shell casings and tamping down the detonators. There were hundreds of 'canary' girls and women hard at it, and scarcely a man to be seen in the great echoing cavern of the filling room. Most of the local men were off to the war the papers said would end all wars. It was exacting work, the forewoman had warned. If there were pockets of air in the TNT the shells could explode in the gun barrels and blow 'our boys' to heaven, and if the women used too much force to press down the detonators the things could blow up in their faces. Not a few wee breadsnappers were missing their mothers as a result.

Annie was looking forward to moving back to Tyneside to take up a new job at Armstrong Whitworth's factory on the Scotswood Road: lathe work, making the shell casings rather than filling them and going yellow in the process. She'd been feeling poorly, and the other girls had told her it was from the explosive. The forewoman had confirmed it: 'It's the poison, hen. It poisons the liver and once it starts ye'll get every bug that's going round. Ye'll have to see the doctor.' She had, and he'd confirmed it: toxic jaundice. She was authorised to leave.

She'd moved up to Glasgow with her mam and the bairn partly because she wanted to do her patriotic duty and partly because the stipend from those she called 'them at the Hall' had been insufficient. The addendum Geordie had negotiated had never been properly witnessed, and the greedy bastards had hit her for rent arrears. Her Da had coughed the last black gobbet of sputum from his lungs so there wasn't any reason to stay in High Fell. Her mam looked after Mary, the bairn, during her shifts and the money was good. The house they shared with another all-female family was comfortable too and she regretted they would have to leave it.

The shift ended and the canary girls swarmed through the streets, some on bicycles, some on foot. It was raining by the time she got home. It seemed to rain all the time in Glasgow, but she made it indoors just before a real deluge began. The bairn skipped up and she enfolded her in her arms. 'She's nee bother, pet,' said Annie's mam. 'We played in the park, and she helped me with the messages.'

Mary was a bonnie wee lassie. People thought she was Italian with her tumbling red hair, dark blue eyes, and olive complexion. They assumed her da was away in the forces and Annie didn't correct them. Mary was her father's daughter alright, thought Annie, and a wave of sadness and anger welled up inside her. She'd waited for him, that bastard Geordie Stubbs, but he'd vanished as if he were dead. Frankie Cunningham would have married her, she knew, but she'd not encouraged him, lovely man though he was. That London policeman had shouted at her, but she couldn't tell him where Geordie was. Not that she would have told him if she knew. Sometimes, just before she went to sleep, she would take his photograph from the drawer and look at it for a long time.

The Western Front, 1915

Geordie and his mates were dozing, taking advantage of the weak spring sunshine for a bit of kip and a cigarette. A few daffodils had bloomed by the farmhouse wall and some birds were singing in the apple tree, which was sprouting fresh green foliage. Geordie had turned twenty-one, but he was so dog-tired that he imagined himself an old man. They had charged the big black cooking pot with meat and vegetables, and for some reason the guns had fallen silent. Sergeant Wilson had fallen fast asleep, and Geordie wondered if the fly buzzing round the man's head would land in his open mouth. It did, and it was just as well because an open motorcar sporting the Union Jack suddenly bounced into the farmyard. Wilson spat out the fly and shot to his feet, hissing for the others to do the same. The chauffeur, a spindly corporal, jumped from the vehicle and opened the rear door for his passengers, who piled out donning their white pigskin gloves and arranging their swagger sticks under their arms.

'Attention!' Wilson hissed at his semi-somnolent crew, adding, sotto voce, 'Get your bleedin' act together! It's Colonel Tambling-Goggins and the bleedin' general!'

The men formed a straight-ish line and saluted the Great Ones. The general, a peevish old cove with a monocle and a white moustache, gazed at his surroundings with distaste. He gave a perfunctory salute and conversed with the colonel in muted tones. The gormless Jumbo – Lieutenant Coker-Williams – had also climbed out of the motorcar and was fussing round his superiors. Tambling-Goggins sent him over to Sergeant Wilson.

'You are to instruct your men to ready themselves for interrogation,' Jumbo mumbled. 'General Fox-Hamilton and Colonel Tambling-Goggins will interview each one separately ...'

Wilson saluted and ordered his men to stand easy. He did not ask the purpose of the interviews and neither did Jumbo offer any explanation. The chances were he'd forgotten.

'Righty-o,' said Wilson, keeping one eye on the officers, who were smoking nearby. 'We'll do this in alphabetical order of names ... Allsopp, on the double you go, Private, and make sure you mind yer fuckin' p's and q's!'

Allsopp gave the officers a ragged salute. They questioned him briefly, before shaking their heads and dismissing him. When Geordie's turn came, he stood at attention. He had a low opinion of staff officers, but he executed a snappy salute and clicked his heels together.

'Stand easy, soldier,' mumbled Tambling-Goggins. 'Now, we are a man down in the staff officers' kitchens ...'

'Bloke went mad, and we had to ship him out!' the general barked. 'Bad show all round.' He lit a cigarette and seemed to lose interest in the proceedings.

'Tell us, my man,' Tambling-Goggins asked Geordie. 'What was your occupation before you joined up?'

A jolt of hope shot through Geordie's brain. 'Chef, sir,' he replied.

'Worked at the Carlton, sir!'

Tambling-Goggins nudged the general, who seemed to have drifted off. 'Darkie worked at the Carlton,' he murmured.

'The Carlton? Why, I know it well!' chirped Fox-Hamilton. 'Best escalopes of veal in London!'

'Jolly good show.' The colonel beamed, turning back to Private Stubbs. 'We'll give you a week's trial. Report to headquarters at twelve hundred hours. Chap will come to collect you. Dismissed!'

The officers climbed back into their car, and it jolted away towards the rear. Meanwhile, Jerry's guns had opened fire again and the horizon – such as it was – filled with smoke and tumult. An offensive by one side or the other was in progress and soon bloodied men were streaming past to the field hospital. Others lay on stretchers, some already passed over to eternity, others well on the way. The kitchen squad envied Geordie his good luck, but they shook his hand and wished him well.

Château Mazengarbe, Pas de Calais

The loquacious Cockney lorry driver introduced himself to Geordie as Lance Corporal Fred Belcher. He had a fag slotted into the corner of his mouth and it spilled ash down the front of his uniform as he prattled on.

'You've landed on yer feet, Jock. All mod-cons where you're goin'.'

The lorry rattled along a sunken lane, then past peasants working in the fields, oblivious to the war. They were entering France, Belcher informed his passenger, and would soon be 'Ome, squire, or what passes for it these days.'

Geordie gaped at 'Ome', which was a vast building at the end of a long, white-gravelled drive lined with severely pollarded trees. He eyed the ducks swimming and diving in a large reflecting pool like a fox before turning his attention back to the stately pile. Built from whitish-grey stone, it towered four storeys above the flat Flemish countryside and was surmounted with a plethora of turrets and spires. Several vast wings radiated from a central core, at the apex of which three flags were fluttering in the slight breeze: the Union Jack and both the French tricolour and the Fleur de Lys. A bored sentry signalled the lorry through.

''Ere we are, squire,' said Belcher, waving a proprietorial hand and spraying Geordie with cigarette ash. 'Château Mazengarbe! Bigger'n St Pancras fuckin' Station!'

The British high command had requisitioned a wing of the château as divisional headquarters. Belcher handed Geordie on to a gaunt old boy with two stripes, who led him down a flight of stone steps to the basement.

'Here you are, soldier,' the old boy muttered in a thick Scots burr. He bade Geordie enter a low-ceilinged kitchen in which some insolent-looking boys were poking at black kettles suspended on chains above a smoky fire. An obese woman was chopping onions and paused to berate the boys in a strange patois. A silver tabby cat was rubbing against her ankles.

'That's Madame Merckx,' the old boy muttered. 'She doesnae speak English. Them's her sons,' he added, jerking his thumb towards the lounging adolescents. 'Sergeant Nethercott's aboot somewhere, probably oot for a wee smoke. I'm Corporal Woodhead, by the way – Cameron Woodhead, the headwaiter.'

With that, he glided away like a grey ghost. The cook was looking at Geordie with a sour look on her fleshy jowls. '*Nou dan, blijf daar niet staan staren!*' she snapped. Geordie didn't understand Dutch. The woman switched to French, which he could follow: '*Et bien, ne restez pas là!*' She waved a knife at the onions. Geordie shook his head and the woman advanced threateningly. The teenagers sniggered and the cat scowled at him, looking like she was preparing to spring. Geordie was spared whatever retribution this harpy and her familiar planned by the sudden entrance of a skinny NCO he took to be Sergeant Nethercott, who hobbled up to the woman and shouted '*Fous le camp!*' – hop it! The woman squawked but she wobbled back over to her bench and attacked the vegetables savagely.

'Don't mind 'er,' laughed Nethercott. 'She's bin 'ere forever and finks she owns the bleedin' place. She knows how to cook, which is more'n me. I was wounded at Wipers, so they put me here.' He peered at Geordie with soft brown eyes and asked, 'Done any cookin' yerself?'

Delighted with the reply, he gestured grandly round the kitchen. It was, Geordie, realised, very well appointed, with rows of gleaming copper-bottomed pots and pans and a huge oaken dresser loaded with cooking implements. Even the Merckx woman was not a problem, because Nethercott's mother was French, and he could threaten her in her own language. Nethercott informed her that Stubbs had worked as a chef, no doubt embellishing his credentials, and she softened a little towards the interloper. His predecessor, Nethercott said, had indeed 'gorn mad' and fried the officers' pancakes in motorcar oil.

Madame Merckx had prepared most of the dinner; *carbonnade de boeuf*, a traditional Flemish dish. She had stewed best quality beef with garlic and onions in beer with thyme, bay leaves, and a little brown sugar. Last, she topped the mixture with a sliced baguette slathered with Dijon mustard and put it in the oven to brown. Preceded by a hearty vegetable potage and with a platter of Lille *mimolette* cheese and a strong Flemish *bière de garde* to finish, it was a fine meal indeed. Madame Merckx had gone up in his estimation, but he could not help but contrast the repast with the rubbish the men in the trenches were eating. Still, he explored the kitchens and cellars with delight. There was a well-stocked larder, and a cobwebbed basement contained a treasure trove of fine wines, bottled, and stored long before Geordie was born.

An officer arrived and put Lance Corporal Belcher at Geordie's disposal to fetch whatever he needed from the nearby towns and villages. Then a pimply young private arrived and reported for duty. Robbie Pascoe by name, he hailed from Truro in Cornwall, but had been an apprentice in the Savoy kitchens in London. The division of labour was that Madame Merckx would prepare the breakfasts, while

Geordie and Pascoe would cook the main meals. After he had eaten and Madame Merckx and her boys had gone home, Geordie sat at the huge kitchen table and pondered what he would cook for the next day's dinner. 'Keep it simple,' Auguste Escoffier had exhorted, and so Geordie suppressed the urge to make elaborate sauces to impress the officers. For dinner, he would offer *petite marmite, filets de sole, selle d'agneau de Pauillac, légumes de saison,* with *pêches et fraises Melba* to finish. There were plenty of fine wines to match the courses. He would go to Calais or Hazebrouck with Belcher to fetch whatever ingredients were not already in the larder.

'By Jove,' enthused Colonel Tambling-Goggins. 'As you were, soldier. Meal was absolutely topping!' He screwed in his monocle to get a better look at Geordie. 'General's over the moon!'

'Thank you, sir,' Geordie replied, raising his wooden spoon to his temple in an unconscious parody of a salute.

After a week, the colonel informed Private Stubbs that he was up for promotion. 'Can't have a talented feller like you staying a mere private,' he said. 'Won't be long before you make sergeant.'

Even Madame Merckx was impressed, and the silver tabby regarded him less malevolently. With Nethercott and Belcher scouring the countryside for supplies, and Pascoe and two other commis chefs working diligently, Geordie presided over the finest kitchen in the Pas de Calais. Only the distant rumble of the guns reminded him that there was a war on. He slept in silk sheets in a boudoir which, if not the match of those allocated to the officers, was far superior to his garret at the Carlton – not to mention the dismal farmhouse where he'd snatched a bit of kip on the Belgian battlefield. Most nights, the cat curled up at his feet. Sometimes she went missing and he wondered if she crossed over to the enemy lines, using up some of her nine lives, but if so, she always came back and demanded a plate of food.

With the kitchen running like clockwork, Geordie, promoted to sergeant, delegated much of the cooking to his subordinates and spent more of his time procuring ingredients. He had learned to cook with what was available, and the ingredients often included the region's herring, rabbit, potatoes, root and leafy vegetables, and beer – the *blanche, gueuze lambic*, and Trois-Monts. He learned to judge the quality of the Maroilles cheese, which came in hard squares, the fine Ménapien ham, and the mussels that came dripping from the sea. Madame Merckx was proud of her region's cuisine and soon his notebook was bulging with her recipes: including the *caudière* and *waterzooï* fish soups; Maroilles tart; rabbit with prunes; *anguilleau verte à la flamande*; *hochepoche*; *tarte aux mirabelles*; the apple and rhubarb pies; and *speculoos* biscuits. Geordie often served the hot and spicy juniper eau-de-vie when the dishes were cleared. He made sure the Other Ranks ate as well or better than the officers.

In Hazebrouck one afternoon, he espied a line of Tommies queueing up half a block from a lighted doorway. A familiar figure averted his eyes as they drove past.

'It's a Red Lamp place,' Belcher said with his buck teeth bared in a lascivious grin. 'Approved by the army and everythink …' He noticed the familiar figure. 'Ay, look, there's old Cameron Woodhead come to get his leg over! Dirty old Scotch geezer!'

Belcher raised an inquiring eyebrow at Geordie. 'Blokes never know if they'll be alive for long,' he said, puffing hard on his fag. 'Hofficers 'ave the blue lamp place with a bar an' piano and everythink. Guvmint done it secret, like, 'cos there'd be an uproar back 'ome if word got out. I've dropped Jumbo off there a couple of times. The Froggies call it "Au Bonheur du Jour".'

Geordie refused to take the hint. He never indulged in the carnal delights promised by the Other Ranks' establishment and as an NCO, he could not visit its blue lamp equivalent. He had heard there was a VD clinic run by the army somewhere near Dunkirk. The thought of syphilis was an effective deterrent, but he also recoiled at the thought of the industrial sex dispensed inside the *maison close*. Prostitution was illegal back in Blighty, but the British military had authorised it for the troops and Geordie wondered at the morality of it. Despite this, he became intimately embroiled in the lupanar's affairs. One hot summer day, when he was sitting in a bar, he struck up a conversation with a young woman called Celestine, who was drinking a glass of beer. She was reluctant to tell him much about herself. 'Oh, I work in a textile mill, monsieur,' she said. Indeed, she had worked in a factory, but better pay had lured her to the Au Bonheur du Jour, where she worked as the receptionist-cum-bookkeeper. Geordie suspected she pitched in at the boudoir in busy periods. This Celestine De Smet was a big Flemish brunette with a throaty laugh and sly brown eyes that told she was up for anything. They had a brief fling but neither of them had their heart in it and besides, she had a beau who was trapped behind the German lines in Lille. However, the relationship presented Sergeant Stubbs with a promising business opportunity, which he rationalised as a way of getting back at the generals for the deaths of Albert Grossman and other friends. Geordie was now over-seeing the meals for a great number of staff officers in several different centres strung out behind the static lines and had a huge budget at his disposal. Celestine approached the madam, who was a cousin of Madame Merckx, and they agreed to provide her establishment with provisions at below market prices. Soon, Geordie – with the assistance of Celestine, Belcher, and Nethercott – was doing business as far afield as Calais. The commanders were quite unaware that anything shady was happening and Geordie and his cronies had soon amassed con-siderable riches. When necessary, Geordie forged signatures, keeping this detail to himself. Nobody suffered from the arrangement, he told himself. Well, maybe the British taxpayers lost out, but wasn't he helping the French economy with his little enterprise? Still, in the dead of night when sleep would not come, he admitted that he was a 'wide boy' and tried to make amends by donating money to the nuns running an orphanage near Hazebrouck. He shuddered to think what Father Flynn back on Tyneside would think.

He also felt better about himself after an incident on the front lines. Promoted to sergeant, he made periodic trips to the front lines to make sure that the troops were receiving hot food and other rations, for if he were guilty of defrauding the officers, he drew the line at harming the poor devils in the trenches. During one such trip, he was speaking with a captain called Brocklehurst when he noticed a sudden flash of light from the German lines. Instinctively, he dropped to the ground, taking the captain with him. Had he not done so the captain would have taken a sniper's bullet.

'Don't know how I could ever repay you,' said Brocklehurst, shaking Geordie's hand. With that, the divisions of class and caste fell away. Oxbridge-educated toff and Tyneside pitman faced each other as equals.

High Fell, 1916

When Geordie was due some leave, he decided to take it in England so that he could travel up to Tyneside. Maybe he could make things right with Annie and the bairn? He cut a fine figure, sitting on the train going north in his best uniform with the sergeant's stripes and his blazing red hair under a khaki cap. He no longer feared arrest, for Chief Inspector Verte must be back at the Yard in London and the Gateshead peelers would be unlikely to recognise him, probably Richardson and the Gorringe twins too. He bought some flowers and chocolates in the Gateshead High Street and wondered what he could get for the bairn. Nothing yet, he reasoned, as he didn't know the gender of the child. He was in the Half-Moon pub when the headline of the *Evening Chronicle* caught his eye: FELLING PERVERTS SENTENCED. Judge Cholmondley-Devereaux had gaoled two local men, his tormentors from the High Fell colliery, Adam Tudge and Scott Joyce, for 'interfering with children'.

Back at High Fell, everything seemed a bit unreal – strange and familiar at the same time. Everything seemed smaller and his previous life seemed like someone else's. He hesitated before knocking on the front door of his old house in Calcutta Row. Finally, he lifted the brass knocker and let it fall. Silence. He knocked again and this time he heard footsteps and a muffled voice. The door creaked open, and a wizened old face stared up at him. 'Aye?' said the old woman who owned it. He didn't know her. Whoever she was, she wasn't Annie's mam. She was impatient. 'Well, divvent stand there lettin' flies in yor gob,' she snapped. 'I've just lifted dinner off the stove. Tell us what ye want.'

Geordie found his voice – just. 'I'm looking for Annie Ross.'

The woman squinted and declared, 'I divvent knaa neebody by that name.' With that, she shut the door in his face.

Geordie stood there for a minute or two before backing off and almost colliding with an old fellow who was trotting along the pavement. Geordie apologised profusely. The old fellow went to walk past but took a double take. It was Moses Parker, the banksman from the mine, a chum of Billy, his stepfather.

'Well, I nivver,' Parker marvelled. 'It's young Geordie Stubbs come back as a soldier.'

From Parker, Geordie learned that his uncle Anthony was back at sea on the HMS *Cornwallis*. There were rumours the battleship had been torpedoed off the coast of Malta. Parker shook his head when Geordie asked about Annie.

'They moved awa', her an' her ma and an' the bairn, but I divvent know where.'

Parker had no idea if the child was a boy or a girl, but he volunteered that, 'Frankie Cunningham might have known – he was elwis fond o' the lassie – but he's in his grave these last three months, killed in France.'

'How … how did it happen?'

'I divvent knaa exact, like,' Parker replied. 'Machine-gunned, they say. He were elwis a bonnie lad.'

He shook his head sadly and bade Geordie farewell.

The knowledge crushed Geordie. He could still hear Frankie's voice. Although he asked round in the pubs, nobody knew where Annie had gone. He had had it all worked out in his mind: Annie would forgive him; he would be a father to the bairn, and they would set up house somewhere down in the South when he got his discharge papers. He walked blindly through the old streets he had known so well, dumped the flowers and chocolates on the Miners' Welfare steps, and trudged back to the railway station to make the long journey south.

He spent much of the train journey drinking in the buffet car. He hardly noticed when the train called at York and when it passed through Stevenage, once the scene of some unpleasantness for him, he was too drunk to care. He took a room in a cheap hotel near King's Cross Station and spent the next week either drunk, getting drunk, or nursing ferocious hangovers. He later had a vague memory of meeting a woman but try as he might, he could never quite recall her face, her name, or remember what they had done. One week later, sick in body and mind, he boarded a train at Waterloo Station then vomited his way across the Channel aboard a rusting freighter.

When he returned to the Château Mazengarbe, depressed and paranoid, he imagined that the silver tabby was sneering at him. The guns still rumbled like distant thunder and the trains still left the station at Hazebrouck laden with the dead, the maimed and the dying – and pulled back in to disgorge fresh supplies of munitions and men. In the fields around the town, there were forests of white crosses. Sometimes a stray howitzer shell would land on the cemetery and disinter the dead. Back home, Kitchener still exhorted men to do their duty and young women handed white feathers to young men who had not enlisted. Geordie lay down on his bed, faced the wall, and cried. He also resolved to 'go straight'; to put the scams behind him. For her part, the silver tabby sat on the window ledge, washing herself, perhaps dreaming of catching mice, serenely indifferent to the concerns of men – even the one who provided her with generous portions of fish and milk.

The Western Front, 1918

Geordie threw himself into his work. His official duties had expanded, and he found himself in the role of de facto quartermaster for the division. There were fresh opportunities for corruption, but he kept to his resolution to live honestly. Meanwhile, the awful war of attrition ground on. There were rumours of mutinies and of Germany's imminent surrender. The Americans entered the war. There was revolution in Russia followed by Russia's withdrawal from the war. Germany sued for peace and the word came round that the guns would fall silent at 1100 hours on November 11, 1918.

Geordie did not know what to think. The Armistice seemed too good to be true. When dawn came on the appointed date, the guns still roared, and men were still dying. Geordie roused Lance Corporal Belcher from his quarters, and they drove down towards the front. Nothing appeared to have changed. The Tommies were as grim faced as ever and in one sector, after 1000 hours, some gung-ho officers had sent men over the top to their deaths. Geordie and Belcher handed out cigarettes, rum, cake, and extra rations to all the men they met, and Captain Lysander Brocklehurst even helped them dish out the goodies.

When the guns fell silent, the lack of noise was somehow deafening, and Geordie rejoiced to hear birds singing in the shell-torn woods.

November 12 dawned dark and cold. Colonel Tambling-Goggins ordered all available men to the front. They were to search no-man's-land for corpses and give them a decent burial. Geordie never forgot the grim task. In one hole, he found the cadavers of two young men who had bayoneted each other to death.

The recruits were anxious to get home, but they were soon disappointed. Orders had come for the 77th to form part of an occupation force in the Rhineland. Colonel Tambling-Goggins handed Geordie a cigarette and asked him how the men had taken the news.

'Naturally they're disappointed, sir,' Geordie replied. 'It's easier for me, as I have no home to return to.'

The colonel had taken a shine to Geordie and liked to chat with him, but he had serious business on his mind. 'Jolly good show,' he said, stamping his fag butt underfoot. 'Now, the army needs chaps of your ability, so I'm offering you a commission. We'll fix it up before we leave for Germany.'

Geordie was flabbergasted. The army was class and caste bound and although NCOs had been promoted because of the appalling death rate of lieutenants, he had not expected this to outlast the war.

'You'll have more responsibility, of course,' Goggins continued, 'but the pay will be better, not to mention the err … prestige.'

Marching home through Belgium and France at night, the Germans covered up to twenty miles in every twenty-four-hour period. The Allied occupation forces followed, among them George William Marmaduke Stubbs, a newly minted second lieutenant with the British Army of the Rhine. He'd patted the silver tabby cat goodbye and imagined that the mercenary beast had gone back to Madame Merckx's pantry. He travelled in a first-class compartment with some Hooray Henrys and wondered how many Geordie officers there were in King George's army. Calcutta Row belonged to another life, but when he spoke, he revealed his ungentlemanly origins. Then again, he mused, his biological father was the son of a titled judge.

The Hooray Henrys regarded him uncertainly, and he was content to ignore them and read his book as the train jolted and rattled through war-damaged and newly liberated lands. Girls and young women lined station platforms and threw flowers to the young men leaning from the train windows. This made Geordie uneasy given that he had had a soft war and had used the army to enrich himself. Despite his atheism, he had inherited a strong dose of Catholic guilt from his mother and thoughts of Annie and their child filled him with shame.

Geordie had left Château Mazengarbe in the nick of time. The day after the regiment departed, Detective Chief Inspector James Arthur Verte barrelled up the gravelled drive in a hired pony trap, his breath steaming on the frigid air, his hair a flame of red against the monochrome winter landscape. He bade the driver wait in bad French and an old gardener directed him to the regimental headquarters. He felt a pleasant sense of anticipation as he strode through the doors, but to his chagrin he found only a private and a corporal, who were sweeping the empty apartments before leaving to join the regiment in Germany.

'Where is Geordie Stubbs?' he demanded. 'I have a warrant for his arrest!'

The Tommies knew 'nuffink', or so they told the bossy rozzer. He screamed at them for their dumb Cockney insolence, which only made them smirk.

'Fuck, fuck, fucking fuck!' he yelled, storming around opening and closing doors and darting into bedrooms and cupboards.

'Careful guv'nor,' advised the corporal, afraid – or perhaps hoping – that Verte would 'blow a bleedin' gasket.'

After half an hour of storming about, Verte had to concede that the bird had flown.

'One day,' he sputtered at the bemused Tommies, 'One day, I will feel that black bastard's collar.'

Verte had no idea where the 77th had gone and even if he did, the commanders would not have allowed him to follow the regiment to Germany. He returned to Dover on the evening steam packet, taking the long view that one day his quarry would return to London and his arrest record would be perfect. Corporal Belcher and Private Abbott had a good laugh about it when he left.

Meanwhile, Geordie's train had crossed the German border near Aachen and covered the fifty miles to the Rhine in under two hours. Tambling-Goggins assembled his officers in the train's dining car and informed them that the Allied armies would occupy the entire left bank of German territory on the Rhine. After arrival at the Cologne station, a short march took the regiment to an abandoned German barracks. After an indifferent meal scrounged from what the Germans had left behind, Geordie ventured out into the rainy evening to explore the city. He gazed in awe at the twin spires of the ancient cathedral, which rose over five hundred feet into the dark sky above the city's Altstadt. Except for the architecture, the warren of shops and houses reminded Geordie of the medieval lanes of York. The streets were deserted, although faces peered from windows, perhaps as frightened of the invaders as they were of the influenza epidemic that was ravaging the city. Nothing was open – it was a Sunday evening after all – but some trams were running. Squads of British soldiers clad in rubber capes were patrolling, their hobnailed boots clattering on the cobblestones. Night fell. Fog swirled up from the river and a greasy rain began to fall, spattering the cobbled streets and drenching Geordie and his companions. If there were any bars open, they didn't find them. Here and there, a few streetlights tried half-heartedly to dispel the gloom. Geordie gave up and returned to the barracks, wondering what the morrow would bring in this strange place.

Cologne, Germany, 1918–19

Lieutenant Stubbs greeted the dawn with relief after an uncomfortable night under a smelly blanket. The barracks was perhaps colder than outside, where it was sleeting hard. Breakfast over, he got down to work. He replaced Kaiser Wilhelm II's portrait with one of his cousin King George V, and spent the morning filling out order forms, inspecting the stores the Germans had left behind, and organising a kitchen roster. Things were a lot cheerier when stocks of coal had been located and fires lit.

After lunch, Geordie conferred via an army interpreter with a city councillor, an older man named Paul Schmidt. He wanted a list of houses and apartments in which officers could be billeted. Schmidt clearly resented having to cooperate with the British. He only answered direct questions and volunteered nothing, his glacial blue eyes staring out the window at the sleety day. Tiring of this, Geordie offered him a cigarette and bade the interpreter translate exactly what he said. Schmidt hesitated but took the cigarette gratefully – it was a vast improvement on what Germans were smoking because of the Allied shipping blockade.

'Tell Herr Schmidt,' Geordie ordered, 'that I sympathise with the people of his city … I understand that it is hard to accept a foreign occupation … We would like to go home but until the orders come, we must stay.'

Schmidt unbent a little. He was a Social Democrat and hated militarism in any form. He feared that the occupation and the exorbitant demands of the French government could only breed resentment and more war. 'Believe it or not, Herr Leutnant, I am a moderate regarding you British. I will help you in order that you are sooner gone, but for every person such as I, there are ten others who will not cooperate.'

It was true, Geordie found. Local officials dragged their feet, and some refused to cooperate and in this, they were encouraged by the government in Berlin. When he ventured into the streets, many of the passers-by averted their faces and the bolder among them spat on the pavement. Shopkeepers' faces turned stony when he entered their stores, and bartenders banged glasses down as aggressively as they dared. Only the children stared with open curiosity. The people in the streets were grey-faced and drawn, dull eyed, their hair lank, their expressions listless, many of them exuding pungent body odour, which testified to the shortage of soap and of coal to heat water. Many were malnourished and thousands had died of starvation because of the continuing blockade. To make matters worse, people were falling ill from the Spanish flu, and mask wearing was becoming common. Over the coming months, however, they began to accept the occupation as the normal state of affairs. They went to school, worked in their shops and factories, drank pale Kölsch beer in the local Kneipen and braved the icy winds to walk in the parks and along the Rhine path.

Thanks to Paul Schmidt, Geordie had found a billet with a young war widow who lived with her little son in a large apartment near the Haymarket. Unlike many people in the city, Frau Fischer did not appear to hold his colour against him. Her husband Klaus was missing in action, presumed dead in the last great slaughter at Ypres. A gloomy British major had also moved into the apartment, but Geordie seldom saw him except at meals. The major had been wounded at Cambrai, but while his physical injuries had healed, psychological damage remained. He was the saddest man Geordie had ever met.

Frau Fischer was politely formal, but she seldom spoke. Except when she served Geordie his meals, she stayed in her section of the apartment. Sometimes at night, he heard the child, Heinz, laughing and he felt a desperate longing, sadness, and guilt for the loss of his own bairn. Nevertheless, he kept himself busy with a German grammar when he was not at the barracks, shaking his head in frustration at the endless inflections. Soon he was able to hold simple conversations and Frau Fischer half smiled at his clumsy attempts to thank her for the meals she served. She was fine boned and dark haired, with beautiful green eyes – but not the least flirtatious. She had a little black-and-white dog called Hansi that followed her everywhere but would only bark when Geordie attempted to befriend him.

Spring had arrived after the long dark winter. Geordie was walking home by the river after a long day's work at the barracks. Entering the Haymarket, he saw Hansi racing across the cobbles to greet his mistress, who had just left a greengrocer's shop. To his horror, he saw that Hansi was running straight into the path of a heavily laden brewery dray. Frau Fischer dropped her purchases and stood with her hand pressed to her mouth. Time seemed to have stopped, but Geordie scooped up the dog with a millisecond to spare and stood panting by the side of the square. Frau Fischer ran up, with a look of joy and relief on her face, drawing her gloves from her hands. She took the dog gratefully, cuddled him, and thanked Geordie profusely. He realised she was speaking English! A café owner steered them towards a table, and they ordered coffee.

'My mother was English,' Frau Fischer said by way of explanation, stroking the little dog and smiling shyly at Geordie. 'She came from

Kew. My father is German – but my mother taught me English from when I was little.'

Her name, she volunteered, was Elisabeth, and she worked as a secretary in a toy factory. Her husband had been a lieutenant in a Rhenish infantry regiment. At this, her face clouded over. She had to go, she said, to prepare the dinner. With that, she stood, lifted Hansi into her arms, and left Geordie sitting at the café table deep in thought.

Frau Fischer – or Elisabeth as he now thought of her – often spoke with him in English after that, but she remained distant despite her gratitude for him putting himself at risk to save her dog. Like Paul Schmidt, she was a Social Democrat, but regretted that she couldn't leave her little boy, Heinz, to attend party meetings. Geordie suggested that so long as she gave him notice, he would be very happy to look after the child. After that, once or twice a week, he babysat while she was out. Heinz had a rather serious and curious nature. It did Geordie's German good to have to explain things about the world to him, and he would listen, unsmiling, with serious blue eyes while Geordie told him what he knew of history and geography. When something particularly interested him, Heinz's face would light up and he would speak so quickly that Geordie could not understand. He was of course curious about the war. If this was Germany, why was Herr Stubbs here? Why did he have red hair? Why was his skin dark? Did he know his father, and would his father come home? Would there be another war? Why were there wars? There was no end to his questions and Geordie thought that if adults had asked them, perhaps the catastrophe might never have happened.

One bright May evening, Heinz asked Geordie if he would take him to the re-opened Luna-Park. Geordie agreed but cautioned that he would have to obtain permission from his mother. She returned shortly afterwards from her meeting and bustled around getting the child ready for bed. Meanwhile, Geordie retired to his room and began to read. He became absorbed in the book – Somerset Maugham's

The Moon and Sixpence – and it was a while before he became aware of sobbing in the major's room next door. When the noise showed no signs of abating, Geordie knocked and entered to find the major kneeling on the floor weeping with his revolver pressed to his temple. Horrified, Geordie begged the man to give him the weapon. The poor man turned to him with his face wet with tears and begged him to explain what the point of it all was. Geordie could not answer, but he managed to take the revolver and lay the man gently down on his bed. Half an hour later, after an army doctor had given the major a sedative, two orderlies took him away on a stretcher. Geordie never saw nor heard of the man again, and he cursed the wretched war that was still taking victims.

The incident cast a pall over breakfast, but Frau Fischer nervously broached her son's request regarding Luna-Park as she was clearing away the dishes. 'I'm sure you'll be far too busy,' she said, but Geordie insisted that he would be delighted to take the boy and that he would like her to come too. The next Saturday afternoon, the three of them set off for the amusement park. A few people scowled at them – this German woman, the British officer, and the child – and one old man shouted that she was the black Tommy's whore. Frau Fischer reddened, and the child demanded to know, 'Why is that man shouting at us, Mutti?' She stuck out her chin defiantly and boarded the tram that would take them to the park. Geordie felt guilty for exposing her to this unpleasantness, but he admired her pluck. They smiled at each other as she handed Heinz down to him at their stop.

The child had a wonderful time. He rode the roller coaster, nervously exuberant, took three rides on a carousel, whooped with delight on the giant Ferris wheel and devoured a large ice cream. He won prizes in the shooting gallery after Geordie showed him how to aim and fire.

'He's a soldier,' Heinz said proudly, holding Geordie's hand and posing for a photographer.

The child went to sleep on the tram going home, clutching his trophies, snuggled up between his Mutti and the English soldier. They didn't notice the frog-faced youth eyeing them with hatred.

'Thank you so much, Geordie Stubbs,' Frau Fischer said, touching his hand gently before leading her son off to bed. 'I haven't had so much fun in … oh, a long, long time.'

Geordie lay awake that night, thinking of her and wondering if she was thinking of him, and drifted into a deep sleep. The next morning, he was gazing out of the barracks window, tapping his pen on his teeth, when Tambling-Goggins breezed in carrying a sheaf of papers.

'As you were, Lieutenant.' The colonel motioned Geordie to remain seated. 'Orders just in.' He waved the sheets of paper. 'We leave tomorrow for Paris, Versailles, actually. There's a big conference there and we have the honour of providing part of the guard. So, go to your billet now and pack some things.'

'All of them?' Geordie wondered aloud.

'No, I shouldn't think so,' replied Tambling-Goggins. 'Temporary assignment and we'll be back in a few weeks.'

'Yessir!' said Geordie with a big smile.

Versailles, France, January 1919

The contingent from the 77th disembarked from the train at the Versailles–Rive Gauche station and marched smartly through the streets to their barracks. Passers-by eyed them curiously and drinkers at pavement cafés toasted them. Swarms of well-wishers welcomed David Lloyd George, Georges Clemenceau, and the American President, Woodrow Wilson, who spoke eloquently of 'peace without annexations or indemnities'.

Shortly after arriving, Geordie was taking the warm evening air near the open-air Notre Dame market. He sat at a vacant table in a kerbside café and ordered an Alsatian beer. His eyes were drawn to a man at a nearby table. It was the way the man sat that caught his attention. When the man half-turned to signal the waiter, Geordie realised that he was Nguyễn Tất Thành, his Annamite friend from London. Nguyễn did not recognise him at first – which was not surprising, given that Geordie was dressed in British army officer's uniform – but recognition dawned, and the two friends clasped hands with genuine warmth. Nguyễn knew, of course, that Geordie had fled when the police raided the Carlton, but he had not been sure of his fate. He recalled Chief Inspector Verte as a boor who had made disparaging remarks about his race.

'Anyway,' said Geordie after Nguyễn had run out of questions. 'What have you been doing?'

Nguyễn sketched his doings for the past years in broad brushstrokes. He had left for Paris in 1917 and thrown himself into anti-colonial agitation, which was why he was here in Versailles. Now going by the name Nguyễn Ái Quốc, he had spent the last weeks lobbying the various delegations at Versailles to support self-determination for his people. Some were indifferent. Some mumbled vaguely about the *mission civilisatrice* and others were downright rude and hostile, even threatening.

When they went their separate ways, Geordie carefully folded the letter of introduction that Nguyễn had written and stowed it inside his tunic. Written in French with a pen and paper borrowed from the café proprietor, it introduced Monsieur George Stubbs as a good friend who would always be welcome in Nguyễn's country. Both felt it unlikely, however, that they would ever see each other again. Three days later, the rival delegations met in the glittering Hall of Mirrors and signed the Treaty of Versailles. The crowds were ecstatic, but after listening to his old friend, Geordie wondered if the treaty really embodied the principles that Woodrow Wilson claimed to uphold.

~ 28 ~

Cologne, 1919

Geordie knew something had changed when Frau Fischer opened the door on his return from Versailles. He had walked back quickly from the railway station, stopping on the way to purchase a gingerbread man as a gift for the child.

'My husband is back,' she said in a low voice.

Geordie opened his mouth but found he could not speak. She poured him a cup of coffee and pushed it over the kitchen table. Klaus had been found almost dead, by some Belgian nuns. The army believed he was dead, and Frau Fischer had accepted this.

She bit her lip before continuing. 'He came back last week. He is blind and he has lost an arm. He was gassed. He sits and weeps and only speaks when he cries out in his dreams.'

Klaus Fischer haunted the apartment, tottering from room to room, tapping his white cane and feeling his way round the walls with his good hand. At times he would call out 'Elisabeth!' like a frightened child. One day, the two men encountered each other at the doorway to the parlour.

'*Wer ist das?*' Klaus demanded, and when Geordie explained who he was, Klaus leaned his cane against the wall and felt the contours of his face. Elisabeth had come up behind them and was standing with her hand to her mouth. Klaus slowly turned and went back to his room, his breath rattling in his gas-ravaged lungs. Lieutenant Stubbs and Frau Fischer were politely formal with each other now, and although he sometimes took Heinz on excursions to the park or the cinema, she never again accompanied them. She no longer went out to meetings and when she was not at work, she devoted her time to caring for her husband.

The summer ended abruptly. Cold rains fell, followed by frosts, snow, and bitter winds. It was Geordie's habit to walk back to the apartment, rugged up in his army greatcoat. One day, deep in thought, he passed the red brick walls of a small factory, from which came the whirr of woodworking machinery and the smell of paint, glue, and sawdust. A sign above the main door identified the premises as HARTMANN, BLOEHM & SOHN, SPIELZEUGHERSTELLER. It was Elisabeth Fischer's workplace, a riverside toy factory. Just then, she left the building, pulling on her gloves and adjusting her hat. Geordie apologised for startling her and offered to accompany her home. She smiled and was about to reply when a youth erupted from the factory door and stood glaring at them. Geordie could not quite place him but thought he had seen him somewhere before: a repellent character with a broad face, a wide, frog-like mouth and a pair of colourless eyes that were glittering with malice.

'Slut!' he spat. 'You disgrace Germany!'

When Geordie stepped forward to remonstrate, the youth abused him as a 'dirty black swine' and shoved him violently in the chest. An older employee ran up and seized the youth by the arm and motioned for Geordie and Frau Fischer to leave.

'Thank you,' sighed Frau Fischer. 'That young salesman – Josef Grohé – is the bane of my life. He started to follow me round like a lovestruck puppy but when I politely rejected his advances, he started to hate me. The next thing was, he joined the *Deutschvölkischer Schutz und Trutzbund*. That lot hate Social Democrats – they say we stabbed Germany in the back – and now he's insufferable.'

Geordie apologised if he had made things worse, but Frau Fischer shook her head and slipped her arm through his. 'Come,' she said. 'I must pick up Heinz. Let's forget about Josef Grohé and his kind.'

They walked on in companionable silence.

Klaus Fischer's condition did not improve, but neither did it get worse. Geordie could hear him coughing at night and little Heinz asked him gravely if his daddy was going to die. Somehow, the poor man held on. Geordie did not know what to say to the child. The doctors came and went, looking grim throughout the long dark winter, but when spring put in a half-hearted appearance, Fischer's condition improved slightly. He took to sitting at the parlour window wrapped in a blanket, gazing with sightless eyes on horrors they could only guess at. He seldom spoke except to request something from his wife in a painful, rasping voice.

One evening, he spoke to Geordie for the first time. 'You seem like a good man … for an Englander,' he wheezed through his ravaged throat. Geordie realised that Fischer had made a little joke, so he laughed politely. Fischer had more to say. 'Elisabeth seems to like you and I'm glad she has a friend.'

Two weeks later, Colonel Tambling-Goggins made an important announcement. 'Good news, chaps,' he told his assembled officers. 'We're going home!' They cheered spontaneously and toasted King and Country with Rhine wine. Replacements would arrive within the week, then trains would take them to Ostend and the ferry for home. Geordie made his excuses as soon as was decent and trudged slowly to the Fischer apartment, unaware of the birds singing brightly in the calm spring evening. Frau Fischer smiled sadly when he informed her of his impending departure. She made him promise to write with his address as soon as he was able to do so, thanked him for all he had done for her and the child, kissed him on the cheek, and bade him good night.

Just days later, he shouldered his kitbag and closed the apartment door behind him. Klaus Fischer was still sleeping, Heinz was at school, and Frau Fischer had left for work. It was a fine sunny day when his train pulled out of the main railway station, the Hauptbahnhof, with the Gothic steeples of the Cologne cathedral receding into the distance, and he wondered if he would see them again.

London, 1920

Geordie's discharge papers came through smartly, and he found a comfortable bedsit in Carter Lane near St Paul's Cathedral. He spent his time wandering through the city streets or supping ale in the 'Rising Sun' pub and reading form guides. The army had provided structure to his life and now that he had been 'demobbed' there seemed to be little purpose to the days. He had managed to accumulate a fair sum of money (honestly, it must be said) but he realised he needed to find a job to prevent him from drifting aimlessly. With his army discharge papers in order and a fine testimonial from his commanding officer, it was not long before he secured employment as head chef in La Perruque et la Robe, a fine French restaurant near Chancery much frequented by the legal fraternity. He threw himself into the work, partly to banish hopeless thoughts from his head, and partly because he enjoyed being back in a well-appointed kitchen. He also lashed out and bought himself a splendid fiddle from J & A Beare in Queen Anne Street and would sometimes entertain the diners with selections from his repertoire of Celtic airs and English folk tunes.

One midweek evening, Cedric the sous-chef puffed into the kitchen and announced, 'They're 'ere, gaffer!' Geordie looked up from testing some bouillon and raised an eyebrow. 'Great big gang o' toffs comin' dahn the street!'

Geordie turned off the gas. Two weeks earlier, some swells down from Oxford had rioted in a nearby Italian restaurant. It started with them throwing food at each other and escalated to total mayhem.

'They always gits away wiv it,' Cedric moaned. 'Daddy pays the damages an' if the restaurants call the rozzers 'e gits on the blower to the chief constable and nuffink's ever done.' He gestured to where the youths were milling around outside and peering through the windows.

The toffs began chanting: 'Buller Buller Buller!' One staggered over to a lamppost and urinated copiously to ironic cheers from his friends. 'Ha ha! I say, Birtwhistle major's pissin' like a horse.' Another youth tousled his blond hair and opened the restaurant door to find Geordie standing with folded arms. The customers were watching developments with trepidation.

'Ye're not coming in here, laddie,' said Geordie.

'Don't be impertinent,' sneered the youth. 'You need debagging, little man.'

'I'm warning you, Sonny Jim. Piss off where ye came from.'

The youth went purple in the face. 'Do you know who I am?' he demanded.

'Nay, laddie, and I divvent care,' said Geordie, pointing to the door.

'Let's have you, black bastard!' The youth was shaping up, Queensberry style.

'Buller Buller Buller!' chanted his mates. 'Clobber him, Johnson!'

Johnson swung his fist, but Geordie leaned back contemptuously, jabbed him on the chest and punched him fair in the centre of his face. Johnson fell on his bum and sat there in blubbering bewilderment. There was astonished shock on the faces outside the window.

'Watch him, bonnie lad,' Geordie ordered Cedric as he walked around the youth to lean out the door and shout 'You and you! Yes you, laddie! Gerrin 'ere and get your mate oot o' ma restaurant!'

The two he had fingered half carried Johnson through the door with his bottom wobbling and the restaurant staff and customers broke into hearty applause.

Calm reigned, but late one afternoon as Geordie was preparing a hollandaise sauce, a shadow announced the presence of a stranger in the kitchen doorway. Geordie's heart sank. The man's ferocious bulldog jowls and red hair were instantly recognisable, and his blue eyes were icier than ever. He had put on weight and his tweed suit was straining against his bulk.

'Detective Chief Inspector Verte,' he rasped, 'and this is Inspector Pickles.' Verte smiled mirthlessly, baring a set of teeth that were stained brown from pipe smoke. 'I've long relished this day. That bit of a ruckus you had with the Bullingdon Boys drew my attention.'

He nodded to Pickles, who addressed Geordie in a curiously high-pitched, Cockney voice: 'George William Marmaduke Stubbs, I am arresting you for a series of offences, including burglaries in Gateshead, Newcastle, and York. You do not 'ave to say anything, but anything you do say may be taken down and used in evidence against you. Do you understand?'

'Aye,' Geordie sighed, offering his wrists for the handcuffs. 'I do.'

The detectives had a car and driver waiting at the kerb. They squeezed their prisoner into the back seat between them and the vehicle set off through thick traffic towards Scotland Yard. When Geordie had last seen that building, it had been part of the London Reception Centre and was absorbing a steady stream of army recruits. It seemed a life-time ago. The charge room sergeant, who looked like he had served since the time of Jack the Ripper, signed Geordie in. He gloated like an angler viewing a prize fish.

'Well, well, well, if it ain't Geordie Stubbs,' he observed. 'Mr Verte 'as been after your collar for a long time, but like the Mounties, 'e always gits 'is man! Now, Mr McGooley 'ere will look after you.'

McGooley was a lugubrious old turnkey. After he had escorted Geordie to his cell, he offered him an evening meal. When it arrived, Geordie threw up his hands at the horrible mess on the plate. 'Haddaway man,' he remonstrated. 'Pigs wouldn't eat that!'

'Suit yerself, squire,' muttered the turnkey. 'Mebbe you won't be so partickler after a night in the cells.'

The cell contained a bed with a stained mattress, a hard, wooden chair, and a rancid slop bucket in one corner. The bed and chair were bolted to the floor, presumably to prevent prisoners from using them as weapons. The next morning, McGooley rapped on the bars with a baton and proffered a bowl of burgoo and a mug of black tea. Geordie declined politely, whereupon the turnkey made off, muttering something about 'Lord Muck needin' to know 'is place.'

The lawyer they fetched him was funny little Yorkshireman called Boris Godbehere. He had a deceptively slow way of speaking, but his mind was sharp.

'First of all,' he whispered, punctuating his words with a wagging finger, 'do not admit to anything. This might seem obvious, but you would be surprised how many people forget this advice. The only evidence against you is fingerprints. There are no witnesses to anything Jim Verte's accused you of, so he will be counting on a confession. Confess to anything, no matter how small, and you are lost. Lost, I say!'

'Thank you, Mr Godbehere,' Geordie replied. 'May I ask, though, if you believe I'm guilty?'

Godbehere shook his billiard ball of a head. 'That is neither here nor there,' he declared. 'My job is to represent you and the prosecution's job is to provide evidence to convict you.'

Geordie promised that come what may, he would refuse to confess – and he stuck to it. Verte and Pickles tried everything in their considerable repertoire to get him to admit to the charges, but he parried every move they made.

'Doesn't matter, Stubbs,' Verte muttered as they left the interview room for the last time. 'We have enough evidence to convict you and put you away for a long time.'

The magistrate remanded Geordie to HM Prison Wormwood Scrubs until his trial in the Old Bailey. Life in the Scrubs was a deeply unpleasant experience, in which boredom vied with claustrophobia. The warders – many of them former soldiers – were humourless martinets who took great delight in humiliating anyone foolish enough to question the clockwork rules of the institution. They did, however, treat Geordie, as an ex-officer, with a certain amount of respect. He put his head down and resolved to endure the incarceration without complaint. Every day was the same, except for Sundays, when the prisoners were forced to attend religious services and received a small extra portion of meat on their tin plates.

One morning, however, when trudging round the exercise yard under a leaden sky, Geordie fell in with a slight, bespectacled fellow whose name, he learned, was Hamish Raeburn. Doctor Raeburn. To say that Raeburn – an Oxford don charged with 'unnatural vice' – was out of place in that purgatory is a colossal understatement. Daily threatened with rape by some of the crims and sometimes assaulted by the screws, Raeburn eventually hanged himself; but not before he had re-awakened Geordie's innate thirst for literature. A previous prison governor had begun to stock the library with the classics and Geordie read his way along the short shelf, his choice guided by his donnish friend. Christopher Marlowe and the other great Elizabethans were Raeburn's passion, and he urged his unlikely student to read them when he was out of that place. In a very real way, the Scrubs was like a university for Geordie Stubbs.

London, 1920–22

The day came when Geordie and three other prisoners were loaded into a Black Maria, which trundled through the West London streets to the Old Bailey. The judge regarded Geordie sourly when he entered the dock. With the jury empanelled, the prosecutor outlined the case against the defendant. A preening peacock of a man called Montgomery Stevens Haugh, he was given to extravagant gestures and florid turns of phrase. Geordie sat impassively as the fellow strutted about enjoying his hour on the stage. Geordie's brief, Boris Godbehere, was restrained and formal. He declared that any evidence against his client was tainted; that his client denied all the charges; and that he was a former army officer who had risen from the ranks because of his impeccable character and high intelligence to serve His Majesty with distinction. Montgomery Stevens Haugh rolled his eyes and smiled owlishly at the jury as he called his first witness.

Detective Chief Inspector James Arthur Verte clambered stoutly into the witness box, confirmed his identity, and swore 'by Almighty God that the evidence I shall give shall be the truth, the whole truth, and nothing but the truth.' He agreed that he had been seconded to

171

the Gateshead Constabulary back in 1912 to investigate a series of burglaries carried out by a person the press had dubbed 'the Human Fly.' He also agreed that he had evidence linking the activities of the Fly with crimes committed in the city of York, including the theft of the King James II chamber pot. A titter of laughter broke out and the judge threatened to clear the court if it happened again. Cross-examined by Boris Godbehere, Verte admitted that there were no witnesses to any of the crimes and that the defendant had not admitted anything. He asserted, however, that certain forensic evidence would prove the defendant's guilt.

After a recess, Montgomery Stevens Haugh called his second witness, a bald, bespectacled little boffin whose fluffy ear tufts made him look like a koala. He confirmed that he worked at Scotland Yard as a fingerprint and forensics expert, for which he had received specialist training in America. Despite this, the Koala looked uncomfortable and kept running his finger inside his celluloid collar. Yes, he had taken the defendant's fingerprints with a view to comparing them with prints found at the various crime scenes, but – and here he cleared his throat and reached for a glass of water – the crime scene prints had vanished. 'Vanished?' Stevens Haugh demanded incredulously. The courtroom dissolved into a storm of buzzing voices, with the beak banging his gavel and shouting for order. When order was restored, Stevens Haugh asked the Koala how, when and where this had happened, all the time shaking his head sorrowfully.

'In the last day or so,' the Koala replied, mopping his brow with a big red hankie. 'They were stored in a locked cupboard at Scotland Yard, but when I went to check this morning, they were missing.'

The courtroom again descended into chaos. When he could be heard, the judge declared a recess and directed the police to make a thorough search for the missing evidence. Geordie was perplexed and relieved in equal measure and Boris Godbehere grinned discreetly and essayed a surreptitious wink. The missing evidence remained missing and much against his inclinations, the judge had to declare a mistrial and Geordie walked free. He had spent the best part of four months in custody and even the dirty air of the London streets smelled sweet when he bade Boris Godbehere farewell and walked back to see if his lodgings in Carter Lane were still available.

The newspapers were full of the story, with newsboys shouting the headlines: 'READ ALL ABAHT IT! YEWMAN FLY WALKS FREE AT THE BAILEY!' Nevertheless, despite or perhaps because of his notoriety, the owner of La Perruque et la Robe readily took Geordie back on, declaring that he had never had any doubts about his innocence. This was probably untrue, but Geordie's notoriety was a drawcard for diners from Chancery. Geordie vowed that he would continue to go straight. He later learned that his friend from the trenches, Captain Lysander Brocklehurst, had taken a leading position with the Metropolitan Police following his discharge from the army. Geordie remembered saving his life – so perhaps he was repaying the debt?

As for James Verte, he sat, smoked, and raged in his office at Scotland Yard. He had been so certain he would send Stubbs down for a long stretch. The little bastard was guilty as hell, and he had somehow managed to pervert the course of justice. Sooner or later, though, the creature would make a mistake and next time he wouldn't get away with it. Not even the promotion to Commander could make Verte forget his rage and pain. He put discreet surveillance on Stubbs, but the man seemed to be living an honest life. 'Seemed' was the operative word. He had to be up to something.

In fact, Geordie's life was uneventful for the next year or so. Business boomed at La Perruque and the proprietor offered him a share in the business, which he was thinking of accepting. One day, however, when he returned to his lodgings after work, there was a letter with German stamps waiting for him on the hall table. Written in English, but in *Sütterlinschrift* on thick, good quality paper, it was from Elisabeth Fischer in Cologne. She informed him that her husband, Klaus, had died two years previously. It had, she said, been a blessing because in the end he could not rise from his bed, refused all food, and 'was a mere skeleton'. On the advice of her good friend Paul Schmidt, she had taken the liberty of writing to Geordie. She would be visiting London to stay with her English aunt in Richmond and wondered if they might catch up.

Three weeks later, Geordie took the tube out to Kew – daring for him given his fears of dark tunnels – and walked from the station to the Gardens. They had arranged to meet at the Temperate House, and he could scarcely contain his excitement as he drew near. At first, he could not see her, but then she emerged from where she had been sitting and walked towards him. They shook hands shyly, then stepped back to take a close look at each other. She was an attractive woman, with her dark hair peeking from around her Tam O'Shanter hat and her green eyes sparkling. There were, he noticed, a few grey hairs among the mass of darker ones, for she was a few years older than the 27-year-old Geordie.

She spoke first. 'I have missed you, Geordie,' she said in her soft Rhineland tones. He mumbled something inconsequential, and they walked arm in arm towards the Great Pagoda. They took tea in one of the Gardens cafés – he with milk and she with lemon in the German fashion – and began to tell each other what they had been doing since he left Cologne. After Klaus's death, she had thrown herself into her political work. It was pressing, she believed, to stop the Nazis, who were hell-bent on seizing power and imposing a dictatorship. Did he remember the Grohé boy, she asked? Geordie recalled the frog-faced youth who had abused her. Grohé was now a leading light in the new fascist party. He still worked for Hartmann & Bloehm, and his hatred had escalated since he discovered that her grandmother was Jewish.

Geordie was afraid that she would reject him if he told her about his sojourn at Wormwood Scrubs, and the reason for his arrest and trial, and he lacked the courage to tell her anything of that part of what had happened to him since he left Germany. Always lurking at the back of his mind, too, was his deep shame for abandoning Annie and his unborn child. Elisabeth was honest, straightforward, and utterly decent. He feared that if he told her the truth, she would want nothing more to do with him. He spoke in general terms instead of his work and how he had been saving his money with the aim of setting up his own restaurant. She was never far from his thoughts, but he had hoped for her sake that Klaus had recovered. The evening shadows had lengthened by the time they finished telling each other their stories.

She invited Geordie to afternoon tea with her and her Aunt Felicity, who turned out to be a formidable dowager who lived in a beautiful Georgian house near Richmond Green. Felicity, who was still strikingly handsome despite her advanced years, was frostily formal, but Geordie soon charmed her. She laughed at his jokes and teased him about his Geordie accent, and it seemed clear that he had passed whatever test she had devised.

'Elisabeth is my nearest living relative,' Felicity told him. 'It was dreadful to be separated during that terrible war and I do feel for her losing Klaus. I met him before the war, you know. He was a good man even if I could never agree with his politics. We've always been Tory.'

Elisabeth stayed in London for three weeks. Hartmann & Bloehm had given her special leave, but she had to get back to Cologne and she needed to be with Heinz. When the day of her departure came round, Geordie saw her off at London Victoria Station. As she was about to board the train, she hugged Geordie and kissed him, then placed her hands on his shoulders and asked him to come to Germany to be with her. He agreed without hesitation. He would give notice at La Perruque and leave as soon as he could. He also resolved to tell her about Annie and the bairn, for he could not bear to think of deceiving her.

Cologne and Munich, 1922

The sun was burning off the fog on the Rhine when Geordie's train pulled into the Cologne railway station. He was expecting Elisabeth to welcome him at the Café Imperial in the domed entrance hall, but there was no sign of her at any of the tables. He ordered coffee and sat on a plush banquette to wait for her. Although he waited for over an hour, she did not appear. By now mildly anxious, he took a taxi to her apartment block in Beckerstraße and rang the doorbell. There was no answer, but a neighbour allowed him to leave his luggage in the hallway. He hurried to the Rathausplatz to seek out Elisabeth's friend Paul Schmidt at the city hall. Geordie dismissed the thought that she had changed her mind. If she had, she surely would have written to tell him.

Paul Schmidt was dictating to his secretary, but he stopped what he was doing and came out into the outer office looking grave. 'Herr Leutnant,' he said, extending his hand. 'Please come with me.'

He ushered Geordie into his office and bade him sit at a low table next to the window with a fine view of the Old Town.

'It is good to see you,' said Schmidt, filling a cup with coffee and sliding it over the table to Geordie, 'but I am afraid that I have some terrible news.' He pushed his glasses up from his nose and blinked tired blue eyes. 'There is no easy way to say this, Herr Stubbs, but Elisabeth is dead.'

'Dead?' gasped Geordie. 'That cannot be … How did it happen?'

Schmidt shook his head sadly. 'Frau Fischer was last seen leaving work two days ago. She told a colleague that she would call in at the fish markets on her way to collect young Heinz from school, but she did not appear. After a while, the teachers contacted me and I took the boy to his grandfather's house—'

'And is Heinz okay?'

'Yes, yes. He's fine.' Schmidt smoothed his hair and continued. 'Well, I know that Frau Fischer would never neglect the child, so I reported her disappearance to the police. The desk sergeant tried to fob me off: "People turn up", "She hasn't been missing for long", "There must be an explanation." So, I pulled rank and demanded to see my friend Captain Honecker. He agreed to put out an urgent alert.'

Geordie found his voice. 'And did … did they find anything?'

'No, there were no leads. They got the *Hausmeister* to open her apartment but they found nothing. Nor had anyone seen her after she left work.' Schmidt swigged some coffee and set the saucer down. 'I'm sorry to have to tell you this, but the following day a barge skipper recovered her body from the river downstream near Düsseldorf.'

'So, she drowned?'

Schmidt shrugged. 'I cannot say. There is to be an autopsy tomorrow and I fear that she might have been thrown in.'

'But who would want to harm her?'

'We can only speculate at this stage, Herr Stubbs. There are always perverts around, but I have a theory. There was a young man at her work. He hated her, both for her political opinions and because she had rejected him …'

'Yes.' Geordie nodded, recalling the altercation with the frog-faced young man outside the toy factory a few years earlier.

'The fellow is a fanatical fascist. These people are becoming bolder by the day … always parading with swastika flags and bellowing about the so-called "stab in the back" … we lost the war because of the Jews and socialists and all that blather. They're starting to beat up left-wingers and Jews. My guess is that the Grohé fellow murdered Elisabeth for both personal and political reasons.

'Anyway, Herr Stubbs, Captain Honecker hauled the fellow in, but he maintained his innocence. What could he do? He had to let him go. He'll keep an eye on him, but—' Schmidt spread his hands wide and smiled wanly.

Geordie had little recollection of how he spent the next few days. He booked into a small pension and wandered the winding streets of the Altstadt in a daze. A few days later, Paul Schmidt called on him and informed him that although Elisabeth's body was found in the river, the cause of death was a massive blow to the back of her head with a blunt object. It seemed that the murderer had attempted to hide evidence of the crime by throwing her body in the river, hoping that the current would take it far from Cologne.

The funeral was a melancholy affair. Elisabeth was interred in the family plot in the Südfriedhof – the vast cemetery in the south of the city. Geordie travelled out to the cemetery with Paul Schmidt, who had hired a taxi for the occasion. It was a beautiful day, with a clear sky from which the mild winter sun strove to melt the glittering frost that covered the graveyard. There was a decent turnout of mourners – family, friends, work colleagues, a sprinkling of Klaus Fischer's brother officers, and Elisabeth's political associates. Heinz was there, clutching the hand of a tall, distinguished looking man who Geordie took to be Elisabeth's father, Herr Keller. Geordie did not feel like disturbing them and left as soon as the formalities were over, declining Schmidt's offer to share his taxi. He did not trust himself not to break down and cry in front of Heinz.

Back in the Old Town, he took refuge in a riverside pub, where he downed several shots of Schnapps and wondered what he would do. The noise of a passing procession awoke him from his reverie – first the monotonous thump-thump of a big bass drum, then the brazen blare of trumpets. He downed his Schnapps, paid the waiter with a wedge of absurdly inflated Papiermarks, and sidled out into the street to see what the commotion was. It was a Nazi parade behind a swastika banner ballooning between two elaborately carved poles. A pair of bruisers toted the poles, their expressions like constipated rats. Other marchers carried banners inscribed with slogans such as 'Germany Awake!' and 'Perish Judah!' and they were bawling out the words of some ultranationalist song, backed by the blaring trumpets, a tuba, and the pounding drums. Onlookers lined the street, some with admiring looks, others openly contemptuous. Geordie caught sight of Josef Grohé just as the youth noticed him. Grohé was dressed up in the shit-brown Stormtrooper uniform with a peaked cap, high black boots, and jodhpurs. When he had marched past, he took a double take and grinned insolently at Geordie. It was tacit admission, Geordie felt sure, that the bastard had killed Elisabeth.

Three days later, Geordie bade Herr Schmidt goodbye. He had already spoken with Elisabeth's father, who promised to keep him informed about young Heinz. He had decided against returning to London and would make his way instead to Munich with the vague intention of opening a restaurant. He had heard that it was a beautiful city and he believed he could make a new start there. Having some time to kill before his train left, he wandered the streets and alleys of the Old Town. Turning from the Filzengraben into Holzgasse, he almost literally ran into Josef Grohé. The Stormtrooper tried to run, but Geordie seized him by the shoulder and spun him round.

'*Bitte,*' the youth bleated. '*Ich habe*—' He did not finish the sentence. Geordie punched him hard, and he slid down the wall and lay still on the cobblestones. Geordie took a deep breath, stepped over him and made his way back to the station to catch his train to Munich. It was only with great difficulty that he had resisted the urge to kick the creature into eternity.

Lambton Hall, County Durham

Mary Ross was a beautiful child. She had inherited her father's red hair and her mother's blue eyes. Her olive complexion was unusual on Tyneside. She was a good child but could be wilful and mischievous. Her mother, Annie, was proud of her but she was also just a little afraid of the child's quick intelligence and mercurial temperament. They had been living for some time in the gatehouse at the foot of the Lambton Hall driveway; a six-room dwelling far beyond anything to be found at High Fell. Annie had been put off by the Armstrong munition works after Armistice Day and she had struggled to find other work. Although Annie pretended that Mary's father had died in the war, malicious tongues wagged. To be an unwed mother branded her as a tart and she had had to summon every ounce of resolve to refuse Father Flynn's demand to hand over her baby to the nuns for adoption – and herself to enter an institution for 'fallen women'. Geordie's granda Tim Allen had been supportive, but he had perished in the Spanish flu pandemic, grieving to the end over his grandson's betrayal.

When Mary was a toddler, Annie had walked to Lambton Hall to ask for an increase in her stipend. There was no sign of Jeremiah and his sister had been married off and moved away. Lady Agatha had recently died, and the old judge, Sir Cuthbert, was in lonely retirement. He had received Annie in the drawing room and was considering her request for increased remuneration when he caught sight of Mary – his great-granddaughter – playing in the garden under the supervision of one of the servants. He called her in and was instantly smitten with the girl and decided there and then to make amends for his – and his son's – neglect of those who were after all their own flesh and blood. Annie and the bairn moved into the gatehouse and the judge saw to it that they lacked for nothing. When the child was older, he arranged for a private tutor for her and a little later he enrolled her in an expensive private girls' school to which she was transported every day by pony trap. She also had the run of the Hall and grounds and would spend a great deal of time in her great-grandfather's company, entertaining him with singing and dancing, reciting poetry and astonishing him with her burgeoning intelligence. Her mother soon tired of a life of idleness and found work in the local shop and post office. She was happy, but the thought of Geordie Stubbs lurked always at the threshold of her consciousness. She had read accounts of his trial and sensational acquittal at the Old Bailey, but London was for her a foreign land, and she had no desire to go there in search of the man who had deserted her and the child. The affair had left her with an abiding distrust of men, but sometimes she dreamed of times past when she and Geordie had roamed the lanes round High Fell and she had thought they would be together forever.

Munich, late 1922–1933

Geordie's train had pulled into the Munich station in a whirling snowstorm. With visibility down to a couple of feet, he blundered around for some time before stumbling on a cheap pension in nearby Schillerstraße. The storm blew itself out by the evening, so he wandered out and found himself in a fairy-tale streetscape. Christmas was drawing near and the big shops along Bayerstraße and Neuhauserstraße had festooned their windows with bright lights and colourful decorations that contrasted with the vivid white of the snowdrifts banked up against the walls. Children swaddled in colourful clothing squealed with delight. *'Mutti, Mutti! Schau! Alles ist wunderschön!'* – Mummy! Mummy! Look! Everything is beautiful!

The sight stabbed his heart, but the crowds of rugged-up Müncheners entering a narrow alley off Bayerstraße caught his eye. A jolly looking old fellow clad in traditional Bavarian costume informed him it was the entrance to the Mathäserbräustadt. Geordie had read about the beer hall in a book by the American writer H.L. Mencken describing a 'beeriad' around the Teutonic world a decade earlier. Geordie could not resist. Entering the alley, he passed a line of booths staffed by radish sellers; 'ancient dames of incredible diameter' in Mencken's telling. A wide staircase led to a vast beer hall, said to seat up to 3000 drinkers. He purchased a beer and a pretzel and found a seat at a long wooden table. Mencken had raved about Munich beer as 'unique, incomparable, sui generis … consummate, transcendental, übernatürlich', and Geordie had to agree as he supped the delicious elixir. He marvelled at the buxom dirndl-clad waitresses carrying long rows of beer mugs on each arm, and at the lines of people swaying with linked arms to the beat of the oompah band. He ordered a second litre of dark beer and matched it with another thick pretzel stuffed with salted radish – a staple of the Munich tippler – and fell into conversation with an off-duty waiter. Geordie struggled to understand his thick Bavarian accent but learned that the Hotel Bayerischer Hof was seeking staff. After his third litre, Geordie decided that he liked Munich and would apply for a job in the famous hotel. A few more beers, and he parted as best friends from the waiter, but never saw him again.

The Bayerischer Hof stood on the Promenadeplatz, a few hundred metres from the Alte Rathaus and a bit further from the two great cylindrical brick towers of the Munich cathedral. The hotel's interior had been described by Mencken as 'a masterpiece of the Munich glass cutters and upholsterers,' but this failed to do justice to the splendours of the establishment. Geordie was impressed. The place was a step up even on some of the places he'd worked in London. He took a seat under a portrait of the Kaiser and lit a cigarette. Herr Alois Egger, the maître d', raised his eyebrows when he saw him, not expecting a brown man, but ushered him courteously through the great breakfast room and into the tearooms, with their splendid domed roof and immense potted palms, and plonked him down on a plush banquette beneath an ornate window. Egger was thorough and finicky, probing to ascertain if Geordie knew his business. He was impressed, and Geordie's command of French and German clinched it. He hired Geordie at a very reasonable salary with room and board thrown in.

Within a couple of hours, Geordie had fetched his baggage by taxi and had taken possession of his comfortable room with views over the snow-blanketed Old City. Perhaps he could be happy here, he thought. Come to terms with Elisabeth's murder and start life afresh. Work, he knew, would banish obsessive thoughts from his mind.

A few days later, the proprietor, Herr Hermann Volkhardt, came to see him in the kitchens and complimented him on the quality of the meals. Volkhardt was delighted to inform his customers discreetly that the new chef had learned his trade – or rather art – at the feet of the great Escoffier. Geordie's fame grew. Not even the large-scale renovations that the hotel underwent in the New Year stopped the customers flocking to partake of the delights '*der wunderbare englischer Koch*' created for them.

The years passed by. In his spare time, Geordie went for long walks, up or down the Isar River or through the English Gardens, stopping at the Chinese Tower beer garden for a litre or two of Löwenbräu. He learned to ski, and in the winter would often venture out to the Grünwald, or further afield by train to the alpine towns of Klais or Garmisch. He found solace, too, in his music, and on many evenings sad Celtic airs would echo over the rooftops of the Bavarian city. He lived a solitary life, although Munich during those years embraced the passions and fashions of the Jazz Age. Crowds of people thronged the streets, which were full of thundering trams and noisy motorcars. Germany, like the rest of the capitalist world, had entered the frenetic economic boom of the Roaring Twenties and for many Müncheners the war and its bleak aftermath were a rapidly fading nightmare. Geordie began to wonder about a change from the ordered routine at the Bayerischer Hof.

Late in 1930, Geordie's colleague, Christian Seidl, asked if they could meet after work in the tearooms to discuss a business proposition.

As they sipped their orange pekoe under the palm trees, Christian cut to the chase. An upmarket restaurant in Schwabing, an inner northern suburb of the city, would soon be up for sale. It would be a great honour if Herr Stubbs would agree to go into a partnership to buy the restaurant. Geordie was interested and the two men took the tram out to Schwabing to inspect the premises, which stood on an ancient, cobbled street in a quaint precinct. A sign proclaimed the restaurant's name to be Die Goldene Gans – The Golden Goose – and after inspecting the premises carefully the two friends made the proprietor an offer. The kitchen was well-equipped and spotlessly clean, the dining rooms comfortable, with dark mahogany tables, polished floors, discreet lighting, and gleaming plate glass windows. The glasses and silverware sparkled. There were also two small flats above the restaurant – one each for the new partners. After a bit of haggling, a price was agreed.

The partners took over management with gusto. They retained the existing staff – including old Manfred Vogelwaid – 'call me Freddie' – a waiter who had been there since the turn of the century – and soon had to hire extra help to deal with the flood of customers. Freddie raised a white eyebrow at the prospect of learning the names of 'so many new French dishes at my age' but got on with the job and Geordie soon came to view the old chap with affection. It turned out that he had lived for a while at Windhoek in Southwest Africa but had come home disillusioned by the brutality of German rule over the 'natives'. He was reliable, courteous, and even managed to speak *Hochdeutsch* – standard German – when required.

Schwabing was the city's bohemian quarter – fast-paced and raffish, and frequented by poets, writers, artists, and intellectuals, many of them left leaning. It lived twenty-four hours a day, with a pulsing nightlife, cabarets, theatre, and musical performances. As the restaurant's fame grew, many of these people came to eat at the Goose. Geordie did not go out much but one evening Seidl persuaded him to go to Das Nackte Ei – The Naked Egg – a nearby cabaret venue. After they had finished work for the evening, they went round the corner and descended a flight of steps leading down into the club. A big no-nonsense butch woman took their coats and entrance money and waved them through a thick curtain to where a pretty usherette dressed as a pageboy took them to their seats. They ordered a bottle of Sekt and settled down to watch the performers through a blue haze of cigarette smoke.

After a brief intermission, the androgynous MC introduced the next act, 'the well-known singer and dancer Fräulein Ilona Esterházy!' to loud and sustained applause. Ilona skipped lightly onto the stage, blowing kisses to the audience, shaking her abundant masses of hair, to grasp the microphone in a white-gloved hand. She was perhaps twenty-five, certainly no older than thirty. She was lissom, callipygian, she was beautiful, and she knew it. The four-piece band struck up and Ilona began to sing a cabaret ditty written by the Berliner Mischa Spoliansky. Her voice was sultry, and the song reflected the cynical, seen-it-all-but-what-can-you-do? worldliness of the times.

The audience loved it and loved Ilona even more. By the time she had finished her bracket of songs and tap-danced her way around the stage with cane and top hat, waggling her shapely bum, they would have done anything for her. A bald old gent pushed some large denomination notes into her hand, shouting 'Bravo! Bravo!', and she had offers of drinks from all quarters of the room.

Geordie was aware that Ilona had been looking at him from time to time and he was delighted when she chose to sit at the table he was sharing with Christian Seidl.

'Hallo, Rotschopf,' she said, with a wink.

'Hallo, Redhead yourself,' Geordie replied, smiling.

She lit a cigarette and studied him brazenly, crossing one long leg over the other and blowing smoke rings. The quick sketch he had made of her won her heart. Seidl raised an eyebrow and excused himself. He had seen a friend across the room, he said, and left them to it. Later, when they were smooching, Ilona confessed that her name was not Esterházy, nor was she Ilona, and nor had she been anywhere near Hungary as her stage name implied. She was plain Mitzi Maierhofer, from a farm up in the Bavarian Alps. Geordie said he liked her by any name, and she became his on-again off-again girlfriend. She might have been a hill farmer's daughter, but Geordie soon learned that she was a fiercely independent young woman of considerable intellect and always up for an argument. She had run away from home when she was just sixteen, unwilling to tolerate her surly father and the prospect of life as some farmer's drudge. She laughed that she had had a sugar daddy for a while but had left when he started to treat her as his property. Next came a stint as a chorus girl and artists' model before a friend convinced her she could sing. She was in no hurry to marry, though she was not short of offers, she said, and Geordie took the hint. She was impulsive, fiery, generous, romantic, histrionic at times, and a good hater and a good friend. She hinted that her temper had landed her in trouble on more than one occasion. When she got to know old Freddie, she announced that had he been a younger man, she would have taken off with him like a shot.

Geordie had gone native, although Mitzi called him her '*dunkeler Englischer Schatz*'. He had begun to dream in German, even in Bavarian! and he now went about the streets clad in a thick green Loden coat and joked that he was considering Lederhosen and a Tyrolean hat. He'd also learned to play some Bavarian folk tunes on his fiddle, and Mitzi was badgering him to learn some Hungarian melodies and accompany her at the Naked Egg. As both he and Mitzi were redheads, they made a striking couple and were a well-known sight sauntering in Schwabing or strolling arm in arm down Ludwigstraße to the Old Town. She taught him colloquial Austro-Bavarian, including swear words, and generally took him out of himself. Although she was a garrulous extrovert, she had a sensitive side. She knew he harboured a deep sadness and did not pry too much.

Geordie read the *Münchner Neueste Nachrichten* and other more liberal and left-wing newspapers and was concerned about the steady growth of Nazi influence. One day he rescued an injured Reichsbanner man, hiding him inside the restaurant to save him from another beating by Nazi Stormtroopers. Geordie sat the man down, patched up his cuts and bruises and gave him several shots of Schnapps. He had hated the Nazis since Elisabeth's murder, and he would have voted for the Social Democrats had he been a German citizen. This became the cause of countless arguments with Mitzi. She was not particularly political when they first met, but she took more notice of politics as German society became increasingly polarised. Perhaps as a further act of rebellion against her conservative rural background – and certainly out of genuine horror at the advances of Hitlerism – she started to vote for the candidates of the KPD, the Communist Party, and even to attend their meetings. She was Red Mitzi in more than one sense, Geordie teased. One day, she saw a caricature of Hitler that he had dashed off for his amusement. With a few pencil strokes, he had captured the vicious creature's essence. 'Can I borrow this?' she asked, and Geordie nodded his approval. A few days later, the drawing appeared on a KPD poster plastered around the city and it was rumoured that the Stormtroopers had put a price on the artist's head. Geordie declined Mitzi's suggestion that he could become a regular contributor to *Die Rote Fahne*, the Communist newspaper. He put the original drawing on his sideboard and forgot about it.

Geordie, however, was not leading an entirely virtuous life. He had bribed workers at the Munich abattoirs and the Viktualienmarkt to provide the restaurant with cheap but high-quality meat, fruit and vegetables, cheese and smallgoods, and other ingredients, and this meant that he and Seidl were making substantial profits.

When Adolf Hitler became Chancellor of the Republic on January 30, 1933, Mitzi and Geordie had a blazing row. It was a matter of common sense, he insisted, that the Social Democrats and Communists should make common cause against the Nazis. Mitzi parroted the Comintern line that the Social Democrats were 'social fascists' and that the Nazis' rule would be short-lived before the Communists seized power.

'It's always "Comrade Stalin said this", or "Comrade Thälmann believes that" with you,' Geordie taunted. 'Why not think for yourself? Besides,' he continued, 'Stalin has the blood of countless innocents on his hands.'

At this, Mitzi flew out of the room in a rage, and he did not see her for several days. He had to admit, though, that the Social Democrats were no more inclined to form a united front than their Communist rivals and seemed to think that the legal system and the political machinery of the Weimar Republic could block the brown terror.

Munich, 1933–34

When she re-surfaced from an epic sulk, Mitzi called Geordie a 'social fascist', but she didn't seem too serious about it. His fears about Hitler and the disastrous failures of the left proved correct. As every school history student knows, the Nazis seized power and turned Germany by degrees into a totalitarian state. The anti-fascist united front Geordie had advocated came into being – albeit too late and in the regime's concentration camps. He worried himself sick about Mitzi. She was outspoken on stage at Das Nackte Ei and although he hoped that reason would prevail and the Nazis would retreat from their worst excesses, he was filled with a sense of doom.

After the rigged March elections, the Nazis abandoned all restraint. Drunk with success and booze, brown-clad thugs paraded everywhere, bawling the Horst Wessel Lied and bashing anyone who failed to return their Hitler salutes or who looked Jewish or was a real or imagined Kommi or Sozi. Hundreds, perhaps thousands of Müncheners were rounded up and incarcerated in rudimentary prisons, where they were subjected to every indignity and abuse. Still, Geordie imagined that if he kept his head down, he could live a private life. He did, however, take the precaution of transferring his savings to a Swiss bank.

One evening, the New Order crashed into Die Goldene Gans when a bunch of Brownshirts swaggered into the restaurant and demanded service. Already half cut and rowdy, they proposed endless toasts to their Führer, slapped the waitresses on their bottoms and made lewd suggestions. From the kitchen, Geordie watched the proceedings with dismay. He recognised many of the revellers from newspaper photographs: including the coarse fatheaded former trench fighter Ernst Röhm, the baby-faced psychopath Edmund Heines, and the boozy August Schneidhuber, the newly appointed Munich police chief. They became increasingly boisterous, guzzled fine wines and mugs of beer indiscriminately and gobbled plates of food like drunken hyenas. The other customers had discreetly left. Röhm swayed to his feet and recited a dirty ditty, licking his fat chops lasciviously. A vaguely familiar Brownshirt got up and led a rendition of the Horst Wessel Lied – the anthem glorifying a Nazi pimp killed by Communists. Schneidhuber proposed a toast to 'good bürgerlich German cooking' and demanded that the chef present himself to the assembly. An ironic cheer went up as Geordie entered the dining room. Edmund Heines demanded to know if he'd blacked his face with boot polish and they found this extraordinarily funny.

Geordie suddenly recalled with a chill who the SA man was that he had been racking his brains to place. Ten years older now and thicker around the waist, it was the frog-faced Josef Grohé, promoted to Gauleiter of Aachen and Cologne, and in Munich to attend celebrations of some sort or the other. Grohé peered drunkenly at Geordie and a gloating leer spread over his face. He mounted the polished table unsteadily in his jackboots and screamed for silence. When the din had abated, he pointed a fat finger at Geordie and denounced him as an anti-fascist Englishman who had caused trouble for the Nazis back in Cologne. His friends started to throw food and smash crockery, working themselves up into a righteous rage. One of them had found Geordie's fiddle and was producing excruciating noises. They forced old Freddie Vogelwaid to crawl round the floor on his hands and knees braying like a donkey. Geordie was appalled. When one of them jumped on Freddie's back and rode him up and down the room, he exploded with rage. He seized the roughrider by the scruff and threw him onto the floor. The lout lay there, shocked, and his friends rushed to belabour Geordie. He managed to land a few decent punches, including a powerful right cross to Röhm's sweaty mug, but there were too many of them. His chef's hat flew off and he fell back towards the kitchen, where he collapsed under the rain of blows. Then Grohé rushed up and kicked him around the floor until he lost consciousness. After urinating on the floor and smashing the cuckoo clock, the mob moved on to some serious drinking at the Bürgerbräukeller, the Stormtroopers' favourite watering hole.

Mitzi found Geordie lying battered and unconscious when she arrived from the Naked Egg. The waitresses had fled, and old Freddie was sitting on the floor sobbing hopelessly. Fearing that the Nazis would return, she telephoned for help and some of her friends whisked Geordie off by car to a private clinic in the Grünwald Forest. Geordie regained consciousness but felt like someone had poured acid into his brain, and every corner of his body was aching. He looked round fearfully but saw only Mitzi and a tall fellow in a white coat – or rather several of him, coming in and out of focus. Mitzi was crying and stroking his hand.

'I am Doctor Löwy,' said the man in the white coat. 'You are safe here for the moment.' Geordie tried to speak but a stab of pain erupted in his jaw. 'I'm afraid we had to wire you up because your jaw is broken,' Löwy explained. 'You also have a broken arm, several broken ribs, severe bruising, and concussion. I have given you painkillers and it is best that you lie quietly. Don't try to speak.' The doctor was also worried that the beating may have caused internal injuries.

Geordie indicated that he wanted a mirror. 'Haddaway, pet!' he winced, lapsing into Tyneside dialect as he peered into the mirror Mitzi held up before his face, which was a mass of purple bruises, his eyes puffy slits and his mouth swollen to several times its normal size. Making a supreme effort, he managed to whisper in English 'Bloody Nazis … smashing up the restaurant … The fucking Bullingdon Club has nothing on these goons.'

Mitzi and Löwy shook their heads and shrugged. After an hour or so, Mitzi kissed his good hand, his face being too sore to touch. She promised to return the next day. Christian Seidl came to see him next, worrying that Mitzi had turned her nightclub act into an anti-Nazi demonstration. She had raised her arm in a clenched fist salute and shouted '*Freiheit!*' – Freedom! The evening had descended into a brawl, and she was lucky not to be arrested. Geordie went to sleep then and when he awoke Mitzi was back. He begged her to be careful, mumbling through his injured jaw, and she made a half-hearted promise not to antagonise the Nazis.

Over the next few weeks, his injuries gradually healed, although he had a persistent ringing in his ears and aches that would not go away. He worried about where he would go when he was better, but Doctor Löwy said it would not be a problem. Geordie remembered, too, that he had transferred the bulk of his savings into a Swiss bank in Zürich. He knew that he was a marked man, so he also decided to sign over his share of the restaurant to Christian and Freddie. Christian, good friend that he was, brought two suitcases filled with Geordie's important possessions and arranged to cover his medical expenses. He also brought some very unwelcome news. The police and SA had searched the Goldene Gans restaurant and although Christian had convinced them that he was apolitical, they had found the savage caricature of Hitler on the sideboard where Geordie had left it, and his 'crime' was compounded by some Communist leaflets Mitzi had absent-mindedly left in a bag next to the bed. If the Stormtroopers found him, he could expect a sojourn in the new concentration camp at Dachau – if he survived that long. When Christian left, Geordie wondered if they would ever see each other again, but Mitzi had already agreed to meet him at the Bar au Lac Hotel in Zürich.

Late the next night, Doctor Löwy's driver – a silent family retainer called Hans – drove Geordie many miles south along dark back lanes before parking the car in a barn and leading him on foot over a narrow mountain track into Austria. There, as dawn was breaking over the soaring alpine peaks, Hans introduced him to an ancient farmer – evidently a family member or old friend – and bade him good luck and farewell. The farmer gave Geordie breakfast – for which he refused payment – and drove him by horse and cart into Innsbruck. There, Geordie bought a train ticket for Zürich, where he went to the hotel to wait for Mitzi and savour the fresh air of freedom.

Munich, 1934

Several days passed. Then a week, and Geordie began to get very worried. Not even strolls along the lakeside, with his injuries healing, could lift his spirits. When a month had crawled by, he risked a telephone call to Dr Löwy in Munich to see if he knew anything. A coarse female voice told him that 'the fucking Jew doctor's gone and good riddance'. The clinic had been 'Aryanised' she said and hung up with a shouted 'Heil Hitler'. After that, he didn't dare to ring Christian Seidl lest the line was tapped, and he feared that Mitzi had been arrested.

Shortly afterwards, Geordie took the train to Innsbruck and set off with a rucksack on his back over the mountain paths back to Bavaria, avoiding border checkpoints. A pair of black-rimmed spectacles with clear lenses and a fedora pulled low over his ears went some way towards disguising his identity. His slow train trundled into Munich without him facing any problems from the conductor, but it was not so easy in the city. There were Brownshirts everywhere, and he had to duck into shops and laneways to avoid them. His skin colour would draw them to him instantly. By the time he got to Schwabing, he was sweating from the heat and nervous tension. The Golden Goose was boarded up and there was no sign of Christian or the other staff. He walked on, intending to question Mitzi's neighbours, but when he asked a woman coming out of her apartment block if she had seen her, the woman shook her head and scurried off. Mitzi's flat had been sealed up, BY ORDER OF THE MUNICH POLICE. Another woman snapped 'I dunno where the Kommi whore is and good riddance to her', so Geordie skulked off through the back streets and the English Gardens towards the central station.

On the way there, he espied a familiar bulky red-headed man coming out of an hotel, nestled in a phalanx of German policemen and Stormtroopers. A banner above the entrance informed the public that an international police conference entitled 'Scientific Detection in the Third Reich' was underway. Verte took a double take at Geordie and pointed him out gleefully to August Schneidhuber, the Nazi police chief who had joined him at the door. Schneidhuber's face twisted in a savage leer; he perhaps remembered Geordie from the night he and his friends had wrecked the Goldene Gans and recalled there was a warrant out for his arrest. He crooked a finger at Geordie while Verte stood by, with an ironically raised eyebrow, smoking a cigarette.

Bugger that, thought Geordie. He fled round the nearest corner and was soon picking his way between the provision stalls in the Viktualienmarkt. A harsh voice called on him to stop and a hand brushed his collar. Geordie feinted to the left and then dashed off in the other direction, knocking over a fruit stall in his haste. His closest pursuer skidded on a bunch of bananas and pitched face first on the flagstones. An enormous red-faced stallholder had seized a straw broom and was belabouring the Stormtrooper with it. 'Bloody hooligan,' she squawked, bringing the broom down smartly on his backside, 'I don't care if you're Adolf himself, you can't go wrecking a decent body's business!' Police whistles sounded and the market erupted into an uproar, but no one attempted to stop the little brown man who was sprinting between the stalls like Jesse Owens. When Geordie rounded another corner, an elderly Ford lorry pulled up with a squeal of brakes and the driver gestured urgently for him to get up in the cab. Geordie leapt aboard and the truck lurched away.

'Name's Willi,' said the driver, a young blond blue-eyed man who stood out as the epitome of the Aryan ideal among the swarthy Bavarians. He was no Nazi, however. 'Saw them bastards after you,' he said in his thick Bavarian accent. 'Only too happy to help.' With that, he piloted the lorry expertly through the city's southern suburbs, checking in the rear vision from time to time to see if they were being followed. They seemed to have shaken off any pursuers, so Willi relaxed, and they lit up cigarettes.

'I hate them,' said Willi. 'My dad is, or should I say was, a Social Democrat city councillor. They came barging in one night and carted him off to Dachau.'

'Dachau? Isn't that a town?'

'Yes, it is. But the bastards have built a concentration camp there. It's a horrible place.' Willi smoked quietly for a while and then changed the subject. 'I'm headed out to Bad Tölz.' He jerked his thumb back to the truck's tray. 'Load of expensive building materials, probably for some Nazi bigwig's new house being built with taxpayers' money. Anyway, I'll be able to get you out of the city.'

He slowed at a bridge over the River Isar, close to the Munich zoo in Thalkirchen.

Just then, they heard a volley of shots from somewhere up the river, then the sound of distant shouting. Willi accelerated just as more shots rang out. 'They've got some poor bastard,' he sighed. 'Let's hope he took some of them with him.'

All over Germany the Brownshirts were out hunting; arresting beating, torturing, raping, and murdering, untrammelled by law. They had commandeered disused factories and offices as makeshift prisons and camps, and nobody had any power to stop them. Geordie found himself praying that Mitzi had not fallen into their clutches.

That morning, Sturmtruppführer Fritz Noagl had been rudely awoken with yet another godawful hangover, for he and his cronies had been boozing until the early hours before returning to the barracks to torment their prisoners. 'Get up, you drunken swine!' an aristocratic voice had shouted. Shit! thought Noagl, it was Sturmbannführer Alois von Pranckh auf Hochstadt; he of the vast estates at Rosenheim and Neuschwanstein. Noagl stood, attempting feebly to straighten his shit-brown uniform, hoping to mollify the red-faced officer who was roaring obscenities at him.

'Get your men and follow me,' yelled Hochstadt. 'We've cornered some Red bitches out near the zoo.'

Noagl licked his fat lips. Now they were cooking with gas. He quite forgot his hangover and was soon rousing his men from their drunken slumbers. They fell in, formed a raggedy line, and slung their rifles over their shoulders. The Sturmbannführer pranced about before them, his uniform neatly pressed and his belt and boots gleaming to a high gloss that would satisfy even the most fastidious Prussian martinet. Hochstadt had been too young for the Great War, but he had devoted himself to rooting out those he believed had betrayed Germany. He marched his men – *Links, Rechts!* – through the Thalkirchen streets, his head held high, fingering the long-barrelled Mauser pistol his father had brought back from the war.

Their quarry – two young women – were hiding in a disused woodcutter's hut in the Grünwald, the forest in the Isar River valley south of the city. The young blonde woman was carrying a rucksack and was wearing hiking boots. She'd feared the Nazis would come for her and so had prepared for her escape. With her long golden hair, she looked nothing like the Nazi stereotype of a Jew, but the old bat of a *Portierfrau* in her apartment block had given the Nazis a good description. She was both a Jew and a Communist and could expect no mercy from the brutes. Her companion had dyed her flaming red hair black. This disguise did not work, because a sly-boots neighbour had informed the Stormtroopers of the change.

The two women had managed to kindle a fire in the hut just as night was falling and ate some bread and cheese, along with the chocolate they had grabbed when they fled. Their plan was to keep to the paths and back roads and slip over the border into Austria. Luckily it wasn't cold, so they were able to settle down for a reasonably comfortable night, disturbed only by the roaring of big cats from the nearby zoo. They found themselves wondering out loud what they would do if the Stormtroopers captured them. Part of them couldn't believe that the reports of beatings, rapes and executions were true – surely Germany was a civilised country? – but little voices at the back of their minds said the opposite.

'Well, dear,' the blonde woman sighed. 'The bastards will never take me alive.' She opened her rucksack and brought out her father's long-barrelled service pistol. 'My father brought it back from the war, and here is my uncle's revolver; captured from the British at Ypres. My dad showed me how to use them on the firing range.'

Her friend was – or had been – a farm girl. She'd never handled a pistol before, but she was familiar with the shotguns and small-bore rifles her father kept on the farm. She was quick on the uptake too and listened carefully as the other girl explained how to use the pistol. After that, they'd huddled together and fallen fast asleep, thankfully without dreams of the nightmare that had befallen Germany. They hadn't seen the old man watching them from his allotment.

When they awoke with daylight streaming through the cracks in the walls, they shared the last of the chocolate and washed their faces in a rain barrel. The plan was to hug the riverbank south to Bad Tölz and try to sneak aboard a southbound train to Lenggries near the

Austrian border. Many of the railwaymen were Sozis, and besides they couldn't think of a better plan. They had just pulled the door closed behind them when they heard male voices and caught a glimpse of brown uniforms moving towards them through the trees. Worse, they also heard the deep-throated bark of a big police dog: even if they managed to sneak away through the forest, the dog would track them. They pushed their way through the bushes towards the riverbank and crouched behind a fallen log. The blonde girl handed the revolver to her friend and checked that the magazine of her Mauser pistol was full. She smiled sadly and they trained their weapons in the direction of the Brownshirts.

The dark-haired girl willed her hands to stop shaking and when Truppführer Noagl swaggered into the clearing, accompanied by a police dog handler and his huge beast straining at the leash, she squeezed the trigger of the pistol as instructed. The savage recoil surprised her, but she had aimed well, and the bullet caught Noagl in the middle of the chest, killing him instantly. The dog handler turned and fled, pulling his dog behind him, but Sturmbannführer Hochstadt signalled to his men to drop and squeezed off several shots in the direction of the women, who were hidden in the trees. The blonde girl, meanwhile, had trained her long-barrelled Mauser on the kneeling form of the Sturmbannführer. The training she had put in with her father on the firing range paid off. She fired and the bullet blew the top off the Nazi's head. In reply, a fusillade of rifle shots whistled through the leaves above her head. The next volley was lower and smacked into the trunk of the fallen tree. She picked off another Nazi and smiled grimly when she saw the Brownshirts retreating. But it wouldn't last. They had won the first round, but they knew the thugs would be back with another officer to tell them what to do.

They took flight through the undergrowth, which tore at their clothing, and although their breaths came in great, panting gasps they kept going. A gravelled footpath appeared, and they followed it upstream until they emerged at a hydro dam and powerhouse. Maybe they would escape after all! The railway line, they knew, was just up the steep slope of the river valley and the closest station was not far away. From behind them came the barking of several dogs – the Nazis were back on their trail, and they would be thirsting for revenge. The slope got steeper, but they kept going until they reached the railway line, which gleamed silver in the sunlight. Just up ahead was a railway fettler's hut, painted green and with hearts carved into the wooden door and window shutters – a homely piece of Bavarian kitsch that mocked their predicament. 'Out!' they shouted at the old railwayman, whom they had surprised as he was brewing a pot of coffee on a spirit stove. They pointed along the railway line in the opposite direction from which they had come. 'Get going, now!' His mouth was a huge O, and his brown eyes were wide with shock, but he scurried off up the line just as the first Brownshirt's kepi-clad head emerged over the side of the slope down to the river. They fired but missed and the head withdrew. After that, the Nazis kept their heads down, but they could hear them crashing around and swearing in the trees. It was only a matter of time before some of them worked their way around the back of the hut.

The amplified voice, when it came, was startlingly loud. One of the Nazis was bellowing through a bullhorn. '*Rote Schlampen*' – Red bitches! he taunted, his accent broad Bavarian. 'There's nowhere for you to go. Best you turn yourselves in.' He kept up his threats, clearly enjoying himself and causing great amusement for his fellows. 'We're decent German soldiers,' he shouted, sounding anything but. 'Give yourselves up and we'll treat you right!'

In reply, they fired into the trees, causing an outburst of swearing and renewed threats through the bullhorn. They caught sight just then of a couple of Brownshirts working their way towards them further along the railway line. When they got closer, they fired again and one of the SA men dropped onto the railway ballast, writhing and groaning. By now, however, others had crawled closer on their bellies and were firing their rifles at the hut. There was nothing for it. They had almost run out of ammunition and the Nazis were closing in. The two women embraced, shouted '*Freiheit* – Freedom!' and raised their arms in clenched fist salutes before pushing their gun barrels into their mouths. They died just before the first Stormtroopers burst through the door with its carved hearts and flowers, cursing that their prey had escaped.

Willi dropped Geordie off at a village on the railway line, safely out of the city. They shook hands, and Willi took off in a cloud of exhaust. Geordie was soon on another D-Zug trundling up to the Alps. He disembarked at the little hamlet of Lenggries, keeping an eye open for Stormtroopers. He spent the night hunched up against the alpine chill by a glacial stream and set off at dawn along a mountain track towards the border. A farmer picked him up in an old jalopy near the Austrian village of Achenkirch and dropped him off in Jenbach, where he bought a ticket for a fast train back to Zürich, all the while wondering at his luck in evading James Verte and the Nazi police.

Someone had left a copy of the *Völkischer Beobachter* in the waiting room, and the screaming headline caught his eye: RED TERROR GANG WIPED OUT NEAR MUNICH ZOO! The Nazi journalist wove a lurid tale of how 'heroic Stormtroopers' had been ambushed by a much larger gang of well-armed Communists in the Grünwald. Several SA men – including Sturmbannführer Alois von Pranckh auf Hochstadt – had made the supreme sacrifice for Germany, but some twenty Reds had perished including the Jewess Elfriede Rubenstein and the so-called singer and dancer Mitzi Maierhofer aka Ilona Esterházy, who had dyed her flaming red hair black. There was a photo of Mitzi, looking sultry, apparently taken when she was onstage at the Naked Egg, to spice up the piece. Geordie wondered about the shots he had heard the previous day. The Grünwald – it was the same area his train had just travelled through. He saw nothing of the splendid alpine scenery as the train steamed towards Switzerland. He hurled the paper aside when he saw the page two article extolling Commander James Verte of the London Met, who had been a keynote speaker at the international police conference in Munich. SS Reichsführer Heinrich Himmler gloated that the gathering showed the world that Germany was in good hands, governed by civilised men. When the train pulled into the Zürich station, the conductor had to remind Geordie to disembark.

Heartsick, Geordie tossed a coin. If it came down heads, he would return to England. His letters to Annie had been returned unopened and the cheques he had sent were never cashed, but perhaps he could still make amends? It was tails. Geordie would put Old Europe behind him. He was mourning poor, brave, gallant Mitzi and he hoped she hadn't suffered at the hands of the Nazis. Then again, it seemed that she had taken a few of the bastards with her, and he hoped they had suffered a bit of what they dished out to others. Mitzi had exasperated and delighted him by turns and although she'd made it clear she wasn't the marrying kind, he felt that she'd loved him in her way, and he had reciprocated the feeling. Perhaps one day he would be able to avenge her – and Elisabeth, who had also died at the Nazis' hands. In a mood of black despair, he wondered if he were perhaps jinxed; that he was fated to bring misfortune to the women he met. After moping for a few days, he withdrew his savings from the Swiss bank and a Cook's travel agent arranged his fare to Genoa in Italy, to board SS *Rex*, a crack Italian liner bound for New York.

New York, 1934

Geordie had splashed out and booked a first-class cabin in what Cook's called 'the Riviera afloat' – a floating hotel designed along the lines of a trout to speed through the waves. The *Rex* crossed the Atlantic in just six and a half days. She was the showpiece of Fascist Italy, with portraits of Mussolini adorning the walls of the ship's public spaces. Geordie hated the sight of him but knew that the voyage would be brief. From the ship's deck, awestruck, he watched the towers of New York draw near. Here, humans had built on an altogether different scale to London, Paris, Munich and the other cities of the old world, fashioning steel and concrete into structures the size of small mountains with deep canyons between.

After clearing customs, Geordie took a taxi and booked into a small but select hotel in Greenwich Village; a district built on a more human scale. The desk clerk passed him his room key with a polite injunction to have a good stay. Geordie's considerable savings would allow him to play the gentleman of leisure indefinitely if he were judicious. He walked across the Brooklyn Bridge and up Fifth Avenue, gawking. He should have been enjoying himself, but there was a feeling of loss and emptiness within him – and a nagging guilt that he had escaped while his friends had to endure the Nazis, and Mitzi had died fighting them. At the back of everything, too, was the memory of Elisabeth, and he had never forgotten Annie and the child either. He wondered again if he jinxed every woman he came across. He found an Irish bar in the Village and drank deep, but the alcohol could not wash away the guilt. Winter was coming on and he still ached physically, too, from the beating by the Nazis. The days were long and empty; perhaps he should move on and maybe lose himself in the vast interior of America, but he was overcome with grief and inertia, and stayed on in the hotel, shunning human company and spending much of his time asleep.

Some weeks later, crouched gloomily over his breakfast eggs and coffee in the hotel dining room, he didn't see the young woman standing at his table. 'Hi,' she chirruped, breezily American. 'Would you mind if I sit here? All the other tables are taken.'

'Of course. Please do.'

She smiled her thanks and sat demurely. She was very pretty, he saw, with shoulder-length brown hair and a snub nose with freckles.

'I'm Glenys,' she said, proffering a slim hand and fixing him with guileless blue eyes.

'Geordie,' he replied, taking her hand. It was cool and soft. 'Geordie Stubbs.'

'Oh, a Scotchman,' she chirped. 'I'm part German, part Scotch myself.'

He laughed. 'Actually, I'm a Geordie, and my name is Geordie.'

She might not have heard, for she had turned to order coffee and toast from the waiter who was hovering nearby.

'Well Geordie Stubbs,' she said, turning back to the table. 'It's nice to meet you. Are you staying long in New York?'

Glenys, it turned out, was from Ohio. She was in town to shop at Macy's and take in the shows on Broadway. Had he seen *King Kong*? Her girlfriends said it was a hoot. Geordie had not. Maybe they could go together, she suggested, and he thought why not. He was lost in a strange and bewildering place, and she seemed nice. She didn't want to seem forward, she said, but her girlfriend had had to cancel the trip and now she was alone in New York. He assured her it was fine.

'Well, that's settled,' she said, pecking delicately at her toast and jam and sipping her coffee.

The film was ridiculous. A gigantic ape fell in love with a golden-haired girl and ended up swinging off the top of the Empire State Building, fighting off biplanes after dropping another girl to her death. Glenys, however, was wide-eyed – or pretended to be. Over martinis in a bar, she told him more about herself. Her full name was Glenys Seiberling and she lived in Akron, Ohio.

'Don't they make motorcar tyres there?' Geordie asked.

'Yes indeedy,' she said brightly. 'My family set up the Goodyear, you know. We're not with them anymore, but we still run Seiberling Tire & Rubber and it's a big concern.'

They parted back at the hotel – she to her room and he to his. He liked her well enough, but thought her a little gauche and naïve – or was that just the way American girls were?

He agreed to meet her for lunch the next day. 'Just a little place with coffee and bagels,' she explained. 'You like bagels? Never had one? My oh my! You'll love them. Bagels with lox and cream cheese.'

He did like the bagels. 'They're Jewish?' he asked, wiping his mouth and dropping the napkin onto his plate.

She hadn't heard about Hitler's hatred of Jews. The world stopped at Long Island, it seemed.

A few nights later, when he was dropping off to sleep, she knocked softly on his door. She couldn't sleep, she said, and did he mind if she sat with him a while? It was raining outside, and lightning lit up the walls of the huge red brick apartment building behind the hotel. She was afraid of thunderstorms, she said. He found himself telling her about Mitzi. About how he had fled from Munich over the mountains.

She gave him a searching look and took his hand. You poor baby, she said. She came close to be kissed and her tongue slid warm and wet into his mouth. Accidental lovers, he thought – she over on a visit from Ohio and he wandering the earth to this city on the edge of the New World.

She showed him Coney Island. She took him to the viewing platform atop the Empire State Building and they laughed at the daft memory of the giant ape swatting the airplanes like flies. They made love in the evenings and lay in a tangle of sheets until the dawn and the snow came. She had to return to Akron soon and he wondered if he would see her again when she did. He was more than a bit in love with her, he decided. One day shortly before she was due to return to Akron, she sat in the hotel lobby to read some letters.

'This one's from my brother Robert,' she said brightly. 'He's an engineering student in Chicago.'

She slit open the envelope and tugged out the letter eagerly. The smile left her pretty face after she started reading. She pressed her hand to her mouth.

'What's wrong?'

She held out the letter. 'You can read it,' she sighed, wiping her eyes. 'He'll be the death of me, he really will.'

The handwriting was squiggly and erratic – loops and whorls that spun out over the page like a spider's web: 'Dear Sis, I'm in a bit of a jam again. I know what I promised last time, but you know how it is. Anyway, to cut a long story short, I owe Bugs Moran big time and he's mobbed up.'

Glenys had screwed up her handkerchief and was biting on it. 'Daddy told him it was the end last time. Robert isn't a bad young man, but he's weak. The horses are an addiction with him. He spends his allowance then goes to loan sharks for more. Oh, it's a sure thing, he says, and sometimes it is but then he'll go and put his winnings on another horse.'

Geordie knew all about it. 'How much does he owe?' he asked. She named a sum and he whistled.

'I can raise the money, I guess, but it'll take a bit of juggling.'

'Look,' said Geordie. 'I can loan you the money. I've had some problems with the horses myself.'

She protested. No. She could not possibly accept, but he insisted, and she reluctantly agreed, but only on condition that he come to stay with her family back in Akron.

Geordie saw her off at Penn Station. 'I'll miss you,' she said after kissing him and climbing up into her coach. She hated goodbyes, she said, and besides, they would be seeing each other in a week's time, so he didn't wait round until the train departed. He walked back all the way from Midtown to the hotel, wondering exactly what their relationship was. He liked her, that was sure, but he wasn't sure that he really knew her. Part of her she kept secret. Not like Mitzi and certainly not like Elisabeth. And Annie, asked the small voice at the back of his mind, what about Annie? He thrust the thought away. He would travel to Akron and things would turn out as they would. Go West, Young Man!

Akron, Ohio, 1934

A week later, Geordie arrived at Akron's bustling Union Station. There was a strange smell in the air, but he was looking forward to meeting Glenys and he scarcely noticed it. Akron was in the North – or the Midwest as the Americans called the region – but many of the people milling around spoke with Southern, 'cracker' accents, and some of them scowled at him. The sky was dark though it was only early afternoon, and the smell was stronger – a sickly pong that reminded him of dirty nappies. Still, he jostled for room on the station platform and scanned the concourse for Glenys. There was no sign of her, but he recalled the adage that it was a woman's prerogative to be late and settled down in the trackside diner with a coffee and a copy of the local paper, the *Beacon-Journal*. When he had finished his coffee, he folded up the paper and went outside to see if Glenys had arrived. She hadn't, so he fished around in his pockets for the address she had given him. Stan Hywet Hall – a vast Tudor revival mansion, she had said.

He hailed a taxi and asked the driver if he knew the place. 'Sure do,' the man drawled in a Southern accent. 'You cain't miss it and ever-body knows it. It sets out on North Portage, pretty as a pitcher. British ain't ya. I don't normally pick up nigras, but you could durn near pass as white.' He meant it as a compliment, Geordie realised. By the time they pulled up outside the Hall, if Geordie read between the lines, he had a reasonably comprehensive picture of local affairs.

'You have a nice day now,' said the driver, pocketing the tip with a wide smile and tipping his cap. No doubt he would regale his wife with the story of how he had picked up a British 'high yalla'.

Geordie had expected a mansion, but not one as beautiful as this. Stan Hywet Hall sat in large, meticulously manicured gardens, a masterpiece of American Tudor, and not just a tacky replica with bogus beams and bullseye windowpanes. The property was surrounded by a high wall and access passed by a gatehouse out of which an elderly retainer came wiping his mouth with a napkin.

'He'p you, boy?' the gatekeeper asked, stifling a belch. 'Just finishing my dinner,' he said by way of apology. He, like many others in this northern city, had a Southern accent.

'Yes please,' Geordie replied, keeping his temper at the thoughtless insult under control. 'My name is Stubbs, Mister George Stubbs. Miss Glenys is expecting me.'

The man eyed him curiously. 'If you'll wait here *Mister* Stubbs, I'll phone through to the Hall and see what they know. Shouldn't be a minute.' He turned and waddled back inside, but not before giving Geordie another long stare. Geordie could hear him talking on the phone but couldn't make out the words. A few minutes passed and the man came back out, shaking his head.

'I'm sorry,' he said, not looking it. 'There is nobody of that name here.'

Geordie tried again. 'Her name is Glenys Seiberling. We met in New York, and she invited me to visit.'

The man shook his head again. 'It's the Seiberling house, but nobody knows no Glenys here.'

The truth was dawning on Geordie. The bloody woman should

have been in Hollywood! He had thought of himself as worldly-wise, but he was as gullible as the next man. The letter from 'Robert' was postmarked Akron, but he hadn't noticed the date. It was an organised scam. She'd lain in wait at the posh hotel for victims and he had been easy meat – sitting depressed and lonely, a solitary man as much out of place in New York as a Papuan tribesman with a penis gourd in Trafalgar Square. She had cleaned him out, as the Americans would say. He sighed, bade the man good day, and turned on his heel, hefting his two suitcases. It crossed his mind to say something to the man, but nobody likes to be gulled and even more so doesn't want anyone else to know it. The man watched Geordie with a faint smile as he walked slowly down the Portage Path through the snow, wondering what to do next.

Geordie spent the night in a flophouse on East Market Street, the cheaper end of town; lucky to find it after landladies slammed the door in his black face. The walls were paper-thin, and he could hear his neighbours snoring and tossing and turning in their sleep. He discovered that the beds were rented out by the shift or for brief liaisons when a grimy face peered round the door and said he had to 'git up and let a body git some shuteye'. Geordie washed his face at a grubby sink and went out to face the day – only it wasn't much of a day for a time that was supposed to be day. A dense smoky pall hung over the street, depositing smuts on every available horizontal surface, and turning the snow black. The nappy stink was stronger than ever when greasy sleet began to leak from the low-hanging clouds. Farther along East Market, he could see a line of factory chimneys belching smoke and make out some colossal brick buildings, over which an enormous electric sign spelled out the name GOODYEAR, together with the Winged Foot symbol. The blowsy old landlady had ignored him when he enquired about breakfast, but he found a cheap workingman's diner where he drank a coffee and ate some pie. Both tasted like rubber, but he was hungry and thirsty enough for anything. He pulled the newspaper he had bought the previous day from his pocket and scanned it. He needed a job and fast. Among the ads for machinists, drivers, and beauticians there was an ad for a chef. 'Must be capable of preparing fine cuisine,' it read, and asked suitably qualified people to ring a local telephone number. It was early, so Geordie hung round the diner, sipping a second coffee before using the pay phone in the lobby.

A woman picked up after two rings. 'Yairs?' she said. 'Missus Fewersteen's office. Margaret Atwater speaking.' The woman directed him to come out to Hareth Manor on West Exchange Street for an interview. The short-order cook looked up from flipping hamburgers when Geordie asked him where it was. 'Long ways, brother,' said the cook, wiping sweat from his brow with the back of his hand. 'Streetcars'll take y'all day with the union trouble. Best ketch a cab.'

Half an hour later a cab deposited him outside Hareth Manor; perhaps the most peculiar building he had ever seen. 'Here we are,' said the driver wistfully. 'Hareth Manor. Sure is grand.'

It certainly was grand – bigger than Stan Hywet and Lambton Hall put together with maybe half of Château Mazengarbe thrown in – but it was a veritable hodgepodge of styles tacked together by someone with inexhaustible supplies of money and the taste of a parvenu. It reared three and sometimes four storeys above street level with art deco bits, Tudor bits, classical Greek bits, a Cape Cod bit, and some other bits that followed no style but were models of unsurpassable ugliness. Geordie recalled H.L. Mencken's quip that 'Nobody ever went broke underestimating the taste of the American public.' Out the back, however, a beautiful American colonial style bungalow lurked in the shrubbery, embarrassed by the company.

A coal-black butler took Geordie's coat and directed him up a flight of marble stairs that swept up to Miss Atwater's office. The woman was busy on the telephone, so she motioned for Geordie to sit on what he imagined was a genuine Louis XV chair. He studied her covertly, taking in the carefully permed blue-rinse hair, the prim, rather plain face, and the thick glasses with huge white frames that magnified her bright blue eyes. She had a rectangular badge on her right breast that read MISS MARGARET ATWATER, and Geordie puzzled why such an adornment was necessary. Her desk, he noticed, had a similar sign on it. As the call appeared to be lasting longer than she had anticipated, Miss Atwater pushed a piece of paper across the desk, and waved a pen in his direction.

'Personal details,' she mouthed before speaking rapidly to whoever was on the other end of the phone line. Geordie complied and Atwater, evidently what the Americans would call a 'multitasker', scanned what he had written while attending to the phone caller. He had added copies of testimonials and she glanced through these and clipped them to the sheet.

'Some people!' she sighed when the call ended. 'Now, Mr Stubbs, I have your details here and will just take them through to Mrs Fewersteen.' She didn't seem fazed by his colour, unlike so many of the people he had met in the city. She stood and walked over to an internal door. 'Come!' said a peremptory female voice when she knocked. After a few minutes, Miss Atwater emerged and announced, 'Mrs Fewersteen will see you now.'

Geordie was puzzled by the strange name but he followed the secretary through the door. Mrs Fewersteen was sitting behind an enormous mahogany desk in a vast, thickly carpeted room. Behind her, a floor-to-ceiling plate glass window gave views east towards Akron's Downtown and the smokestacks beyond. It must have cost easily a thousand dollars. A sign on the desk identified this middle-aged bottle blonde as MRS ETHEL FEUERSTEIN. (Ah! Geordie had worked it out – Fewersteen was the American corruption of the German name Feuerstein.) She did not rise to greet Geordie but studied him through ornate spectacles like an owl perched on a twig observing a mouse. She did not hoot, however, but purred like a cat with an American accent.

'Please sit, Mr George Stubbs,' she ordered, waving him to another Louis XV chair. 'Now, I have looked over your particulars and I have to say, I like what I see.'

He thanked her and allowed her to continue.

'You're a Scotchman,' she said. 'A high yalla Scotchman. We've just been to Scotland looking for stuff for the house. My husband is quite the collector and Scotland's full of things we just had to have.'

'Err, I'm actually a Geordie,' ventured Geordie, but she ploughed on regardless, bemoaning the exorbitant costs of shipping 'stuff' from Scotland and burbling about the Loch Ness monster, haggis, Robbie Burns, and pipers at Edinburgh Castle. After a while, she tapered off, apparently remembering what Geordie was doing there. She named a salary, which seemed more than reasonable, and said that he would live in the colonial-style bungalow rent-free, sharing it with Harris, the butler.

'Because of my husband's business, we often entertain, and we like to impress. Oh, we have all kinds of VIPs here, I can tell you. Folks from the government. Captains of industry. The cream of the cream of our Republic. Why, just last week we had Henry Ford to dinner. He and my husband are best friends, I can tell you. Henry said to me, "Why, Mrs Fewersteen, there are few men in the business world who can match your Hal."' She rambled on like this for some time, not thinking it necessary to ask Geordie if he was happy with the offer. She eventually dismissed him, and as he left the room, she picked up the phone and chirped, 'Well, Hal, we've hired us a black Scotchman to do the cooking. If he's any good, we'll keep him on.'

Miss Atwater made him sign a contract and took him for a tour of the house. Inside was as much a juxtaposition of styles as outside and was crammed with Mrs Feuerstein's 'finds' from across the oceans. These included tiger skin rugs, stags' heads with huge antlers, Carrara marble fireplaces, enormous Flemish oil paintings in gilt frames depicting nymphs cavorting with satyrs or the angelic baby Jesus looking adoringly at his mother, stuffed birds and animals, and even something that looked like first cousin to the King James II bedpan from Mansion House in York. There were lines of leather-bound books, antique pistols and arquebuses, and a curious brass device that looked suspiciously like a thumbscrew. One large room was a veritable museum of American colonial expansion, with a covered wagon crammed under its lofty ceiling, cart axles, rusty iron pumps, bullwhips, slave neck halters and more. A photograph given prominent place showed a dour-looking family group perched on and around a horse-drawn wagon. 'These fine folks,' Miss Atwater explained in reverential tones, 'are Mr Fewersteen's ancestors, when they had just arrived at their farm after emigrating from Alsace.' In yet another large chamber sat a huge machine that Miss Atwater said vaguely had something to do with rubber and which still smelled like it. Another room featured dozens of bottles of various sizes, shapes, and colours. They were patent medicines, and included Daffy's Elixir, Mug-Wump Specific for Venereal Diseases, William Radam's Microbe Killer, and Bonnore's Electro Magnetic Bathing Fluid, which claimed to cure and prevent a whole gamut of illnesses, including cholera, rheumatism, measles, scarlet fever, hip disease, 'female complaints', necrosis and chronic abscesses, mercurial eruptions, and epilepsy. Pride of place was given to a large bottle of Clark Stanley's Snake Oil Liniment, next to which was a photograph of a beaming Hal Feuerstein shaking hands with the cowboy-hatted Clark Stanley, 'the Rattlesnake King', who had invented the concoction. A large portrait of an older-looking Feuerstein hung on the back wall, with the inscription 'Hard Work and Thrift Made America Great'. Smaller print informed the reader that Mr Feuerstein had amassed the seeding capital for his industrial empire by hawking such elixirs round farmhouse doors in rural Ohio. Phineas T. Barnum's motto 'there's a sucker born every day' sprang to mind, but Geordie kept the thought to himself. Hucksterism had made Feuerstein rich as much as the hard effort and frugality he extolled.

Geordie's brain reeled from the overload, but to his pleasant surprise the huge kitchen was a cook's delight, with a gleaming array of expensive American gadgets. Miss Atwater whispered that some big New York establishment had poached Geordie's predecessor, and that his sudden departure had rather left them in the lurch.

'Well, what do you think?' she said when they concluded the tour. Geordie replied that it was rather big. 'Yes indeedy,' she laughed. 'Mr Fewersteen likes to say that something drives him to keep adding rooms. Then once he's built 'em, he has to find things to put in 'em!'

Geordie smiled politely and they arranged for him to fetch his luggage and move in that afternoon. Late that evening, sitting on his bed and rummaging through his luggage, he thanked whatever deity there might be for his good luck in finding the position with these people, odd though they were. A strong wind had blown up outside. The snow was sparkling in the streetlights – clean out here away from the pollution – and the wind had blown away the smog. Down in the valley, a giant sign spelled FEUERSTEIN TIRE & RUBBER in coloured lights on one of the huge factories.

Akron, 1935–37

Geordie lived an uneventful life in Akron. He found the butler, Norman Harris, amiable, so they got along just fine, although they were separated by the proverbial common language. Geordie was saving up with the aim of leasing an upmarket restaurant in New York City, so he didn't go out or spend much. He bought a mail order fiddle from Sears Roebuck and was moderately satisfied by the quality. He had given up trying to explain that he was a Geordie not a Scot, and how he came to be 'coloured', and fantasised that he would call the restaurant 'The Scotchman' and decorate it in tartan wallpaper with claymores and sporrans and pictures of men in kilts shooting grouse. His quarters were comfortable even if they overlooked the hideous 120-room monstrosity that was Hareth Manor. Some builders had arrived and were adding yet another extension and he wondered if Hal Feuerstein had in mind a replica of the half-timbered abode of his Alsatian ancestors – Strasbourg on the Cuyahoga. On the positive side, the mansion was just far enough out of central Akron to escape much of the rubber mills' stench.

The city both fascinated and appalled him. It was still reeling from the Great Crash and the atmosphere of gloom was palpable. The mills were working short time and men begged in the streets or sold apples in a desperate bid to retain some dignity. He was shocked to read in the *Beacon* about 'dance-a-thons' at Summit Lake Park, where couples danced non-stop for days for prize money. Unemployed men jumped to their deaths off the North Hill Viaduct, but business revived to some extent after Geordie had been there for a couple of years. The mills took on additional labour and the streets came alive again, but the people were jittery, fearing the upturn would not last.

Initially, the pint-sized mogul Hal Feuerstein treated Geordie only as 'hired help'; he was 'coloured', and a foreigner, after all. Even smaller than Geordie, he strutted about wearing bow ties and straw boaters, his fat little legs clad in tweed trousers held up by thick braces above his two-tone shoes. The clownish appearance was deceptive, though: he was a veritable human dynamo; an apostle of the American business gospel. Geordie endured his uplifting breakfast homilies. 'Hard work and thrift,' he said, waving a forkful of egg or grits, 'is what made America great. Never forget what our great President Calvin Coolidge said: "The chief business of America is business." That is true wisdom, my friend.' It was tiresome but the money was good. The little man was ignorant of just about everything except business, but for him ignorance was a virtue: 'I didn't get to where I am by reading books,' he boasted. Indeed, barring the Holy Bible, some eugenics tracts, and *Popular Mechanics*–type magazines there was not a book in sight in the intellectual wilderness that was Hareth Manor. The leather-bound 'books' in the 'study' were fakes; the pages burned or pulped, and the covers pasted on boards and sold by the yard. Geordie learned Feuerstein's biography off by heart. After attending business school in his teenage years – 'all that a man needs in the way of education' – Hal Feuerstein spent several years hawking patent medicines and gewgaws door-to-door. Unperturbed by hostile housewives, ornery dogs, and the grim Ohio winters, he squirrelled away his money to set up in rubber manufacturing in a modest way. He chose well, for America had entered the motorcar boom and he rose from Ohio farm boy and snake oil salesman to American tycoon with the ear of presidents. A fanatical workaholic, Feuerstein left early each morning after dining on eggs, toast and coffee, the preparation of which taxed Geordie not one bit.

Feuerstein's wife and grown-up children were also undemanding – 'Nothing fancy, just good plain American food, if you please!' – but as the mogul frequently entertained his business associates and potential clients at home in Hareth Manor, Geordie was often busy creating more imaginative fare. Alas, the opportunity came at a cost. Ethel Feuerstein would come into the kitchen and announce the arrival of the great and good of American industry and often show him off to the guests: 'Our marvellous black Scotchman who worked with Escofferino in London.' He felt like one of the trophies stuffed into the mansion. The guests included the Detroit motorcar magnate Henry Ford, local rubber moguls, local politicians, and an ageing Episcopalian minister called George Atwater, who haunted the table like a gigantic, black-coated bat and ate as much as an army of locusts. Their table talk (which Geordie could not help overhearing) often revolved around family matters, for these people socialised and took their holidays together.

When the men retired to Hal's Native American–themed 'den' to take their coffee and cigars, their talk took a more serious turn, and Geordie was often invited to listen. Sitting four-square within a vast tepee purchased cheaply or stolen from dispossessed Plains Indians, they held forth on market trends, stocks & shares, and speculated about recovery from the Depression. Invariably, too, they would turn to politics, puffing on their cheroots, and whingeing about something called 'Section 7(a) of the National Recovery Act', which they regarded as the root of all industrial evil.

'This Roosevelt fella is no better than a goddamned Communist!'

Ford roared, banging the arm of his chair. 'He's under the thumb of International Jewry!'

The man would get along fine with the Munich Brownshirts, thought Geordie, but he smiled like many generations of African American folks had done to give the racialist philistines the impression that they loved and respected them.

'Goddamned un-American!' Feuerstein agreed.

The Goodyear man – a well-scrubbed, more urbane New Englander – would nod gravely. 'The Act allows Red agitators to lead honest American workingmen astray. Hal and I are in absolute agreement that no matter what Roosevelt and that Wagner guy say, we will keep the open shop in Akron.' This was said in a tone of almost religious reverence, and Geordie had to fight hard not to snort.

The Reverend Atwater broke in here and they listened deferentially to the speech they had heard many times before. 'We saw the I Won't Work Reds off back in 1913 when they were ruining the city with their strikes,' he said fiercely. 'There are just as many staunch men today willing to crack heads and I dare say that we will have to muscle up again soon.'

Geordie was appalled that the codger had half the tureen of château-briand down his front. He had also consumed several large tumblers of bourbon and was reaching for more.

The moguls agreed that foreigners were the cause of much of the unrest, and that 'Eye-talians', 'Bohunks', 'Polacks', 'Nigras', and 'god-damn Jews' were a threat to the purity of the Anglo-Saxon race and American ideals. (Geordie bit his tongue at this, realising that he had become invisible.) Many of them were double-dyed Commies, too, they agreed, nodding their heads sagely.

The city was on the verge of large-scale industrial strife. Geordie read about it in the *Beacon-Journal* and listened to some very angry workingmen in bars, who swore that they would no longer take what the rubber companies dished out to them. Geordie kept his mouth firmly shut, not that the Feuersteins or their guests asked for his opinion. He sympathised with the union but felt there was little he could do to help.

Hal and Ethel had several grown-up sons and daughters and they, like their parents, seemed to think that Geordie was a piece of equipment put there for their convenience. Hal Junior resembled his father, worked diligently in the family business and shared his views. The daughters were spoilt creatures who spent their time socialising, tripping off to New York, and 'wintering' at the family compound in Florida. One of them sent her dirty clothes to Paris for laundering. There was, perhaps inevitably, a black sheep in this family. Bobby Feuerstein was a quiet, skinny young man who had dropped out of a law degree at Princeton a few years before. His father and brother treated him with open contempt and his sisters regarded him with haughty disdain. His mother doted on him, but she worried that he would never 'make something of himself'. Bobby went to bed late and slept late, partly to avoid his father and brother and partly because it suited his lifestyle.

One warm spring day Geordie was sitting on the back porch, reading the *Akron Times-Press* and smoking a cigarette, when Bobby Feuerstein sidled from the main house. 'You'd be the Scotchman,' he observed. 'Me, I'm Robert Fewersteen: Bobby Fewersteen – not quite master of all I survey!' He extended a hand theatrically towards the factories smoking in the valley below.

'Why aye, but I'm not a Scotchman.'

'Does it matter? Everyone calls you that.'

He had taken a silver hip flask from his pocket, taken a swig, and offered it to Geordie, who declined: 'Too early, bonny lad.'

'Never too early for me.' Bobby laughed, taking a greedy suck like a calf at the udder. He put the flask away and regarded Geordie through narrowed blue eyes. 'Tell me, Scotchman, what do you make of our beautiful Hareth Manor?'

Fearing a trap, Geordie was non-committal. 'It's big … err … impressive,' he ventured.

Bobby whinnied like a horse. 'Goddamned ugly if you ask me! My father has as much taste as a gorilla! He's a philistine who "knows the price of everything and the value of nothing!"'

Geordie was impressed that a 'Fewersteen' could quote Oscar Wilde. Bobby confided that he hated business and that his father was a tyrant who had insisted that he study law and become 'an asset to the firm'. 'My choice would be literature – or even to be a pilot – but Daddy would not allow it. Now, I am cooling my heels while he decides what to do with me. My much-esteemed big brother would put me in the tire-curing pits.'

Geordie had heard that the curing pits were one of the worst jobs in the rubber mills. He ventured that perhaps Hal Junior was exaggerating, but Bobby insisted that his brother hated him. 'Anyway,' he added, striking a theatrical pose. '"Here I stand, I can do no other. God help me. Amen."' Geordie stared, so he explained, 'Martin Luther. Speech at the Diet of Worms, 1521. I liked history at school, but my father agrees with his fascist buddy Henry Ford that it's bunk. Incidentally, speaking of diets, thanks for the marvels you cook up in your kitchen, Scotchman.'

Bobby spent much of his time in bars and betting shops, where he wore old clothes. The idea was that he would not stand out as a rich man's son, but he chuckled that he stood out as a rich man's son wearing old clothes. After their first meeting, he often came to chat with Geordie and when he suggested that they take a trip to the Ohio Derby, Geordie agreed, albeit after a mental tussle with himself. The memory of the bother the nags had caused him back on Tyneside was still strong in his mind. The Derby was held each year at the Jack Thistledown Racino at North Randall on the outskirts of Cleveland. Geordie had imagined that they would travel down to Cleveland by the electric streetcar and then take a taxi out to the racecourse, but

Bobby had other ideas. He drew up outside Hareth Manor in a splendid custard-coloured Isotto Fraschini convertible roadster. 'Well, what do you think?' he asked as they drove off in the fine Italian machine. Geordie wondered where it had come from, but Bobby waved his hand airily, and laughed that his family had a stable of automobiles and would never know it was gone. Geordie felt uneasy but went along for the ride. Bobby was an appalling driver and when they motored down the North Portage Path towards the Cuyahoga Valley, Geordie worried that he would lose control of the car. They passed Stan Hywet Hall and Geordie wondered what had happened to the bogus 'Glenys Seiberling'. Bobby stalled several times driving up out of the valley but somehow, they made it to North Randall without mishap.

Geordie had not set foot on a racecourse for some years, and he felt uneasy as they parked the car and entered the grounds. The horses had almost been his downfall before, and he feared they could be again. The smells were reminiscent of High Gosforth racecourse on Tyneside. Akron was the birthplace of Alcoholics Anonymous and he wondered if there was an equivalent for gamblers, as once he succumbed to the lure of the betting slip, he didn't know if he would be able to stop. He brushed aside his fears and walked up to the nearest bookmaker. He had studied the form guides and placed a hefty bet on a Kentucky outsider called Arctic Fox, ignoring the favourite, the local horse Euclid Star. The horses thundered round the track with Arctic Fox trailing, but when they entered the final straight, Arctic Fox put on an impressive surge of speed and passed the finishing post ahead of the favourite. Most of the punters ripped up their betting receipts in disgust, but Geordie made a packet. His luck held and he left the grounds substantially richer than when he had arrived. The small voice at the back of his head was now inaudible.

When they got back to the car, Geordie realised that Bobby was very drunk. Bobby dangled the keys to him and insisted that he drive home. Geordie had sometimes driven Corporal Belcher's army lorry in Flanders years before but had not been behind the wheel since. He managed to switch on the ignition, put the car into gear and was terrified when it leapt forward with an almost lion-like roar. He kangaroo-hopped out onto the main road with Bobby giggling like a maniac. Bobby fell into a stupor and somehow Geordie managed to pilot the powerful car to its destination, despite almost driving off the road into Cuyahoga River near Boston Mills. He pulled up outside Hareth Manor bathed in sweat and attempted without success to wake his snoring friend. In the end, he had to leave the car out in the street and half carry Bobby to the house. Old Hal wanted to fire him on the spot, but Ethel persuaded him that Geordie had looked after their son and that the car was unscathed by the outing. After this, Geordie insisted that he and Bobby should confine their betting to bookmakers' shops. He also suggested that Bobby might like to go easy on the booze, but the young man confessed that he could not stop or moderate his intake.

By 1936, downtown Akron was humming. Thirsty men flooded into the bars and speakeasies at every shift change in the giant mills, and the stores along Main Street did a roaring trade. There were cinemas and vaudeville with dancing girls atop stages under glittering ceilings depicting the heavens. Bobby Feuerstein introduced Geordie to many of these establishments, and to a circle of bohemian friends who shared his tastes for alcohol and fast cars. One evening, he took Geordie up a fire escape at the rear of an old warehouse off Mill Street and introduced him to a fat man known as Whiskey Dick, the 'captain' of an illicit poker club. Dick – whose mother knew him as Liborio Percoco – made a good living from various dubious activities. He had arrived at Ellis Island from Bari in 1911, shoeless and without any English, and still spoke with an Italian accent. He informed Geordie proudly that they had let him out of the penitentiary early for his part in cutting down on pilferage from the prison kitchens and reforming the menus. Geordie became a regular at the card sessions and the two men became friendly, in large part because of Whiskey Dick's Calabrian respect for Geordie's profession. He introduced him to his wife, who passed on a few of the family's recipes, including *zeppole*, cannelloni with veal, eggplant *alla Calabrese*, and *tonno alla Alessandra*. Dick and his wife also appreciated Geordie's fiddle playing and urged him to learn some Italian folk tunes.

It was an open secret that Whiskey Dick was on good terms with the Akron underworld. After all, his business depended on it. Geordie encountered some of these characters at the poker games. 'Doncha worry, *amico mio*,' said Whiskey Dick. 'Whatever my friends do outside dis room, we plays an honest game inside, an' dere's no guns at table.' Honest or not, between the poker games and the betting shops, Geordie never managed to save any money, and his New York restaurant plans receded faster than Hal Feuerstein's hairline.

Lambton Hall, 1936

Annie Ross's heart brimmed with love and pride for her beautiful and clever daughter, but she baulked at attending Mary's graduation ceremony at Newcastle University. 'Howay, lass, I canna,' she wailed. 'I'm nobbut a pitman's daughter. I've no business with all them professors and doctors!' Mary was quietly insistent. 'Well, Mammy, if you won't go, neither will I.' They went into the high street and bought Annie a new dress, a pretty hat, new shoes, and a pair of white gloves. 'You'll do, Mam,' said Mary. 'A tuck at the back of the dress here and ye'll turn heads.'

It was the spring of 1936, and the earth was waking up from its winter sleep. There were new buds on the leafless trees in the grounds of Lambton Hall. Sir Cuthbert was long in his grave and his wastrel son was in some faraway place. Annie and Mary were the mistresses of the hall, which the old judge had bequeathed them in his will. The day of the graduation came, and Annie sat in the auditorium with tears in her eyes. The woman sitting next to her smiled reassuringly. 'It's quite alright, dear,' she said, her accent placing her as a resident of leafy Jesmond Dene. 'You can be proud of your daughter, and she's won the prize.'

Mary had graduated with honours in medicine and surgery from the university's prestigious medical school. She could have entered any practice of her choice, but she was her great-grandfather Tim's leftie girl, and it was sad that he had not lived to see her achievements. The idea of prescribing pills to Tory dowagers and rich hypochondriacs did not appeal to this medical Narodnik. Together with her classmate Alice Dixon, she rented a surgery down by the river in one of the poorest neighbourhoods on Tyneside. The bleak Depression ground on. They made little money, but she had a fine place to live, a doting mother to care for her needs, and room enough for Alice at Lambton Hall. Yet Mary was restless. One day, she entrusted the practice to Alice and took the train south to Dover, to catch a fast ferry to France. Her mother's heart was broken, but Mary reckoned she was made of strong stuff and would recover. Like many of the best of her generation, Mary had Spain in her heart.

Akron, Ohio, 1937–38

Meanwhile, Akron had become an industrial war zone. There were daily reports of sit-down strikes in the rubber mills and Hal Feuerstein ranted at the 'un-American activities' of the Congress of Industrial Organizations unions. He had floodlit his factories, fortified them with barbed wire and machine guns, and brought in Pinkerton armed 'detectives'. Their boss, Colonel Joseph J. Johnston, became a fixture at dinners in the Manor and vied with old man Atwater in bloodthirsty rhetoric. 'Time to crack skulls,' agreed the old cleric, spilling gravy down his shirtfront and scraping it off with his knife. 'Back in 1913 we had them on the run! Yes indeedy!' Old Hal bragged about providing Franco with cheap tyres on credit. Geordie was disgusted to hear Henry Ford propose a toast to Franco, Hitler, and Mussolini as 'the saviours of Christian civilisation' and watch the gathering spring to their feet and raise their glasses.

One evening, when Geordie was at the poker school, the workers at Feuerstein Tire & Rubber walked off the job and set up picket lines right around the sprawling perimeter of the plant. Whiskey Dick confided that he had heard on the grapevine that Old Hal was planning to bribe Wilmer Tate, the firebrand leader of the industrial union movement in the city, using a local gangster as a go-between. If so, he was wasting his time, for Geordie had heard that Tate was a 'sea-green incorruptible' who lived and breathed union. Geordie admired Tate – a fellow redhead – and after enduring Feuerstein's table talk, he wondered what he could do to help the union.

Soon after the strike began, Hal Feuerstein left town on a business trip to Florida, taking Ethel with him – a pointed hint that he would not negotiate with the strikers. Bobby took the opportunity to rummage around in his father's study, where he found a thick chequebook. He took this to Geordie, along with a sample of Hal's handwriting. Geordie couldn't believe his luck: here was a wonderful chance to undermine the little autocrat. He forged Old Hal's signature on several cheques, which Bobby cashed in banks around Akron, Canton, and Cleveland. They sent the money anonymously to the union strike fund and to Republican Aid for Spain, keeping back small amounts for themselves. Geordie had also been fiddling with the safe in Hal's study and one evening it sprang open. Tucked inside was a thick buff envelope stuffed with cash. Old Hal was due back the following day, so Geordie took the money to Bobby's room and the two conspirators counted it out into piles. It came to $15,000 – a small fortune at the time. Again, they kept some for themselves, but Bobby agreed to mail $3750 to the union and $7,500 to Republican Aid for Spain in a series of batches. It was time for Geordie to leave.

Old Hal exploded with rage when he discovered the thefts and forged cheques. He was in a foul mood already because the union was on the verge of victory. He called the police and as Geordie had disappeared, there was little doubt about who was responsible. The next day, the city's paperboys shouted the headlines on Main Street: READ ALL ABOUT IT! FEWERSTEEN HEIST! POLICE HUNT SCOTCHMAN!

The police combed the city and raided the card school and Geordie's other haunts, but he was hunkered down thirty-five miles away in a Cleveland apartment Bobby Feuerstein rented under an assumed name for his trysts with his male lovers. After a week or so, having dyed his flaming red locks black and wearing plain glass spectacles, Geordie ventured out into the Cleveland streets, dressed like your average Ohio 'coloured' man. He had cultivated a passable American drawl too. The Feuerstein heist had been relegated to the inside pages and although the Cleveland police had been enlisted, the manhunt had been scaled back.

One day, Bobby arrived at the apartment bearing bags of groceries and bottles of beer. His father, he chortled, was still in a vile humour and spent much of his time on the telephone urging the police chief and sheriff to continue the hunt for 'that goddamn Scotch nigger' and complaining to his wife that she should never have hired him. They had a good laugh about that, but the next time Bobby came, he was looking grim. 'Whiskey Dick told me that there is a contract out on you with the Mayfield Road Mob. You don't want to mess with them guys. It would be best if you left town.'

The Mayfield Mob were fearsome gangsters based in Cleveland's Little Italy. They had a finger in every criminal pie in town and the capo, Freddie Polizzi, was suspected of dozens of murders. The problem was, where could Geordie go? He dared not venture outside, and he was terrified that every passer-by he saw through the lace curtains might be either a Mafia assassin or an undercover cop. Bobby, however, came the next day with some good news. A sailor friend had informed him that the cook of a British freighter had jumped ship at the Cleveland docks and the crew were refusing to sail without a replacement.

SS *Loch Fyne* was a rusty old tramp steamer that had seen better days, but Geordie was anxious to depart, and Captain Angus Macleod was desperate for a cook. Geordie bade farewell to Bobby, the crew cast off the mooring lines, and the ship nosed out onto the shallow waters of Lake Erie. She picked up cargo in Toronto and unloaded it in Montreal, then juddered along at nine knots down the wide

St Lawrence River to St Johns in Newfoundland. By this time, the newspapers had lost interest in 'the Scotchman'. Nevertheless, he was relieved when the coast receded over the horizon and the *Loch Fyne* steamed out into the wide Atlantic, bound for Scotland. The Scottish crew were ecstatic about the standard of the meals Geordie prepared and delighted by his Celtic fiddle playing. When they reached Greenock, Captain Macleod begged him to stay on, but he declined politely, and took the train south to London. He had half believed the crew when they joked that they would have to shanghai him to keep up the ship's culinary standards and provide them with music.

~ 41 ~

London, 1938–39

Geordie stood under the great pillars at Euston Station, contemplating the driving rain. It was late 1938. Winter had set in, and London seemed as gloomy as when he had left fifteen years earlier. Shortly afterwards, he sat in the Lord John Russell pub, sipping a pint of Bass, and looking out at rainswept Marchmont Street. He checked for the American dollars sewn into the lining of his jacket and pondered his next move. Someone had left a copy of *The Times* on the bar, and he scanned the headlines. He flipped through the pages for the To Let columns, but a small page five article caught his eye. US POLICE STILL HUNT ELUSIVE SCOTCHMAN it read, with a fuzzy photo of himself clad in chef's attire. Geordie looked around furtively, but the photo was too blurry to identify him, and the pretty young Welsh barmaid was keen for a chat with a fellow redhead. Her name was Becky Griffiths and she had arrived the week before from the Rhondda Valley. She looked eighteen if she was a day and had worked in a Pontypridd draper's shop before leaving for London. Geordie told her his name was George Fraser-Smith and that he had just resigned his officer's commission.

'Ooh, very posh for a Geordie,' she chirruped. 'Was it exciting work?'

'Oh aye, lass, it was.' He touched the side of his nose. 'I can't say too much but it was liaison work in France.'

'Ooh, fancy that.'

What a cad, he thought, lying to this lovely, naïve creature, but the newspaper article had put him on his guard. He'd have to steer the conversation into safer waters. He ordered another beer and when she brought it, he asked if she knew of anyone offering lodgings nearby.

'Well, look you, isn't it a coincidence because there's a flat just become vacant where I live near Russell Square. If you'll wait, I can take you there.'

Later, when she had finished her shift, she walked with him to her apartment block, sharing her umbrella and chattering brightly about her family back in Wales and how she would like to bring her cat but didn't know how it would take to the move and how would she get it here. She was seventeen and a half, she said with smile and a toss of her red hair. He felt even more of a bounder for lying to this innocent child and worried that people would take advantage of her. She rattled on and he found himself wondering about his own child.

'Here we are, now,' Becky said proudly, pointing to a dark brick, rain-washed block that rose five or six storeys above the street. An ornate but slightly dilapidated sign identified it as The Coniston. The caretaker was a middle-aged Cockney geezer called Wally Beecroft, who chained smoked Woodbines, squinting his intelligent, currant eyes. He had hobbled out of his little office, smelling strongly of gin, but Becky greeted him cheerfully and gushed that her friend Mr Fraser-Smith was looking for accommodation and she thought maybe the top flat, look you, would be just the job. Beecroft doted on the girl and readily agreed to help.

'Yes, guvnor,' he coughed, spraying cigarette ash down a tattered cardigan that had fed generations of moths. 'Number twenty-six 'as jist become vacant, so if you'd like to come wiv me, I'll do the honours.'

He led 'Fraser-Smith' and Becky to an astonishingly ancient lift, which creaked slowly to the top floor. The corridor smelled of boiled cabbage and mildewed carpet, but Number 26 was a surprisingly pleasant furnished bedsit with a view over the trees of Russell Square towards the British Museum. Geordie took it on the spot and agreed to the reasonable rent Beecroft was asking. Beecroft left, counting the month's rent Geordie had paid in advance, and Becky took her leave, saying that she hoped to see him again.

Geordie holed up all winter in The Coniston, looking out at the dripping trees and the sullen sky as he prepared simple meals on his one-ring gas stove, wrote in his diary, or practised Italian folk tunes on his fiddle. Marchmont Street was full of bookshops, and he bought a plentiful supply of reading matter. He particularly liked the melancholy novels of Patrick Hamilton, which held up a mirror to the times. He found an antique dealer and jeweller who was happy to exchange dollars for sterling without asking awkward questions. He often spent time with Becky in Lyons teahouses and grew fond of the naïvely honest soul. She was a reminder that human beings could be decent even in dark times. The Zeitgeist of the time disturbed and depressed him. London had almost, but not quite, limped out of the Depression. The streets were cold and unfriendly, and an air of foreboding hung over everything. War was on the horizon, and he once saw a squad of Blackshirts emerging from the Russell Square tube station. They eyed him with naked hostility, muttering about blacks and Jews thinking they owned the place. One of them looked familiar but Geordie couldn't place him. They were a shabby lot and Geordie recalled the English fascist leader's former opinion of his new legionary mates as 'black-shirted buffoons making a cheap imitation of ice cream sellers.' Reading Patrick Hamilton's novels did little to lift Geordie's spirits, although he was fond of the books.

A shocking incident down at the Thames Embankment did nothing to improve his mood. An old man had mounted the parapet above the river and was ranting and brandishing a Bible in one claw-like hand. The voice sounded familiar and as Geordie drew closer, he realised its owner was Miserable Mick Armstrong, the former mechanics' charge-hand who had once harangued indifferent shoppers in the Gateshead High Street and bullied him at work. The man had also helped drive him out of the York carriage shops. Geordie was concerned, despite this, because he saw that the stones of the embankment wall were greasy with rain and Mick's leather-soled shoes had little if any grip. Mick had just opened his Bible at Zechariah and bawled out 'Ho, ho, come forth, and flee from the land of the north!' when he slipped. Geordie rushed to save him, but he toppled backwards down into the raging ebb tide. Several people had stopped to listen to the ranter, but their amusement turned to horror. They hung over the parapet, pointing and shouting, but none dared jump in to save him; indeed, it would have been suicidal to do so. A nurse dashed off to call the police but even if the elderly bobby who arrived puffing and panting could have done anything, he was too late. 'He'll wash up down Wapping way,' said the policeman, wiping the perspiration from the rim of his helmet. 'We'll send out the police launch but …' The black waters had closed over Mick's head, and it was as if he had never existed. Geordie felt an aching existential sadness. He had disliked the man intensely, yet somehow, he found himself grieving for him.

One misty spring evening, after the sun had almost shown its face over the grey city, he went for a stroll through the park, intending to take his tea in a Lyons teashop and perhaps find a cinema showing *Mr Smith Goes to Washington*. A couple of prostitutes accosted him, but he declined politely albeit with a broad wink and kept walking. There was a sudden high-pitched scream and he rushed to investigate. A little man wearing a brown overcoat had pushed a red-haired young woman up against the park railings and was groping at her clothing. It was Becky Griffiths, and her assailant was one of the Blackshirts Geordie had seen near the tube station. He sprinted across the grass, but the man saw him coming and ran off into the fog. Becky was unharmed.

Becky couldn't understand why the man had attacked her. Geordie had to explain gently that there were some very nasty people in London. She should avoid the park after dark, he advised. Being so honest herself, she thought everyone else was the same. Becky stared at him with her huge blue eyes as it dawned on her what the man had wanted. Geordie fretted that he could not always be there to protect her. The assault had given her such a fright, however, that she decided to return to Wales – a decision that relieved him no end, though he knew he would miss her. She was too innocent for this world, but she should be safe with her parents in the close-knit Rhondda community. He saw her off at Paddington Station. She would write, she promised, and tell him how she was getting on.

The thought of family and parents revived the old feelings of guilt, and Becky's departure left a hole in Geordie's life. He decided to travel back up to Tyneside to locate Annie and the child – his child – although he or she would be in their mid-twenties by now and would be a stranger to him.

It was twenty-odd years since Geordie had last seen High Fell. Everything was strange and familiar at the same time. It seemed grubbier and smaller. The north wind blew soot and cinders down the narrow streets and a greasy rain dripped from the low clouds. It smelled of smoke and gas. Machinery clattered endlessly over at the pit and a locomotive whistle echoed mournfully off the fellside. Walking through High Fell, he recognised a few faces, but the young people were total strangers; presumably they had been babies or had not even been born when he left. He had plucked up the courage to visit Annie's fierce mother, but the man who opened the door said he'd never heard of her. Geordie wondered what his so-called father, Jeremiah, would know, so he trudged through the lanes to Lambton Hall, despite his promise never to bother him again. The Hall, however, was deserted. Nobody answered when he drew down the great bellpull and hammered on the big front door, which caused a parliament of rooks to flutter skyward. A simple young man clipping hedges stared at him with his mouth hanging open and could or would not tell him anything except that the judge was 'lang deid'. Geordie gave up when it began to get dark, left a scribbled note under the front door of the gatehouse and went back to Felling. When he inquired in the local pubs about his uncle Anthony, drinkers just shrugged. One old man said he remembered him, but when Geordie pressed him for details it seemed that the codger had confused him with someone else.

London, 1939

Geordie returned to The Coniston in London under a cloud of depression. He realised that he had too much time on his hands, so he took himself off around the local restaurants and soon secured a position at Parnell's, a fine dining establishment near Russell Square. 'Eventually anybody who's anybody ends up here,' boasted Albert Parnell, the fat proprietor, as he showed Geordie around. After he sampled the results of Geordie's skills, Albert gave him a free hand, and the other staff treated him with deference. Geordie was going through a 'Burgundy' period, and he turned out a delicious array of that region's specialties, many of them prepared with the region's famous red wines. There was *boeuf Bourguignon, coq-au-vin, escargots de Bourgogne, jambon persillé, pôchouse, oeufs en meurette,* and much more besides, served with crisp baguettes and creamy butter and washed down with fine French wines. For dessert, Geordie produced wondrous puddings featuring cassis and blackberries when he could get hold of them. Parnell's takings soared and when he offered to take Geordie on as a partner, Geordie promised to think about it.

Meanwhile, Geordie's gambling itch had returned, and demanded to be scratched. He had read about the London racecourses and his American loot was burning a hole in his pocket. Early one Saturday, he awoke early and took the train from Waterloo Station out to Ascot and walked the mile or so to the racecourse. He'd studied the form guides in the Lord John Russell and reckoned he could make a killing by backing a rank Irish outsider called Donegal Blue. The horse won by a good length and a half. He was hooked. Everything about the races conspired to lure him back – the smell of horseflesh, liniment, beer, and fish and chips with salt and vinegar; and the hissing of the crowd as their favourites failed to win or their excited cheers as they won. His winning streak continued at Epsom, and he pocketed a small fortune at Alexandra Park. Thus fortified, Geordie began to haunt Alexandra Park of a Monday evening.

One morning, he read in *The Times* that the northern industrialist Norman Barnes MP would be visiting London to open a state-of-the-art engineering factory in West Ham. Geordie sipped his coffee and pondered the report. This Barnes, the paper reported, had settled in a Lancashire mill town some years before and bought into a successful spinning mill and acquired a profitable real estate portfolio and a stack of gilt-edged shares. He had purchased a Gothic pile overlooking the town and married a young woman from an impoverished aristocratic family. After election to the town council, Barnes was elected as the borough's Tory MP. Geordie mused that the man's career proved Balzac's assertion that 'behind every great fortune is a great crime', for he had little doubt that Barnes, MP, was the same man who had defrauded him in York years before.

One warm Monday evening as Geordie walked towards the gates of the Alexandra Park racecourse, he recognised a fellow alighting from an Austin 'Flash Lot' taxi. 'Bastard,' muttered Geordie. Norman Barnes had been a stick-thin figure, but even though he'd piled on the weight and was dressed like a toff, he still had the mean horse-face and shrewd eyes that devoured everything in their sight. Geordie strode over and planted himself in his path.

'Here!' protested Barnes. 'Get out of my way, fellow!' He did a double take and muttered 'Don't I know you?' The voice was Yorkshire overlain with posh – bangers and mash masquerading as haute cuisine.

'Too bloody right you do,' shot back Geordie. 'You're the arsehole who disappeared with my money back in York. Remember – after the royal chamber pot incident.'

'On second thoughts,' huffed Barnes, 'I never set eyes on you before. Now, out of my way!'

'Bloody liar! You're the same Norman Barnes alright.'

Barnes was a bigger man than Geordie and he sneered in his face. 'Well, what of it, ye little black bastard? I'm not a man to be trifled with. Move or I'll knock you down.'

He went to shove Geordie out of the way, but Geordie was far too quick for him and jabbed him hard in the ribs. Infuriated, Barnes took a swing, but Geordie stepped aside and punched him in the solar plexus. Barnes doubled up in pain with his monocle dangling on his chest, spluttering about pressing charges for assault, his voice now broad Yorkshire.

A policeman was shoving his way through the crowd that had formed around the combatants. 'What's goin' on, sir?' he demanded of Barnes.

'This fellow … assaulted me,' Barnes wheezed. 'Old employee … Disgruntled … Name o' Stubbs … Passes himself off as Cyril Toward … Criminal …'

The policeman swivelled his head, but Geordie had vanished and was hurtling through the Haringey Woods as fast as his little legs would carry him. He arrived back at The Coniston in a lather of sweat and plumped down in his armchair to work out what to do. He'd been on the verge of taking up Albert Parnell's offer to buy into the business, but now he'd have to bugger off and hide. He'd have to give notice, but he dithered, not wanting to hurt Albert's feelings. Preparing the next evening's menu almost took his mind off his worry about the law, but had he seen the squat little American waddling down Great Scotland Yard, he would have left Parnell's employment there and then.

'I ain't got time to waste on the monkey!' snarled the dapper little Yank in spats, tapping the charge room counter with a stubby forefinger. 'I wanna see the organ grinder. Gottit?' The old desk sergeant started to protest but shut up when he took in the speaker's expensive suit and air of authority. He raised his eyebrows when the little man gave his name as Hal Feuerstein.

'Yes, *that* Fewersteen,' he confirmed. 'I believe our Embassy has been in touch.'

'One moment, sir,' fawned the sergeant. He lifted the telephone and spoke quietly before hanging up.

Commander James Verte strode into the vestibule, his hobnails clattering, with a strained smile on his bulldog jowls. His girth had expanded with age and his once red hair was sparse and shot through with white, but he still exuded power and menace. He held out a red paw in greeting and ushered Feuerstein along the corridor to his office with a view of chimney pots and the Clarence pub.

When they were settled, Verte rang to order tea, and invited the rubber magnate to state his business. He was not obsequious, Feuerstein noted with approval – this British Bulldog would get things done. The tea arrived and Feuerstein regarded it with apprehension. He preferred coffee, but he sipped the astringent brew and set aside his cup and saucer. He caught Verte's attention the moment he mentioned Geordie's name. 'Hmm, Geordie Stubbs you say? What has he done?'

'Well, Commander,' said Feuerstein. 'That goddamned nigger Scotchman stole a substantial sum of my money. I have reason to believe that he gave some of it to the Reds in Spain, and some to some goddamn strikers. He disappeared from my hometown – Akron, Ohio, that is – and slipped through the police dragnet. Rumour has it that he's back in Great Britain.' He took a sip of the tea, winced, and continued. 'He's a dangerous criminal, Mr Verte. I employed him in a position of trust, but he repaid me and my wife by breaking into our safe and forging cheques worth multiple thousands of dollars.'

'Go on,' Verte prompted, slurping his tea with relish, blue eyes glittering.

'I believe that the Scotchman hid in Cleveland and that he signed on as crew on a Limey ship. Anyways, Commander, he plumb vanished and I'm hoping that you can catch him.'

'Leave it to me, sir,' said Verte. 'I'm sorry for what happened and although I suspect you will never get your money back, you can rest assured that if Stubbs is in this country, we will find him, charge him, and gaol him.'

When he had ushered Feuerstein out of the building, Verte returned to his office and made a series of telephone calls. If that conniving little bastard was in England, he'd find him. After setting the investigation in train, the commander went home in what for him passed as a good mood. Grunting at his wife when she asked if roast fowl was okay for dinner, he climbed the stairs and locked himself in his study. Mugshots of the criminals he'd collared occupied most of the walls; among them the Tyneside gangster Ebenezer Richardson glowered, framed in a horrid triptych with the Gorringe twins, who had fed their victims to the Chollerford pigs. Richardson had died of peritonitis in Durham Gaol, and the Gorringes were safely banged up in the Broadmoor Asylum for the Criminally Insane. Yet, like an angler lamenting the fish that got away, Verte had tacked up photographs of the one villain he'd failed to convict: George Stubbs, the little Geordie with the wonky green eye, the thick red hair, and the insolent leering black face. Humph. Stubbs was older now, but he would recognise the Human Fly. The criminal had evaded a long stretch because someone had tampered with evidence. This time, Verte promised his young son Simon, Stubbs would be an old man before he emerged from prison.

When Verte consented to go down for dinner, he sat grimly at the table, answering his wife in monosyllables if at all, before shoving his plate to the side and declaring that he could not eat such muck. He took his hat and coat and went out to the pub, ignoring the woman who stood twisting her handkerchief in her hands and staring out of the kitchen window at the gathering gloom.

He arrived at the Yard with a hangover the next morning. 'Best leave him be,' said the old desk sergeant. 'Bugger's like a bear with a sore head.'

Just then, a ferrety little man entered the vestibule and said he wanted to speak with a detective. His accent was Geordie and when the front of his mac opened, the old sergeant saw he was wearing a black shirt. 'I've come aboot the reward, like,' said the ferret, when the sergeant asked him to state his business. 'I seen the Human Fly the other day at Russell Square.' A halitotic belch revealed rotten brown teeth.

'Take a seat, sir,' said the sergeant, recoiling. 'I'll get someone to see you.'

The fascist's information gelled with what James Verte had learned from the Tory MP Norman Barnes, who had arrived in high dudgeon a day or so earlier, demanding justice. Verte summoned the police sketch artist and very soon a poster with a fair likeness of Geordie Stubbs's features was circulating around the city's nicks.

Albert Parnell's boast that anybody who was anybody eventually came to his restaurant seemed to be the case. One evening, with the kitchen humming along, Geordie took himself out into the dining room as was his occasional wont, to check that the customers were enjoying their food. This wasn't just to stroke his ego, as some of the more discerning diners had on occasion made useful suggestions and although he prided himself that he was at the pinnacle of his profession, Geordie was not too arrogant to listen. He was listening with half an ear to an opinionated old dowager when he caught sight of a familiar-looking fellow enjoying some crème brûlée at a table under the potted palms in the window. It was Bobby Feuerstein, his good friend from his Akron days. Half-cut from an afternoon's boozing, Bobby threw his arms around Geordie, told him he loved him, and declared that he should have known he was the chef from the quality of the food. Geordie disentangled himself from the maudlin embrace and arranged to meet Bobby in the pub the following afternoon.

It was warm enough to sit outside when the two friends met and quaffed several pints of Bass, which was a cut above the 'bug's piss they call beer Stateside,' Bobby reckoned. 'I'm over here with the Old Man,' he continued, smacking his chops after a long pull on his ale. 'He's put his foot down and given me an ultimatum. Either I shape up in the British branch of the firm, or he'll ship me out without a cent. Bastard means it too.

'Anyway, it's a damn good job that I walked into that restaurant and met you, because the Old Man is still mad as hell about what happened.' Bobby giggled and insisted on buying another round before he continued.

'I shouldn't laugh,' he said when he returned with the pints. 'The old bastard went to the Limey police – what's that place? – yeah, Scotland Yard – and demanded to know if you had returned from the States and if so, what they proposed to do about you. He's got a lot of clout so if I were you, I'd make myself scarce because he's not going to rest until he gets revenge.'

Bobby had to travel out to Brentford with his father that day, so the two friends parted with regret and Geordie wandered off with a feeling of foreboding. The next day he noticed a man loitering across the road from the entrance to The Coniston and read in the *Daily*

Herald that the US Consul-General had raised the 'Scotchman' issue with the British authorities. He wondered if James Verte was still on the force and decided to go into hiding. He paid Wally Beecroft a couple of months' rent up front and Wally agreed to store his possessions. Wally didn't ask why he had to leave in such a hurry, but winked and said, 'Any friend of Miss Griffiths is a friend of mine and you're a real gent, Geordie.' The revelation that George Fraser-Smith was Geordie Stubbs hadn't fazed him and he promised to look after Geordie's fiddle 'like it's your Straddivarian.' The next morning Geordie left by the back entrance of the flats with two suitcases. He found a miserable little room over a butcher's shop in Whitechapel and hoped that the matter would blow over. He also took to pulling his cap down low over his red hair and turning up his coat collar. A pair of thick black spectacle frames and a bogus Indian accent completed a fair disguise.

London, 1939

Geordie had not forgotten the swindler, Norman Barnes. To add insult to injury, the bastard had set the police onto him at Alexandra Park. He'd fix him up, so he would. He'd check out Barnes's new engineering works, which he'd heard was built on waste ground near the main outfall sewer alignment at West Ham, just five stops up the District Line from Geordie's Whitechapel room. Reconnaissance from the sewer greenway established that the factory night-watchman's rounds were regular as clockwork and that he spent long periods sleeping or drinking beer in his hutch in the factory grounds. Geordie watched through the window as Barnes sat in the red brick office signing documents a secretary placed in front of him. There was a pile of builder's waste under the wall. It would ignite easily … but no, setting fire to the gaff might be satisfying but it would be too dangerous. Anyway, Barnes would claim on insurance … No, Geordie would use the old loaf to get even with the wazzock.

Geordie crept out along the greenway on a moonless night that promised rain. He had a rucksack on his shoulder and a set of lockpicks he had purchased from a shady Whitechapel trader. When he had ascertained that the watchman was asleep, he climbed the wire fence and was soon standing on the soft grass outside the factory offices. Apart from shunting noises from the rail yards and the rumble of distant factories, all was quiet. Geordie made short work of the lock on the front door and crept up the main flight of stairs. He'd masked the beam of his torch with blue cloth and played it on the doors he passed in the main corridor. There it was – a plate on a large wooden door announcing that this was the office of Norman Barnes, Esq., MP, Managing Director. The lock picks did their job again and soon he was sitting at Barnes's desk, rooting through stacks of documents with his gloved hands. His torch showed that Barnes's out tray contained a stack of signed letters waiting for the post. There were also some notes in Barnes's hand. Geordie helped himself to a few and pocketed a sheaf of unused sheets bearing the letterhead:

NORMAN BARNES & SONS, LONDON HEAVY ENGINEERING WORKS,

HEAD OFFICE, ABBEY LANE E15.

A fistful of embossed envelopes completed his haul. As a calling card, he dashed off a wicked caricature of the fat proprietor and left it on the desk next to a photograph of Mrs Barnes. She must have been after the ugly bugger's money, he snorted. Satisfied that he had left everything as he found it, bar the purloined stationery, Geordie retraced his steps and, save for a scare when the watchman lurched drunkenly from his hutch for a wee, he made it back to the greenway and then the Underground station without mishap. He had not lost the touch.

Back in his room above the butcher's shop, Geordie spent some time practising Barnes's handwriting before composing several letters on the letterhead paper he'd stolen from the factory offices. The first letter, addressed to the Prime Minister with a copy to the Tory Party chief whip in the House of Commons, announced that he, Norman Charles Barnes, was resigning forthwith as Member for his Lancashire constituency. He had had a religious epiphany, the letter explained. Wretched sinner that he was, he confessed that he had obtained his start-up capital by theft, fraud, and deception. He would atone by devoting his life to Jesus and would be giving away the lion's share of his wealth to charity. He apologised for the inconvenience to the Party, which he still felt stood for the Bulldog values that had made Great Britain the envy of the world. The second letter, to the editor of *The Times*, repeated the gist of the first. When he had finished, Geordie was satisfied that even a handwriting expert would not be able to tell that the letters were forgeries, and he had been careful not to leave his fingerprints on the paper. The next morning, he bought stamps in Dulwich and posted the letters from across the city in Notting Hill Gate and in case the Establishment killed the story, he also tipped off the pro-Labour *Daily Herald* and the Communist Party's *Daily Worker*.

Although *The Times* did not immediately report the story, Willie Gallacher, the Scottish Communist MP, used Question Time to quiz the Prime Minister on the rumour of Barnes's resignation and confession of criminality. Gallacher would not be deflected, and *The Times* reported the affair in an explosive front-page article that confirmed reports in the two left-wing papers. A tearful Norman Barnes denied that he had written the letters and the Prime Minister stonewalled. The Opposition demanded an expert examination of the letters. Two graphologists reported that the letters appeared to be genuine. A third was unsure, but Barnes's career was in tatters. He announced that he would not seek re-election, his wife left him, his profits plummeted, and his sons disassociated themselves from the firm. Six months later, he had drunk himself to death. Geordie did not feel guilty for exposing him as a fraud, but he felt uneasy about the manner of his death.

Dover, England, Late Autumn 1938

The young woman with striking red hair and olive skin looked dog-tired. She was queueing up at the Customs barrier at the port of Dover, with the ferry she had just left at the end of the pier getting up steam for the return voyage to Calais. The look she had given to the famous White Cliffs when they drew close was unutterably sad, but there was a quiet strength about her that demanded respect and her blue eyes were direct and clear. If you looked closely, you could see incipient grey hairs in the mass of red curls, yet her age, surely, could not have been thirty. The queue inched forward obediently – not like the animated surges she had become accustomed to – and eventually she stood at a table before a po-faced customs officer. He flicked through her passport and looked up with a frown.

'You've been in Spain,' he observed.

She nodded agreement.

'With the Reds?' he asked, his expression sour as week-old milk.

'With the Republic,' she replied evenly.

'Doing what?' he demanded, his tone now insolent.

'I'm a doctor,' she replied. 'I was working in hospitals in Barcelona and at the front. You know, treating wounded soldiers, but also children maimed by Nazi bombing …'

She trailed off, for the customs man was plainly uninterested.

'You sure you're English?' he demanded. 'You could be Syrian.'

'Why aye, quite sure,' she replied, her singsong tones redolent of a coaly landscape and the grey North Sea.

'You're dark,' he observed suspiciously. 'English people aren't dark.'

'Tyneside born and bred,' she offered. 'If you call that English.'

He slapped her passport down smartly on the desk between them. She took this as an invitation to go but he motioned her brusquely into a grim little waiting room. The woman who eventually entered had the face of every wardress since the Tower of London was built; grey and dull-eyed, but eager to be about her business. Especially with this Red from Spain. She'd just searched some German and Austrian Jews and wondered why they had to accept them.

'In 'ere, miss,' she ordered, pointing to a windowless anteroom, and pulling on a pair of rubber gloves. 'Take your clothes off.'

The young doctor wearily complied and stood shivering while the ogress poked stubby fingers into her mouth and bade her bend over. Next, the woman rummaged through her suitcase, throwing out clothes and books, until she weighed a knotted handkerchief on the palm of one red paw, a 'gotcha' look on her Hovis-bread face.

'Wot's this?' she demanded, perhaps fearing it was an anarchist bomb.

'It's Spanish earth.'

'Earth?' The customs officer sniffed the handkerchief suspiciously. 'Why do you want it?'

The doctor flared up. 'My friends are buried in Spanish earth. One day I will return and kiss that earth!'

The woman shifted her eyes uncomfortably, crammed everything back in the case and told Mary Ross to go, thinking that these people were too clever by half. Mary paused in the street, taking in the strangely familiar sights: the homely English architecture, the looming cliffs, and wheeling seagulls; the smells wafting from the fish and chip shop and the pub; and the small-town peaceful ordinariness of it all. She sat in a Lyons teashop and ordered tea and muffins and her mind went back to Spain and the Ohio boy who had died on the Ebro. She wasn't aware that she was crying until the grey-haired waitress asked her kindly what the matter was. A half-remembered quote flashed through her mind – 'You may not be interested in war, but war is interested in you' – but she smiled at the woman's well-meant words and savoured the first decent cup of tea she'd had for some time.

London, 1939 and France, 1940

Geordie was terrified of arrest and deportation to America. He had to get away. He hated the army, but he hated the Nazis more and the meaty stinks wafting up from the butcher's shop below his flat had almost turned him vegetarian. When Britain declared war on Germany, he rejoined his old regiment, the 77th, and reported to the same Wiltshire base where he had undergone basic training twenty-five years earlier. RSM Clark and Colonel Tambling-Goggins had gone to the great barracks in the sky, but Gilbert Coker-Williams was still there with the same gormless air about him, which hadn't stopped his promotion to Major. Soon afterwards, the regiment left via Plymouth for Nantes in France.

The troopship *Vulcan* steamed slowly up the Loire, gulls wheeling in its wake, trailing a long cloud of black smoke. Nantes was peaceful despite the state of war. London – and the wrath of Commander James Verte – seemed a long way away. Geordie's regiment was billeted in an old French barracks, and he settled down into his work organising the regimental stores. Geordie's driver – a cheerful Cockney lance corporal known as 'Banger' Smith – believed that the war would not last long. Geordie did not share his optimism. Nevertheless, this was the period of the 'phoney war' and Geordie enjoyed a quiet life in Nantes. He even found time to refresh his French and discuss the local cuisine in the cafés and markets:

'These buckwheat crêpes are *très agréable*, mademoiselle.'

'Thank you, monsieur. You must try this Mâchecoulais cheese with a glass of our local dry white Muscadet.'

'Ah madame, could you please give me the recipe for this *gâteau Nantais*?'

Geordie wandered into a fishmongers and surprised the proprietor with his knowledge of the *fruits de mer*. 'Yes, monsieur, I have used the *beurre blanc* sauce with fish many times.'

One day he bought some star-shaped *fouacre* from a handsome blonde woman who ran a brioche stall in the Talesac market. They got talking and she introduced herself as Nolwenn Tanguy.

'You are Breton, madame?'

'How did you know?'

'You have the same name as the surrealist painter, but you are much prettier.'

It wasn't much of a line, but Madame Tanguy was susceptible to flattery and up for anything. The liaison was light-hearted and they broke it off when her gendarme husband became suspicious. Geordie sat facing the doors in cafés and bars for a while afterwards in case he needed to make a fast getaway.

One day, idly browsing an old copy of *The Times*, Geordie suddenly sat up straight and peered intently at an article on page three, which read:

The City Coroner, Mr Harold Cromarty, found yesterday that Commander James Arthur Verte, 59, of Hedgegate Court, Powis Terrace, London W10, had taken his own life while of unsound mind. Mr Verte, he said, had drowned in the ebb tide after throwing himself off Westminster Bridge.

Commander Verte is remembered as an innovator. He pushed for the adoption of scientific methods of detection, such as fingerprinting and profiling, and built up an immense card index on suspects. Thanks to these methods, he was able to bring many of the country's most notorious criminals to justice, including the notorious Butcher of Barking and the Gorringe twins.

Sources at Scotland Yard indicate that the detective had been obsessed with a master criminal who had defrauded a famous American industrialist of thousands of dollars, some of which he had given to the losing side in the recent Spanish Civil War.

'James never let up on a case,' said a colleague. 'This fellow had got to him alright and it broke him.

'He was one of the best. Had he been born earlier I believe he would have apprehended Jack the Ripper. He will be sadly missed.'

Commander Verte was buried with full honours in the South Ealing cemetery and the eulogy was delivered by the Met Commissioner, Sir Philip Game. Verte was divorced, but is survived by his two sons, one of whom is an officer with the City of London Police. The other son emigrated to Australia, where he followed in his father's footsteps as a detective.

Geordie felt a wave of sadness mingled with relief wash over him as he put the paper to one side and re-focused on his coffee and brioche. Something was gone from his life, but he could draw a line under the years in which J.A. Verte had relentlessly hunted him. He wondered if his policeman sons were as obsessive as their father.

The Nantes idyll ended abruptly. In May 1940, the Germans stormed into France and Belgium and put the Allied forces to headlong flight. The 77th received orders to move immediately to the front. Geordie threw together a parcel containing his diaries and personal papers and took it to the post office. He addressed it to *Wally Beecroft, Concierge, The Coniston* with a covering note and hoped that it would make it back to London.

The journey to the front was depressing. Refugees pushing barrows, bicycles and even wheeled bedsteads crammed the roads around Paris and they passed groups of dazed-looking French soldiers, who begged for cigarettes – and hope. Somewhere near the Ile de France, a Messerschmitt fighter zoomed down to strafe the road. Geordie was unhurt but he saw that half of Banger Smith's head was missing. It was so sudden and brutal that Geordie couldn't quite grasp it had happened. He staggered from the car and vomited, so overcome with the horror that he didn't care that the enemy aeroplane might re-appear at any moment. The only sounds were the wind in the trees and the hissing of the damaged radiator of his car. He felt helpless but managed to pull Smith's big body from the front seat and lay it on the grass verge. Poor old Banger. He had liked the good-natured Cockney. He had kids back in Stepney, Geordie recalled him saying. He should bury him, he thought, but he lacked a shovel and there was no sign of life in the farmhouses in the great flat fields. He hoped some local peasants would appear and give Banger an honourable burial. He saluted the lance corporal and set off, hoping to find his regiment.

Farther ahead, beyond a wood that obscured the view, some machine guns began to chatter and he feared that his brother officers had run slap bang into the enemy. He climbed a towering lime tree and saw that this was indeed the case. Major Coker-Williams was standing with his hands up, guarded by German soldiers under the barrels of a line of Panzer tanks. Fearful that they would soon come barrelling down the road, Geordie set off through the woods and across a turnip field without any plan other than to get away from them. He trudged for hours across fields, through hedgerows and spinneys, and forded a couple of knee-deep streams. As the sun was falling towards the western horizon, he came across a deserted farmhouse. A dozen or so dairy cows were bawling at the gate and chickens were running around the yard but there was no sign of human life. After making a half-hearted attempt to milk one of the cows, Geordie hunted through the kitchen cupboards and found a loaf of coarse bread and some honey, some of which he devoured while sipping from a pitcher of milk. He spent an anxious night fully clothed in a four-poster bed, dozing off then waking in fear, imagining that he had heard German boots outside.

When a rooster woke him at dawn, he breakfasted on the remains of the bread and honey and set off again, hoping to find British or French troops. He could hear the distant sounds of battle as he crossed the fields, but he saw nobody except an elderly farmer who was pollarding some trees.

'Do you have anything to eat?' Geordie wanted to know.

'Only some apples, monsieur, but you're welcome to them.' The farmer gave Geordie a quizzical look. 'Are you lost, then?'

'My regiment ran into a whole German armoured division. Messerschmitt fighters too. I'm trying to find some other British force.'

'Sorry, but I can't help. There is a road to the south just over there.' He pointed to a line of trees and shrugged. 'I'll take my chances with the Boche. I'm eighty-eight years-old, monsieur. The Prussians came this way when I was a boy. They'll go away again.'

'Not for a while, it seems. They are too strong for us.'

'No, well all I can say is *bonne chance*, my friend.'

Geordie wished he could afford the old man's sang-froid.

Ten minutes later, Geordie stumbled out through a hedge and into the road just as a splendid bottle green-and-black Stutz Vertical Eight roadster slowed to take a corner. He stuck out his hand to flag the car down, but the driver swerved, with no intention of stopping. His heart fell but to his great joy, the car rolled to a halt and a hand beckoned him to come forward.

'You're jolly lucky,' said a posh English voice from within as the liveried chauffeur scurried to open the rear door. 'François here wasn't going to stop, but we saw your uniform.'

Geordie did a double take as he climbed inside the car's roomy interior. The voice's owner was a man with enormous eyes who was recognisable around the world. He smelled strongly of drink.

'My name is Windsor,' the toff said, proffering a well-manicured hand, 'and this is my wife.'

Geordie was dumbfounded as he took in the slim, dark-haired figure sitting opposite him. Some popular doggerel jumped into his head: *Hark the herald angels sing – Mrs Simpson's pinched our King!*

'Jolly bad show, what?' said Windsor. 'I could have told them if they'd only listened.' Geordie murmured something non-committal and the man continued what was a well-worn theme. 'We met old Adolf, you know, and he was jolly decent. There was absolutely no need for us to go to war. He wanted us to be friends, but the damned Jews queered the pitch for us. Best bet now is for us to sue for peace and give Adolf a free hand in Europe while we rule the seas and get on with running our empire. Why we should concern ourselves with the damned Poles is beyond me. We were in Germany a few years back, weren't we my dear?' He turned to his wife, who rewarded him with an indulgent smile. 'What the Nazis have done for Germany is what the rest of us should have done, don't you think?'

Geordie did not 'think.' He replied that Hitler was a dictator, and that Britain was enough of a democracy to be worth defending. As for Windsor, he bore out Huckleberry Finn's opinion that 'All kings is mostly rapscallions', but Geordie kept the thought to himself.

Windsor cut him off. 'Tosh, old man! The German people worship their Führer. He has put the country back on its feet; put the Four-by-Twos in their place and stopped Bolshevism. In the last ten years he has totally reorganised the order of German society ...' Here Windsor adopted a steely pose and stared out the window. 'Countries which are unwilling to accept such reorganisation with its concomitant sacrifices should direct their policies accordingly.' He went on in this vein for some time as the big car sped through the countryside, addressing Geordie as if he were the audience at a fascist rally. Geordie said nothing. When Windsor's peroration ran out of steam, he asked the driver where they were. François replied that they were drawing close to Orléans. Would His Highness wish to stop for refreshment, he asked? Windsor did not bother to reply but turned his gaze back to Geordie.

'Geordie, eh?' he observed. 'Not seen a Geordie officer before. Nor a nig … err a coloured one. Now, I should have asked what you want to do instead of running orf at the mouth.'

Geordie said that he planned to find a British unit and report for duty, but Windsor brayed like a horse and scoffed that it was all over.

'Jerries are cutting through our lines like a hot knife through butter. Froggies never stood a chance. Rotten to the core. The Germans are disciplined, Lieutenant Stubbs. They haven't been weakened by Jewish democracy and socialism. They are the future and we had best get used to it. Best thing we can do now is to sue for peace.' Here, he paused. 'Oh, I should have said, we are headed for Lisbon via Biarritz, and you're welcome to accompany us there. Or we can drop you off at Bordeaux and you can report for duty there if you wish.'

Geordie thanked him and said Bordeaux would suit him fine. Windsor continued his monologue. 'Marvellous car, this. American you know, like my wife. Eight cylinders, overhead-cam engine, a double-drop chassis frame, a worm gear rear axle, safety glass, and four-wheel hydraulic brakes. By Jove, she's a beauty! I think a German must have designed her!'

Geordie knew 'she' was designed by a Hungarian, but he kept silent.

Windsor dropped off and snored with his mouth open, revealing a line of gold fillings in perfectly manicured teeth. His wife sighed and shook her head. 'He's been drinking, you know,' she said. She had a tinny, high-pitched American voice. 'He hated leaving the house in Paris but there was little choice with the Germans closing in so fast. I've been thinking, Lieutenant, that if you don't manage to leave the country at Bordeaux, you could travel across to our house on the

Riviera. I hate to think of it standing empty and you could hunker down there.'

It was an idea, Geordie agreed, so she wrote the address and caretaker's details with a Mont Blanc fountain pen on expensive cream paper. She had the air of a woman used to getting her way. She too believed that Great Britain should sue for peace and hoped that the United States would stay out of the war. Roosevelt, she opined, was practically a communist and would have to be constrained.

~ 46 ~

Valence and Marseilles, 1940

It was dark when the strange pair and their chauffeur dropped Geordie off at the British Consulate in Bordeaux. Staff were rushing round with armfuls of documents and burning them in the garden. Telephones rang incessantly, unanswered, and a frazzled young fellow wearing plus fours and a diamond-pattern jumper shook his head when Geordie enquired about the state of the war. 'Haven't you heard?' he brayed, Eton-style. 'The Froggies are finished, and Jerry has our chaps cornered at Dunkirk. Now, if you don't mind, I have work to do!'

Dismissed as a nuisance, Geordie wondered what to do next. He could try to get to Gibraltar, but a better bet might be to head to Marseilles and pick up a ship to cross the Mediterranean to meet British forces. Then again, he had the address on the Riviera the Duchess had given him. Money was no problem with Feuerstein's dollars sewn into his uniform. He tossed a coin and Marseilles it was. After spending the night in a cheap hotel, he wandered over to the Gare Saint-Jean, only to find regular services in chaos. He found a seat on a train bound for Montauban but for some reason it took him to Périgueux before chuffing away in the wrong direction towards Limoges.

After a week of wandering across the face of France, Geordie found himself one sunny afternoon near Lyon in the Rhône valley. A sign informed him that he was now in the South: '*à Valence le Midi commence*.' Marseilles was close now. He was beginning to smell but was reluctant to abandon his British uniform and find a new place for his nest egg. He read in a newspaper that Paris had fallen. Gloom hung thick as treacle over the town, and the newsagent muttered that it was only a matter of time before France surrendered. Geordie bought some new clothes, along with an expensive brass and leather suitcase, and booked a room in an old hotel near the station. The Armenian hotelier raised an eyebrow at the sight of the unusual-looking British officer standing before him but slid the key across the counter.

'Terrible times, *mon capitaine*,' he sighed. 'I have a son at the front, and I was at Verdun in the last war. My parents escaped the 1896 pogroms in Turkey. We owe everything to this country.' So distressed was he that Geordie didn't bother to correct him about his rank.

A few days later, when Geordie was eating breakfast, the hotelier accosted him. The blazing headline in the newspaper he unfolded declared that France had signed an armistice with the invaders. Oh fuck, thought Geordie, wondering what it meant for him as a British soldier in the new Vichy zone. He soon found out. He was taking a stroll through the Jouvet Park, when two gendarmes jumped out from the trees. They permitted him to take his things from his room and the manager bade him a melancholy goodbye. There were some fascist youths nearby, he whispered, and they must have tipped off the gendarmes. The two *pandores* marched Geordie to their barracks, searched him, and wrote his details in a ledger. They were very sorry, they said, but they had orders to intern English soldiers at Fort Saint-Jean in Marseilles for the duration of the war. Geordie smiled wryly: he would make it to the city, but not under his own steam.

Fort Saint-Jean had stood guard at the entrance to the old port of Marseilles for three hundred years. Built of the local white limestone, it looked as if it had grown there. Colonel Maurice Liger-Belair, the fort's commander, gave a Gallic shrug of his broad shoulders and said he had his orders – and what could he do? Lieutenant Stubbs was an officer and a gentleman, so he would be treated with the privileges due to his rank, but he was still a prisoner. He escorted Geordie to a large room overlooking the sea, with another window facing the quay. From outside came the sounds of soldiers drilling and the soft voice of the sea. Liger-Belair did not lock the door. Things could be worse. He had just unpacked his suitcase when a blond head appeared round the door and to Geordie's great surprise addressed him in Tyneside-accented English.

'Howay man,' said the visitor. 'I'm Captain Bill Maxwell and you – so the colonel tells me – are Lieutenant Stubbs.'

There were about a dozen British soldiers at the fort – five officers, an NCO and a few privates, Maxwell said. The grub was good, with wine of course, and Liger-Belair allowed his charges to wander the city streets so long as they observed a strict curfew. Anyway, there was nowhere for them to go if they did escape.

'So, bonnie lad,' Maxwell sighed, 'we must make the best of it. Once things become clear, I intend to bugger off to fight Jerry, but in the meantime, I spend the afternoons in a bar not far from here and you're very welcome to join me. Mind you, the colonel insists that we wear civvies when we're in the town. Questions would be asked if we got around in uniform.'

Later that afternoon, Geordie and Maxwell strolled along the quayside and turned right into the Canabière, the main street of the central city. Maxwell, Geordie noticed, had an occasional slight facial tic. A few blocks farther on, Maxwell stopped and pointed at the façade of a large building.

'There you are, bonnie lad,' he enthused. 'L'Hôtel du Louvre et Paix. It's my pleasure to introduce you to the best bar in the city.'

The hotel was grand indeed. Six storeys high including the attics, and built out of the light-coloured local stone, it had graceful wrought iron balconies and high, well-proportioned windows. It was surmounted by an ornate clock featuring four caryatides representing four continents – a winged fish for Europe, an elephant for Asia, a dromedary for Africa, and, for some peculiar reason, a sphinx for America. The sculptor had overlooked Australia, making Maxwell quip that they should have added a kangaroo for geographical accuracy. The bar was cool, hushed and elegantly furnished. Maxwell steered Geordie to a table and a waiter took their orders.

'Aha,' Maxwell whispered, inclining his head towards the door. 'Here comes Nancy Wake. She's a smasher.'

Geordie followed his gaze to the attractive dark-haired young woman coming towards them and smiled his appreciation.

'Down boy!' Maxwell hissed. 'She's married to a rich Frenchman, so don't get ideas.'

Nancy studied Geordie with keen interest as she extended a slim hand for him to shake. She spoke 'educated Australian' and was not in the least shy or retiring.

'Another denizen of Fort Saint-Jean,' she teased, her green eyes sparkling. 'I do hope you're not a spy like our Captain Maxwell here.' Maxwell went to open his mouth, but she hastened to assure Geordie that she was joking. 'When I first saw Captain Maxwell, he was sitting over in the corner, reading an English book as if he were in a Lyons teashop. He wasn't in uniform, and I feared that he was either a Boche spy or an agent provocateur.'

She ordered a gin martini from the hovering waiter – the first of many, for she seemed fond of a drink – and proceeded to grill Geordie about how he came to be in Marseilles. He found her intriguing. He learned that she was part Māori (which explained her lovely complexion) and that she was married to a prominent French industrialist. Later, when she mentioned that she had worked as a reporter in Germany and Austria, they compared notes about the Nazis. She was intrigued to hear of his meeting with the Duke of Windsor and declared most emphatically that she did not share his fascist views. She had been in Vienna during the Anschluß in 1938 and had seen Jews strapped to a wooden wheel, which was trundled through the streets while Brownshirts flogged them to the jeers of passers-by.

'I swore,' she said, 'that one day I would get revenge on those swine.'

Nancy was fascinating, but the life of enforced idleness in Fort Saint-Jean began to pall. Geordie also felt a little guilty, for here he was sitting in Marseilles eating and drinking well while the Nazi jackboot was stamping across Europe and Britain was under siege. He had learned that the Messageries Maritimes shipping line was still sending vessels out to the Far East: perhaps he could sneak aboard to get out of a city that was an open prison? In any case, it was unlikely that they would enjoy the liberties permitted by Colonel Liger-Belair for long. The Etat Français was consolidating its hold and the Vichy militia – the Milice – was flexing its fascist muscles.

The Messageries Maritimes ships berthed at the Bassin de la Grande Joliette just west of the Old Port. Geordie spoke with a docker and learned that the *Ville de Verdun* would soon be sailing to Saigon. The docker pointed her out – an ungainly, one-funnelled ship of around 7000 tons displacement that was loading at the dockside. She had been a Boche ship said the docker, spitting into the dock, and likely would be again – if they wanted the old tub. Geordie went up the gangplank and asked for the skipper, who turned out to be a morose old seadog called Monsieur Garrigues, who spoke with a thick Provençal accent and sported a luxuriant handlebar moustache. Garrigues shook his head when Geordie asked to book a passage on the ship. There was no room and besides, Monsieur Sterbs was a foreigner – an Englishman even, and a black one to boot. Geordie had expected such a response and when he drew a fistful of US dollars from his pocketbook, the old skipper's eyes glittered. He reached out for the notes, but Geordie put the money away.

'Sorry, skipper,' he countered. 'Half now and half when we're out of French waters.'

Garrigues agreed and they shook on the deal. The ship was due to sail the next day at 1400 hours, and if Monsieur Stubbs would report one hour before, he would keep the customs and passport officers busy. Things appeared to be going well, but as Geordie was walking back to the fort along the docks, head down, deep in thought, a young man dressed in a brown shirt and blue beret stepped up behind him and thrust a pistol at his neck.

'Hands up, *nègre!*' the man ordered.

He shoved Geordie up against a wall and patted him down, all the time squinting from the smoke from the Gaulois stuck in his mouth.

'How much?' Geordie asked. 'I can pay you in American dollars.'

'*Sale noir,*' the militiaman spat; a zealot who had the power to take the money for nothing. He waved the pistol in the direction of the Old Port and gave Geordie another shove for emphasis. Geordie's brain was working hard. Escape was not right out of the question, but he obeyed, and spread his hands in a gesture of surrender. Just then, there was a shout from over near an old warehouse next to the seawall.

'Hey, *blaireau!*'

A docker's hook sailed through the air, grazed the *milicien*'s head, and fell to the concrete path with a clatter. Geordie didn't hesitate. He chopped his fist down hard on the militiaman's hand, sending the pistol clattering to the ground. The longshoreman he had met earlier sprinted up, grabbed the pistol and without hesitation, shot the fascist in the head.

'Quickly m'sieur,' he ordered, stuffing the pistol into his belt. 'Help me get rid of this bastard.'

Together, they pulled the corpse over behind the warehouse and rolled it over the seawall into the water, but not before the docker frisked the young man's pockets, taking his papers and spare ammunition. The corpse sank but the blue beret bobbed on the waves.

'Now, let's go,' said the docker; a man weather-beaten by decades spent working in the open air, with fierce blue eyes and broad shoulders.

Geordie stuttered his thanks, shocked at the brutal dispatch of the young militiaman – who was just a boy – yet relieved at the same time. He guessed that the docker was a Communist, so he mumbled 'I thought that the Party was neutral in this war?'

'*Pfui*,' snorted the docker. 'The Party is misguided, but strong enough to see the error of its ways and change course.' He stood to attention and raised his fist in a clenched fist salute. 'I was in Spain, m'sieur. *Mort au fascisme!*'

With that, the two men shook hands and went in opposite directions. As far as Geordie could see, there were no witnesses, and he made his way back to the fort without further trouble. He had seen what he later believed might have been the first blow struck by the Resistance in Marseilles, but he couldn't get the sight of the blue beret bobbing on the swell out of his mind. On the way back to the fort, he espied a Mercedes touring car sporting the swastika flag and ducked into an alley. The car drove by, carrying five thugs, their leather coats and hard faces shouting Gestapo. He hurried back to the fort and knocked on Bill Maxwell's door.

'Jesus Christ, man,' muttered Maxwell. 'I was in Spain with the International Brigades and was part of a prisoner swap. I'm done for if those bastards get their hands on me again.'

Geordie offered him his berth on the *Ville de Verdun*. Maxwell demurred, but Geordie was insistent. He would not allow his friend to fall into Gestapo hands. He would take his chances there in the Midi, perhaps in the Windsors' holiday house. His French was passable enough to fool the Boche; even the *miliciens* if he mumbled. Geordie was always light on his feet and later that day he startled Maxwell on the stairs outside their rooms. Maxwell spun round and the slight tic that Geordie had noticed earlier had turned his friend's face into a twitching grimace. He muttered his apologies, but Maxwell waved them aside.

'It's alright, bonnie lad,' he whispered. 'I've never been the same, really, since I came back from Spain. Let's sit down and I'll tell you about it over a coffee and a glass of Armagnac.'

They wandered down to the Louvre et Paix and as they took their seats, Nancy Wake entered the bar. 'There you are boys,' she said. 'I don't know about you, but I'm parched.' She signalled to the waiter and gave an enquiring look.

'You may as well hear it too,' said Maxwell. 'I was just about to explain why I have this twitch.'

Nancy nodded. 'Yes, I've wondered about that but you never talk about yourself.'

She exchanged glances with Geordie and waited for Maxwell to begin.

'I was in Spain, you know. When Franco revolted, I volunteered for the International Brigades. I was a trained soldier from the Great War and more or less on the Left. It seemed the right thing to do though our government had other ideas.' He took a sip of his Armagnac. 'It was a bad show. I'll spare you the details, but we were outgunned. Franco was armed to the teeth by Mussolini and Hitler. I won't carry on about what the democracies did. Or didn't do.

'Anyway, I was taken prisoner during the Battle of Guadalajara.'

'That was the early spring of 1937, wasn't it?' asked Nancy.

'Yes, it was.' He took another sip of his drink and the twitch returned. 'A bomb blast knocked me unconscious. Italian plane. Italian regulars found me, and I was lucky because if the Moors or the Blackshirts had found me they would have cut my throat.'

'Poor boy,' said Nancy, taking his hand.

'They put me in a concentration camp.' He shuddered at the memory. 'Horrible place on a godforsaken plain somewhere west of Madrid. Either freezing or hot as hell. Bad food and not enough of it. Beatings. Outbreaks of disease. One day two of those stinking guards came into the barracks and grabbed me. They frogmarched me over to the commandant's office. He wasn't there, but another Spanish officer was sitting behind his desk. I doubt he'd ever seen action. His uniform was crisply pressed and his belt and boots gleamed. A right dandy he was but you could sense a how should I say, a viciousness about him. He didn't know me from Adam, but he looked at me like he hated me.

'There were some other men in the room – a Spanish regular NCO and a couple of Blueshirts. Then the door opened and two Nazis came in. SS men smoking cigarettes and gibbering in German. Ugly buggers. One of 'em looked like a frog.'

Maxwell finished his drink and reached for his cigarettes. When he had lit up, he continued his story. 'Anyway, I saluted the Spanish officer, but he just stared at me for a while and said something to one of the Blueshirts. The militiaman spoke in English and told me that the capitán was an army doctor who was studying the *mentalidad* of captured rebel soldiers.

'I objected because the fascists were the rebels. They had revolted against the elected government. The dandy sneered; the Republicans were Red scum, he said, and Franco was the saviour of Spain. I had picked up enough of the language to follow what he was saying. He wanted to know everything about the *Inglese* mercenary, especially about my political views.

'I butted in there. I told the little rat that I was not a mercenary. I'd come to Spain because I wanted to help the Spanish people fight fascism. He looked ready to explode and the NCO started tapping the truncheon into his hand, so I shut up.

'He went on in a monotone. He wanted to know everything about me. Where I lived. My sex life. If I drank alcohol or took drugs. There were some papers on the desk and he tapped them. Intelligence test papers.

'I interrupted again and told him that under the Geneva Convention I was only required to give my name and rank. That did it. He started to rant that I was an illegal combatant and could not hide behind what he called the "Jew Convention".

'Naturally I started to object, so the next thing was the dandy signalled to the NCO and he came up and belted me in the face with the truncheon. The dandy didn't seem happy about my blood spurting onto his desk so they dragged me into a corner where the NCO belted the shit out of me while the Blueshirts held my arms behind my back. The SS men had a go too. Bastards were laughing.'

Nancy shook her head. It sounded just like what went on in Germany, she said, and she'd seen the Stormtroopers beating Jews in Vienna. Now they were taking over all of Europe.

'When they'd had their fun, they made me stand at attention and the little bastard snarled at me that I would answer all his questions or I'd really regret it. They gave me another hiding then before frog-marching me off and throwing me into a cell and throwing a bucket of water over me for good measure.'

Maxwell ran his hand over his face and took a sip of the coffee he'd ordered.

'I was a mess, but a little soldier came in with some bread and water. I guessed he was just a conscript and no fascist because he took one look at me and went away and came back with a basin of warm water and some cloth. He washed the worst of the blood away and told me to be strong. He told me the officer had been in the camp for some months, and he believed he was the Devil, he was so vicious with the prisoners.

'It was the same again the next day and the day after and so on. They did some things I can't tell you about. I realised those bastards would kill me, so I decided to play along. I invented details of my life and when he wanted to know about my sex life, I made out I was a veritable satyr and all kinds of pervert. I really went to town. Yes, I was always drunk. I'd been in a reformatory as a boy, and I'd been court martialled for desertion under fire – even though I was a decorated veteran of the Somme!

'The swine lapped it up but after a while he lost interest. I guess he had all the material he wanted. The little soldier who'd been kind to me said the man's name was Doctor Vallejo Nájera, and I never forgot it.'

He fell silent. They hadn't noticed it was getting dark outside. After a while, Geordie found his voice. 'Ye survived though, bonnie lad.'

'Aye, I did,' Maxwell agreed. ''There was a prisoner swap late in the war and I got back to England.'

Early the next morning, Geordie was awoken by an urgent thumping on his door. It was the French commandant, Colonel Liger-Belair. 'Quickly, Lieutenant,' he hissed. 'The Nazis are downstairs. Get dressed and follow me.'

Geordie scampered along the corridor, clutching his baggage. When they passed a window, Geordie saw that the Gestapo men were in the courtyard below, shoving Captain Maxwell at gunpoint into their car.

'Too late,' whispered Liger-Belair. 'We will go down the back stairs. You can sneak out along the sea path. After that, bonne chance! Keep to the back streets and head for the hills.'

They saluted and shook hands at the door. The Nazis, however, had anticipated that their prey might try to sneak out the back, so they had stationed a man just round the first corner of the sea path. He was young and powerfully built, with thick blond hair and big hands inside black gloves. A swastika badge gleamed on the lapel of his leather coat. His eyes were an icy blue, but they widened when he took in Geordie's face.

'*Du!*' he mumbled before switching to English. 'I remember you …'

Geordie recognised him at the same time: it was Heinz, the son of Elisabeth Fischer from Cologne. Whatever would she make of her son, he wondered, but Fischer gave him no chance to reflect.

'*Schnell,*' he hissed, flapping his hands towards the path. 'Go! I didn't see you.'

When he was safely away from the Fort along the sea path, Geordie's knees gave way and he had to sit on the stone wall near where the fascist militiaman's body was thrown. His mind was whirling, comparing the Gestapo man with the child he'd known so long ago. He would be sailing aboard the *Ville de Verdun* after all, but he did not feel like celebrating given that Bill Maxwell was back in Gestapo hands. Nancy, he felt sure, would be fine. Her French was fluent and she was intelligent enough to outwit the militiamen. Half an hour later, he was walking up the gangplank of the little ship. The captain hid him from the customs men behind a bulkhead on the lower deck and when the ship sailed on schedule, Geordie was ensconced in his stateroom, with a considerably lighter wallet.

The rusty old *Ville de Verdun* made only ten knots in fair weather and that taxed her elderly engines and caused her to shudder from bow to stern. Even the *Loch Fyne* was, in comparison, a greyhound of the seas. Geordie felt a stab of emotion when they steamed past Gibraltar – with its British garrison – and turned south into the Atlantic Ocean along the African coast bound for the Cape of Good Hope. She called in at a few Vichy ports, taking on and discharging passengers, and re-coaling and stocking up with supplies and fresh water.

~ 47 ~

Saigon, French Indochina, 1940

After an interminable crossing of the Indian Ocean, the scruffy little ship steamed up the Saigon River and berthed at the Nha Rong wharf in the city that the French called the Paris of the Orient. It was a relief to stand at last on firm ground after the eternal rocking of the ship. Geordie agreed with Somerset Maugham that Saigon had the air of a little provincial town in the South of France rather than the feel of Paris claimed by the guidebooks, but he found it agreeable, with its broad tree-lined streets and handsome colonial architecture. He took a rickshaw from the wharf to the nearby rue Catinat – described in his Baedeker as the city's Champs Elysée – and booked into the art deco Saigon Palace Hotel. The border police had waved him through customs, taking him, perhaps, for a middle-ranking *métis* civil servant or businessman returning from leave in *la métropole*. He did not disabuse them.

After washing away the lingering soupçon of ocean salt on his skin in the claw-footed bath in his private bathroom, Geordie wandered out to play the part of a *boulevardier*. The heat hung in a solid block over the town, so he promised to buy himself a set of tropical whites. He

273

strolled on up the street, hugging the shade of the trees, admiring the Opera House, and lingering in the cool vestibule of the neo-classical General Post Office. Strange oriental scents mingled with the smells of coffee and French cigarettes – and, it must be said, the odd whiff from the drains. He took in the grand Hôtel de Ville and the fashionable shops, in which fine French ladies scrutinized the (almost) latest fashions from Paris or Lille. At the farthest end of the street from the river, the two towers of the red brick Catholic church rose high into the sky, glowing pink in the afternoon sun. Close to it was a building which he later learned had a gruesome reputation – 'Hell next to Heaven' – the Direction de la Police et de la Sûreté. It being almost the 'hour of the aperitif,' he took a table under the striped awning of the Continental Palace Café terrace and watched the bustling traffic in the street. Pony traps clip-clopped past at speed, interspersed with Citroëns, Renaults, Peugeots and the odd Berliet motor lorry. Rickshaws were drawing up, discharging nattily dressed men and women keen for a drink and some gossip. Some old Frenchmen who had been playing *quatre-vingt-et-un* packed their boxes of dice and shuffled off home. Geordie ordered a Dubonnet. The terrace was soon full of cigarette smoke and chatter in rapid, Southern-accented French. Save for the scurrying waiters and the odd *métisse* leaning on the arm of a planter or businessman, there was not an Asian-looking face on the terrace. Most of the Vietnamese people in the street were labourers and servants. All this, Geordie the flâneur saw as he sipped his drink and luxuriated in the cool breeze from the overhead fans.

The woman had been watching him for some time and Geordie was flattered by the attention – despite a voice at the back of his mind warning him to remember the *soi-disant* Glenys Seiberling. They sipped their drinks for perhaps twenty minutes before she stood and made her way to his table. She was much taller than him.

'Do you have a light, m'sieur?' Geordie hastened to produce his silver cigarette lighter. 'Do you mind if I join you? She had a throaty voice with the accent of the Midi. 'My silly girlfriend has failed to appear.' She rolled her eyes and took a puff on her Gaulois. Geordie was entranced. She was an attractive brunette with sleepy brown eyes and a light olive complexion. Her chin was slightly too prominent and her features too irregular to be called beautiful, but she was stunning, nevertheless, with a slim figure and prominent breasts. He put her age at mid-thirties – perhaps a decade younger than himself.

She looked him directly in the eyes. 'You are *un Anglais*, but you seem to speak good French. Do you recognise my accent?'

'You are from the South.'

She nodded. 'I am from Cassis in Provence. My name is Nathalie Cazenave. Home now is a little village in up-country Cambodia. It is so utterly tedious that I nag my husband: "Get a promotion, *chéri*, or I will go mad from boredom," but he just laughs. So, I come down to Saigon when I can to escape the ennui. But what of you. Monsieur, oh, forgive me, I don't know your name.'

'George William Marmaduke Stubbs, but call me Geordie.' He bowed and she laughed, revealing sharp white teeth. He found himself talking freely with this beguiling woman. He liked her, but despite her air of sophistication, there was a jaded edge to her. Still, she was a powerfully attractive woman and he felt himself drawn to her. They nattered on and it was *l'heure bleu* when she stood to take her leave.

'You will be here tomorrow?' She would have liked to stay, she said, but she had some business to attend to that would not wait. With that, she left, her shapely bottom swaying in her expensive blue dress, and she turned to give him an intimate little wave as she disappeared up the street.

The next afternoon, Nathalie Cazenave was observing Geordie through sleepy eyelids and puffing on a Gaulois. She was naked on the bed next to him, her head propped on her elbow, a large breast resting on his chest.

'Tell me, M'sieur Geordie Sterbs,' she teased, 'are you an English spy?'

'And you, Madame Cazenave,' Geordie laughed, 'are you with the Sûreté?'

'I might be,' she replied. 'Do you want me to arrest you?'

He kissed her nipple. 'You can arrest me any time you want to.'

'*Pfui*,' she said with mock severity. 'I would be more interesting as a *flic*. Better than a housewife from Kratié!' She sighed and extinguished her cigarette. 'Kratié,' she said, sighing again. 'I must go back there tomorrow. Back to the sheer unending boredom of it … but in the meantime, Monsieur Sterbs, I am going to fuck you rotten!'

With that, she pushed him onto his back and rode him slowly until they both came and lay sweatily in each other's arms.

Nathalie had promised to return in a month or two and he found that he missed her – not just the sex but also her sleepy, ironic nature and the way she teased him. She was in a bad mood when he saw her again.

'I don't mind telling you, Geordie, that I married too young. Far too young. My parents were idiots. "Ooh, Nathalie, 'e is such a good catch." Oh yes, my husband is solid, dependable, but oh so *ennuyeux*. You have no idea. He works such long hours. He sets off every morning at precisely the same time; returns for lunch on the dot at 1300 hours; finishes work at the same time every evening.' She imitated his heavy tread on the veranda. 'The sun goes down and he drinks an apéritif – one small glass, never two, and always vermouth – and reads *l'Echo du Cambodge*, reading aloud little snippets about the greatness of Marshal Pétain or the perfidy of Churchill and Albion. Oh, you have no idea. If Henri knew my grandmother was Jewish, he would divorce me.

'He makes love to me once a week on Sunday nights with the lights off, at the same time, and then rolls off and snores. A good catch? Pfui! He is only ten years older than me, but I swear he was middle-aged at twenty and now he's an old man at forty-six.' Nathalie ground out her Gaulois savagely. 'Oh Geordie, I swear the man's a human metronome.

Have you read that book, the one by Karel Čapek about the robots? That's him to a tee!'

'Well, if he's that bad, why don't you divorce him?'

Nathalie snorted. 'What would I do and where would I go? He cradle-snatched me straight from school, thanks to my silly parents who just wanted me off their hands. So I have no profession, no qualifications, and no experience of paid work. Mon Dieu! You men, you know nothing.' She mimicked Geordie's voice. '"Why don't you leave him?" Bah!' She drank her coffee. 'To be fair, though, he never objects when I take off for Phnom Penh or Saigon.'

Geordie was contrite. He realised that it was easy when the man was the one leaving. He'd done it himself. He went quiet and when Nathalie saw him looking so despondent, she kissed him and said he was her silly Anglais booby. He wished it were so simple.

Geordie soon found the life of a flâneur was beginning to bore him. The rue Catinat was lovely, but he had little to do, especially when Nathalie was away. As the saying goes, the devil finds work for idle hands and the old hankering for wagers and dice returned. He had heard that there were gambling schools over in the Chinese quarter of Cholon on the west bank of the river and could not resist the temptation to go there to try his luck. The bouncer at the first place he went to mistook him for a flic – the man was Chinese, and his knowledge of French was not good enough for him to pick Geordie as English. Nevertheless, after passing several establishments that he suspected were opium dens, Geordie found an illicit casino in an alley behind some shophouses and joined a poker game. The Chinese gamblers were po-faced and deadly serious, but Geordie could dissimulate with the best of them and was still flush with funds. He placed some large bets, and his luck was in that day. He returned to his hotel much richer than he had left it but failed to notice that a hard-faced Asian man was tailing him. He returned to the casino several times over the next week and each time won substantial amounts of French

Indochinese piastres. Nathalie, down from Cambodia, warned him that it was unwise for him to continue. Cholon, she said, was unsafe after dark and as he was neither Chinese nor Annamite, he was a conspicuous mark.

Her advice was sound, but he refused to listen. '*Eh bien, Monsieur Tough Guy,*' she warned, miming washing her hands. 'You will see what I mean!'

One starless night as Geordie was strolling past a stinking rubber warehouse someone smashed him over the head from behind and he slumped unconscious into the gutter. When he came to, suffering from an excruciating headache, he found that his assailant had stolen his wallet, his hotel key, and all the money he was carrying. His clothes were torn and bloodstained. He reported the assault and robbery to the police in the rue Catinat but the ancient *perdreau* behind the counter – a scruffy old boy with the look of an absinthe drinker – shook his head lugubriously. M'sieur Sterbs, he regretted to say, would not see his money again. He had not seen his assailant, had he? *Mais non, mon ami!* The Indian moneylenders would have laundered the money and asked no questions about its provenance.

Worse was to come for Geordie. When he arrived back at his hotel room, the Annamite chambermaid was chattering to the manager. She turned to face Geordie and pointed to the interior of the room. His assailant had used his room key and ransacked it. Geordie searched the room with trembling hands, anticipating the worst and as he feared, the thieves had taken most of his money – piastres, francs, sterling, and US dollars. He had enough hidden away behind a cupboard to pay his way for a few weeks, but after that he would have to find a job and move out of the Saigon Palace Hotel and into something much cheaper. Nathalie arrived back later that day and insisted on accompanying him to the police station. The same old *poulet* at the counter attempted to fob her off but she was a formidable woman and he acceded to her demand to see his boss after sniffing her perfume and ogling her breasts. The chief fell over himself to oblige her and sent a detective – a gloomy *métis* – to examine the crime scene. The detective was pessimistic about recovering the money but wrote down the details and picked through the debris. He would put the word out among his snouts, but he could not promise anything. Geordie never knew the outcome of the investigation because Nathalie – showing a practical head – persuaded him to travel up to Phnom Penh with her. She had reliable information, she said, that there was a chef's position vacant that should prove eminently suitable for him and, of course, mean they would be closer together.

Phnom Penh, Cambodia, 1941–45

Geordie and Nathalie disembarked from the Messageries Fluviales steamer at the Phnom Penh pontoon wharf, where the river flowed past slowly, the colour of cocoa, its far bank lined with trees. The heat was immense, the sun a flaming eye in the vast blue dome of the sky. Strange scents wafted on the wind, and urchins vied to carry their baggage. They took a rickshaw to the Royal Hotel, a jewel of modern French colonial architecture, marrying French architecture with oriental designs and featuring sloping tiled roofs and triangular dormer windows. Silent fans cooled its corridors and its luxurious guest rooms. Geordie had wanted to stay somewhere cheaper, but Nathalie insisted that they stay at the Royal for a day or two until she left for Kratié. She would pay. She also promised to find him nice lodgings in the European Quarter.

She was true to her word. The next day she took him to see her old friend Madame Francine Sargentini, a Corsican widow who supplemented her pension by renting out rooms. Her house, which overlooked the Boeng Kak – a lake to the west of the European Quarter – was comfortable, and Geordie arranged to move in. Nathalie had also heard that there was a vacancy for a chef at the Résidence Supérieure – the offices and the home of the chief French administrator in Cambodia. The Résident Supérieur himself interviewed Geordie and found him satisfactory (or else was desperate) for he hired him on the spot.

Thus, Geordie Stubbs began an almost four-year sojourn in Phnom Penh, the city the French called 'the pearl of Asia'. It was situated at the Quatre-Bras, where the Tonlé Sap, Mekong and Bassac Rivers come together to form a giant St Andrew's cross. The colonial buildings were tasteful confections painted in whites and yellows, with shady verandas and often set in beautifully manicured gardens – the French had plenty of poorly paid servants to keep things shipshape. The teeming Khmer, Vietnamese and Chinese quarters were shantytowns save for the Celestials' shop houses along the Quai Sisowath.

Geordie found working at the Résidence Supérieure congenial. The kitchens were clean and modern, and he had a staff of two competent Annamite sous-chefs and two Khmer scullery hands. Phạm Văn Đức and Ngô Quyền were quite capable of running the kitchens, but it was policy to have a European in charge. He learned a great deal about Annamite and Cambodian cooking from his colleagues. He could soon turn out the Khmer fish *amok* and *nom banh chok* and the Annamite chilli and lemongrass beef, along with bowls of fragrant *phở* and thick and tasty *gỏi cuốn* with the best of them. However, his boss, Monsieur Léon Thibaudeau, preferred French food. This was fortunate for Geordie as it allowed him to see more of Cambodia. European fruits and vegetables did not grow in the tropical climate, but they could be cultivated in the cooler climate at Bokor, the French hill station in the mountains between Phnom Penh and the Gulf of Siam. Sometimes, in the hottest months, he drove up the steep and winding road built by convict and corvée labour to cook for gatherings of settlers and officials.

It was a happy time in Geordie's life. Nathalie came down frequently from Kratié and as Madame Sargentini was no prude, Nathalie was able to share his bed. Nathalie was fond of her husband despite everything and had no plans to leave him, and Geordie had no wish to form a more regular relationship. They were discreet, and the French population chose to see nothing.

Some months after Geordie's arrival, the Japanese decided to occupy the country. In theory, they were allies of Vichy France through their alliance with Nazi Germany, so they allowed the French to continue to administer the colony – or protectorate as France preferred to call it. The Résident often entertained high-ranking members of the Japanese garrison and expected Geordie to produce some classic Japanese dishes such as yakitori, sukiyaki, tempura, and sushi. The Vichy officials claimed to hate the occupiers, but Geordie knew that but for his cooking, they would have interned him. They organised a youth militia they called the Yuvan, which paraded about the city like some oriental version of the Hitler Youth and rounded up a few hapless Jews to prove their ideological purity.

The Résident also entertained members of the Khmer elite including the young king, Norodom Sihanouk. The chubby youth tried hard to assume an air of gravitas but was prone to fits of giggles and did not seem altogether comfortable with the role that the French had thrust upon him. He had a child's fondness for desserts and visited Geordie in the kitchen one evening. They spoke at length about the intricacies of French cooking, but Geordie realised there was a ruthless streak under the young man's charmingly gauche façade. Indeed, he could hardly contain his anger when Geordie refused his offer of employment at the Palace.

Sometimes, Geordie had to cater for gatherings of officials in from the provinces for conferences. He learned that the tall gloomy man with a pencil moustache who attended these meetings was Henri Cazenave, Nathalie's husband. They never had reason to speak, but one evening Geordie noticed the man scrutinising him through narrowed eyes. It seemed that he knew about Geordie's affair with Nathalie. Cazenave was a powerful man, so it pleased Geordie to learn that he had a Khmer mistress in Kompong Chhnang – knowledge that he could use as counter-ammunition if necessary.

One day in July 1942, Geordie was distracted from his work by a great hubbub in the streets outside the Résidence. He ran to the window and saw that an elderly Buddhist monk had clambered onto a wall and was delivering an impassioned speech to a milling crowd of Khmers, many of them monks sheltering from the fierce sun under their parasols. 'Down with the French!' shouted the monk and the crowd roared their approval. The speaker went on in this vein for several minutes, but then Geordie heard whistle blasts and saw a line of French police advancing up the street wielding long truncheons. The speaker appealed for help from a squad of Japanese soldiers who were standing nearby, but they ignored him. The demonstrators fell back but the police ran amok, mercilessly clubbing them down. Within minutes, the street was cleared except for the prone forms of seriously injured protestors. Geordie was horrified to see the Résident standing at the main gate smiling and joking with the police commander.

Geordie's Annamite colleagues became thoughtful after the 'revolt'. Phạm Văn Đức muttered that he was surprised that the Khmers had it in them to oppose the French. Phạm was a conscientious worker, but he was not at all obsequious and had an erudite air about him. They had become friendly and one evening, when they were sharing a bottle of wine after work, Geordie mentioned to Phạm that he had known the revolutionary, Nguyễn Ái Quốc, in London and had met him during the negotiations in Versailles following the Great War. Phạm raised his eyebrows and didn't say anything. After that, Geordie wondered if Phạm was a Việt Minh agent but kept his suspicions to himself. He had no wish for his friend to fall into the hands of the Sûreté.

The dry and the wet monsoons came and went, and in June 1944, the electrifying word came that the Allies had landed in Normandy. Monsieur Gauthier, the new Résident Supérieur, stopped by to chat with Geordie and hinted that the Vichy administration might turn its coat and side with the Allies. It was complicated, he said, because of the Japanese military occupation and the Việt Minh's alliance with the United States. Nevertheless, it did seem to Geordie that an end to the war was in sight.

Meanwhile, he had to deal with a distressing personal problem. Nathalie had become distant, and she did not always come to him when she was down from Kratié. She also began to borrow money from him – something she had not done before. He suspected that she had another lover, and when he caught a glimpse of her sidling into the Chinese Quarter late one afternoon, he decided to follow. She crossed the wide street near the Phnom into an alley near the river. When she entered a Chinese shophouse the truth dawned on him; she was smoking opium and borrowing money to pay for her habit.

'You're chasing the dragon,' he said bluntly when he next saw her, and he wondered how he could have missed the signs. Her skin had taken on a yellowish tinge, and she had lost weight through not eating. She did not bother to deny it but shrugged and slumped on the edge of his bed with her head in her hands.

'When did it start?' Geordie demanded.

'It was quite recently. I thought I could handle it, but—'

'And Henri, your husband, does he know?'

'He would not notice if I stood on my head at the table and yodelled like a Swiss but I'm worried that even he will find out.' She lit a Gaulois and blew a long stream of smoke towards the ceiling. 'The habit's not cheap and sooner or later he will find out. I've been borrowing from Peter to pay Paul as you English say.'

Geordie raised an eyebrow. 'So, you're in debt?'

'Yes. To the Chinese triads. I borrowed from the Tamil moneylenders to pay them, and they are all demanding their money.'

Geordie was very fond of Nathalie, and she had been good to him. 'I'd like to help,' he said, 'but I'm not sure how I can raise the money.'

She looked at him despairingly. 'Oh Geordie, I'm so scared. Those gangsters are ruthless. One day, if I don't pay, I'll end up dead in an alleyway, or they'll dump me in the Mekong.'

Geordie nodded thoughtfully. Monsieur Cazenave, he knew by repute to be a straitlaced person who would not be sympathetic to his wife's plight.

'Okay,' he said. 'I will find the money but on one condition. You must seek medical help because if you don't you won't break the cycle.'

Nathalie stubbed out her cigarette and hugged him. She swore she would get clean, and he hoped she had the strength to overcome her cravings. First things first, though. He'd whistled when she told him how much she owed. He'd have to find the money, but the question was how. His savings wouldn't cover it.

His first idea was to try to win the money at dice or cards. There were horse races in Saigon and the Khmers would bet on anything. The Chinese shophouses, too, often sheltered illicit gambling clubs. His experiences in Cholon had made him wary, but he did place the odd bet before he realised that he would not clear Nathalie's debts that way. Meanwhile, her creditors were threatening extreme violence if she failed to pay.

Geordie was no longer the agile youth who had once gone on burglary sprees, incurred the wrath of James Verte, and earned the nickname of the Human Fly. He had thickened around the waist for a start, and he doubted he still had the arm strength to climb sheer walls. Nevertheless, the thought of Nathalie's plight spurred him on. He had always been a nocturnal walker and did not raise any suspicions when he sauntered around casing residential neighbourhoods. There were two promising targets – one an up-country French planter's elegant pied-a-terre near the Quai Sisowath, and the other a garish monstrosity owned by a rich Tamil moneylender. He discounted the

Royal Palace as it was under heavy guard and its treasures would be too traceable. He'd never be able to pull something like the Mansion House burglary again. Another problem would be finding someone willing to fence the stolen goods. A Chinese gambler with whom he had played cards suggested an Indian merchant named Balakrishnan.

Geordie was in luck, for Balakrishnan hailed from Madras and spoke fluent English. He invited Geordie to take tea with him and made small talk.

'Cricket is the sport of gods, isn't it?' he said, pouring Geordie a cup of Darjeeling and passing him a plate of jaggery cakes. 'I'm eternally grateful to the British for bequeathing us the gift of the game.'

Geordie took a bite of cake. It was excellent and he wondered about getting the recipe, but Balakrishnan was in full flight about cricket and the lamentable effects of the war on the game. Geordie agreed with Kipling about 'the flannelled fools at the wicket' but did not interrupt. When he had run out of steam, Geordie hinted at the reason for his visit. Balakrishnan pretended not to understand, but Geordie could see the sly calculation in the man's eyes. After some circling around, he agreed to help and they settled down to serious haggling. All smiles, he agreed to take anything that Geordie could provide. He would pass on the goods to his contacts in Saigon and Bangkok. He had proposed a forty per cent commission, but Geordie beat him down to thirty-five and they shook hands on the deal.

One pitch-black night, with the monsoon rain thundering down, Geordie sneaked out of his lodgings in a rubber cape, equipped with a short crowbar, an electric torch, a pair of pliers, and a set of lock-picks provided by Balakrishnan, all of which he carried in a jute sack on his back. He had ascertained that the planter, an elderly Savoyard called Gérard Morel, was not in residence. There were two ancient Annamite servants, but they lived in a small wooden building behind the main house and never stirred after dark. Geordie vaulted the high wall surrounding the property and was soon inside the house. There was little chance that the servants would hear anything over the roar of the rain, and he was able to go about his business undisturbed. There was a safe in Morel's study, but it was as ancient as its owner, and Geordie soon had it open and saw by the light of his torch that it contained several thick bundles of piastre and franc notes. There were also some rings but although they looked expensive, he did not have the heart to steal them. They were, he assumed, the wedding rings of Morel's parents. He had no such scruples, however, about lifting some necklaces, and gold cufflinks engraved with the planter's initials.

Balakrishnan's eyes gleamed when Geordie laid out the treasure on his desk. He handed over a wodge of cash and this, together with the currency Geordie had stolen, was enough to pay off Nathalie's debts with some left over for her treatment. She clung to him and professed her undying love. She had booked into the clinic of an Alsatian physician who specialised in treating addiction and told her husband the problem was malaria. It seemed that the crisis was over and that the Human Fly could retire for good.

Nathalie relapsed shortly after she left Dr Schneider's clinic. She had returned to her old haunts to prove to herself that she had kicked the drug. As the physician had warned, she succumbed and was soon a regular user again and running a sort of pyramid scheme to pay her debts. Geordie had no wish to return to burglary on a permanent basis and the thought of falling into the hands of the colonial police was a terrifying prospect. On the other hand, Balakrishnan – 'call me Salman, Geordie' – was delighted to resume business. The trouble was that Monsieur Morel was a well-connected and vengeful man. Wealthy householders had become more vigilant, and the police had doubled their patrols. One night, the flics nearly caught him when he was running away in horror from a cobra that he had surprised on the veranda of a house he was about to enter. That was it, he swore.

After a second session in Dr Schneider's clinic Nathalie swore that she had seen off the dragon. She still had large debts to repay with no way of raising the money, and her husband was becoming suspicious. In desperation, Geordie stole a silver coffeepot from the Résidence and took it to Balakrishnan. There were no repercussions, so he decided to lift some more silverware. It would be the last time, he promised himself. Alas, the coffeepot was a great favourite of Madame Berjoan, the wife of the new Résident Supérieur. Monsieur Berjoan arranged for a detective to hide behind a screen in the dining room and he caught Geordie sneaking out the side door with a fistful of silver cutlery.

Geordie was frogmarched to the Sûreté building and interrogated by a pair of hardboiled flics. He had been caught red-handed with the cutlery, but he refused to admit to taking the coffeepot. They snorted derisively, but moved on: who was the fence, they demanded? Geordie said there was no fence as he had taken the silverware on a sudden, mad impulse. They roughed him up a little, but he stayed silent, so they put him in a squalid cell to await trial. He could hear screams at night and rats and spiders disturbed his sleep. The toilet was a hole in the corner and the bed was a steel frame with a thin rubber mattress and filthy blanket. Compared to that awful place, the St Albans Gaol and Wormwood Scrubs were palaces. Nevertheless, Nathalie had arranged for a lawyer and bribed the turnkey – a silent fellow called Delahaye – to bring him some cigarettes and decent food.

Geordie never met the advocate, because early one morning Warder Delahaye flung open the door to his cell and motioned him to follow him through to a side entrance. To Geordie's amazement, the turnkey pushed his suitcase across the front office counter. There was no sign of flics about the place. He was free to go, said Delahaye, but should mind how he went because the Japanese had staged a *coup de force* and were rounding up all the French. He gave Geordie a straw hat to pull down over his ears and pushed him out onto the street. 'A friend will be along shortly,' he said, before disappearing towards the Annamite quarter. As a *métis*, Delahaye could hide among the Asian population but with his blazing red hair and brown complexion, Geordie would stand out like the proverbial dog's balls. There was the sound of distant shots and just as Geordie feared the Japanese would soon appear, Phạm Văn Đức ran up. He was short of breath but managed to beckon Geordie to follow him. They raced through some back streets and narrowly avoided a patrol of Japanese Kempeitai – fearsome military police – who were pushing some terrified Frenchmen before them at gunpoint. One of the French turned and looked at Geordie, who froze – it was Henri Cazenave, who flicked his head to indicate that Geordie should make himself scarce. Geordie wished he could thank him, and often thought about his decency over the following years. An Annamite chaloupe was standing with steam up at the wharf and Phạm shooed Geordie aboard, all the while talking rapidly in his language with the skipper. He handed a roll of banknotes to the man and turned to Geordie.

'Good luck, Geordie Sterbs,' he said. 'You're a fool, but any friend of Nathalie is a friend of mine.'

He shook Geordie's hand and went ashore. He did not look back. A deckhand cast off the mooring lines and the little vessel swung away from the wharf and into the current, which took it down past the Quai Sisowath and the Royal Palace and into the main channel of the Mekong. The skipper, who spoke broken French, instructed Geordie to go below and stay out of sight. If the Japanese boarded the vessel, he was to tell them he had stowed away. *Compris?* Geordie nodded and sat on a coil of rope, clutching his suitcase, and listened to the throb of the donkey engine and the swish of the water on the hull of the little craft.

~ 49 ~

Jungles of Cochinchina, 1945

Despite the oppressive heat below decks on the little steamboat, Geordie nodded off to sleep. Troubled by his conscience, he dreamed that the women in his life were staring at him with reproach, and he woke up dribbling and confused. He wondered if he would ever see Nathalie again and had a sudden vision of Mitzi with her red hair and bright blue eyes. Annie joined her. Elisabeth too. They were all talking at once and none of them had anything good to say about him. The throbbing of the engine had slowed, and another vessel had bumped the wooden side of the chaloupe, startling Geordie from his reverie. The skipper began an animated conversation in rapid-fire Vietnamese with someone else close by. Water lapped against the hull and the heat hung thick and heavy in the hold. After a few minutes, he heard the other vessel pulling away. The skipper climbed down the ladder – a small, neat man with a birthmark on one side of his face. He was looking scared. The skipper of the other vessel, heading upstream from Saigon to Phnom Penh, had warned him there were two Japanese gunboats stationed a few kilometres downstream. They were stopping and searching every vessel that passed.

'Kempeitai!' said the skipper, drawing his forefinger across his throat. 'So sorry, but you no stay on boat!'

He motioned for Geordie to follow him up the ladder.

The river here – one of the Mekong delta distributaries – was immense, the current barely discernible. The skipper spun the wheel and accelerated towards the left bank. He pulled in at a rickety jetty. It was growing dark, and Geordie just managed to keep his footing on the slippery bamboo and almost dropped his suitcase into the water.

'So sorry,' repeated the skipper. 'Village here.'

With that, he steered the chaloupe out into the stream and soon the sound of the engine faded. Geordie was at a loss what to do next. He had very little money, didn't know the language, and was very hungry and thirsty. The beam of a searchlight downstream in the gathering dark concentrated his mind. He clambered off the jetty and made his way up the bank, hoping there weren't crocodiles about, and saw a house ahead. Sitting on stilts, it had a palm thatch roof and walls. Beyond, in the twilight, he could make out a paddy field, and beyond that again, the forest pressed in.

As he came closer, he saw a family of five or six people sitting and eating at a rough table in the light of a kerosene lamp. They viewed him warily, but he smiled tentatively, and they beckoned him to join them for their meal of rice, vegetables, and *nước mắm*. A teenage boy with a smattering of French asked who he was and where he was going. Geordie tried to explain that he was British, not French, but the boy misunderstood. '*Oui, vous Français!*' he said in bad French. For this Annamite peasant boy, all Europeans were French.

Geordie applied himself to the frugal meal and did not see or hear the group of armed men approach from the forest until a harsh voice addressed him in staccato Vietnamese. He turned round and saw that a group of men had their Sten guns trained on him and they did not look friendly. Việt Minh irregulars, Geordie surmised. He raised his arms and spoke in French, trying to make them understand that he was British, but they knew even less French than the boy, so he shrugged and gave a lop-sided smile.

The leader motioned brusquely for Geordie to stand. He picked up his suitcase and they marched him, stumbling, down a path past the paddy field and into the jungle. He could see nothing, but the guerrillas knew every twist and turn in the path. He had a sudden terrible fear that they were going to execute him, but when they kept going, his hopes rose. The moon came up and lit up the forest with spectral silvery light. The guerrillas strode on ahead never breaking their stride, except when the leader cocked his head to one side to listen for any unusual sounds. After what must have been two hours, they came to another small clearing surrounded by dense thickets of bamboo, and marched Geordie straight up to a house set on stilts. Without ceremony, they pushed him through a primitive gate into the space under it.

He was in a kind of prison, with vertical bamboo poles serving as bars. There was no chair, only a woven straw mat, so he sat on his brass-bound suitcase and pondered his situation. A teenage guerrilla brought him a cup of water and a ball of rice and muttered something in Vietnamese when Geordie thanked him. There was nothing else to do, so Geordie stretched out on the mat and fell asleep. He dreamed of Nathalie and woke in terror, wondering what had happened to her. The Kempeitai had taken her husband and he feared the worst for her too. Sometime before dawn, he dozed off with these thoughts roiling inside his brain and awoke again when the dawn was streaming in from the east. He could hear footsteps on the floor above and one of the guerrillas appeared and unlocked the gate. He motioned for Geordie to follow him to a latrine ditch. Upon his return to the cage, there was a bowl of rice and some water waiting for his breakfast. Thus did Geordie spend the next three days, hot and anxious, with nothing to do. His captors ignored him, and they did not share a common language even if they had wanted to speak with him. One would stand guard while cleaning and oiling the guerrillas' weapons. He soon had cause to be grateful for their attention, for in the heat of the day he was horrified to see a cobra slither between the bars of his prison. He backed away with a scream, but just as the serpent raised its hood and began to rear up to its full, terrifying height, the guard came running and shot it in the head. The young man smiled and dragged the creature away by its tail, leaving Geordie stammering his thanks.

Late one morning, when he was dozing on his mat, he awoke to find a young man scrutinising him from outside the cage. He had an air of authority and sported military fatigues and a peaked cap with a five-pointed red star. A wide leather belt with a pistol in a holster completed his rig. On his feet, he wore the customary Hồ Chí Minh sandals fashioned from rubber tyres. He observed Geordie for some minutes, before addressing him fluently in French. His name – or at least the nom-de-guerre he gave – was Lieutenant Trần Hùng. Geordie stood and told him who he was and how it was that he came to be in that place. He had not spoken with anyone for days and he found himself gabbling, but a sudden thought hit him. He rummaged in his suitcase and pulled out the letter Nguyễn Ái Quốc had written over a quarter of a century earlier. Trần took the yellowing paper and spent some time studying it, looking up searchingly from time to time at Geordie.

'Where did you get this?' he demanded and after Geordie had told him of how he knew Nguyễn, Trần called to one of the guerrillas and the man opened the gate. 'I shall have to verify this,' Trần said, brandishing the letter. 'In the meantime, you will have to give me an undertaking that you will do as you're told. Don't try to leave, because the Japanese would shoot you. The Kempeitai massacred some Europeans down by the riverbank in Phnom Penh.'

The lieutenant knew nothing of what had happened to French-women in the city, but Geordie feared the worst. He found himself muttering a half-forgotten prayer for Nathalie's safety. After another frugal lunch had been prepared and eaten, Lieutenant Trân and a couple of other guerrillas left the compound. They would be back in several days, he said.

Jungles of Cochinchina, 1945

It was a good week before Trần returned. This time he strode up to Geordie and held out his hand. 'Welcome to the Revolution, comrade,' he said, with a broad smile. 'You will understand that we must be careful. Some of the French have sold themselves to the Japanese to save their skins. You might have been a spy. Some other French soldiers refused to surrender and took to the hills. We don't trust them either.'

Geordie felt a great relief wash over him, but he was bemused that Trần – like Phạm back in Phnom Penh – took him for a Communist. He was an anarchist or perhaps more accurately, a 'Stubbsist'.

'Now,' Trần continued, 'you must accompany us to our base. We have heard that the Japanese are coming this way.'

Later that day, Geordie marched with Trần and his escort deep into the jungle. They walked and walked, sleeping rough and eating balls of cold boiled rice that the guerrillas carried in hessian bags. They might have been ragtag irregulars, but they were the toughest soldiers Geordie had ever seen. They marched without complaint on a diet that could not have sustained the Tommies he had served with in Flanders. He staggered behind them and sometimes cursed the suitcase he was carrying, but he clung to it grimly. The heat was incessant and the humidity beneath the forest canopy was intense. The smell of humus, damp earth, and decaying vegetation was overpowering. At times, they were plagued with swarms of mosquitoes. Snakes slithered across the path and there were scorpions and other loathsome forms of life. One night it rained and although the guerrillas rigged up a shelter from saplings and interwoven fronds, it was impossible to keep dry. Geordie's city shoes began to disintegrate, and his suitcase was mildewed. Sensing his distress, Trần reassured him that they were almost at their destination. The land had begun to slope gently upwards, and they were leaving the flat delta lands behind, Geordie realised, although he had no idea of where they were. The dense jungle canopy shut out the sky and he only had a general idea of where the sun was, so he didn't know the direction of the march. Trần was taciturn, but he did question Geordie about Europe. He hoped one day to visit to see the cities and the industrial miracles he had read about in books and magazines.

The Việt Minh base was so well camouflaged that Geordie had no idea that it was there until they arrived. Trần took him to the commanding officer, past an artillery battery concealed from the air with nets and branches, and into a tunnel sloping into the side of a hill. Geordie hesitated before following Trần inside; memories of the High Fell mine were surging up into his conscious mind. There were rooms dug out of the earth – some with maps affixed to the walls and others stocked with weapons and ammunition. Still others appeared to be sleeping and eating quarters and one, he saw, was a medical facility. Low wattage electric globes cast light and shadows throughout the complex, which meant there was a generator nearby. Soldiers, some of them Việt Minh regulars, went about their business, and gave him curious looks.

The Việt Minh commander was a grey-haired veteran. He sat behind a desk covered with maps and papers and motioned for Geordie to sit. He introduced himself as Colonel Hoàng and offered Geordie a cigarette. He too spoke fluent French. He carried himself like a soldier but there was a donnish air about him. Geordie noticed a rack of books with Vietnamese and French titles on the wall behind him: Marx, Engels, and other left-wing writers he hadn't heard of. He questioned Geordie at length about his past and was very interested in how he had met Nguyễn in London. He gave Geordie a searching look and asked, 'Are you a Communist, Monsieur Sterbs?'

Geordie had never been a Party member, but he sympathised with its aims. He said that during his life he had seen much injustice. His own mother was Irish. The Irish had fought hard for their freedom and so he understood why the Annamites – or rather the Vietnamese – wanted the French out of their country. All of this was generally true, although it rather overstated how much attention Geordie paid to politics. He didn't think it prudent to mention the Moscow Trials, and he recalled sadly the arguments he had had with Mitzi Maierhofer back in Munich. She'd called him a social fascist, but he had an idea that the party line had changed.

Colonel Hoàng looked disappointed but nodded to show that he understood. It would be impossible for Geordie to travel to Saigon, he said. The Japanese would arrest him, and the chances were that they would execute him as a spy. However, as he would know, the Axis would soon be finished. The Red Army, he said with pride, had fought its way into Poland and Germany. The British and Americans had the Nazis on the run in the West, and they were advancing on Japan in the Pacific. In the meantime, he wanted to know how Geordie could make himself useful until the liberation of Vietnam. Geordie had a ready answer for that. He was a professional chef and more than happy to offer his services in that capacity. This pleased the colonel no end.

Lieutenant Trần took Geordie to the kitchen and introduced him to the staff – four or five peasant boys clad in dirty smocks. Water bubbled in huge, blackened pots and there were large bags of rice stacked around the walls. The place smelled strongly of *nước mắm* – the pungent fermented fish sauce beloved of the Vietnamese. The kitchens were deep inside a cave excavated from the hillside. An ingenious tunnel system took the smoke from the cooking fires and dispersed it through several vents into the forest. As a professional, however, Geordie was not impressed by either the kitchen layout or the hygiene and he set to work to reorganise things. Trần translated and although the boys sometimes looked puzzled and perhaps miffed, they carried out Geordie's instructions without complaint. Geordie asked Trần to procure disinfectant and soap. This took a few days and then he set the kitchen hands to work scrubbing the work surfaces and sluicing them down with fresh water. He instituted regular hand washing, with buckets of water and soap always kept ready at the kitchen entrance. Next, he reorganised the actual cooking processes so that meals were prepared according to a flow system. The quality of the meals improved markedly. The colonel was ecstatic, for unlike in the British army, all ranks in the Việt Minh ate the same food.

Soon, Geordie's helpers were bringing regular supplies of catfish, along with spices and condiments and the fish sauce staple. Phạm Văn Đức had trained Geordie well in Vietnamese cooking, so he was able to serve simple but nutritious meals based on the local diet. The *cá kho tộ* – braised catfish – was a hit with the colonel, who hailed from Tonkin in the north of the country and was keen to try the southern cuisine.

'You will spoil us, Comrade Stubbs,' he said, not altogether in jest. 'We will get too soft to fight the French or the Japanese.'

The monsoon rains set in with a vengeance. When Geordie went outside for some fresh air, he was astounded at the sheer force and volume of the rain. Lieutenant Trần came out for a cigarette. 'The war is almost over,' he said. 'And not before time.'

'I'm surprised,' Geordie replied. 'As far as I know, the Japanese still occupy much of China and Southeast Asia. I can't see them surrendering any time soon.'

'Yes, that is what I thought too, but the Americans have dropped a terrible new bomb on Japan. The Japanese don't have a choice. Their army here in Indochina is intact, but now they must surrender. One bomb can destroy a whole city.' Trần shook his head and finished his cigarette.

Geordie had been standing, but a sudden wave of fatigue forced him to sit down. He had earlier developed a rash on his ankles, and he had the beginnings of a bad headache. Trần looked very worried and insisted on taking him to the sick bay. The elderly nurse on duty took his temperature and raised his eyebrows. Trần translated the old man's instructions. Geordie was not to leave his sickbed and was to drink plenty of water. He had no intention of disobeying. There were sharp pains in his wrists and ankles and a dull ache in his shoulders. The nurse gave him analgesics and apologised that he had nothing better to offer. By evening, Geordie was delirious, with an elevated temperature. The nurse told Lieutenant Trần that Geordie was suffering either from dengue fever or chikungunya, both caused by bites from infected mosquitoes.

Three days later, the crisis had passed. Geordie woke to find that his headache and fever were gone and the pains in his joints had abated. The nurse insisted that he rest and assured him in broken French that the kitchen staff were adhering to the new regime he had imposed. Geordie went back to sleep, and when he awoke, he had visitors. A lanky European man was standing with Lieutenant Trần at the end of his bed. When he saw that Geordie was awake, a broad smile creased the man's ruddy features, and he came round to shake hands.

'Back in the land of the living, Lieutenant Stubbs,' he observed. His accent was American. 'I'm Rory Nelson.'

This Nelson was a boyish, sandy haired man with the rank of captain in the OSS – the Office of Strategic Services. Geordie had

never heard of it, but Nelson explained that he was a liaison officer
with the Việt Minh. His commanding officer was General 'Wild Bill'
Donovan. They operated behind enemy lines and Wild Bill 'did not
give a shit' that the Việt Minh were led by Communists so long as
they fought the Japanese.

'Anyway,' he smiled, 'we have some good news. The Japs have surrendered. The war is over!'

Indeed, as they spoke, Việt Minh forces were occupying Saigon,
Trần added. Vietnam was free! With that, they left to allow Geordie
to rest, and he dozed happily, until he sat up with a start, recalling
that Nathalie was still in Phnom Penh. Lieutenant Trần knew nothing
about her specifically, but he did know that the Kempeitai had interned
French civilians in a concentration camp at Pich Nil on a low pass
between the Kirirom and Elephant Mountains south of Phnom Penh.
Frenchwomen had been raped and a group of French warders were
dragged away by string threaded through their nasal septae, dripping
blood, and executed in the forest. Much later, after the war had ended,
Geordie learned what had happened. Nathalie had almost given up on
life. The rains had poured through the broken thatch of the barracks
roof and she had almost died when an outbreak of dysentery swept
through the camp. One day, she told him in a letter written from her
new home in France, two Khmer men came, introduced themselves
in fluent French as representatives of the independent Cambodian
state, and drove her and her fellow survivors to Phnom Penh. Some
weeks later, General Gracey's British forces arrived and swatted the
Khmer administration aside. It had been an awful ordeal, but Nathalie's
sojourn at Pich Nil had broken her craving for opium.

Vietnam and Singapore, 1945–48

After several days, a Việt Minh soldier came with orders to escort Geordie through the jungle to a rubber plantation. Colonel Hoàng and Lieutenant Trần had already left for Saigon. The soldier took Geordie's suitcase and they set off at a brisk pace along a narrow path in the rain. It took half a day to reach the plantation, their progress slowed by flooding. The plantation was huge and strangely beautiful with endless rows of hevea trees stretching in dead straight rows under the dark sky to the distant forest. The French planter had either fled or been interned by the Japanese and his property was showing signs of neglect, with weeds growing between the rubber trees and uncut lawns around the house. The Việt Minh flag was flying, and some guerrillas had set up camp in the coolie barracks and inside the house. Geordie sat on a big cane chair on the veranda to wait. A slightly built man came out through the French windows just then and Geordie's jaw really did drop with surprise.

'Welcome, my friend,' said Nguyễn Tất Thành, extending his hand. He had an enigmatic look on his thin face, but his eyes were smiling. 'It's a long way from Dracula's Castle and the Carlton Hotel!' The revolutionary leader still had the large, liquid brown eyes and the same wispy beard Geordie well remembered, although it was grey now. They chatted for a while, recalling the old days back in London and their chance meeting in Versailles, before Nguyễn pointed over the lawns to an approaching European man clad in khaki military fatigues. 'You've met your American OSS escort, I believe,' he said, before clasping Geordie's hand and disappearing back inside the house. On an afterthought, he turned back, and spoke. 'I hope we treated you well. Please do not speak badly of us when you go back to your country. Vietnam needs friends.' Later, putting two and two together, Geordie realised that his friend was now known to the world by his new alias of Hồ Chí Minh.

The OSS man, Rory Nelson, led Geordie to a waiting jeep, and they set off in pouring rain along a tarmac road to an airstrip where a Curtiss-Wright Commando C-46 twin prop aeroplane was waiting. They were flying non-stop to Singapore, 650 air miles away, Nelson explained. Some other Americans were already aboard, but Nelson did not introduce them. They had the manner of VIPs despite their military fatigues. As the aircraft was taxiing to the end of the runway, he told Geordie that his orders were to deliver him to the British military authorities, as he was still a serving British officer, suspected of desertion. That gave Geordie considerable food for thought.

The C-46 climbed steeply up through the rain clouds, its fuselage rattling with the effort. Up above the clouds the sun blazed but the plane continued to climb until it reached its cruising altitude of some 27,000 feet and its motors settled into a steady drone. Geordie was apprehensive. He had never flown before, and he dared not think of the enormous gulf of air just under his seat. In just under three hours, the C-46 touched down on solid earth and he mumbled a prayer and almost crossed himself. They climbed into a waiting jeep driven by a black GI, who whisked them away towards the town, looking very surprised to see a black, red-haired officer. On the way, large numbers of Japanese POWs were repairing the roads, guarded by British and Indian soldiers, and in one place a mob of Chinese civilians were jeering and hooting at the prisoners. There were signs of heavy bombing along the way. The driver drew up outside a line of Nissen huts flying the Union Jack and Geordie climbed down, clutching his suitcase. He shook hands with Nelson and the jeep roared off. The Royal Marine sentry regarded him quizzically but waved him through when he saluted and introduced himself as Lieutenant Geordie Stubbs. Hearing the rank sounded strange to his own ears. A tough Military Police sergeant escorted him along the corridor and knocked on an office door. Inside, a tall, gaunt, grey-haired officer with major's pips looked up from practising cricket batting strokes. He was wearing voluminous Bombay Bloomers and a khaki battledress. This apparition squinted at Geordie and bade him sit in a visitor's chair at the tatty desk, which was piled high with papers, including many in Japanese or Chinese. The officer introduced himself as Major Horace Walpole-Crawford and leaned forward in his own chair with an owlish look on his face. He might have looked like an idiot, but Geordie soon found that the appearance was deceptive. Twiddling his RAF-style moustache, the major asked if he played cricket and looked disappointed at the reply. He then proceeded to interrogate him in a very professional manner, albeit in a lazy Eton drawl. Geordie realised he was an intelligence officer. He was very interested in the details of how Geordie had become separated from his unit in France. He shook his head sadly at Geordie's account of the death of his driver and raised his eyebrows at his account of his meeting with the Duke of Windsor.

He looked pensive when Geordie told him of his time with the Việt Minh. 'Jolly bad show,' he muttered. 'You do know, old man, that the blighters are Communists?' Geordie admitted that he knew but that without their help he would either have starved in the jungle or been captured or worse by the Japanese.

'Hmmm,' drawled Walpole-Crawford, still playing with the ends of his moustache. 'Our chaps have gone there, you know. To Saigon, I mean. The orders are to secure the city and hand the colony back to France. The Yanks don't much like it, but then it's not their property to give away.'

The knowledge saddened Geordie, but Walpole-Crawford's plummy voice broke into his dismal musings. 'You do realise,' the major was saying, 'that I'm going to have to treat you as a deserter until I can verify that your story is true?'

Geordie nodded. He had half-expected this, but Walpole-Crawford hastened to assure him that in the meantime he would be treated as an officer and a gentleman. He managed to convey that this was regardless of Geordie's colour and accent: 'Scotchman or not, I jolly well hope we don't have to put you in the glasshouse!'

A few days later, Walpole-Crawford received a telegram informing him that Lieutenant George Stubbs had been reported missing in action in France in 1940.

'Looks like that part of your story checks out, old boy,' said the major over dinner in the officers' mess. Returning POWs reported that they had not seen Geordie after the attack. It took rather longer for word to come from the French military authorities that Geordie had escaped from Vichy custody at Fort Saint-Jean in Marseilles. After this, Geordie was reinstated in the British army with his former rank. He would even receive back pay. Naturally, he told the major nothing about his misfortunes in Phnom Penh. Walpole-Crawford questioned him further about his time with the Việt Minh, but Geordie could not tell him much. He wondered if he would have told the man anything even if he did know anything of military value.

Orders came from on high that Lieutenant Stubbs was to remain in Singapore to work as a quartermaster in the massive task of reconstruction. He would have preferred to be shipped off back home, but the army gave him no choice. The days passed uneventfully, save for increased Communist activity, and Geordie's life became routine.

Naturally gregarious, he soon knew most of his fellow officers and quite a few NCOs by name. He spent most evenings in the refurbished officers' club, drinking gin and tonic on the wide verandas or beer at the bar. Alas, when the Singapore Turf Club resumed track races in 1947, Geordie returned to his old tricks, running an illicit book on the horses, and amassing a considerable store of 'the readies', which he kept in a wooden ammunition box under the floorboards of his room. He was aided in the racket by the Redcap NCO, Sergeant Keith Pitt, whom he had first encountered at his interview with Major Walpole-Crawford. Pitt was as tough as he looked. When the local triad gangsters attempted to muscle in on the betting racket, Pitt shot two of them dead and took their leader into custody. He could explain, quite plausibly, that his assault on the triad was part of his police duties.

Chastened by a spell in the Military Police glasshouse, the triad boss gave Geordie's racket a wide berth and he had to start filling a second ammunition box with money. He did not stop at running the SP bookie racket. Using his quartermaster's position, he began to siphon off foodstuffs and alcoholic drinks from the officers' supplies and sell them at below market rates to Chinese restaurateurs and shopkeepers. By now, he was employing some assistants besides Sergeant Pitt, and he had leased a small warehouse near the docks to store the produce. The ammunition boxes were now quite inadequate to store his growing wealth, so he arranged with a shady Indian banker to launder the proceeds.

Had Geordie confined himself to the fixed-odds bookmaking racket, he would have escaped detection. Alas, however, the deceptively languid Major Walpole-Crawford was watching and weighing up his options. One hot and humid evening as Geordie was enjoying a snifter on the veranda of the Officers' Club, the major suggested that they should retire to a secluded gazebo overlooking the river. Geordie asked if it could wait, but the major was insistent. When they reached the gazebo, the major looked round to ensure that they would not be overheard.

He came straight to the point. 'I know what you're up to, old boy,' he chided, staring out over the river through the curtain of rain that had begun falling, and twiddling with his moustache. Geordie feigned incomprehension but the major laughed out loud. 'No, don't attempt to deny it. You've been on the fiddle, and I know all about the nags as well. I've already interrogated your friend Sergeant Pitt and he's admitted everything.' He gave Geordie time to take this all in before continuing. 'Terribly sorry, old chap, but I have enough to put the pair of you away for a very long time.'

Geordie half-heartedly denied the allegations, but Walpole-Crawford waved him aside with a sniggering laugh. 'Like I say, your goose is cooked, unless ...' He left the words hanging and fixed Geordie with a penetrating stare.

'Unless what?' replied Geordie, hope springing up.

'Well, Lieutenant, I'm a reasonable man and if you are prepared to, err, come to the party, we can put this, how should I put it, unpleasantness aside.' He raised an eyebrow and waited for a response.

'Party?'

'Well, walk with me down along the river and I'll explain. The rain's eased.' The two men strolled like two old pals along the river trail, deep in conversation. They saluted when some brother officers passed by on their way to the club and resumed their talk. 'You've been most enterprising, Lieutenant; a real *chevalier d'industrie* if I may say so, but the bubble is about to burst. Keep it up for much longer and it won't be just me you have to worry about. The trouble is that you've got too greedy. I always have my ear to the ground, and I have other ears listening too. You've begun to make a lot of noise!

'Here is my offer. You can either agree or disagree, but you really don't have a choice.' The major paused here and turned to look Geordie full in the face. 'The deal is that you hand over the proceeds of your little enterprises to me – all of it, mind! – and in return I will allow you to resign your commission and leave Singapore. To this end, I have already booked you a one-way passage, second class, to Melbourne, in Australia. It'll be an honourable discharge.'

Geordie opened his mouth to protest, but the major's eyes were hard. 'No ifs or buts, Lieutenant Stubbs. I know all about your little scam with that crooked Indian banker, so don't think you can hold out on me. If you decline, I will have you arrested. Do I make myself clear?'

'Perfectly clear, you bastard!' Geordie muttered. The major raised a languid eyebrow, and the two officers retraced their footsteps to the club, where a celebration of some kind was in full swing. Geordie feigned a headache and retired to his room. That night, he lay awake with major's words swirling round his brain, but he could not see any way out of the dilemma. He dozed off and awoke exhausted at the sound of the reveille bugle. That very morning, he resigned his commission and the following week he embarked aboard the SS *Strathmore*, bound for Melbourne via Fremantle. He had little more than his discharge money, having left most of the proceeds of his criminal enterprises to the bent Walpole-Crawford. He could only hope, Micawber-like, that something would turn up in Australia.

~ 52 ~

Bombay and Australia, 1948

Just as Geordie's army career was coming to an end in Singapore, a broken-down old toff shambled up the gangplank of SS *Orcades* in Bombay, clutching a battered suitcase, grateful to escape the rain. He had spent the night huddled under the archway at the Victoria Gardens and was looking forward to a long sleep in a proper bed. After a snifter of course. Maybe two or three. He attempted to bluff his way into First Class but was directed towards a four-berth cabin on the lowest deck in Tourist Class. His cabin mates snored and dropped their aitches, and one of them was a 'half-breed with a chichi accent', he sniffed. It was a fine way to treat an English gentleman, he moaned to anyone who would listen in the Verandah Café or the smoking lounge. A Kiwi bloke told him he was a pain in the arse and pushed him aside when he took a swing at him. Never trust a colonial, the toff muttered when a steward intervened.

Jeremiah Archibald Leslie Cholmondley-Devereaux had spent the war years scrounging in European bars in Bombay and Madras, eking out his paltry stipend. He hadn't seen his family for years and had difficulty recalling their names. His gorgeous auburn locks had faded, and he had egg yolk eyes wandering in a moonscape face. His hands shook and his skin was dipsomaniac yellow. His pinstripe suit smelled, and his shoes gasped for air like the mouths of the salmon he'd once landed in the River Tweed. Aboard the *Orcades*, he cadged drinks and cigarettes before people tired of it and turned away when they saw him coming. After he drank half a bottle of Glenfiddich that he stole from behind the bar, he contemplated throwing himself overboard but baulked when he thought of drowning alone in the immensity of the ocean. He didn't fancy the sharks either; he'd seen the horrid creatures following the ship to eat the rubbish the lascars threw overboard. His ticket was valid as far as Fremantle, but he stowed away just before the ship sailed east again. The Master had planned to hand him over to the Port Adelaide police but instead put him ashore with a couple of quid and a stern warning. Catching sight of Jeremiah's footwear, he added a pair of almost new shoes from the ship's lost and found. Jeremiah had only a hazy memory of how he travelled to Melbourne from Adelaide. People had given him lifts and he'd ridden on a tractor at some point in the journey. Pillion on a 1913 Beezer at another – Christ knows how he didn't fall off after the beer the chap had plied him with. When he arrived, he staggered into the GPO and withdrew his stipend. Showing admirable restraint, he walked past numerous pubs, and took a room in a squalid boarding house at the dockland end of Flinders Street. He sometimes dreamed of Lambton Hall and would wake up crying. Increasingly forgetful, he dimly remembered an Irish wench, a real looker even if she was part darkie. There was a child, maybe? His memory wasn't the way it used to be. Often, he would put his tattered homburg at a jaunty angle and shamble off up Flinders Street hoping someone would stand him drinks.

Melbourne and Tasmania, 1948

Geordie had been honourably discharged just as Major Walpole-Crawford had promised. He had turned 54 years of age and was beginning to slow down. The voyage to Australia was uneventful. He drank the odd pint of English bitter, read his way through the ship's library, played the part of Neptune in a crossing-the-line ceremony, and made a start on writing his memoirs, spicing things up with a view to finding a sensationalist publisher. Early one winter morning, SS *Strathmore* steamed through the Port Phillip Heads and churned up the wide bay to the Yarra River docks. The immigration officer was distracted by a young woman and waved Geordie through. Had he not been side-tracked by the woman's pulchritude, there was every chance that he would have denied Geordie entry. This was the time of the White Australia Policy and Geordie Stubbs was not white.

Geordie had imagined he would arrive in a land of sunshine, but Melbourne was grey and gloomy, with factory chimneys belching smoke into low-hanging clouds. The first place he tried refused him a room, but he secured accommodation in the Rendezvous Hotel in Flinders Street and watched the rain drizzle down the window-panes. A mild depression settled down on him as it often did when he was not busy. One evening, he walked up the street to Chloe's Bar in Young & Jackson's Hotel, where he fell into conversation with a youngish, ruddy-faced Englishman who was drinking a gin and tonic and studying a form guide.

'Major Harry Rolls,' said the Englishman, shaking Geordie's hand. 'A Scotchman by the sound of you. Just got here meself. Got demobbed in India and went to London but couldn't hack it. Nothing but rain and bombed-out buildings, so I asked myself why not go to sunny Australia?'

Major Rolls had been born in Calcutta and served as a PT instructor in the British Indian Army. A thickset, jolly chap, he radiated bonhomie and was delighted to meet a fellow British ex-officer, 'coloured' and 'Scotchman' or not. He was planning to go to Tasmania and after a few more drinks he suggested that Geordie could accompany him. He waxed enthusiastic about becoming a 'dairy wallah'; there had been a dairy farm at Poona, and it seemed like just the job. Why not, thought Geordie, downing his drink, and shaking Harry's hand. Who knows, maybe I could go into cheese making or something like that? It was settled. The two men went on pub crawls and later took in an Australian Rules football game, which mystified the pair of them.

One cold afternoon, a doddery old bloke came up when Geordie was reading *The Age* newspaper in Chloe's Bar. 'I don't suppose you could stand an old soldier a drink?' wheedled the man. The accent was posh English, the voice a wheezy rasp from years of cigarettes and whisky. Geordie looked up and took in a pair of rheumy blue eyes and a bald pate, fringed with remnants of what had once been red hair. The voice seemed familiar, despite the ravaged vocal cords.

'Okay,' Geordie replied. 'What can I get you?'

'A double whisky would hit the spot.'

The man had been out in the rain, and he was shivering. He claimed to have served in Malaya and India with the Gurkhas. Geordie doubted it, but he made polite conversation with the old wreck. When he went to the loo, the truth hit him – the man was Jeremiah Cholmondley-Devereaux, his biological father! What strange currents had washed him up on this far southern shore? When Geordie returned to the bar, Jeremiah had left. Though Geordie searched the nearby streets, he never saw him again. A few weeks later, *The Argus* reported that a dog walker had found the body of a homeless man on the Yarra bank. The coroner found he had died of multiple organ failure compounded by sleeping rough on a frosty night. His shoes were missing, presumed stolen, and the Savile Row label in the inside pocket of his filthy suit hinted at a silvertail down on his luck. His identity was never established.

Meanwhile, Harry and Geordie had taken the tram down to Port Melbourne and boarded SS *Taroona* for the voyage to Devonport in Tasmania. Harry fell violently seasick when the ship steamed out through the Port Phillip Heads and into stormy Bass Strait. He groaned as the ship rode up the giant waves and moaned as it crashed into the deep troughs. Crouched retching over a bucket, he wailed that he should never have left India, where *dhobi wallahs* had washed his clothes, servants had waited on him at table and the sea was a distant thing he had never seen except on trips to Madras.

'Haddaway man,' Geordie remonstrated. 'Once you set foot on shore, you'll feel better.'

When the ship docked at Devonport – a clean little town with a rocky mountain on the horizon – Harry did indeed perk up. 'Spot of whisky would be just the job,' he enthused as they pushed through the doors of the Formby Hotel lounge bar. 'Spot of single malt and a curry to go with it.' Curry they could not get in Devonport, but the menu boasted:

YE BESTE FAYRE IN TOWNE

Cream of Tomato Soup
Roast Mutton and Gravy with Three Veg
Silverside and White Sauce with three Veg
Lamb's Fry and Bacon
Pie of the Day with Chip's
Fruit Salad with vanilla Ice Cream
Golden syrup Pudding with Custard
Lamingtons
Tea or Coffee

The soup and fruit salad came out of tins and the fruit salad was swimming in sugar syrup. Geordie's professional sensibilities recoiled but Harry tucked in. Still, they did have Scotch, so they managed to polish off the best part of a bottle of the stuff, washing it all down with Boag's beer.

The next day, Harry took a taxi out to Spreyton, a village that boasted a spanking new Ovaltine factory set among orchards. He was meeting the owner of a dairy farm, who was to teach him the dairyman's trade. He had saved up in India with the aim of buying his own farm when he was familiar with the work of running one. Geordie, for his part, wondered if there might be a position for him at the Ovaltine factory, but he was out of luck.

Harry returned to the Formby looking pensive. There was a farm labour shortage, so the farmer had agreed to employ him, with a house thrown in, and he was to start work the following day. 'Rum sort of cove,' Harry ruminated. 'Didn't look anything like the fella in charge of the dairy at Poona. Scruffy. Wears overalls. Not sure that he washes his hands when he's been to the toilet. Not sure, either, where he keeps the darkies … Err, no offence meant, Geordie …'

Geordie spent the next day sightseeing. He walked round the Bluff and took the little ferry over the Mersey River. There wasn't much to see after that. The town appeared to be asleep. Meanwhile, Harry Rolls had reported for work on the dairy farm, dressed in Oxford bags and tweed sports jacket. Barry Chugg the dairyman was indeed a scruffy old goat who wore frayed bib-and-brace overalls and sprouted a week's grey stubble on his weather-beaten chin. A moth-eaten trilby sat on his head. His spectacles were held together with red insulation tape and Harry swore that he switched his roll-your-own cigarette from side to side with his tongue. He complained about the low prices for milk and studied Harry's attire with thinly veiled amazement.

'Cows just come in to the milkin' shed,' he told Harry. 'Yous best git yer arse over there an' start milkin' 'em.'

Harry was dumbfounded. How dare the man speak to him like that! Didn't the bounder have darkies to milk the cows? Shaking his head, Harry wandered over to the milking shed and observed the animals milling around mooing. He approached the nearest cow, a big Frisian with a colossal pair of udders straining with milk. He vaguely recalled that milkmaids sat on stools and saw that one was waiting.

'Easy there, girl,' he muttered, plonking the stool down next to the cow. 'Now then,' he said, stretching out a hand and prodding her teats, 'nothing ventured, nothing gained.'

He was nervous and the cow even more so. She bellowed loudly so Harry shouted at her to bloody well shut up and stand still. Meanwhile, the other cows were restless, demanding their turn. Harry positioned the milking bucket under the cow's udder and grasped a teat. Nothing happened, whereupon he squeezed tighter, and the outraged animal bawled and kicked the pail towards her neighbour, a little Jersey, who promptly voided copious amounts of green poo into it. Harry swore and looked for a tap to wash the bucket. Bugger this, he thought, turning his head towards the door where Barry Chugg was standing.

'Reckon ya know yer way about a dairy farm!' Chugg sneered. 'Yer useless as tits on a bull!'

'This is no sort of job for an English officer and gentleman!' retorted Harry, and with that he was off, kicking milk churns aside, leaving the farmer standing with his mouth open.

When he arrived back at the hotel with his face and clothes spattered with cow dung, Geordie laughed uproariously. Harry was priceless. His dream of becoming a dairy wallah had foundered on shoals of cow poo and the unrealistic expectations of a Taswegian farmer. After drowning his sorrows that evening, Harry just escaped being caught weeing on the police station door with Geordie standing by laughing. It was difficult to say which one was the worst influence on the other. The next morning the two rogues bought tickets on the *Tasman Limited*, the crack Tasmanian express train. Sitting up in window seats nursing hangovers, they observed the beautiful Tasmanian countryside as the train trundled along at up to 40 miles per hour on a narrow-gauge track. They were bound for Hobart, the state capital, 200 miles by rail to the south.

Hobart, 1948

Many hours after leaving Devonport, the two reprobates stood in the station forecourt taking in the view over the Hobart harbour. A high mountain loomed over the city and to the left were the wharves of Sullivan's Cove, clogged with ships, their funnels spouting plumes of smoke. The sweet aroma of boiling fruit hung over everything, reminding Geordie of the smell of York many years before. He learned that it came from the IXL jam factory. It was very cold, with a chill wind blowing off the mountain and the promise of a frost. Trams rattled past, with blue sparks flashing from the overhead wires. It was much more of a metropolis than sleepy Devonport, but it had the air of a city at the edge of the world. They took rooms in the Hollydene Guest House in Campbell Street, happy for an early night.

They were up bright and early the next morning, Harry chirruping happily as he tucked into a steaming plate of lamb's fry and bacon, which he washed down with huge mugs of sugary tea. Geordie viewed the stewed offal with distaste and settled for a bowl of Weet-Bix and an ambivalent fluid that called itself coffee. Thus fortified, they strolled off into town, ogling the pretty nurses going in and out of the nearby hospital. The two boulevardiers explored the town centre and wandered around Salamanca Place before catching the tram to Lower Sandy Bay, where the people were more English than the English; a far cry from Wapping – just down the street from their guesthouse – which was inhabited by the descendants of convicts. They jumped off the returning tram and wandered into the Royal Exchange Hotel in Campbell Street for a few pre-lunch drinks. The public bar was full of off-duty police officers playing darts and what the locals called Eight Ball – pool to the rest of the English-speaking world. As one team lacked members, they invited the pair to join them. Geordie was wary of cops, but Harry struck up a rapport with them. After a round of drinks and much discussion about what they wanted to do in Tasmania – and much merriment over Harry's adventures at Barry Chugg's dairy farm – one of the wallopers informed them that there were positions vacant for trainee constables and civilian auxiliary office staff with the local police force. This did not interest Geordie in the slightest, but Harry's ears pricked up and he arranged to visit the nearby police station later that afternoon.

'Don't fancy myself as a rozzer,' he said over scallops and chips in the Carlton café, 'but I wouldn't mind being an office wallah.' When Geordie reminded him that he had been a PT instructor in the army and ought to be fit, Harry laughed. 'My dear chap,' he chuckled. 'I didn't have to do the PT exercises; I just made the darkies do them, beggin' your pardon! I'm not just bone idle; I was born idle!'

Later that afternoon, Geordie wandered off without any real aim in mind. He had developed a taste for the local Cascade beer, although he was puzzled why they served it in small six-ounce glasses and had never heard of pints. He visited some of the city's many pubs, including the Alabama, the Brunswick, the Ship's infamous 'Snakepit', Hadley's Orient, the Victoria Tavern, the Lord Nelson, and the Cornish Mount, and came to rest in the Coronation Hotel up in West Hobart. By this time, he was feeling decidedly merry. He was sitting at the bar minding his own business when a bloke with no front teeth and a football beanie on his head came up and said, 'G'day, Bluey'. Geordie didn't like the look of him, but he nodded politely and waited for him to state his business.

'New chum is yer?' the man demanded after swigging down half his beer. 'What are ya, Abo or what?'

Geordie said that yes, he was new in town and no, he wasn't an Aborigine.

The man's face creased in a sneer when he heard Geordie's accent. 'Whaddarya?' he demanded. 'A black Scotchman?'

Several of the other drinkers were leaning forward over their beers and smirking. Geordie was sober enough to finish his drink and look around for the nearest exit.

'Where d'ya think you're goan?' demanded football beanie. 'Pub not good enough for ya?' With that, he turned his glass upside down on the bar, the signal that he wanted to fight. 'Carn ya black bastard!' he growled. 'Let's 'ave ya.'

He swung a punch at Geordie's head, but Geordie was too quick for him despite the drink he had taken. He thumped the bloke swiftly – one, two, three! – in the ribs and stepped back like a pro. Alas, he jostled the drinker standing behind him, spilling the man's drink in the process.

'Hey!' snapped the man. 'That's me beer, you bastard.'

Geordie biffed him too and turned just in time to ward off his initial antagonist, who had recovered from Geordie's blows and was spoiling for revenge. Things went rapidly downhill after that. Soon it seemed that the entire bar was fighting. Glasses smashed on the floor, and someone hurled a stool at the 'top shelf' bottles behind the bar, sending the two barmaids rushing for cover. Geordie didn't have time to lament the shocking waste because someone hit him over the head with a billiard cue and he slumped unconscious onto the beer-sodden carpet. He came to when someone threw a bucket of water over him. When he could focus, the large red face of an angry constable swam into view. The officer pulled him to his feet and snapped a pair of handcuffs round his wrists. Other big flatfeet were frogmarching brawlers out through the pub doors and into a line of paddy wagons waiting on the street.

The sergeant in the charge room ignored Geordie's outraged claims of innocence. 'I was attacked and defended myself,' Geordie squawked.

'Yeah, yeah,' scoffed the sergeant wearily. 'I've 'eard it all before.'

He wrote Geordie's details in a massive charge book, licking his lips in concentration, and signalled for a lounging constable to escort the prisoner to the cells.

'You've 'ad a skinful,' jeered the constable, steering Geordie down a urine-coloured corridor. 'You can sleep it off an' then you'll be up before the magistrate in the morning.'

The cells were already half full and more of the Coronation pub scrappers piled into the dismal place, making them double up. Geordie's cellmates kept their distance from him, muttered together in the corners and gave him shifty looks. They seemed to be regulars both in the nick and the Coronation. He didn't get much sleep, fearful as he was of a nocturnal attack.

The magistrate, Mr Crisp, glared at Geordie when he shuffled into the dock the next morning. With his torn clothing, black eyes, and unshaven face, Geordie did not look his best. His head was throbbing like the engines of the *Ville de Verdun,* and he felt tired and ill.

'There's too much of this kind of thing,' snapped the beak, studying the charge sheet. He looked irritated when Geordie pleaded not guilty.

Senior Constable Lyell Bishop took the stand and swore on oath of how the police had attended a disturbance at the Coronation Hotel and 'found him over there, that coloured bloke, lying unconscious on the floor.' The next witness was a skinny middle-aged woman who gave her name as Mrs Mavis Devine. Geordie recognised her as one of the barmaids at the Coronation Hotel. Mavis perjured herself blind that day, insisting that 'that darkie there' had provoked the fight and caused most of the damage. She had seen him throw the barstool at the top shelf bottles. The other barmaid, who gave her name as Jane Forbes, claimed that Geordie had thrown a bottle at her. Geordie objected but kept quiet when the beak warned him against further interruptions. He learned later that Mavis was the sister-in-law of his antagonist in the football beanie, a man called Max Johnstone. Mr Crisp thanked her for her evidence and gave Geordie a stern look.

'Mr Stubbs,' he said, leaning forward with a business-like air. 'You are a former British officer, and I would have expected more from you. You arrive in our peaceful city and proceed to destroy a hostelry and assault the patrons. You should be ashamed of yourself. You are not some young buck who doesn't know better. I find the evidence you have given on your own behalf not credible.

'Mrs Devine and Miss Forbes, on the other hand, impress as honest and upright women. I would have thought, Mr Stubbs, that you as a former officer, would have been aware of your duty to defend the fairer sex from unsavoury scenes such as broke out at the hotel.

'I've a mind to send you to prison but because you were previously unknown to this court and served in His Majesty's forces, I propose an alternative.

'I will make an order for you to pay for the damage you caused to the hotel. I will also sentence you to three months' imprisonment, wholly suspended on condition that you agree to take employment for a period of at least one calendar year up on the hydro-electric schemes in the centre of this state. Should you breach these conditions, you will go to gaol. You are, I believe, a qualified chef and so you will be able to make yourself useful in that capacity.'

It was not the most auspicious start to Geordie's stay in the island.

Bronte Park, 1948

And so it happened that Geordie Stubbs's peregrinations took him to Bronte Park, a remote construction town on the Tasmanian Central Plateau. The instruction was to proceed to the Hydro Electric Commission's head office and wait for the bus. Geordie stood there clutching his suitcase, impressed by the Art Deco building's façade, with its mouldings of electrical insulators. He had said goodbye to Harry, who had secured a civilian position with the police in Hobart, and they promised to keep in touch.

Men were milling round on the footpath, some of them wearing khaki army tunics and caps. They were Poles who had fought against Hitler but did not wish to go back to what was now Communist Poland. This was a time when politicians declaimed the need for Australia to 'populate or perish', and British migrants – the so-called Ten Pound Poms – were lured on assisted passages. Several of these were grumbling about the weather, which had turned blustery with a threat of rain, and did not match their expectations of a sunlit idyll Down Under.

The bus was a sluggish monstrosity of Great War vintage, painted grey and emblazoned with the HEC logo. It jolted off, coughing great clouds of exhaust at startled passers-by. The highway was sealed as far as New Norfolk, twenty-one miles upriver, but after that it degenerated into a narrow dirt road. There was snow on the mountains and the heaters strained to provide some warmth against the damp cold that crept in through the cracked windows. The Poles had lapsed into a morose silence, and several were muttering prayers to the Black Madonna of Częstochowa and crossing themselves. They weren't friendly, perhaps because of Geordie's colour. The landscape was starkly beautiful, but he was too cold and depressed to pay it much attention.

It was mid-afternoon when the driver turned off what had the temerity to call itself the Lyell Highway and made for a settlement nestled in the wooded hills. 'Here we are, men,' he said, pausing to take the cigarette from his mouth. 'Home sweet fuckin' 'ome – Bronte fuckin' Park. Gawd knows where the Park is!' The Poles gazed stoically on their new surroundings, but the so-called Pommies were visibly shocked by what they saw. Bronte was an assortment of wooden office buildings, behind which were lines of small, unpainted wooden shacks. Behind these again were some large, corrugated iron workshops and even farther away were the wooden houses of the married employees. There was an acute labour shortage, which had led the Premier, a knighted grocer, to promise British migrants a place that strongly resembled Scotland but for the thickly wooded hills. It was a reminder that the transplanted colonists had never really felt at home in vistas far removed from the gentler landscapes of the Old Country and helped explain why Australians still carried British passports and talked of 'Going Home' to a place they had never seen.

There was not a blade of grass to be seen in the township and much of the ground was covered in blue gravel, interspersed with patches of red mud. It looked dreary, but it beat the gaol cell that was the alternative for Geordie Stubbs. A little weasel of a man marched the new recruits over to the veranda of an office and bade them wait for induction interviews. A Union Jack hung limply from a flagpole. The wind blew, it began to rain heavily, and it was very cold. Geordie figured the Poles had endured far worse in Tobruk and Monte Cassino. Some of the English recruits muttered about going home, and indeed several of them would 'snatch it' within the week. Geordie found himself near the end of the line and it was over an hour before his turn came to enter the office.

'To the right, cobber,' ordered a bored clerk at the door. 'Mr Newcombe'll see you in his office.'

This Newcombe peered up at Geordie with hostile yellow eyes. He had a foxy complexion and his gingery hair clung to his scalp in tight waves. He was wearing a grey tweed jacket and baggy grey trousers. After that, Geordie never saw him wearing anything different. He was abrupt to the point of rudeness.

'Name?' he barked.

He muttered something about Scotchmen and scribbled something on a form. 'Here,' he said, shoving the paper across his desk. 'Take this to the stores. They'll tell you what to do from there.'

He turned back to a pile of paperwork.

Geordie read the slip of paper twice. It gave his occupation as 'P & S Lab'.

'Excuse me,' he said to the top of Newcombe's dandruffy head. 'What does this mean?' He turned the paper to show it to Newcombe.

'It means,' Newcombe replied curtly, 'that you're a pick and shovel labourer. You're on the fuckin' banjo, tiger!'

He bowed his frizzy head to the paperwork and ignored Geordie, who hovered by the door.

'Haddaway man,' Geordie remonstrated. 'I'm not a pick and shovel labourer.'

Newcombe looked ready to explode. 'You're what I say you are, ya cheeky black bastard! Unless you want to get the arse, get out of my office!'

Geordie slapped a sheaf of papers on Newcombe's desk. 'It's Lieutenant George Stubbs to you,' he snapped. 'Honourable discharge from His Majesty's forces. These are my papers as a chef. I understood that I was coming here in that capacity.'

Anger fought with incredulity on Newcombe's sour features. 'Well,' he sputtered. 'Why didn't you say so?'

'I tried to, man,' said Geordie coldly.

Newcombe rose from his seat and roared. 'Dessie, get in 'ere and take this man to the back office. Get his particulars. Show 'im the way to the mess hall an' the stores.'

As soon as they were out of Newcombe's sight, Dessie's face broke into a wide grin. 'Jeez, mate,' he chuckled. 'You certainly got old Grinner's goat in there. Anyway, Dessie Delphin's the name.'

'Grinner,' said Geordie, shaking the man's hand. 'That suits him!'

'Yairs,' Dessie agreed. 'The bastard's face would crack if he smiled.'

Dessie took Geordie to the stores, where he was issued with chef's uniforms and a pile of sheets and blankets. Next, he introduced him to the kitchen staff and then showed him to his 'camp' – a dreary wooden shack with a bed, a chair, and a desk – one of hundreds set on the gravel. At least it had a heater, for which Geordie was thankful, because it had started to snow, and frigid night was falling. He couldn't know it, but his enforced sojourn in this remote place was to become a waking nightmare.

Hobart, August 1954

Let us skip forward some years here. The psychiatrist Doctor Stuart Hetherington, aka Kanga, was sitting at his beautiful Huon Pine desk in his surgery in Hobart's Macquarie Street medical precinct. It was a world away from the tough construction town of Bronte Park, but the place was of great interest to the psychiatrist. Hetherington had eagerly accepted Judge Dicer's request to report on Geordie Stubbs's mental condition, for like most Tasmanians he was fascinated by the spate of murders that had struck the state, and it had piqued his professional curiosity. Now the time had come for him to write what would be a rigorous case study of the morbid effects of genetics on human behaviour. It would help validate his mentor Professor Vallejo-Nájera's hypothesis of the red gene and expose the deleterious effects of miscegenation on individuals and its pernicious consequences for society. The report he was about to write for the judge would have to be couched in layman's language but would form the basis for the more rigorous scientific study he had in mind for a professional journal – a study that would make his name and clinch his claim to the directorship of the New Norfolk mental hospital.

Hetherington had been impressed by Professor Nájera's 1939 study of leftist prisoners captured during Spain's civil war. Its conclusions had gelled strongly with his own observations of the Red Peril, and it would provide the intellectual underpinning for his own work. He arranged his books neatly on his desk, took up his Parker fountain pen and began to draft his report for the judge, pausing now and then to clarify his thoughts, cross something out or craft an apposite phrase. He was very aware, too, that the matter was not purely academic, or restricted to summarising his findings on one criminal. He strongly believed that he was an intellectual warrior in a world-historic struggle and the Stubbs case was one skirmish in that conflict. The French in Indochina were fighting a losing battle against the Communist hordes, and had he not so recently seen wharfies in this very city being led by the nose by agitators? By Jove, he could be relied on to fight his corner! He took up his pen again and inserted some quotes from Nájera about the 'intimate relations between Marxism and mental inferiority', then paused to ponder the matter of Stubbs's admittedly high intelligence. That didn't seem to fit in with the professor's theory, but there could be no doubt about Stubbs's psychopathology, and the link with the fellow's leftist politics was crystal clear. It was genetic, he felt sure. Stubbs's maternal grandfather had been a socialist and, Hetherington strongly suspected, a follower of the Irish terrorist James Connolly who had revolted against the Crown in 1916. And again, birds of a leftist feather flocked together, and Stubbs's personal relationships with the Mitzi woman in Munich and the Oriental Red in London revealed that despite his denials the man was a Communist. QED.

Hetherington's pen raced across the page, then he paused. Professor Vallejo-Nájera had also argued that the admixture of Moorish blood contributed to deviancy in the Spanish lower classes, and here Hetherington saw a clear parallel in the criminality of the mestizo George Stubbs. The patriotic doctor had never forgiven the ungrateful Irish for revolting against the Crown, and Stubbs had a strong dose of wild Irishry. This, Hetherington wrote, further predisposed him to antisocial behaviour. This was important, he noted, for miscegenation had been proven to bring out *the worst of both races*. He made a note and underlined it three times. Stubbs had inherited his brown skin from his wayward mother, whose Jamaican grandfather had jumped ship at Belfast. Hmm, this made Stubbs an octoroon, Hetherington calculated, ticking off the generations on his fingers before adding this point to the draft. Normally such a relatively slight proportion of African blood would allow a person to 'pass for white', so the little man's dark skin marked him as a throwback to his African ancestors. The matter of the man's African genes was crucial to an understanding of his behaviour. Now, where was it? That passage in the American psychologist Frank Bruner's book about the mentality of African Americans? He thumbed quickly through the volume. Yes, here it was, a succinct summary of the mentality of those people, who were

> lacking in filial affection [with] strong migratory instincts and tendencies; little sense of veneration, integrity, or honor; shiftless, indolent, untidy, improvident, extravagant, lazy, lacking in persistence and initiative and unwilling to work continuously at details.

He quoted the whole passage in full and sat back to read over what he'd written. He mulled over the section he'd written on Stubbs's Irish blood again and stared out of the window at the mountain. He recalled a passage in the copy of *Lady Chatterley's Lover* that he had recently purchased and kept locked away from Mrs Rattray's prying eyes. Couldn't mention the book in his report, of course, which was a pity. The writer, Mr Lawrence, had described the Irish as 'rats swimming through in a dark river' and that reminded Hetherington that other writers had seen the Irish as a contagion. He could steer clear of that pornographic novel while making the point. The Irish were often darkish white, after all, scarcely civilised, and had spread plague-like throughout the Empire like the Chinese and other 'lesser breeds without the law'. Prognathous-jawed, of dim intellect, prone to violence, and marked by simian features, they had bitten the hand that fed them with their nonsensical Republic, the doctor believed. It was all coming together: the Irish attributes, the shiftless negro mentality, the miscegenation, the pernicious politics. All of these, he wrote, were concentrated in the case of atavistic reversion that was George Stubbs. He listed some of the symptoms of the man's degeneracy:

> His peregrinations have been seemingly endless. He sneers at tradition and authority, religion, and royalty, and he prefers to play the fiddle rather than knuckle down to a regular existence. He has done time for theft and vagrancy. He is a gambler. His drinking caused him to be arrested for affray and 'sentenced to the Hydro' as Taswegians call it. He deserted his pregnant lover and has never seen the child. One strongly suspects that he has fathered and abandoned other children. He also exhibits a dangerously lax attitude towards the homosexual perversion, which is rightly criminalised in Tasmania.

The matter of Stubbs's peculiar physiognomic features could not be overlooked. These, he wrote, were further evidence of the man's inherited criminality. Now, where was that book? Hetherington rummaged around in the broom closet and pulled out the little step-ladder the cleaner kept there. He propped it under the tall corner bookshelf and scanned the topmost line of books. There it was. The battered copy of Cesare Lombroso's classic study, *L'Uomo Delinquente*. He'd found it in one of those bookstalls by the river in Paris and pored over it through long evenings armed with an Italian-English dictionary. Professor Kretschmer's taxonomy came to mind, too, so Hetherington made a note about the peculiar jumble of body types that made Stubbs a classic dysplastic. He could recall the reference off by heart. He hummed to himself as he wrote of Stubbs's peculiar physical attributes: the strabismus, the rhotacism, and the heterochromia. With these, the outward signs of the man's extreme deviancy were startlingly clear and he explained how,

> Professor Lombroso insisted that criminals are distinguished from the rest of humanity by physical anomalies; that criminals are born rather than made in most instances, that their features have much in common with the apes, and that they are congenitally incapable of following the rules of civilised society.

The answer to the problem of the deviants among us, Hetherington wrote, lay in a vigorous application of eugenic principles, such as Professor Vallejo-Nájera was enforcing following the defeat of the Reds in Spain. He wasn't sure that it was strictly necessary to include this in his report for Justice Dicer, but it could do no harm to spread the word.

In view of all of this, the doctor reasoned, it was not surprising that Stubbs had carried out his shocking offence. Indeed, he speculated that the Bronte Park murder might only be the tip of a veritable iceberg of crime. He sat back at this point and pondered how best to conclude the report, for here he had come to the interface between law and science. Duty called. The cup of tea would have to wait. He began to jot down points again. He stressed for the judge's benefit that *none of what he had observed in Geordie Stubbs in any way absolved him of responsibility for the murder*. That would have to be underlined in the typed copy and he made a note for Miss Sproule. Monster or not, in layman's language, Stubbs was as sane as the next man.

He continued writing steadily, covering sheet after sheet of notepaper with whorls and squiggles, and crossings out, enveloped in a fog of blue smoke from his Craven A's. He was anxious to follow the Rule of the Four C's – that his report should be Clear, Concise, Complete, and Correct – and that it eschewed language of too technical a nature for the judge. The short winter's day had long since petered out when the good doctor finished writing. He was weary but took the trouble to read through what he had written, pausing every now and then to cross out an infelicitous word or phrase and substitute another. Miss Sproule could decipher his doctor's scrawl, he knew, and although he wouldn't admit it, she often improved on his grammar, spelling, and style. It would do, he sighed, tossing down his pen and lighting another cigarette. He stood, put on his coat and hat, and left the report on Miss Sproule's desk for her to type up the next day. He would dine at the club and an evening spent with his good friends would take his mind off the case.

~ 57 ~

Hobart, August 1954

It was such a gloriously sunny winter's day that Marjorie Sproule left her Battery Point room to walk to work. She sat for a while on a bench in St David's Park to feed the birds with the crumbs she had collected from the breakfast leftovers. She was still trim and slim and save for a few lines at the corner of her blue eyes, she would have passed for a young woman in her twenties. Despite the walk, she still arrived early at the surgery, because she liked to brew herself a pot of tea and read the paper before settling down to work. As usual, she had arrived earlier than the doctor and was looking forward to some peace and quiet. He would have been to his club the night before and the chances were he'd be grumpy and hung over. For all his airs and graces, old Kanga was a boozer, and he was beginning to have the potato nose to prove it. After switching on the electric jug, she went over to her desk to see if he'd left any work for her. He had. She picked it up and wondered not for the first time if they taught 'doctor's handwriting' at medical school. If so, she could be employed to teach it! She sat down with her cup of tea, her brow wrinkling with the effort of deciphering the scrawl. For non-adepts it wouldn't matter if you turned it upside down. It was her custom to read his letters and reports from beginning to end before starting to type, as it was only possible to interpret the scrawl in context.

She couldn't disagree with the first sentence, which concluded that 'GEORGE WILLIAM MARMADUKE STUBBS displays *no clinical signs of psychosis*', but her eyes widened as she deciphered the next sentence, which asserted that 'the prisoner displays an inherited anti-social personality disorder which contributed to the viollent' – she automatically crossed out the extraneous *l* – 'crime of which he is accused and convicted'. It didn't improve as it went on. In a comparatively brief space, Kanga had managed to run the whole gamut of racialism and class snobbery. The report alleged that Geordie was sexually promiscuous to the point of satyriasis and that he displayed a contempt and hatred for his social betters that manifested itself in his communistic beliefs. It damned Geordie as a narcissistic psychopath with a hair-trigger temper, whose lack of impulse control had led him inevitably to the crime of which he had been convicted. His behaviour was genetically determined, and he exemplified the perils of miscegenation. It was possible that if his step-father had been stricter with him – or if his biological father had faced up to his responsibilities – Stubbs might have overcome these burdens, for his antisocial behaviour had first manifested itself in childhood, and by his teenage years had hardened into criminality. The fact that he was an atheist also unmoored him from morality. A whole passage expounded on something called the 'red gene':

> Geordie Stubbs is an octoroon with a great deal of primitive
> African blood running in his veins and this combined with a
> genetic lode of wild Irishry has created an explosive impullsiv-
> ity [sic]. I have consulted with an eminent Spanish colleague
> on these matters and the Professor concurs with my assess-
> ment that Stubbs carries the red gene that predisposes him
> to deviant behaviour and an anti-social personality disorder –
> and communism.

The conclusion damned Geordie to the hangman's noose:

> He is, however, not psychotic and can distinguish right from
> wrong. There are therefore not any extenuating circumstances
> in this case, and *I can see no reason why he should not be pun-
> ished to the full extent of the penalties provided for by the law.*

Miss Sproule shook her head. She made no attempt to begin typing, but sat staring out the window, oblivious to the view of the snow-capped mountain. She had observed Geordie closely throughout the interviews and she simply did not believe he was capable of the horrible crime of which he had been convicted. He was a bit of a lad, she admitted. By his own admission he had done things he was not proud of, but a killer … Not a chance! Nor did she despise his colour, for her left-wing wharfie father had instilled it into her that racial prejudice was stupid and wrong, and her own mother's family were Cape Barren Islanders after all. She wasn't quite clear what it was she felt for the little man: partly her feelings were maternal, but partly they were … She suppressed the thought. Plainly, Lance Giblin's murder was the work of a psychopath, but Geordie Stubbs, she was sure, was not such a creature. Through her work with Hetherington she had encountered several of them, including a dead-eyed child killer who had radiated an aura of evil. She also believed that the police had relied on tainted evidence and should have looked more closely at Stubbs's refusal to divulge his whereabouts at the time of the murder and his lack of motive. While Hetherington's role did not include comment on the legal aspects of the case, he had nevertheless damned Stubbs with this slanted report.

She believed that Hetherington was nowhere near as bright as he thought he was. He was a Stalwart Son of Empire, a direct descendant of upper-class Englishmen transplanted to form a bunyip aristocracy. He displayed all their class, race, and gender prejudices – and then some – which he had dressed up in pseudo-scientific gobbledegook. Whiter than the Queen, unreflective, with distinctive accents quite unlike the transplanted Cockney-Irish speech of the lower orders, Hetherington's ilk were educated in exclusive schools where they were taught that they were born to rule. Women such as herself were not worth a second glance. They were the weaker sex, whom Hetherington's Tory-Anglican god had created to make dutiful wives, mothers, and daughters. She wondered if he was a fascist like his Spanish mentor, and what he would make of the fierce Republican women who had shouldered rifles alongside their male comrades. Her beloved uncle Arthur, who had returned from the Spanish war with sad eyes and a permanent limp, was reticent about his experiences in the POUM militia, but she had questioned him at length and learned a great deal about that tragic conflict. She hurled Hetherington's report down with a silent oath. She had served this man quietly, but she had had enough!

When the doctor entered the surgery, she stood up and waved the handwritten report in his bleary face.

'Yes?' he snapped, wrinkling up his marsupial features.

'I don't think he did it!'

'Oh, and why, pray, is that?' he replied absently, fiddling with his briefcase, and waving a dismissive hand. 'Have you typed up my report?'

'No, I haven't,' she replied, 'and I'm not sorry. I've listened to everything Mr Stubbs has said, and I just know he's innocent.' He stood there without saying anything, so she ploughed on. 'And what bearing, Doctor Hetherington, do his colour or his politics have on the crime he is supposed to have committed?'

'Really!' Hetherington sniffed, exasperated now. 'May I remind you, Miss Sproule, that I am the expert here, not you. Your opinion is of no consequence.' He wagged a finger in her face. 'Apart from that, Miss Sproule, the court found him guilty and it's not up to me – or you – to dispute that ...' He paused, smirked and concluded: 'Now, if that's all, I really do need the report finished and in the judge's hands.'

Miss Sproule's nostrils flared. Her blue eyes flashed with a fierce, cold anger he had never seen or at least never noticed before. 'Damn you, man,' she snarled, quite setting him back. 'You want him to be guilty so that it fits in with your stupid theories.'

'Now, then,' Hetherington warned. 'I'll remind you that—'

'Red gene indeed!' She snorted. 'Nonsense cooked up by a Franco war criminal.'

His jaw hung open and he sputtered like a defective steam valve.

Marjorie Sproule had transformed before his astonished eyes into an angry Boadicea. 'Well … well … b-bugger you, Hetherington!' she fumed. 'May God forgive you because I never will. You know that man is innocent, yet you invented a load of bloody claptrap that will send him to the gallows!'

With that, she stormed out, leaving the door wide open behind her, telling him to type his bloody report himself for she would have no part of it. Hetherington sat opening and closing his briefcase and staring out the window. Miss Sproule had been with him for the past eight years and had come highly recommended by a retiring colleague as an efficient and unobtrusive employee. She had never displayed the slightest sign of insubordination. She was always punctual and had not taken a day off besides her two weeks' annual leave save for when she had come down with the flu a few years earlier. Her flare-up had stunned him as much as if he had been attacked by a sheep.

London, 1953

In the 1950s, London shuffled pale and wan like an elderly patient on crutches. Bomb sites were everywhere, although they sprouted weeds now and scruffy children played wars in the rubble. Here and there, hideous new buildings had been thrown up in the gaps left by exploding bombs. Essential goods were still rationed, and people queuing up outside the shops grumbled that they'd won the war, but you'd never know it. The Coniston was gloomy, for the sun was packing up early to leave the summer foliage of Russell Square in slightly sinister shadow. An old codger dressed in a motheaten cardigan and tartan slippers was smoking a Woodbine on the steps of the apartment block when a slim woman walked up briskly.

'Hello,' she said. 'We spoke on the phone. You must be Mr Beecroft.'

He carefully nipped out his fag and rather cautiously shook her cool hand. 'Call me Wally, miss,' he replied, taking in her flaming red hair and darkish complexion with goggle-eyed appreciation.

'And I'm Mary,' she replied. 'Doctor Ross if you want to be formal.'

Wally doubled over in a fit of coughing and Mary repressed the urge to tell him to stop smoking. They had the National Health Service now and no doubt the doctors at the local clinic had already warned him to quit.

'Constitution like an ox,' he wheezed, patting his chest, and wiping his eyes with a grubby handkerchief. 'You'd better come in and I'll put the kettle on.'

Mary was down in London to give a paper at a conference at St Bartholomew's Hospital. Her recent promotion to full professor was long overdue, for outstanding as she was at her job, she had to overcome the entrenched male chauvinism of a profession steeped in fuddy-duddy conservatism. Her Geordie accent hadn't helped, either, and she still encountered men who expected her to empty the bedpans or make their coffee, and who would raise bushy eyebrows at her 'bolshy' opinions. She stared them down, for she had worked with the best in the field, including Eddie Barsky and Sidney Vogel, treating wounded Republican soldiers and civilians in Spain. When it was Britain's turn for the Nazi bombs to rain down, her services had been greatly in need, and after the war she had been to Germany to treat survivors of the Allied bombing.

Old Wally ushered her into his little office, cleaned off a chair with his handkerchief and busied himself making 'a brew'. When he had served it in cracked cups and apologised for not having milk, Mary produced a yellowing sheet of paper and smoothed it out on his rickety desk. She passed it over and he put on his new NHS spectacles and began to read, before looking up with owl eyes magnified by the thick lenses. The script was remarkably elegant, though the note was brief and apparently dashed off in haste.

'Yes, miss ... err Doctor, should I say.' He coughed. 'I well remember Mr Stubbs. A gentleman and a scholar he was. 'E left a bit of stuff wiv me to forward when 'e wuz settled.'

Hobart, August 1954

After storming out of old Kanga's surgery Marjorie Sproule walked across the city centre to the Carlton Café, which sat across the street from the Royal Hobart Hospital. She was hoping that her friend Eliza Mansell might be there. Miss Mansell was a clinical nurse specialist who lived at Mrs Mahoney's establishment, as the nurses' home was not to her liking. Miss Sproule knew that she sometimes came to the café at this time. They'd often shared a coffee and a joke about the doctors, including 'that silly bloody Kanga'. Eliza was not there, but Miss Sproule ordered a coffee and sat at a table near the window to wait. Her temper had cooled, and she wondered what she was going to do after insulting her boss. Perhaps she would have to give notice to Mrs Mahoney and return to Launceston and stay with her parents until something else turned up. Eliza would know. Miss Sproule's fine blue eyes filled with tears when she thought of the fate awaiting Geordie Stubbs.

'I say,' said a pukka sahib voice. 'I didn't mean to startle you, but are you alright, Miss Sproule?'

It was Mr Rolls – Harry Rolls – a cheery English soul whom she had often encountered in the court buildings and at the police head-quarters when she was running errands for Doctor Hetherington. He was employed in some civilian capacity by the police. She agreed that he could join her at her table when he asked, and he sat and ordered two more coffees from the newfangled Italian machine that hissed and frothed steamily on the front counter under the expert eye of old Luigi the octogenarian barista.

'I don't mean to pry, Miss Sproule,' said Harry, 'but is there anything I can do to help?' He handed her a clean handkerchief and waited until she had blown her nose and composed herself. His voice was kind and she found herself pouring out her heart to him about how an innocent man was going to hang. Harry Rolls listened carefully to what she had to say about his wayward friend.

'Fact is, Miss Sproule, I've been wonderin' what to do myself,' he said, stirring three-and-a-half heaped teaspoons of sugar into his cappuccino. 'You see, Geordie Stubbs is my good friend, and I can't believe he could have done it.' He rummaged in his briefcase and produced a copy of the day's *Mercury*. 'By Jove,' he said, smacking the page, 'this doesn't help. Now they're saying Geordie is a Communist. Here, look at this article by Karl Wollig: "The Beast is Red" indeed!'

'That's not all,' said Miss Sproule, encouraged by Harry's support. 'You've no idea what my boss has written in his report for the judge. He's practically guaranteed that Mr Stubbs will hang.'

Harry nodded sadly. 'Yes, my dear. I can tell you too that the police dossier won't help. The evidence, such as it is, is damning.' He listed the points on his fingers. 'Firstly, Geordie's kitchen knife was found embedded in Lance Giblin's chest. There's no denying that it's Geordie's knife because it's got his initials burned into the handle and he doesn't deny it's his.

'Secondly, there is a witness who claims that he heard Geordie arguing and fighting with Mr Giblin the night before the murder.' Harry gulped his coffee and continued his summary. 'Thirdly, as if what he says isn't bad enough, this witness – someone called Darryl Hall – alleges that he saw Geordie walking away from the scene of the crime shortly after it seems to have happened.'

'But surely Mr Stubbs has an alibi?'

'That's the thing.' Harry shook his head in frustration. 'The silly duffer refuses to say where he was. I don't know what his game is. I've tried to talk some sense into him. His lawyer, Mr Lindsay, has too, but he simply clams up.'

'Well, it does seem like an open and shut case, then.' Miss Sproule looked glum but Harry had no words of comfort.

'I can tell you, too, that the detectives in charge of the case believe Geordie committed at least three other murders.'

'Yes, there was speculation about that in the papers. It seems to me, Mr Rolls, that the evidence is slim, but enough to convict him and enough to torpedo any appeal.'

Harry sighed. 'The law will take its course and I'm not sure there is anything more we can do. I can go to see the silly bugger again but I doubt he'll listen.' He looked at his watch. 'Oh, I say, is that the time? Got to get back to work, but perhaps we could meet again to see what we can do?'

Miss Sproule agreed. They would meet again the following day in the lounge bar of the Alabama Hotel after Mr Rolls had had another go at trying to get Geordie to provide an alibi.

Meanwhile, there being no indication that Miss Sproule would re-appear in the surgery that day, Stuart Hetherington had arranged for a colleague's secretary to type up his report and deliver it urgently to Mr Justice Dicer. This done, the judge read it carefully and went home full of dread for what he would have to do. The matter wrapped up, and it being a quiet afternoon, Hetherington started to write the article the professor in Madrid was urging him to complete. He found, however, that he had developed writer's block and a little voice nagged at the back of his mind, suggesting that Stubbs had not 'dunnit'.

He also realised that he would have to seek out Miss Sproule, for it had suddenly struck him that with her quiet competence she was indispensable. Staring out the window at the snow on the summit of wintry Mount Wellington, he also admitted to himself that the woman practically wrote his reports for him. Perhaps an apology was in order?

With all this washing around in his head, he called in at the Victoria Tavern in Murray Street after work. He was fond of a drink at the best of times and this time he settled in grimly for a session, knocking back beers with whisky chasers. When the barmaid suggested that he'd had enough, he weaved around to the Brunswick, the Alabama, and several other pubs, waxing uncharacteristically garrulous with strangers, and standing them drinks. The booze sapped rational thought. After closing time, he staggered out and took a taxi to Mrs Mahoney's Battery Point boarding house and thumped on the front door, desperate to apologise to Miss Sproule. The building was in darkness and a lonely wind was blowing down the street past Bahr's chocolate shop, which he had haunted in happier times as a Hutchins schoolboy. The Post Office clock solemnly chimed, warning of the late hour, but the alcohol had washed all circumspection from his brain.

'Miss Sproule … Marjorie …' he snivelled. 'I'm sorry.'

A light went on upstairs and heavy footsteps thumped downstairs, muffled by thick carpet and the solid colonial door. A dog woofed, and he was dimly aware that a Siamese cat was watching him disdainfully from a mezzanine window. The door was flung open, and a woman stood there with her hair in curlers and a frosty expression on her face, ready to bite like the bull terrier by her side. Hetherington had not reckoned with meeting the formidable Ethel Mahoney, the former hospital matron who ran the place. She had a poker in her hand and seemed inclined to use it on him.

'This is a respectable house!' she barked in unison with the dog. 'Go away or I'll call the police!'

He backed away, slurring apologies. She slammed the door in

his face, so he reeled unsteadily up Hampden Road. Up near Kelly Street, now at the maudlin stage of inebriation, loving everybody and lamenting his misfortunes, he encountered Knocker Roddy, an old tramp who lived in a sort of kennel in the little park in Francis Street.

'I am a wretch!' Hetherington wailed. 'Eight years Miss Sproule has worked for me, and I have treated her like a skivvy!'

Generous soul that he was, Knocker shared his last bottle of four-penny dark with the doctor, who swore eternal friendship and afterwards lurched off down to Ma Dwyer's Blue House in Salamanca Place. Ma refused him admission, so he lurched off up through St David's Park to Macquarie Street, intending to enter his club. It was closed for the night, and so, desperate for a wee, he proceeded to urinate copiously on the footpath. He hadn't noticed the two constables following him. He awoke in the cold, unforgiving dawn in a Liverpool Street cell with a terrible thirst and a pounding headache, recalling what he had done the night before. A fellow clubman who was high up in the police force arranged for the charges to be withdrawn and advised him to moderate his alcoholic intake.

Hobart, August 1954

'Say ya prayers, ya little black bastard,' Warder Cresswell jeered. 'The old judge is gunna sentence ya to swing today.' With this, he shoved Geordie along the corridor and up some steep stairs into the courtroom. A murmur rippled round the public gallery at the sight of The Beast. *The Mercury*'s Karl Wollig opened his notebook ready to jot down his impressions of the penultimate act of the ghastly drama. All rose when Judge Dicer entered. He had walked the short distance to the court as slowly as Shakespeare's whining schoolboy creeping unwillingly to school, lamenting that on so glorious a morning he had so dark a duty to perform. He had avoided the mob that swirled round the main entrance, sooled on through a loudhailer by the insufferable Alderman Amos. The spectators in the gallery listened in silence as he laboured through a stilted speech, interrupted on occasion by the noise of the mob in the street. In conclusion, Dicer declared, there were no extenuating circumstances to prevent him from performing his melancholy duty. A flunkey stepped forward and placed a black cap on his head, whereupon Dicer recited the time-worn litany: George

William Marmaduke Stubbs would be hanged by the neck until he was dead, and Dicer prayed the Lord would have mercy on his soul.

Geordie's face betrayed no emotion as he was led down the back stairs to the prison. The trial had concluded as he knew it would and although he had dreaded the sentence, he was also relieved that the drawn-out drama was over. He couldn't know it, but Justice Dicer was no hanging Judge Jeffreys and had had no stomach for what the law had forced him to do. He rushed off to the lavatory, where he was violently and miserably sick.

Geordie was sitting behind the wire mesh grill in the prison visiting room when Harry came in and started to rant. 'You're a stubborn fool Geordie. I've known a few blockheads in m' time, but you are insufferable. Look man, if you don't tell Simon Verte where you were, you're done for!'

'Well, good afternoon to you too, Harry.' Geordie went to say something else but started to cough.

Normally solicitous of his friend's needs, Harry didn't notice. 'For the love of Jesus, Geordie, I've heard the hangman is on his way from Melbourne. Dermot Lindsay is a top man. He's lodged an appeal, but it's a mere formality. You're going to swing!'

The warder sitting nearby smirked. Harry stormed out, afraid he'd lose his English sang-froid if he stayed. The screw Miss Sproule called the Lizard came in and took Geordie back to the condemned cell.

The next morning, Harry was at his office desk poking glumly at a ledger of crime statistics when Miss Sproule knocked on the door. There was no sign of tears this time; indeed, there was a steely look in her blue eyes.

'Ah, Miss Sproule,' he said, peering at his watch. 'I thought we had agreed to meet in half an hour or so over at the Alabama, in m' tea break.'

'Well, Mr Rolls,' she replied, 'there's no point in moping around, so I have come with a proposal. Doctor Hetherington has been rather sweet of late, and he has agreed to give me time off with pay.'

'I went to see Geordie.' Harry sighed, pushing up the steel-rimmed reading glasses that lent him a somewhat professorial air. 'Bugger wouldn't budge, so I'm afraid there's nothin' much we can do. 'Cept maybe pray.'

'Nonsense!' she retorted. 'I've borrowed my uncle Arthur's car, and I suggest that we drive up to Bronte Park to make some enquiries.'

'I say,' said Harry, perking up. 'Nothin' ventured; nothin' gained. I'll just grab me coat and we'll be off. I'll just tell Mr Lee next door that I'm takin' the rest of the day off.'

Uncle Arthur's lovingly waxed and polished 1948 E93A four-door black Ford Prefect saloon was parked outside in Liverpool Street. Some young constables were admiring it and they shared knowing glances when Harry and Miss Sproule jumped in. Miss Sproule ignored them and drove away – very competently too, for a woman, Harry marvelled. She changed gear smoothly and accelerated up Argyle Street. There were no mishaps and soon they were motoring up the Lyell Highway from Granton at a fast clip.

'I say, Miss Sproule,' Harry enthused, 'where did you learn to drive like this? Never tried it meself. Never needed to. Had a driver wallah back in India. S'ppose I'll have to learn.'

'My dad taught me,' she replied. 'Anyway, you may call me Marjorie, seeing that we're friends.'

Bronte Park

Several hours later, after Miss Sproule – Marjorie – had skilfully negotiated the winding dirt road up through the Derwent Valley and up onto the Central Plateau, they arrived at Bronte Park. The sun was blazing down from a cloudless sky, but there were deep winter shadows behind the assorted wooden and corrugated iron buildings of the construction town. Miss Sproule parked the Ford Prefect outside what a man told them was the single men's mess and they went inside. Clouds of steam were rising from the kitchen and there was the sound of great activity. One of the cooks saw them and came up wiping his hands on his apron and regarding them quizzically.

'Hello,' he said in a musical Italian accent. 'I'm Gino Biancocini. Can I help-a youse?'

When Harry explained that they were friends of Geordie Stubbs, Gino's face broke into a broad smile. 'You friends of Geordie, you-a my friends!' he enthused. His face fell when he recalled that Geordie was sentenced to hang. They explained that they had come up to find anything that might help at the pending appeal. 'He is a good man,' said Gino. 'He always wants to help the people.' He looked like he was about to cry.

Miss Sproule shook her head and exchanged a glance with Harry. No help here either. They all believed Geordie was innocent but had no proof. They both took an instant dislike to Darryl Hall, the bodgie known as Elvis.

'Sly boots,' said Harry. 'Wouldn't trust the little shit … sorry Marjorie. Army language.'

Marjorie waved a hand. 'Yes. He's lying through his yellow teeth.'

'Should've given him a biff. Man's got a nerve workin' here after what he's said and done.'

Another kitchenhand, Big Joe Ružička, just grinned gormlessly; he was less use than a rain gauge in the Nullarbor. Next, they button-holed Snowy Myers, a big silent kitchenhand whom the police had neglected to question. Myers, who was usually half-cut according to Gino, answered their questions monosyllabically, but when Harry revealed that he was a fellow ex-serviceman, he began to talk. He became even more voluble when he learned that Miss Sproule's fiancé was the famous Lieutenant David McDougall, VC, who had died fighting the Japanese on the Kokoda Trail. Snowy was himself a New Guinea veteran. He too could not believe that Stubbs had murdered the young engineer, and he denied overhearing them arguing and fighting as Elvis had claimed. If they'd done so, he would have heard them. He reckoned that Elvis Hall was a liar and needed to be shot at dawn and his clothes burned.

'He's not wrong,' said Marjorie, 'but it's no help either.'

Gino provided some hope. 'I shoulda have said. Murray Triffitt, he is-a the apprentice cook. A good friend of Geordie's. He shoulda start his shift soon.'

The young man came in shortly afterwards and went to his locker for his chef's regalia. He looked pleased when Miss Sproule said why they wanted to speak to him.

'Good bloke, Geordie,' he said. 'Taught me heaps. I was in a bad way before I met him. My parents had died in a car crash and he was like a father to me. Keeps me awake at night worryin' about him. He didn't kill nobody.'

It looked like more of the same – character references but no evidence – but then Murray gave them the hope they'd been so desperately seeking.

'Them coppers didn't want to know nothing. I went up to them and told them. Told 'em that Geordie had been carrying on with a married woman. He was no poof like they reckoned.'

Miss Sproule put a hand on his arm. 'And do you know who she is, Murray?'

'Got a bloody good idea. It's old Grinner's missus. Grinner Newcombe's that is. Naturally, Geordie kept quiet about it, but I don't miss much.' He scratched his chin. 'Look, come over to me camp. I've got somethin' there that might help.'

They crunched across the gravel to Murray's hut and waited while he rummaged around inside. 'Here y' are. It's his diary. I dunno what's in it. Seemed disrespectful to go looking at it without his permission.'

They felt no such constraint and Marjorie felt like kissing him.

'It's his handwriting alright,' said Harry. 'Recognise it anywhere. Beautiful hand.'

Gino found them a quiet corner of the kitchen and they settled down to read, fortified by cups of the cook's strong Italian coffee. 'By Jove,' said Harry. 'Let's get started.'

Tuesday 9th August 1949

I've settled in well at Bronte Park, tho' that obliging magistrate Mr Morris gave me no choice. 'Sentenced to the Hydro,' as they say. I'm happy to be back in harness. I'm working with two assistant cooks Tas Youd and Gino Biancocini, and there's four kitchenhands. After a couple of days one of them, a teddy boy type or what they call a bodgie here called Elvis – although I'm told his mother called him Darryl – left a newspaper in the lunchroom. I say 'newspaper' but it's just a rag. The Melbourne Truth – horses, scandal, tits, and bums. He left it open at page three for me to see an article headed in big type WILD PUB BRAWL: SCOTCHMAN'S CHOICE: CLINK OR THE HYDRO! There was a photo of me with black eyes and torn shirt. Anyway, I ignored it and they soon forgot about it.

One of the kitchenhands is a young fellow called Murray Triffitt, a farm boy whose parents recently died in a car crash. His dad was always boozing, and they ran off the road at the Dee River. The farm wasn't worth a brass razoo. Murray reckoned if it had been a horse, you would have shot it, and he just walked away. Life's bloody hard for so many here – outside shithouses and dirt floors.

[…]

Thursday 15th September 1949

I've arranged for Grinner to promote Murray to apprentice cook. The bugger ummed and ah-ed a bit but had to agree. Elvis hates me after that. The others are okay, good blokes really. Snowy Myers drinks and fights the Japanese every night in his hut. Tas is an amiable little Taswegian. Gino's an excitable Neapolitan and a first-rate cook. The fourth kitchenhand is a 'New Australian' called Jozef Ružička – Big Joe, we call him. He doesn't say much and despite his size, you don't really notice him. Sometimes he gets pissed and parades around the single men's camp with his shirt off. He's a Slovak and hates Czechs. I don't know what to think of him really, but he never causes me any trouble, although I've seen him looking at me with narrowed eyes a few times.

[…]

Wednesday 5th October 1949

I've redesigned the kitchen layout and begun to reform the menus. I'm determined to phase out the chops and sausages slathered in tomato sauce and replace them with decent tucker – see, I'm picking up the Aussie lingo! Gino's enthusiastically supported the culinary revolution and even Tas and Murray raised on silverside and three veg admit the new stuff's better. But Elvis gets around with a face on him like a wet weekend in Sunderland.

We cook up huge tureens of Boeuf Bourguignon and call it 'stew' and the blokes lap it up. Coq-au-vin. Wine and garlic! 'Givvus another serve o' that chook stuff, Geordie,' they say. Big pans of lasagne! Sauerbraten! Apfelstrudel too! Couscous. Minestrone. Ravioli. Spaghetti that has never seen the inside of a tin! Even pressed duck one time when I got a bargain from a farmer down near Westerway. (Lovely down there in autumn with the English trees turning and a profusion of fruit like you wouldn't believe – raspberries, apples, blueberries, blackberries, pears, plums, peaches. Hops and the smell of good black earth. You could do worse than retire down there.) We serve up Asian food too – stuff the men call chop suey though its origins range from India to Indonesia and Cochinchina. There's chocolate éclairs, and Black Forest cake, Far Breton … The Tour d'Argent in the Tasmanian highlands! The bacon and egg breakfasts are my concession to Taswegian custom, but even then, we've jazzed it up. We tried to get rid of the tomato sauce, but Maurie Duggan the union rep came to see me. 'We love your food, Geordie,' he said, 'but there's just one thing.' 'Yes?' 'The dead horse.' 'Eh?' 'The tomato sauce. Blokes can't do without it.'

Breaks my heart to see blokes slopping it on our creations.

[…]

Friday 16th May 1952

Howay! The old beak 'sentenced' me to 12 months on the Hydro, but 3 years later, I am still here! I have a driving licence and a second-hand Baby Austin, which I take for long drives in my spare time. I've bought a decent fiddle from McCann's in Hobart and often entertain myself and the boys of an evening. Turns out there is quite a tradition of fiddling here, with an American influence from when Yankee ships sat out the Civil War here.

[…]

Saturday 8th November 1952

Old Mick Prendergast is retiring and we're having a bash for him in the Rec. Hall tonight. Mick's a ganger who started back on the Waddamana scheme the best part of 40 years ago. They lived in tents in the snow and rain. Hard man. Quick with his fists and even quicker with his wits, he's run an SP bookie racket from his house. He's asked me to take over for a consideration and he will be the Hobart end of the operation. Suits me.

[…]

Tuesday 23rd December 1952

Last night there was a Christmas dance in the Rec Hall. Typical Aussie do – men down one end of the hall round the barrel. Women down the other end drinking tea or shandies and nibbling on the sandwiches and butterfly cakes.

Ernie Darke's Silvertone Orchestra was up from Hobart. They played things like An Elephant's Nest in a Rhubarb Tree, The Hokey Pokey, The Beer Barrel Polka, Pack Up Your Troubles, and Bing Crosby stuff. Fair play to them, they tried some Fats Domino and Lloyd Price numbers. Arthur Smith's Guitar Boogie too but they made a right hash of that! Elvis Hall was delivering them beer. Seemed to know them. The little blonde singer was guzzling like there was no tomorrow. They didn't sound too bad if you had had a skinful and a tin ear, and couples were up on the dancefloor. Some fool suggested that I join them on fiddle. I pretended not to hear.

Grinner Newcombe was turning nasty with the drink. Typical of that bastard. His missus was serving tea and coffee. Janice. She's ground down by life, I reckon. She's a nice looker but she deliberately tries to make herself unattractive. Nobody had asked Janice. 'Off limits' because of Grinner! Well bugger that. I walked straight up and asked her to dance.

'Oh, I couldn't,' she said.

'Haddaway, bonnie lass,' I coaxed, 'course you can.'

She reckoned she didn't know how to dance, so I said I'd teach her. She was a fast learner. Neither of us saw Grinner lurching up the hall looking nasty. The prick grabbed Janice's arm and dragged her outside. Gino came up then. He told me to back off. Reckoned Grinner was like Hitler for his wife. Bashes her. Gino has seen her with black eyes. Cops won't do anything. They say it's just a domestic.

Anyway, I was sat there fuming for a while before getting another beer. I took more notice of the band because the singer was so pissed that she was forgetting the words of the songs and the drummer was starting to miss the beat. You couldn't really make out their faces through the cigarette smoke, but I recognised the drummer's ugly mug when I got closer. The pianist and the singer too for that matter. Then I went out and studied the poster that was stuck up on the front door. Ernie Darke was the bodgie on guitar, Bert Goss was on double bass and Alf Devine was the one murdering the trumpet. They seemed vaguely familiar but it was the other three that caught my attention: Mavis bloody Devine on piano, Jane Forbes on vocals, kazoo and washboard, and Max fucking Johnstone on drums! The bastards who had stitched me up at the Coronation Hotel. Got me sent to Bronte! Max went out for a piss during a break, so I followed him. He came back in a bit later with two black eyes and a swollen mouth. It almost took my mind off Janice and I decided to call it a night.

Two big Bedford vans were parked out the back, with Ernie Darke's Silvertone Orchestra on them. Anyway, there was a bit of a scuffle and big Sergeant Alomes came round with a wriggling little bloke in each hand, like a hunter with a brace of partridges!

'Howay, Stan,' I said. 'What have ye got there?'

'Burglars,' he replied shaking one by the neck. 'Keep still ya little bastard! Vans are fulla stuff.'

I near pissed myself laughing. Mickey Devine and Brian Goss they were called, family members of the band. Alomes charged them with multiple counts of breaking, entering, and stealing, and the band members themselves were charged as accessories.

While the good folk of Bronte were off dancing, Goss and Devine had snuck into their houses and taken whatever took their fancy. They'd already done over Ouse, Hamilton, and Sorell, so the cops didn't have to be geniuses to work out their game. The arrests couldn't have happened to a nicer pack of bastards!

[…]

Sunday 19th April 1953

I saw Janice again tonight. We were at a 21st birthday party in Tarraleah. Her face lit up, but I made no move to join her, not wishing for her to suffer her husband's anger. Grinner drank so much in so short a time that he passed out in an armchair, sprawled there snoring and spluttering like a surfacing whale, the arsehole.

I went out for a smoke, and she followed me. One thing led to another and soon we were snogging and all over each other like there was no tomorrow. I led her to my Baby Austin, and we drove out into the forest. The little car was cramped but we managed somehow to have sex and curled up there sleepily afterwards until Janice sat up and said, 'Oh Jesus, I'd better get back before he wakes up and notices I'm gone.' Luckily, Grinner was still snoring away, and the party was in full swing, with the new rock and roll music blasting out of the record player and couples jiving.

[…]

Tuesday 11th August 1953

Me and Janice try to be together as often as possible, although sometimes a few weeks go by before it's safe. Sometimes I play my fiddle for her. She says it's lovely and she cries at the slow airs. Careful as we are, Janice says Grinner is getting suspicious.

[…]

Monday 15th March 1954

Grinner came into the mess late this afternoon and told me he wanted a word outside. 'You been paying my missus a bit too much attention,' he said. 'I'm giving you fair warning, Scotchman. She's my wife and you keep your fucking hands off her.'

It was bound to happen. Not much you can keep secret round here! Anyway, I hate the little bastard, so I drew himself up to my full 5'4" and prodded him in the chest. 'Now you listen to me, Newcombe,' I said. 'A little shit like you doesn't deserve a fine woman like Janice and the next time you hurt her, I'll come after you.'

He was stunned. Nobody had ever dared speak to him like that before. He started to arc up but backed off. He reckoned he could sack me and said he knew all about the SP racket. The idiot. I'm pretty sure Sergeant Alomes looks the other way. I was worried though because he went off muttering about 'killing the bitch'.

I'm a bit worried about another thing too. I've developed this cough. Tried Vicks cough mixture. Suck all the time on Irish Moss, but they don't do anything for it. I've been putting off seeing Doc Bryant about it. Maybe he'll just tell me to cut down on the smokes and he'd be right. I'm like a bloody dragon!

[...]

Monday 26th April 1954

Grinner was down in Hobart at a meeting, so Janice and I drove out to a secluded spot near Lake St Clair. She started to cry. She said she'd been reluctant to burden me with her problems, but it all came out. Newcombe had swept her off her feet when she was a trainee nurse and has kept her barefoot and pregnant. He started to beat her, usually when he was drunk, but then even when he was sober, he would give her the odd backhander if she was too slow in serving his dinner or ironing his shirts or had annoyed him some other way. A couple of times he's threatened her with his .22 hunting rifle and another time he held a knife at her throat. She reckons she'd leave him but there are the kids and her parents both died a while back. She has no money, and she never got her nursing qualifications. She doesn't even know how she could get away from Bronte Park without him following her even if she had somewhere to go. She feels trapped.

Although I like Janice well enough, I can't see myself running off with her and the kids. Whether she loves me is another matter too. She's desperate to escape from Grinner. But Grinner is so violent and unpredictable that I really fear for her life. Grinner doesn't know for sure that we've had sex and I fear that if he finds out he'll kill her. I might ask Harry Rolls if he can help. He's got a lot of contacts in the Returned Services League – maybe he could find her a job on the mainland or something.

It was mid-afternoon when Marjorie and Harry visited Janice Newcombe in her neat Hydro prefab. She let them in, glancing up and down the street as she closed the door. The poor woman's face was slathered with make-up, but it couldn't hide the bruises under her eyes. Neither of them were skilled interrogators, but they didn't have to be. Janice broke down under Harry's clumsy but gentle questioning and Marjorie's sympathetic words and admitted that Geordie had been with her in his Baby Austin at the time of Giblin's murder.

'Oh dear,' said Harry. 'You should have said something.'

Janice looked guilty, sad, and defiant at the same time.

'You don't know my husband. He's threatened to kill me and he means it. I was just too scared to come forward. I know I should've, but what about the kids? I even took an overdose of sleeping pills Doc Bryant prescribed but I vomited them up. I don't know what to do.'

'You have to come with us,' said Marjorie. 'You can't stay here, and you must help save Geordie. They'll hang him, you know.'

Janice nodded, then bit her lip. 'But where will I go? And what about Archie and Timmy, the children?'

'Pack some clothes for yourself and the kids,' said Marjorie.

The kids came home from school and within fifteen minutes Janice was standing by the door with two suitcases. They all crammed into Uncle Arthur's car and were soon speeding down the Lyell Highway to Hobart, where Harry put up Janice and the kids in his spare room. 'Let them gossip,' he said when Marjorie worried what his neighbours would think.

Hobart, August 1954

The day after Harry and Marjorie's trip to Bronte, police investigated reports of screaming coming from a rundown weatherboard house in Little Arthur Street, a narrow lane in North Hobart. When loud knocking failed to elicit any response, the police kicked down the door. In the dingy back bedroom, they found the body of Wendy Jones, a 40-year-old prostitute. The young constables had nightmares about what they found. Blood had soaked the bedclothes and was spattered up the peeling wallpaper, apparently from Wendy's severed jugular.

Meanwhile, Harry and Marjorie took Janice Newcombe to see Inspector Simon Verte. They knew Verte by reputation and hoped what they had heard wasn't true. Alas, it was.

'Well, you were shagging the bloke,' Verte sneered. 'It's only natural you want to save him.' He took a drag on his cigarette and declared, 'I think you're making this up, Mrs Newcombe.'

He shooed them out of his office, glared at Marjorie Sproule, and warned Harry to stick to the job he was paid for. With luck, they'd give up and let the case take its course, he thought, grabbing his trilby, and heading for the pub for a quick mid-morning snifter. He had no sympathy for that little bugger, Stubbs. He was the cause of Verte's father's death. Fuck him. He deserved to swing for that.

Harry was enraged by Verte's refusal to help, but Marjorie kept a cool head. At her suggestion, they sought out Geordie's lawyer and found him leaving the Magistrates' Court. Dermot Lindsay, LLB (Hons) was a flamboyant man-about-town whose rakish demeanour and inebriated antics concealed a sharp mind. He was delighted by what they had to say. The appeal was scheduled for the following morning, and he had despaired of the outcome. Now, listening to a pared-down summary of Janice's evidence as they left the court building, he had no doubt that his client would walk free.

Lindsay snorted derisively when they told him of the inspector's response. 'If I had a quid for every collar he *hasn't* felt, I wouldn't have to work again. Anyway, come with me.'

Lindsay was a champion boozer, so he steered them to the lounge bar of the Brisbane Hotel. He scounged a biro from the barmaid and took notes on a succession of beer mats, numbering each one and stowing them in his briefcase in between sips of his ale, muttering about how you never had a notebook when you needed one. When he and the beermats had absorbed all the details of what Janice had to say, he whisked her round the corner to his chambers and she made a sworn statement that Lindsay's secretary recorded in triplicate. Harry sent her to his home in a taxi afterwards and he and Dermot Lindsay settled back at the Brisbane to celebrate. Marjorie left them to it. Somewhere past the sixth round of beers, Lindsay forgot his promise to convey the good news to the so-called Beast, who was brooding in his prison cell unable to shake the awful knowledge of the dangling noose from his mind.

The courtroom was packed the next morning at ten o'clock sharp when Justice Philip Knopwood strutted in, resplendently gowned and bewigged. A portly sexagenarian with the face of a ferocious baby, the judge was descended from a notorious flogging parson of colonial days who would sentence a man to 100 lashes before retiring with good appetite to luncheon. Knopwood was standing in for Justice Dicer, who was off on extended sick leave, and this was one case he would enjoy. He glowered over his half-moon glasses at Geordie, who was sitting small and dark in the dock, just wanting the appeal over and done with. The reporter Karl Wollig checked his watch: like everyone else he expected the appeal to be rejected in a matter of minutes, with the sentence upheld and plenty of time for a few beers before writing it up for the next day's edition. The usual mob was shouting outside, and the prosecutor was looking smug. When the spectators had resumed their seats, Knopwood waved impatiently to Dermot Lindsay to stand and make his case. The old curmudgeon's demeanour stated *Be quick about it, man. I haven't time to waste on tomfool appeals like this.* Geordie clearly agreed, so both were dumbfounded by what Lindsay had to say. Knopwood sat with his mouth open for a good minute before ordering a short recess. Janice was waiting to testify, but when the court re-assembled, the prosecutor rose to state that in the light of new evidence, the Crown was withdrawing all charges against Mr Stubbs. Dermot Lindsay pumped Geordie's hand when the little man stepped down from the dock and Harry Rolls rushed up and in a most un-English display of emotion, engulfed Geordie in a bear hug and danced him round the room. Geordie didn't say anything. He looked small and bewildered. Miss Sproule hung back, but she too was ecstatic. The *Mercury* man rushed off to file his scoop – eschewing the drink he'd promised himself – and soon the news reached the Talbot Hotel in Newtown where the hangman was swilling beer and reading a form guide. He swore a foul oath, downed his drink, and slouched off back to his room, angry that he'd been cheated of his fee. Across in Macquarie Street, Stuart Hetherington took a phone call, cancelled his appointments for the day and went home to work in his garden. Alderman Amos was speechless for once.

As for Detective Inspector Simon Verte, he was carpeted by

Superintendent Jim Doughney. 'Detective?' sneered the big superintendent. 'You couldn't detect shit in a country dunny with a miner's headlamp and a canary. Think about retirement, Verte, because unless you pull your finger out, you're going back on the beat as a constable. In Zeehan. Now get out!'

The following morning, Simon Verte arrested the Bronte Park kitchenhand Jozef Ružička and charged him with the murder of Wendy Jones. It was an open and shut case that not even Verte could bungle. Witnesses testified that they had seen Ružička enter the Little Arthur Street house and leave it after they had heard loud screams. Ružička, who was down from Bronte on a week's leave, was lying on his bed in a boarding house drinking imported *borovička* when the police stormed into his room. They found bloodstained clothing in a box on top of the wardrobe along with a hunting knife, also blood-spattered. Forensic examination identified the blood as that of Wendy Jones and the post-mortem established that the knife was the murder weapon. Ružička's fingerprints matched those found at the scenes of the unsolved murders at Queenstown, Hobart, and New Norfolk. After lengthy interrogation by Inspector Verte and Roy Edensor, Ružička also admitted that he had killed the engineer Lance Giblin at Bronte Park, but he refused to give them any reasons why he had carried out the murders.

Meanwhile, true to his word, Harry had arranged via his RSL contacts for Janice Newcombe – who had reverted to her maiden name of Archer – to take up a position as housekeeper with a wealthy family in the Western Districts of Victoria. Her children would live with her in a cottage on the property. Geordie Stubbs, meanwhile, took a room in the Hollydene guesthouse and pondered his return to Bronte. His hair had turned grey from living in the shadow of the gallows, and he was gaunt faced. Nevertheless, he acquiesced to Harry's suggestion that they celebrate, and they spent much of the day propped up at the bar in Hadley's Hotel with Dermot Lindsay. Marjorie Sproule joined them for a while, but she wasn't a drinker and soon left them to it. As they left the bar, Geordie caught sight of a man exiting the Victoria Tavern. It took him a second to recognise Warder Tommy Cresswell, who was out of uniform and full of drunken bonhomie.

'Jeez,' Cresswell slurred, attempting to fix his close-set eyes on Geordie's face. 'Good to see ya, mate. Always noo you was innocent.'

Geordie repressed the urge to thump him and went on his way.

Lying in bed at night, Stuart Hetherington recalled with shame how he had colluded in a process that had almost sent Geordie Stubbs to his death. He regretted, too, that Marjorie Sproule had put in her notice, ostensibly to prepare for her exams. Hetherington felt sure it was also because she had never forgiven him. She had typed up the transcript of the unsettling interview with the psychopathic Ružička and joked that it would be impossible to find any evidence of the red gene in him. Hetherington had swallowed his pride and attempted a smile.

While the doctor was interviewing the real Beast of Bronte, Simon Verte was skulking in the back bar of the Royal Exchange Hotel. Ružička's arrest had saved him from demotion, but only just, and he was bent on venting his anger. He'd given his poor wife what he called a fourp'ny one and bawled out some young constables, but even he couldn't deny that he had been promoted beyond his ability, and that his father would have been ashamed of him. The thought of his father gave him an idea of how he could stitch up Geordie Stubbs. He'd contact his twin brother, Claude, in London and together they'd fix the little bastard good and proper. He swilled down the remnants of his beer and swayed over to the front door with a vicious grin on his ruddy features.

~ 62 ~

Bronte Park, 1954

By this time, Geordie had been welcomed back at Bronte by his workmates and the diners in the single men's mess, who had missed his creations. Even Sergeant Alomes came to wish him well. 'Never thought you'd dunnit, tiger,' he growled. 'Just between you and me them two that was here are pretty crap detectives.'

Everything felt strange and familiar at the same time and rather anticlimactic after Geordie had cheated the hangman's noose. He derived some satisfaction from the knowledge that the wretched bodgie Elvis Hall was in Campbell Street Gaol, doing twelve months for lying under oath and perverting the course of justice, and he was pleased that Janice was safely out of town. He had debated the wisdom of returning given that Grinner Newcombe was said to be raging about her infidelity and had sworn to get revenge. To forestall this possibility, Geordie used a ruse that he had used years before to get rid of a pair of blackguards at the High Fell colliery. He had plenty of examples of Grinner's handwriting and it was a simple matter to forge a letter of resignation from the man. Grinner vehemently denied writing it, but Resident Engineer Ted Loftus hated him and chose to believe it was genuine. Nobody knew where Grinner had gone, and nobody cared. It was unlikely that he'd ever find Janice, who was not claiming maintenance for the kids lest it help him track her down.

Geordie was distractible. Everything felt flat, and he had a powerful urge to return to the land of his birth. He confessed to Murray Triffitt that more than anything he wanted to make it up to his child for his failure to be a father. After a couple of months, he gave notice. The skipper of a German apple boat had offered him a job because his regular cook had jumped ship, bewitched by a Hobart siren. The ship, however, sailed without Geordie. The cough that Doctor Hetherington had noticed was more persistent, and Geordie had lost a great deal of weight. He was suffering from sharp pains in his chest, was coughing up bloody sputum, and even walking up the short flight of steps into the mess hall winded him. He was not surprised by the sharp deterioration in his health. He had had months to dwell on his health problems. Just a week or so before he had gone to prison, Doc Bryant had called him into the Bronte medical centre.

'I'm afraid, Geordie, that there's no easy way of saying this,' said the doctor, examining the cigarette smouldering between his fingers before crushing it into the ashtray on his desk.

Geordie had nodded. He knew what was coming.

'I can't give you false hope,' Bryant continued. 'The test results came back, and they aren't good. You have squamous cell carcinoma – lung cancer in layman's terms.'

'How long have I got?' Geordie lisped, his mouth a taut line.

'Six months,' Bryant replied. 'I can't say for sure. You might get a bit longer than that.'

Geordie had told nobody and he had brushed off Hetherington's questions about his coughing during the prison interviews. Now, with his symptoms worsening and with perhaps only weeks to live, he decided to say goodbye to Bronte and enter a hospice for the dying in Hobart.

Hobart, Spring 1954

One chilly spring day shortly after Geordie had left Bronte Park, an attractive red-haired woman took a room at Hadley's Hotel, the stately old girl of Hobart's board and lodging establishments. Sitting in the lounge bar, she read in *The Mercury* that the notorious murderer Jozef Ružička had been hanged at Campbell Street Gaol. A sidebar announced that the hangman had lost his footing and drowned in Constitution Dock the same evening after squandering his fee in the Hope and Anchor pub. The woman admitted to herself that she took a certain grim satisfaction in the executioner's watery end, and although she was in principle opposed to the death penalty, Ružička's demise was also no loss. Pushing the newspaper and these grim thoughts aside, she took a thick book from her handbag and was soon absorbed.

Professor Mary Ross had taken leave of absence from her post at Newcastle University to track down her father in this outpost of the Empire. She had learned his whereabouts sometime earlier from old Wally Beecroft, the caretaker at The Coniston flats in London, but had been too busy at work to follow matters up. When the personnel office said she had banked up too much leave, she booked a passage to Melbourne on SS *Orontes* and then flew down to Hobart. The day after her arrival she had rented a car and driven up the winding mountain roads to Bronte Park. It was not a wasted journey, for she learned a great deal about her father from the apprentice Murray Triffitt, and he told her how to locate Geordie back down in Hobart. Murray also gave her a box of Geordie's papers, which he had been keeping until Geordie gave him a permanent forwarding address. She returned to Hadley's late that evening and telephoned Harry Rolls at the number Murray had given her. She stayed up late that night reading through her father's papers, and the following day, while she was out sightseeing on Mount Wellington, Harry dropped off more documents, including Miss Sproule's shorthand notes of her employer's interviews with Geordie. If she were to meet her father, she wanted to know everything about him. The following afternoon, once again sitting in the Hadley's lounge, absorbed in her book, Professor Ross had quite forgotten that she had arranged to meet Harry, so she gave a start when he addressed her. A woman and another man stood by Harry's side.

'Sorry about that,' Harry stammered. 'You were in a bit of a brown study, Professor. Anyway, I'm very pleased to meet you, and this' – here he indicated the woman with him – 'is my good friend Miss Sproule. My other friend here is Mr Lindsay, your father's lawyer.'

They all shook hands (to Harry's mild surprise), and he went with Lindsay to get the drinks in. Neither of the two women were good at small talk and both looked relieved when the men re-appeared with the glasses.

'Okay,' said Mary, taking a sip of her sherry and putting the glass down carefully. 'Please call me Mary. I'm very grateful, Miss Sproule, for the opportunity to read through your notes from the interviews with my father. I must also thank you, Mr Lindsay, for your part in this matter. Now, Miss Sproule, my shorthand is rusty, but I under-stood most of it.'

'That's good, Professor,' replied Miss Sproule. 'It's Marjorie, by the way. As you know, I worked until very recently as secretary to a well-known psychiatrist here in Hobart. I was present when he interviewed your father to prepare a pre-sentence report for the judge in your father's case.'

'And I take it that you didn't believe my father was guilty?'

'That's right. I listened to everything he had to say. Later, I read Doctor Hetherington's handwritten report and I was distressed by it.'

Harry's eyes were smiling at Miss Sproule, Mary noticed. Dermot Lindsay had noticed too, and he gave her a wink. Mary was amused but would not be deflected.

'Why did you come to think this?' she asked Marjorie.

'Well, apart from everything else, the evidence was flimsy. Circumstantial, you might say. The police had made a complete hash of the investigation. They just couldn't be bothered. There was a lot of pressure for a quick conviction and the detectives on the case were hopeless. Now, I do realise that Doctor Hetherington's role was purely to advise the court on the mental state of the accused – your father, that is – but his report not only accepted guilt but constructed a case aimed at proving Geordie Stubbs was capable of such a crime.'

'Did this Hetherington fellow believe it?'

'Yes. Well, I think that he had convinced himself of it against his better judgement.'

Mary changed tack. 'What did you think of my father?' she asked.

Miss Sproule blushed and continued. 'I thought he was a bit of a rogue, but I could not see him as a person capable of such a murder. Geordie was not – is not – a psychopath. Anyway, as you probably know, the real murderer was hanged a day or so ago.'

'Yes,' nodded Mary. 'I'm very grateful to you and Harry here for doing what the police should have done.'

Mary was impressed by Miss Sproule. She couldn't know it, but the woman had blossomed. She had been a meek and unobtrusive presence in Hetherington's surgery and a quiet mouse in other parts of her life, but she was now a forthright woman who spoke her mind. She was considering studying for Matriculation after finishing her commerce course and dreamed of one day graduating with a degree from the university. She had amassed quite a library of the classics and had a keen interest in history.

'Now, Harry,' said the professor. 'I'm not completely clear on why my father refused to produce his alibi. What was going on here? Couldn't the police have protected the woman … er, Janice?'

Marjorie smiled sadly. 'They treat such matters as "domestics". They don't want to know, I'm afraid.'

Mary nodded. She'd seen too many battered women in her surgery.

'Fact is' – Harry put down his empty beer glass and tried to catch the barmaid's eye, much to Dermot Lindsay's relief, for he was parched – 'Fact is, look, your father knew he was terminally ill by that stage. I'm sorry to tell you this, m' dear, but he was going to die anyway, so he thought what did it matter that he would go a few months earlier? Maybe he'd cheat the hangman by dying first of cancer?'

Dermot Lindsay nodded his head. 'Yes, I moved heaven and earth to get him to provide an alibi, but he wouldn't budge.' He wiggled his glass at Harry.

'That is so,' agreed Miss Sproule, 'and I rather think he was burdened by a lifetime of guilt.'

'I think I understand.' Mary nodded. 'He abandoned my mother when she was pregnant with me, so perhaps he believed he deserved his fate.'

'Yes,' said Miss Sproule. 'Precisely because of that, and because he was ashamed of some of the other things he'd done.'

Harry nodded his agreement. 'Complicated fella, your father. Some of the things he got up to … Stole the King James chamber pot you know!'

'Seriously,' cut in Miss Sproule, with a flash of her blue eyes at Harry.

'Some of his antics were not funny and he was ashamed of them.'

'True enough,' nodded Lindsay. 'But some of his antics *were* damned amusing. Stitching up that Yank tycoon for a start, and as Harry says, that chamber pot business …'

They were silent for some minutes then, each one looking out of the windows at St David's Cathedral where a funeral was taking place. Lindsay shuffled off for more beer. It was quiet in the lounge, save for the ticking of the grandfather clock in the corner and the muffled noises of cars outside in the street. When the silence lengthened, Mary spoke.

'Going back to what you were saying earlier, Marjorie, I recall that you said this Hetherington fella "aimed to construct a case to prove that Geordie Stubbs was capable of such a vile crime" or words to that effect. Could you explain what you mean?'

'Hetherington is an obsessive man. He had studied in Madrid under a professor of psychiatry who believed in something he called "the red gene". He believed that Geordie was a textbook case, and he was determined to prove it – and write a scientific paper on the topic.'

'That he was predisposed to behave in a criminal manner?'

'Exactly. According to the Spanish professor, left-wing people are criminal morons, not to put too fine a point on it.'

'And is my father a leftist?'

'Not exactly, but Doctor Hetherington started from the assumption that he is a Communist and therefore a born criminal.'

The professor took a sip of her sherry and looked at each of her companions in turn. 'Do any of you think my father is a born criminal?'

The two men shrugged.

'I doubt he is a congenital criminal,' said Miss Sproule. 'The so-called Human Fly stole because he was under grave threat from gangsters, and he defrauded that Feuerstein man because of what most people would now admit was a justifiable hatred of fascism – although he kept some of the proceeds for himself.'

'Bit of a Robin Hood,' commented Harry.

'A noble bandit,' added Dermot. 'Some of our bushrangers fit that category.'

Marjorie Sproule nodded her agreement. 'Yes, he is. I think, Mary, that your father is basically a good man. His antics during the Great War were inexcusable, but he did have a crisis of conscience and gave the proceeds of his crimes to the nuns at Hazebrouck. Then there were the Phnom Penh burglaries, but in mitigation, we must admit that he was trying to save his lover, the Cazenave woman.'

'I know about the red gene theory,' said the professor after a lull in the conversation. 'I must say that I was delighted to learn that my father had defrauded that awful Feuerstein man and sent the money to the Spanish Republic … I was in Spain during the Civil War, by the way.'

Marjorie raised her eyebrows at this and smiled broadly. Her father and uncle would be interested to hear it, too.

'I know, too, about that fascist Antonio Vallejo-Nájera,' Mary continued. 'He hates leftists and believes as you say, Marjorie, that they are all congenital criminals. The interrogations were often supervised by operatives of the Nazi SS.

'The man's life work was to eradicate the red gene from the Spanish population by killing the carriers and stealing their children. He took at least 30,000 children from socialist families, often after the parents' execution, and gave them to fascist families to rear.'

'So, we beat the Nazis, but their ideas continue,' observed Harry.

'Yes, quite so,' replied the professor. 'For his services to Franco, this Vallejo-Nájera was made Spain's first professor of psychiatry. This is the man your Doctor Hetherington looks up to.'

Miss Sproule laughed. 'I'm afraid that the only red gene Geordie Stubbs has is for his hair!' She took a sip of her Babycham. 'I must say that I had a long conversation with Stuart Hetherington when I left his employment. He has come to regret ever entertaining the theory and he will not be writing the paper he had promised the man in Spain.

'He feels very guilty for failing in his duty to protect an innocent man. He tried to rationalise the report he sent to the court. "I am a psychiatrist" – she made air quotes – "and as an expert witness I was required only to report on Stubbs's mental state. I was not a judge nor a juror, nor a lawyer bound to argue his client's innocence. Nor was I responsible for Stubbs's refusal to save himself by telling the truth about where he was at the time of the murder."

'He now admits, however, that he colluded in a process that would have ended, but for Harry's persistence, with an innocent man swinging on the end of a rope. He was trying to force the facts to fit an untenable theory.'

'I say, Marjorie, that's rather eloquently put,' said Harry. 'But don't forget that it was you more than anyone who saved Geordie. Not me.' He looked pensive. 'Anyway, I have to say that I went to see him yesterday and it doesn't look good.'

Dermot was looking for a chance to speak. 'He didn't help himself though, with that nonsense of refusing to provide an alibi.' He shrugged and finished his beer.

Mary Ross gratefully accepted their offer of an early dinner. Dermot Lindsay knew just the place. 'Italian, with a good drop of sixpenny red – if you can put up with the lawyers.'

Taroona, Spring 1954

The hospice for the dying sat on a low sandstone bluff overlooking the Derwent estuary in the southern suburb of Taroona. Dark clouds had gathered and gusts of wind set the trees shaking and white caps dancing on the water. Behind it all, solidly imperious, the blue mass of Mount Wellington bulked to the sky. Mary parked her rented Austin A40 at the end of an avenue of cypress trees and climbed the low flight of steps to the entrance doors. Inside the building, the sound of the wind was abruptly stilled. The atmosphere was hushed and reverential, and although she was an agnostic, Mary found herself breathing a silent prayer.

'John McCarthy,' said the stooped figure in the white coat advancing towards her from an office doorway. 'Doctor McCarthy. I'm the medical director here, and you, I presume, are Professor Ross. If you would just follow me into my office, we have a few formalities before you can see your father.'

The elderly doctor motioned her graciously to an upholstered chair facing his desk. The floor was thickly carpeted and muffled the sound of Mary's heels. After inquiring whether she would have tea or coffee, he got down to business.

'Now, I expect you will be in for a bit of shock,' he said, peering over his glasses. 'Geordie has lost a lot of weight since you would have seen him last.'

'I have never seen him.'

McCarthy raised his silver eyebrows at this but waited patiently as she explained her relationship with the man who lay dying a few doors along the corridor. Satisfied by her answers to his questions, he gave her some medical details and then rang a little brass bell. After a little while, an elderly nun knocked and entered.

'This is Sister Elizabeth,' he said. 'She will take you to him. Mind, he tires easily and moves in and out of sleep. He was playing his fiddle in the grounds as late as last week, but I'm afraid he's too weak now.'

'Such beautiful airs.' The nun sighed, fingering her rosary. 'They took me back to my childhood in Ireland.'

Geordie's body was a slight hump in the bedclothes. His faded grey-red hair spilled out over the snowy pillowcase, and he was breathing quietly in his sleep. His fiddle and bow sat on the dressing table. Mary Ross sat on the chair by the bedside and the nun retreated, smiling sadly, and whispered that she would be just along the corridor if needed. Mary took in the dark face, its cheekbones prominent, its closed eyes sunken deep into their sockets. His ears looked enormous, but his body looked so small. She felt a turmoil of emotion: sadness, regret, and the old resentment conflicting with the pity she felt for this husk of a man.

Geordie stirred, sensing someone was close by, and his eyes flickered open.

'Sister Elizabeth?' he croaked.

Mary took what seemed an age to reply. 'I'm Mary … your daughter. Would you like me to pour you some water?'

'Mary,' he whispered. 'My daughter? I never thought—' He started to cough then, and it was some minutes before he could raise himself up and reach out for the glass she proffered. He took little birdlike sips and sat the glass down on the bedside table before turning his sunken face towards her.

'Aye,' he said at last after scrutinising her for a minute or so. 'I can see your mother in you.'

'And I can see myself in you,' she replied, feeling awkward. She had rehearsed what she was going to say, but her thoughts had flown away. She was comparing what she saw with the robust man in the Kodachrome photographs Murray Triffitt had given her. She knew from what Doctor McCarthy had told her that his time was near, and so did he, for his voice had become urgent.

'I'm so sorry that I abandoned you and Annie all those years ago,' he said. 'I left because I was terrified of going back down the pit and it was clear that your mam would never leave her da and ma. The polis were after me too, but I should not—' He broke into another fit of coughing. When he had finished and wiped the bloody spittle from his lips he lay back on the pillows.

Mary said nothing, but she reached out and laid her hand on his. It felt skeletal, weightless, like a featherless bird's claw.

'Aye,' he whispered. 'It's ironic. Annie's da was coughing his lungs up with the pneumoconiosis when I left, and here I am coughing my life away.'

'I know that you came looking for us. Twice.'

'And I would have come again, but for—'

When the coughing fit was over, Geordie's voice was urgent: 'Your mother … What did she say about me?'

'I'll not lie to you. She seldom spoke about you except in the most general way, usually about "that bastard your father", and it was not until I became an adult that she told me everything. She told me then about the note you'd left under the gatehouse door. She kept it in her box of important things, and I have it with me.'

Mary fumbled in her handbag, withdrew a yellowing piece of paper, and read it out in her husky contralto voice:

'Dear Annie, I cannot make it up to you for what I have done. I cannot forgive myself, so I can hardly expect you to do so but I do think of you, and I wonder about the child whose name I do not know. I could get no sense out of the young man who was working in the garden, so I have taken the liberty of leaving this note under your door. If you wish, you can write to me at The Coniston in Russell Square, London.

'Also in my mother's things,' she added, 'was her reply, which I have here. I'll read it to you:

'Geordie Stubbs you hurt me more than you can know. We have maid another life for worselves and you have a cheek coming back now. By worselves I mean me and my precious daughter. I don't hate you Geordie Stubbs but cant forgive you either for what you done.

'She didn't send the note. She never married or let anyone else get close to her. Except for me.'

Mary was silent then as her father took in what she had said.

'And how did you manage?' he croaked. 'Did the people from the Hall provide for you like they promised?'

'Well,' she began. 'Despite your absence – or more accurately because of it – I have had a privileged upbringing. The stipend was never enough, and Mam had got put off work at the munitions factory when the war ended, so she took me to the Hall to ask for more. Sir Cuthbert saw us in the grounds.'

Geordie had raised himself up onto his pillows and was listening intently as she spoke.

'Well, Sir Cuthbert was a lonely old man, long retired from the bench and too frail to get out much. My mother said he was smitten with me, for I was a cheeky red-haired lassie. His own flesh and blood, too. He lavished all his love on me, and I never wanted for anything from that time. Perhaps he regretted some of the things he had done in his life, for he had a merciless reputation and maybe wished to atone for it.

'When I was old enough, I went to Newcastle to study medicine. That's where I was when you last came looking for us at Lambton Hall. The young gardener was not quite right in the head and gave you no information, but you left that note with a London address. My dear mother died shortly afterwards, but she had kept the note and I found it some time later when I was sorting through her things.'

Geordie still had a tight grip on her hand but let go when he was wracked with another bout of coughing. When it was over, he asked her to continue.

'I travelled down to London and went to the address at The Coniston,' she said, refilling his glass with water and handing it to him. 'The caretaker was an old man called Wally Beecroft. He spoke highly of you. He had forwarded a box of your possessions out to Australia, and he was able to give me the details of where to find you.'

'I'm very glad you did,' Geordie replied, though his voice was scarcely audible. 'Before ... before I got sick, I was planning to come back and look for you again. I wanted to try to make up for what I had done.'

Mary nodded. She was struggling with herself. Part of her wanted to tell this man that she forgave him, but another part resisted. And yet when all was said and done he was her father. From what she'd heard he wasn't an evil man and she believed him when he said he was ashamed of what he'd done. She leaned forward. 'Well, it's a cliché, but it's true, nevertheless. I forgive you but I can't forget what you did to us. I always felt you somehow. An absence can be a presence and you were always there. A big black question mark over my life.'

'Thank you for coming,' Geordie rasped. 'I don't deserve it but thank you ... daughter.' He sipped some more water and raised himself up on his pillows. His eyes had regained some of their brilliance. 'Now, Mary, could you hand me my fiddle?'

She demurred, but he was insistent. He tucked the violin under his chin, picked up the bow, and began to play a haunting air, Turlough O'Carolan's 'Farewell to Music'. It was, Mary realised, his own farewell to the world. When the last yearning notes had died away, Mary went to put the fiddle on the bedside table but Geordie held up his hand. 'Nay, lass,' he said. 'I'd like you to have it. It's a 1934 Charles Enel. Not a Stradivarius, but it's good.' She thanked him. She would keep it safe, she said. They sat quietly then, for although there was much that she wanted to ask and say, she was afraid of tiring him or causing another coughing fit. Shadows were drawing in. There was some commotion in the corridor – a demanding baritone English voice raised – and it briefly distracted Mary's attention. Through the door she saw Sister Elizabeth, her face red with indignation, shooing a beefy red-haired man out the front door, refusing to take a paper he was holding out. 'Just go,' hissed the nun. 'I'm not giving your silly extradition papers to Mr Stubbs.' When Mary turned back to the bed, there was a crackling, wet sound. Geordie Stubbs was dead.

Acknowledgements

Some years ago, I made a tantalising discovery in the Cambodian National Archives. In 1945, an English chef called Stubbs was arrested for stealing silverware from the kitchen of the French Résidence Superieure in Phnom Penh. Alas, I could find nothing else about him, his sentence, how he came to be in the French Protectorate shortly before the Japanese coup de force against their nominal Vichy allies, or what happened to him afterwards. Mr Stubbs was relegated to a minor footnote in my history of the French colonial period in Cambodia, but on reflection it struck me that I could invent a life for him in a work of fiction.

My friend Professor David Chandler was intrigued by the project, and I must thank him for his encouragement and many suggestions. David is probably the world's foremost English language Cambodia historian, but he also recognised that inventing a life story for the enigmatic cook was great fun. I have incorporated several of his suggestions, including Geordie's meeting with Nancy Wake and having the Rogue have different coloured eyes.

My old friend Tony Dewberry read an early draft of the book and made a number of thoughtful editing suggestions, for which I owe him thanks. Having been a conscript during the Vietnam War era, he was able to correct my errors concerning army ranks and customs.

Nor can I fail to thank Dr Susan Young for her painstaking work of editing the book. We didn't always agree, but I have adopted almost all of her suggestions. She is a meticulous, insightful and indeed inspiring editor and has helped turn the original draft into a much better book.

Finally, thanks are due, too, to my life partner, Professor Dorothy Bruck, for reading drafts of the book and making many pertinent suggestions. More generally, I must thank her for her unstinting encouragement whenever I felt disinclined to persevere with the Rogue's story.

Naturally, any errors, inconsistencies, anachronisms or infelicitous turns of phrase are my own fault.